Hiding Behind The Couch Series

Reverberations

I0652686

by
Mother Goose
(Debbie McGowan)

Beaten Track
www.beatentrackpublishing.com

Dedicated to…

…my alumni, without whom I would undoubtedly
have failed social psychology and statistics but also
would not have been barred from the Buck i'th' Vine.

Author's Note

As a way of making light of how long it's taken me to finish this novel, I've spent the past five(!) years saying, "Josh has been stuck in the loft for [x] years now." That was where I left him at the end of *Reunions*, published in April 2017—dangling from the loft hatch in his former 'surgery', a space he previously rented but now owns.

It might, therefore, be somewhat confusing to find that Josh is *not* stuck in the loft at the beginning of this book. This isn't because he cunningly escaped while the author was under siege from burnout. Rather, the five-chapter epilogue of *Reunions* and the first seven chapters of *Reverberations* (this book) overlap. This was always my intention—to add in the 'how did we get here?' background to events at the end of *Reunions*—but it should, I hope, also serve as something of a *Previously...in Hiding Behind The Couch*.

Either way, all you need to know is that at the start of this story, Josh isn't stuck in the loft...*yet*.

ps. If you're wondering about 'Mother Goose' (on the title page), my youngest daughter is to blame. The story behind it becoming my nickname is too long to tell here, but she changed my name on the manuscript way back in summer 2017 and phoned me a few months later in a panic at the prospect of me having published the book without noticing. I appreciate her optimism, even if she does send me messages that simply say 'Goose!' and my eldest daughter now calls me Goose Face, Goosey and Gooseth in front of her friends.

Contents

1: L'Alouette 1

2: Lovely Girls 12

3: Building In-spectres 25

4: Most Haunted 37

5: Uneventful Vigil......................................47

6: Another Morning......................................57

7: The Only Way is… 67

8: Clocking Out 78

9: Best Behaviour...89

10: To-Do.. 101

11: Privilege Is as Privilege Does.............. 109

12: In Front of Every Good Man…..........120

13: One Man's Treasure 131

14: Into the Light 141

15: Too Much 154

16: The Wrong Side 166

17: Lonely Women....................................177

18: To Love and Friendship......................189

19: Unsettling Symmetry 198

20: By One's Teeth......................................208

21: Abstinence..219

22: Party..232

23: Spa Partners...245

24: Runaround..258

25: Reflections..267

26: Blueprints...279

27: By Degrees...295

28: Law and Disorder...308

29: Tethered...321

30: Into His Own Hands 330

31: Bleeding Out 340

32: Exorcises in Love..353

33: The French Have a Phrase for It 364

34: Getting Up Again..378

35: Entropy 388

36: A Good Thing...399

37: Big Air...407

38: Reconstruction 419

39: Hair of the Dog...433

40: Dirty Money 445

41: Loose Ends 458

42: Size Medium 471

Epilogue: Ellipsis 485

Acknowledgements/Credits...503

About the Author 504

By the Author..505

Beaten Track Publishing 508

I count myself in nothing else so happy
As in a soul rememb'ring my good friends

William Shakespeare
King Richard the Second,
Act II, Scene III

And there reigns love and all love's loving parts,
And all those friends which I thought buried.

William Shakespeare
'Sonnet XXXI'

1: L'Alouette

Rowan Mews
Present Day
Monday, 15th April

PINK DUVET, BLACK headboard, two beanbags—one blue, one yellow—chocolate-brown desk, orange wall units. To Genie Rowan's eye, her daughter's room was reminiscent of an upended box of giant-size Liquorice Allsorts. Phee had chosen the design herself and gabbled for weeks about how excited she was to come home for spring break—all those lie-ins in her plush, comfy, boldly striped pink and black bed.

Two nights, she'd stayed. That was all. In normal circumstances, Genie would've been furious. But these were *far* from normal circumstances. Nor in Phee's absence was the room vacant, for dead centre of the colourful chaos stood the monochrome, slight form of Lord Xander Etherington-Bowes, flapping his hand—palm up, palm down, palm up, palm down—and humming a monotone melody.

"What's he doing?" Genie whispered, consigned to watching from the doorway, her entrance barred by Jonathan's arm. He seemed nice—Jonathan, that is. Xander was the same as ever. But neither man need worry. With all the strange goings-on, Genie had no intention of setting foot in that room.

"Checking for air disturbance." Jonathan inclined his head to return Genie's attention to Xander, still humming and flip-flapping his hand, though he was on the move, his regimented steps spiralling out from his starting point.

"Does it work, whatever it is he's doing?" Genie asked.

1

"If there's anything here."

"There is." Xander stopped both walking and flapping to stare at the air above the queen-size bed. "Where is she?"

Genie shook her head and made a guess. "The poltergeist? That's why I called—"

"No."

"I believe His Lordship means your daughter," Jonathan explained.

"Oh! She's at a friend's for a few days. Why?"

"We will stay here tonight," Xander said.

"Yes, that's…fine." Genie doubted her agreement was required. If she told them to leave, they would, but the entire situation was utter insanity to begin with and certainly couldn't be made more so by having Xander Etherington-Bowes and his personal assistant sleep over. "You will keep it to yourselves, won't you?"

Xander marched across the room and stopped a few feet from her location. No eye contact. She remembered now. He'd been the same when they were children.

"His Lordship speaks to no-one," Jonathan assured her on Xander's behalf.

Or no-one living, Genie thought but refrained from saying lest Xander interpret it as anything other than flippant humour born of ill ease. "But *you* do, Jonathan."

Xander smiled grimly and took another step towards them. "He won't tell anyone about your…poltergeist. Excuse me. Please."

"Sorry." Genie moved aside, and Xander marched past, out of the room and along the hallway to the top of the stairs. Jonathan raised his eyebrows at Genie and strode after Xander; she had to jog to catch up. "Where are you going?"

"To fetch the equipment."

"Equipment?"

"Meters, cameras…"

Xander reached the front door and halted, waiting for someone to open it.

"Hang on!" Breathless from the chase, Genie slid past and stood between him and the door with her arms outstretched. Xander startled and stepped back. "Take the car around to the side of the house," she instructed Jonathan.

He bowed his head. "As you wish, Your Ladyship."

"Margaret?" Genie called. Her assistant appeared a mere second later. "Can you direct Jonathan to the side entrance, please?"

***

Campus Restaurant

MID-AFTERNOON AT THE start of the exam period, the university restaurant was dotted with procrastinating revisers eking out their 'just a quick one before I make a start' coffees. From the dregs of the lunchtime menu, Doctor Sean Tierney selected a chicken salad bowl for himself and a plate of wrinkled chips and mushy baked beans for his surprise guest, paid for both meals and carried them over to the table at which she sat scrolling morosely through social media on her phone. Sean set the plate down next to it. "Here you go, young Phee."

"Thanks."

Scroll. Pause.

Sean slid onto the seat opposite and picked up his fork.

Scroll. Pause.

"Shall we talk while we eat, or wait till we're finished?"

Phee shrugged and switched off her phone screen. "We can eat first."

"All right." Sean speared a tomato slice and put it in his mouth. Being told to reduce his fat intake had transformed his previous indifference towards salad to loathing, and it tasted of nothing, not that it mattered when the stress had done for his appetite. Phee's call had come three hours ago as he was leaving his office for his final lecture of the academic year, so he'd had no time to speculate on why she was on her way to see him, and she seemed in no hurry to explain.

"How's school?" he asked.

"All right. It's school."

"And your A' Levels? Are they going OK?"

"I suppose."

Sean chanced his luck with the cucumber. He couldn't taste that either. He put down his fork and rubbed his eyes, dragging his hands over his cheeks. "Look, Phee, I think you'd be better just telling me why you're here."

She ate the chip on her fork and took her time chewing and swallowing. Sean was sure the heavy-headed sensation was his blood pressure notching upwards.

At last, Phee said, "I need your help."

"OK?"

"I wouldn't ask if I didn't have to."

He was guessing the kind of help she meant was financial, which could be anything from a loan of a few grand to buy a car to a lifetime in maintenance payments. A car he could stretch to without having to rethink his plans. Anything more and he'd be having some difficult conversations later, not that this one was a walk in the park.

Phee was waiting for him to agree to help. It was a trick people generally left behind with their adolescence, attempting to secure someone's agreement without them knowing what it was they were agreeing to. Had he known Phee better, emotional attachment would have made Sean fall for it. As it was, he held his tongue and gestured for her to explain.

"You've met Paul—Mum's boyfriend—haven't you?"

"Only the once." On first impression, he'd seemed a decent guy, but there was more to that question, so Sean kept his opinion to himself and waited for Phee to gather the words or courage or whatever she needed to spit out what she'd travelled 100 miles by train to say.

"He...I mean, I...um..." She cleared her throat. "Me and him are..." She left it there, but she need say no more. The statement completed itself, ticker-tape style, in the airless expanse between them.

Sean's world lost focus while the scenario played out in his head of Phee as the victim of some dirty old man, but Paul was fifteen years younger than her mother, putting him closer to Phee's age. Even so, she wasn't yet eighteen.

"How long's it been going on?" he asked.

"A month. Maybe a bit longer."

"How much longer?"

Phee grimaced and dropped a grainy black-and-white image onto the table. "Twelve weeks."

***

Rowan Mews

XANDER PIVOTED AWKWARDLY on the spot, neither watching Jonathan's departure nor looking Genie's way.

"Would you like a drink, Xander?"

"May I have a Scotch with no ice, please?"

"Of course. Come through to the drawing room." Genie moved off, glancing back to check he was following. "I haven't seen you in such a long time. It would be lovely to catch up."

"Lovely," Xander repeated. "Yes, it would, but you asked me here to look into your..."

Genie couldn't tell if he'd intentionally left off or become distracted mid-sentence. "Poltergeist?" she suggested and opened the drinks cabinet, eyeing the three bottles of whisky, one of which had been her grandmother's; Genie rarely drank the stuff. "Do you have a preferred brand?"

"Ardbeg. You won't have any."

"No, you're quite right. I'm a wine drinker myself."

"I drink wine."

"If you'd rather have whisky—"

"I'd rather you chose for me."

"As you wish." Genie picked up the bottle of red she'd opened at lunchtime and retrieved two clean glasses, watching Xander out of the corner of her eye. He was soundlessly clicking his fingers and circling, inspecting the room.

"When did you move into this house?" he asked.

"Thirteen years ago. It belonged to my grandmother. I needed somewhere to live, and the house was standing empty, so I bought it from my father."

"You didn't inherit it from your grandmother?"

"No, I—"

"Did she die here?"

"No. On the way to the hospital. Why? Do you think—"

"She's not your…poltergeist. How old is your daughter? Seventeen."

Genie had already answered the question but confirmed it again. "Yes. Eighteen next month." She held out one of the glasses to Xander. When he didn't take it, she put it on top of the cabinet and slid it towards him.

"Thank you." He picked it up, took a small sip, and put it down again. "Your daughter wasn't here when it happened, you said."

"That's correct, yes. She slammed the front door—you know how teenagers are, or perhaps you don't—"

"My second cousin is thirteen years old."

"Right." Genie gave herself a mental ticking off. "As I told you, I heard the front door slam, then Phee's bedroom door, and I went up to investigate."

"That was when you saw the bed levitate."

"I may be mistaken about the bed."

"And the lamp flew into the mirror."

"Yes." She'd almost convinced herself it was an acid flashback triggered by Phee's tantrum, but the mirror was crazed, and the lamp was in two pieces. She hadn't been mistaken about that. Hence she'd called Xander, whose attention had drifted again, this time to the grand piano in the bay window.

He pointed at it. "Who plays?"

"Phee sometimes. And Paul. Is *poltergeist* the wrong term?"

"Paul?"

"My partner. I notice you always hesitate—"

"He's not your daughter's father." Xander stalked over to the piano.

"No." Whether he'd missed her question or deliberately ignored it, Genie was growing tired of the constant interruptions. "Do you still play?"

"A little." He tapped one of the keys near the top of the keyboard. "It's out of tune."

"It was tuned less than a month ago."

Xander pressed another key and held it. "I hear perfect pitch. Heat, humidity." He tilted his head back and blinked up at the ceiling. "Reverberation. No piano is ever perfectly in tune." He released the key and hummed the same note, or that was how it sounded to Genie's non-musical ear. Still, she nodded her understanding.

"May I play?" Xander asked.

"Knock yourself out." Genie pursed her lips, tried again. "I mean…yes, by all means, do."

"I'm familiar with figurative speech." Xander moved behind the piano and perched on the stool. "Do you have any music?"

"In the stool."

He rose and opened the lid, transferring all the music to the top of the piano. He closed the lid and sat again, plucking the topmost score from the pile.

Taking her wine with her, Genie sat on the sofa and kept her eyes on the rug as she prepared for Xander's performance, recalling his recitals from their youth. He could play almost any piece put in front of him, but it was always in the same dry, mechanical style, and she didn't wish to insult him. However, as he began, it was apparent he had at some point learned to interpret dynamics: there was surprising musicality to his playing, although still no sense of him *feeling* the music, and he remained starchly upright through to the very end of the piece. By then, Jonathan had returned, and both he and Genie applauded Xander's efforts.

"Bravo! That was marvellous, wasn't it, Jonathan?"

"Yes, Your Ladyship."

"Please, do call me Genie."

"As you wish. Now, if you will excuse me, my lord, Genie, I will set up for tonight."

"Of course. Thank you."

With another head bow, Jonathan retreated.

"What shall I play next?" Xander asked.

Before Genie could reply—and it would only have been to give him free choice—the entire stack of scores flew from the top of the piano, scattering and sliding across the parquet floor.

Genie stared at the mess in astonishment. "Xander! Really!"

He shot from the piano stool as if it were a headstrong horse that had thrown him and backed right up against the bay window, his eyes fixed on where the scores had been. "Who are you?" he demanded. Aside from his rapid blinks, his gaze remained fixed on the same spot. "I asked you a question!"

Fighting to not further voice her annoyance at Xander's outburst, Genie slowly rose to her feet and bent to retrieve the score closest to her, but Jonathan must have opened a door, as a draught wafted the papers out of reach. She tried again; the papers slid another few inches across the floor.

"Xander, what the hell's going on?"

"There's a boy."

"A...*what?*"

"A young boy. Sitting at the piano."

Genie turned, keeping her eyes averted until she was facing the stool. There was nothing for her to see. "Who is he?"

"He won't say. What is the music he has chosen?"

"What do you mean?" When Xander didn't answer, Genie followed his gaze to the score on the music rest. She edged closer. "Can't you read it from there?"

"I dropped my glasses. What is it?"

Genie moved closer still, taking care not to step on Xander's glasses. "L'Alouette."

"'Alouette' or 'The Lark' from *A Farewell to Saint Petersburg*?"

Genie squinted at the subtitle. "'The Lark'."

"What's the significance?"

"None I can think of." Genie couldn't recall ever having heard it played. "But—"

"I wasn't asking you." Xander's voice rose to a shout. "He can't hear me over the music."

Genie eyed the unmoving piano keys, her panic mounting until she thought she might vomit.

"It is not he who is playing, it's..." Xander gasped. "We must leave. Now." Without further warning, he bolted past Genie and the piano and out of the room.

"Xander—wait!" Genie dashed after him, in her haste treading on one of the music scores. She skidded and waved her arms in an attempt to catch herself. The piano lid crashed shut as her back and then her head collided with the hard floor.

***

A Hotel Room

PHEE RETURNED THE ultrasound image to her bag and flipped her phone face down on the duvet. It was easier to lie and say she'd missed the call if she couldn't see it, but it wouldn't stop him calling back. Her gaze drifted up and around the bare cream walls, almost as basic as the dorms though infinitely smaller... cleaner...nobody asking questions.

What's wrong?

Nothing. Just being quiet.

You're lying.

However much she'd wanted to confide in her school friends, she couldn't. One or two had been through terminations, but they'd known they were pregnant almost as soon as it had happened, and they'd been certain they didn't want to stay that way. They'd never understand how she felt. How could they when she didn't understand herself?

Shuffling back on the hard mattress, she crossed her legs and sat, pixie-like, absently tracing the grey stripes on her school socks until she remembered in disgust that she hadn't changed them in three days—since she'd arrived home on Friday claiming she'd caught the sickness bug going around school. Other than bringing her a new bottle of water every couple of hours, her mum had left her 'to sleep it off'—better she thought Phee was hungover than this horrible reality.

Another wave of nausea lapped at her throat, although not enough to send her running to the bathroom, which was an improvement on lunchtime. Still, she should shower; she hadn't had one of those in three days either.

She shouldn't have come, but she couldn't stay at home, staring guiltily at her newly decorated room—exactly how she'd wanted it, and after all those awful things she'd screamed at her mum on Christmas Day. It hadn't even been important—just an ungrateful brat mouthing off because she didn't get what she'd asked for, which somehow got twisted into *no wonder Grandma and Grampy disowned you—as long as you're happy, what do you care?* And now this. Her mum was...*had been* her best friend, but what kind of person slept with their best friend's boyfriend?

So really, three-day-old socks were the least disgusting thing about her. She was the worst, and she shouldn't have come here looking for sympathy she didn't deserve, but she didn't know what else to do. She'd told him, then watched through her eyelashes, waiting for him to react while he'd stared at the salt and pepper pots and pinched his chin.

He'd sighed, laughed bleakly and shaken his head—"God, what a mess"—looked up at the ceiling, at the table next to theirs, anywhere but her face. She'd willed him—*look at me!*—and at last, he had.

"Sorry. You took me by surprise."

She'd broken down then, in a university café, in front of a man she hardly knew; the same man who kept calling, leaving voicemails and text messages to ask if she was doing all right, was the hotel up to scratch, how was the sickness, and had she spoken to her mum yet? No pressure, but she felt it even so, over their uneaten lunch when he'd squeezed her hand, called her sweetheart, said, "We'll go somewhere a bit quieter and talk, OK? Don't you worry, we'll figure it out," and brought her to this hotel, not his home, and why would he? He had no responsibility or obligation to her. He was not much more than a sperm donor, Mum said. But he hadn't sent her away. Not yet.

2: Lovely Girls

Off Campus
Nineteen years ago
May

R IGHT, LET'S SEE what this one's got to say." Moving the papers back and forth in front of his face, Sean found a distance at which he could mostly read the words. Nothing to do with bad eye sight: too much studying, nowhere near enough sleep, and he was hammering the whiskey, but it was the only way he could drag himself through to bedtime each day. The words swam out of focus, though it made little difference when not a single one of them was sinking in.

He needed a break, some time away from the house to recuperate, and he'd have taken it if he'd anywhere close by he could go. Maybe he'd walk up to the uni, dodge into his old halls for a shower, pop into the off-licence on the walk back. It would fill the couple of hours until visiting time and ensure he was in a reasonable state to face it.

"That's what I'll do." Decision made, he shoved the papers back into the folder and pushed it across the desk, his eyes drawn to a coffee ring, like the sun against the horizon of the ocean-blue folder.

Nudging the folder with his finger, he emulated the sunrise, noticing another ring intersecting the first, and another. And another. His eyes roamed to the desktop clutter beyond— dirty mugs and plates, days-old toast crusts, a pizza box, chip wrappers, three empty bottles—and beyond those the mess of the room—his filthy quilt curled on the sofa, a crumpled pair of jeans on the floor and a singular shoe. Books littered the carpet, hardback stepping stones to nowhere, terminating a few feet from where he sat.

"Jesus, what a pit." At some point, before Josh was discharged, he'd give the place a damn good clean. But not today. Today, he couldn't look at it a moment longer. In the absence of a second shoe, he ran up to his room, stepped into the worn-out trainers he should've binned months ago, and left.

***

Post-exams, Lloyd George halls of residence were next to dead, and the few residents Sean saw didn't recognise him, nor he them, though he doubted even the powers-that-be would care that one of their postgrad students was availing himself of the facilities. In the event he was caught, he had a story ready—problem with the boiler, waiting on the landlord. It happened often enough to be plausible. But no-one did ask, today or any other day, as if he were invisible to those he passed by. He wasn't sure if that was better or worse than the alternative.

He was lonely. Lonely and bored. Lonely and tired. Lonely and hungry. Lonely and drunk. Sick of the sound of his own moaning drone, of reading papers so pointless he could no longer remember why he'd wanted to study this shitty subject in the first place. And mad.

Mad as hell.

Who was to blame? Was anyone to blame? What did it matter? It wouldn't change anything. Couldn't rewind.

"Sean!"

He'd almost made it to the gate out onto the road and at first didn't recognise the voice. Lonely as he might be, he was in no mood for socialising, but he was also too polite to pretend he hadn't heard. Imagining some terrible ailment that would offer an excuse to dash off, he turned around, and his heart sank right down into his holey footwear.

"Hello, Hillie." Their research and ethics lecturer. "How are you doing?" Of course it would be someone who knew what had gone on.

"Sean," she said again, quieter this time, accompanied by a warm, caring smile as she came to a stop in front of him. "I'm OK, thanks. How are you?"

She was asking for real, and it whipped every possible response from Sean's head. Every one but the truth, which leapt from his mouth in desperation. "Falling to pieces."

"Oh…Sean."

Christ, if she starts crying, I'm done for.

A group of students neared their location, and Hillie moved to block their line of sight. Her palm landed on his bare, still-damp arm, steadying, comforting. Lonely, yes, but he didn't deserve the company, the sympathy.

Once the students had passed them by, she squeezed gently and said, "My car's just behind those trees. Come and sit with me awhile."

He hadn't the strength to argue. Besides, what would he be arguing for? Another hour of silence in the psych unit followed by more hours of silence in an empty house, followed by whiskey coma and a new day when he'd do it all over again? If he could break the cycle…

"Let me get this junk out of your way." Hillie dodged around him and opened the passenger door, scooping armfuls of folders and papers over the back rest and leaving them wherever they fell before gesturing for Sean to get in. "Sorry it's such a mess. There's rarely anyone in it but me."

"It's plenty tidy enough." He was living in a hovel of his own making; the local tip would have been a step up. He got in and stared out the windscreen, not sure what to say, afraid to talk lest she'd tire of his company too soon. Like a starving man offered a benevolent feast, he wanted to gorge on her kindness.

"Pull that door shut, will you, Sean? The wind's cold."

"Sorry." He was impervious but did as she asked and sat back, letting his eyes close. The lids ached, and his eyeballs felt like they were on fire. The image swam into view, and he opened them again, turning towards her, offering the best smile he could dredge up.

She'd changed, no longer the newly badged PhD who'd prattled for two hours, fuelled by nerves and only vaguely aware of the disdain rising from the undergrads before her. Empathy had arrived with her self-confidence, and it reached over the centre console, tethering him to her.

"Are you receiving any support, Sean?"

"From the hospital?"

"The hospital, university...any at all."

"I didn't request it."

"You shouldn't need to."

"It's not really about me, is it? Josh—"

"Is getting the help he needs," she said. "But I'm not asking about Josh. How can I support *you*, Sean?"

That was an interesting question. How should he answer? *Rewind time, stop me coming home from the conference...* "I'll have to work through it." It was how he'd survived the past month. His thesis crowded out all other thoughts; only when he stopped did they seep into his relaxed mind, infiltrate his dreams. Study, whiskey: the royal road to lost consciousness.

"Do you want to talk about it?"

"I don't know. D'you think it'll help?"

"It might, it might not. But I'm listening if you want to try."

Unsure where to look, his gaze fell to her hands resting on the steering wheel as if the car were waiting at traffic lights. Red, amber...

"I wish I'd remembered my notes. For the conference. I'd have come home to the same bloody mess, but it would've been done and dusted and saved us all a lot of unnecessary grief." The next sentence stalled somewhere between his brain and his mouth. *He hates me.* "I'm sorry, I can't...no, it's not helping, but thank you." He reached for the door handle, pushed the door open with his knee. "I'm grateful."

She watched without argument, said only, "If I can do anything, anything at all…"

"Thanks, Hillie. You're very kind." He closed the door and walked away.

***

"Sean!"

Jesus wept. Can I just get off this fecking campus?

"Evening, ladies. You're looking fine. Are you off celebrating?"

Jess looped his left arm—"Last exam"—Imogen his right.

"Is that you now? All done?"

"Yep." Jess skipped a step or two, light-hearted and joyous. "Graduation, here we come!" The two women high-fived in front of his face and laughed, exhilarated by their achievement.

"Congratulations!" The switch flipped in his head to *Sean the cheeky, chirpy Irish lad.* He had no right to rain on their parade.

"Thanks." Imogen—or Genie, as she preferred—kissed his cheek, lingering to murmur, "Love the beard."

He hadn't grown one intentionally, simply hadn't got around to shaving, since it required going into the bathroom.

"You should come with us," Jess said, glancing past him to check Genie was OK with it. Genie nodded, her heavily made-up eyes transforming from sultry to wide and sparkly.

"Yes, you should."

"You're all dressed up," he protested, painfully conscious of his crumpled T-shirt and jeans that were passable but far from clean, not to mention he felt the gravel underfoot with every step.

"We could go back to your place and—" Jess began, but he cut in.

"No, it's all right. You go on and enjoy yourselves."

"If you're sure…" Genie said.

"I'm sure." Sure he wanted to go with them so desperately it was giving him belly ache.

"We'll walk with you," Jess suggested. It was non-negotiable. He shrugged within their clutches and then listened to their chatter. Like being gently splashed with warm water. He drifted along in a pleasant daze, imagining their perfumy smell, trying not to imagine them drinking and dancing into the night with the dashing young men of this town.

His and Josh's place was down a little side road off the high street, and as they approached the corner, Sean attempted to ease out of their huddle. Simultaneously, they squeezed, tightening their grip on his arms.

"*Please* come with us." Genie pouted and blinked, all heavy lids and lashes.

"But Josh—"

"He can come too," Jess said.

"Oh…he won't want to," Sean blustered. *Tell them what the hell you like*, Josh had said in the spew of awful things, hate, lies, denial, before the pills kicked in and Josh checked out. *They can't know, Sean. Please don't tell them.*

Jess cupped her hand around her ear. "Do I hear the whirr of cogs?"

Genie mimicked, staring into the distance, listened, nodded. "I do believe he's reconsidering."

Sean laughed and sighed. "All right, all right. I'll pop home and change. You go on ahead. Where will you be?"

"The wine bar by the roundabout," Jess said as they finally released him. "If you don't show within half an hour, we'll be back." She flashed a seductive smile over her shoulder, linked arms with Genie, and the two of them sauntered away.

***

Pop anthems blasted from the wine bar's many speakers— background music, allegedly, but Sean could hardly hear himself think, which suited him perfectly. Jess and Genie danced a few feet from the table, sucking on the straws in their drinks, miraculously without spilling a drop. Such beautiful young women, and great company; he'd miss them tremendously. Both were heading home at the weekend, their law degrees completed, jobs already lined up.

An empty glass thumped down on the table, drawing Sean out of his mope-lust stupor.

"Did we get you drunk?" Jess's open-lipped smile had its usual effect.

"Aye, you did," he said, though it was more to do with the swift glug of whiskey he'd taken on his way out of the house, finishing off the last inch in the bottle. He checked the time: almost ten. He'd need to leave now if he was to make the off-licence.

Genie grabbed his hand. "Come on," she said, tugging. "Dance with us."

"I'm a shocking dancer."

Now Jess had his other hand, and he probably could've fended them off, but concerned sideways glances had punctuated their revelry all evening; they wouldn't care how terrible he was as long as he appeared to be having fun.

As it turned out, being pressed between two writhing warm feminine bodies meant 'appearing to have fun' was no longer a problem. His troubles temporarily forgotten, even the guilty nag of missing visiting hour subsided to a grumble. They danced until they were breathless, bought another round, popped to the Ladies' to freshen up, on their return sandwiching him where he sat intoxicated less by the alcohol than their presence.

"We should continue this at home." Genie's thigh slid over Sean's as she intentionally leaned across him for her glass. The flash of flesh caught his eye, and he peered down into her cleavage mere inches beneath his chin. A slight dip of his head and he could have pressed his lips to her soft, plump breast.

The thought that it would be safer—less likely to result in arrest—barely registered when Jess reached over and tugged Genie's shirt shut, her fingers lingering on the edge of the fabric as she met Genie's gaze. "Your nipple's showing."

Genie looked down, as did Sean, at the bumps of nipples pushed against the silky fabric, teased to erectness by Jess's fingertips.

"You're killing me here," Sean mumbled, pulling back on the seat, arousal taking over.

"So what do you think?" Genie asked, watching his face as she poked her thumb in between his shirt buttons and stroked his chest. "Want to come home with us?"

"What do *you* think?" Sean grinned, gladly casting himself upon the whims of the two women who had both—singly—shared his bed on more than a few occasions over the past three and a half years. Whether this was a regular indulgence of theirs or a one-off fuelled by alcohol and celebration? Well, he wouldn't be wasting his efforts on analysis, that was for sure, but he took his time with his drink, not wanting to appear too eager, particularly when he was so turned on he'd shoot in seconds.

And that was precisely what happened. They took a taxi back to Jess and Genie's place. No airs and graces, the three of them were naked and sharing three-way kisses on the sofa almost before the taxi drove away. Genie left the lip foray, licking a trail down Sean's chest and abdomen while Jess's tongue thrust into his mouth, her breasts filling his hands. He muttered a desperate warning as Genie's lips closed around him, sucking his orgasm from him, grunting as she swallowed, smiling as they kissed, moaning as she ground her pelvis against his thigh. They were all one in his climax, no beginning or ending, an all-consuming bliss.

The orgasm never quite relinquished its grasp on his senses; Jess and Genie didn't give it a chance. For the time being, they were done with him, and he assumed a spectator's seat in the middle of the sofa while they cavorted on a sheepskin rug. It was a glorious privilege to witness Genie's enjoyment of oral sex at a near distance and the effect her expert actions had on Jess, who lay back, leaning on her elbows, knees raised, hips lifting to meet the bob of Genie's head between her thighs. She arched and cried out, beauty distorted by the contortions of pleasure until she fell, panting, onto her back.

"Ready for more yet, Sean?" Genie asked, slowly withdrawing. Jess laughed and pulled Genie close again to kiss her.

"Whenever you are," Sean replied. He could have gone again right away, but watching them was easily as much fun.

Genie rose and scooted to where she'd dumped her bag and her clothes, rifled through the pile and pulled out a condom, unwrapping it as she came over to the sofa.

"I want you inside me," she said, already rolling the condom onto him. He nodded his consent and awaited further instruction, but her actions spoke for her. Straddling his thighs, she slid down onto him, pausing as their bodies joined and then slowly tilting her pelvis back and forth, maximising contact. The rhythm steady, she bent to kiss him, the taste of Jess transferring from her mouth to his. His hands found their way to her breasts, cupping, squeezing, weighing them in his palms. She straightened, briefly denying him contact before pushing a nipple against his lips and holding on to the back of the sofa as she lifted and plunged, lifted and plunged.

"Going to bed. See you in a bit," Jess said and stumbled away.

Sean watched out of the corner of his eye, asking in the next brief pause, "Is she all right?"

"Gone to play with her toys. We'll join her when we're done here—if you can handle it."

He was heading rapidly into his second climax and doubted he had any more in him, but if this was his one and only chance to spend the night with the two most beautiful women he knew, he'd do his level best to make the most of it. It occurred to him it wouldn't have been a possibility at all if Josh weren't in the hospital, and the resultant guilt brought a few moments' staying power, along with the realisation that Genie had done all the giving so far. With that thought, he lowered his hand and sought out that spot he'd been told men could never find. More like they'd never tried.

"Oh, God, yes. Keep doing...that..." Genie's up-and-down became jerky and erratic, and then ceased completely as she bore down on him, breath held, eyes closed, her entire body tensed. It was a good twenty seconds before she came out of it, panting and smiling. "Did you come?" she asked. The word always sounded so much dirtier in her plummy accent.

"No, but it's OK." More than OK. He kept hold of the condom as she lifted and climbed off, collapsing beside him.

***

"Morning!" Genie squeezed his hips from behind as she stepped past him to reach the coffee he'd made. "Sleep well?"

"Grand, thanks." Better than he had in months—since Josh's first attempt. No dreams, no recollection of anything after Jess draped a heavy arm over him, until half an hour ago. "Is Jessie still asleep?"

Genie nodded and swallowed down the coffee to answer. "Yes. I don't think we'll see her for a few hours yet. While we're alone, I need to talk to you."

"Oh, right?"

"Actually, I want to ask you a massive favour."

Sean was intrigued but made himself another coffee while he waited for Genie to find her voice. She was unusually nervous and nursing an empty mug before she spoke again. "Would you let me have some of your sperm?"

Sean swayed backwards in his surprise. "I... Could you repeat that?"

"Your sperm. I'm willing to pay for it."

"You want to get pregnant?"

"I do."

"Since when?"

"Since always. I even went to the sperm bank, but it dawned on me. I don't know who any of those men are. However, I do know you."

"What about your career?"

21

"I can do both." Her eyes beseeched his agreement at the same time registering something else. "Ah. Maybe it would help if I explained."

"No, Genie, there's no need. How you live your life is entirely your own business, but can I think about it for a while?"

"Of course. I just thought, with me leaving at the weekend, well...yes. Sorry. I was worried I wouldn't get the chance to ask you."

"You didn't orchestrate last night for this reason, did you?"

She laughed and edged closer. "Not at all. Last night was very much spur of the moment." Her index finger trailed down his chest and came to a rest in his belly button. She leaned in and left a soft, lingering kiss on his lips. "Did you have fun?"

"That I did." He was rising to the possibility of more. "So if we do this thing, are you wanting to go with the whole turkey baster delivery method, or..."

"Natural is good." Her breath was hot on his neck. "You went for the screening, didn't you?"

"Yeah." There had been an outbreak of chlamydia on campus a couple of months earlier, and most of the student body had taken up the offer of the sexual health check. Since then, Sean had been too preoccupied to do anything that might change the clean bill he'd been given.

"Me too. But really, there's no rush, Sean. You take your time. As I say, I will pay you."

"You don't have to do that."

"Will you at least let me clear your student debt?"

"Have you any idea how much—"

"Shhhhh." She kissed him again, more forcefully, and took his hand, leading him out of the kitchen and up to her room. "We can discuss the details later."

***

"I didn't realise you were still here." Jess flopped onto the sofa with a pained moan. "God, I'm so hungover."

"Are you?" Sean asked. It was almost three in the afternoon—several hours since he and Genie had decided to let Nature do with it as she would and had unprotected sex. Genie had left to meet up with friends, and Sean, in no hurry to go home, had hung around waiting for Jess to get out of bed.

"Aren't you?" She studied him dubiously and sniffed. "Still drunk?"

"Maybe." He quickly changed the subject because the alcohol she could smell on him was recent. "What are your plans for the rest of the day?" Only a mouthful. "Anything?" Not even a double.

"I thought I'd spend it with you and Josh. We've hardly seen each other lately. I know, I know. It's my fault."

"You had your exams. It's understandable."

"It's not. I've been neglecting you both. Is that all right?"

Sean floundered, lost for words. "I...I've still got a fair bit of research to do. And I need to do some washing. Plus the house is a mess, and—"

"Ha! I don't believe it for a second."

"Which bit? The research?"

"You're telling me Mr. Neat Freak has finally abandoned his lifelong habits to become a slovenly student?"

"No... Well, see, he's...gone away."

"Really? He didn't say anything. Where?"

"Newcastle? I'm not too sure." It was the only place Sean could think of that Josh had ever been, other than back home.

"Oh, he's gone to see Ellie? When's he due back?"

"Couldn't say for sure."

"You don't sound sure of anything today, Sean."

"Aye, well, you and your girl Genie kind of blew my mind."

Jess laughed and patted his knee. "You're lying—by which I mean I'm sure we did blow your mind, but there's something you're not telling me." She walked her fingers up the inside of his thigh. "I wonder if you could be persuaded..."

"Jessie." He covered her hand with his, stopping her. "Will you let it go? Please? For me?"

For a moment, she watched him, frowning and trying to gauge if she could push him, but—to his relief—relented. "OK. For you."

"Thanks."

"So…what shall we do with our day? How about I give you a hand with the cleaning?"

"You don't know what you're letting yourself in for."

She patted his knee again, no ulterior motive this time. "I know enough to understand you need your friends right now. Come on." She grabbed his hand and pulled as she got up. "Let's get the place in order for when Josh comes home. It'll make you feel better."

He let her haul him upright. "Do you think so?" he asked.

She shrugged and smiled sadly. "It can't possibly make you feel any worse."

3: Building In-spectres

D ID YOU HAVE a couch?" Libby spun on a spot almost dead-centre of what was, in the not-so-distant past—although long enough ago to precede Libby's entrance into their lives—Josh's consultation room. She was enthralled by the place and the glimpse of Josh's history that came with it, while he lingered in the doorway with ghosts clutching at his limbs and refusing to release him. Libby drifted out of his hazy field of vision. At least it had taken her mind off 'Sean's secret love child' for the time being.

"This looks couch-sized," she said.

He blinked and refocused on where she was crouched, examining the lighter rectangle of carpet where once his couch had been.

"Yes," he confirmed and finally stepped into the room. "My desk was over there—" he pointed at the near-right corner "—and the bookshelf was against the back wall."

"Has nobody been in here since you left?"

"A few people came to look around, and one rented it but didn't use it, the landlord said." Or former landlord, seeing as Josh now owned the building.

"It's an amazing space." Libby sprang to her feet and dashed past him. He followed her out and watched on in silence as she circled the expansive hallway at the top of the staircase—what used to be his reception/waiting room—peering in through doorways to inspect, in turn, the kitchenette, bathroom, broom cupboard and storeroom. "*Loads* of space," she said, returning to his location. "You know what I think?"

"What do you think?"

"You've been haunting it."

He folded his arms, made vulnerable by her observation. His adopted daughter shared his knack for people-reading and could hack through his defences in seconds. Even so, he attempted to downplay how astutely she'd given form to his feelings. "Is that right, *Shaunna*?"

Libby gave him a disapproving look. "I'm gonna tell her you took her name in vain. Can't you feel it?" She held up her hands as if she were carrying a beachball. "Shaunna says it's residual energy—"

"That's physical, not *psychic*."

"Why can't it be both? I mean, all that concentrated thinking and talking must leave something behind."

Josh partly drew a breath but thought better of arguing that hard science said she was wrong. He was sceptical himself when the simple act of being there was affecting him more than he'd anticipated, largely in a positive way. For the first time in his life, he felt content, at peace, as if this were the mislaid final piece in the flatpack from which Joshua Sandison-Morley had been constructed.

"You *know* I'm right," Libby said. He didn't appreciate her victorious tone, but she scooted away before he had a chance to tick her off for being cheeky. "It'll need brightening up a bit," she called back, once again in Josh's ex-consultation room.

"It *is* bright," Josh grumbled. It was cream; the only colour brighter than that was white.

"But it's so...boring."

Josh sighed and went to join her, wishing she'd either stay in one place or stop calling for his attention. "It needs to be neutral, not too much colour or clutter."

"Why? Because *you* don't like colour and clutter?"

This time, his response was interrupted by a bang—not loud, but sudden—and it echoed around the empty rooms. They both jumped, clasped hands to chests and stared at each other.

"What was that?" Libby asked, edging closer until she and Josh bumped arms.

"I don't know. Maybe one of the vents is open."

Libby nodded. "Yeah." Neither of them moved. "Are you g—"

Another bang: same kind, but it sounded like it came from a different location. Josh didn't recognise the noise.

"Let's go and investigate," he said, heart in mouth, and stepped off, only then realising he had hold of Libby's hand. She stumbled along behind him, back out to the hallway, where they both paused. The doors to the other three rooms were ajar, as Libby had left them, and there was no discernible draught.

"We should check the windows," Libby suggested.

"Good idea."

They'd barely taken one step when there was a third bang directly behind them.

"Shit!"

"Libby, language!" Josh snapped, but if she hadn't said it, he would have because he recognised that sound all right. He'd caused it often enough himself. It was the slam of his consultation room door. That explanation stretched only as far as knowing the source of the noise but not the cause. There was no draught; the windows were double-glazed. There was no subsidence—he had a surveyor's report to prove it—and the doorframes were square to the floor.

And *there was nobody there.*

"Somebody's playing a joke on us," Libby said.

"Who?"

"I dunno. Sean?"

"No." More than twenty years had passed since the strange goings-on in their uni halls of residence and they still couldn't explain what had happened. But where Josh flat-out refused to believe in the paranormal, then and now, Sean had merely suspended his disbelief until he saw conclusive proof to the contrary. Still, he had as much invested in this new venture as Josh and wouldn't risk it all on a prank that neither would find amusing.

Before Josh could impart his reasoning, there was another noise, not a bang this time, but the rustle of paper, followed by a dull thud.

"That came from the toilet," Libby said. Her expression hardened. "I'm going in. Cover me."

Stunned, he watched her march over to the toilet door and assertively push it open.

"There's nothing in here that—"

"Libby."

She turned to look at him. He pointed downwards. Libby slowly lowered her chin. A roll of toilet paper unfurled at her feet.

"Oh my... Run!" She took flight, grabbing his hand on the way past and pulling him—unnecessarily, he was going as fast as he could—across the hallway and down the stairs. They flew out onto the forecourt, not even thinking to check for moving vehicles. Luckily, there were none.

"I think it's time for a coffee," Josh panted once they'd put a few more feet between them and the building.

"Yeah," Libby agreed, equally breathless. No doubt their expressions matched too, as hers was one of sheer fright. "Where are we gonna go? George has got the car."

"There's a place down the street. We can walk there."

"OK."

It wasn't a long walk, less than five minutes at the speed they were doing, but it was enough for them to calm down and reinstate some sense of rationality. Josh ordered their drinks—cappuccino for him, caramel latte for Libby, no chitchat as the barista was unfamiliar—and they found a table near the front windows.

"This is nice," Libby said, taking in her surroundings. Josh did the same, in his case to refresh his memory. He used to visit this coffee shop thrice daily but had only been in once since he gave up his surgery. His haunted surgery, filled with things that went bump in the middle of the day. He was having flashbacks to his uni halls again.

"Did you notice if the window was open?" he asked. He was desperate for a logical explanation.

Libby shook her head. "It looked like it was shut, but…it had to be open. It just had to be."

"Or the loo roll might've been balanced on the holder and was disturbed when you opened the door the first time."

"Maybe." She sounded far from convinced, and in any case, it only explained the unravelling toilet roll, not the two loud bangs before it or the door that slammed all by itself.

"We'll get Sean to investigate later," Josh said.

"Oh, yeah! I'd forgotten about that!" In an instant, Libby brightened. "Is she really his secret love child?"

Josh laughed. "No. She *is* his daughter, but it's not a secret."

"But nobody knows about her."

"I do."

"Does Sophie?"

"I think…y…I don't know."

"George?"

"We haven't discussed her, so no."

"Shaunna?"

Josh sighed. He genuinely took no issue with Sean confiding in Shaunna, particularly as it meant Sean wasn't bending Josh's ear all the time. However, Shaunna had been Josh's friend first— by some thirty years, seeing as they'd done the entirety of their schooling together—and he envisaged she would have said something if she'd known. "OK. Maybe you have a point, but it's not as if Sean's hidden Phee's existence. He was a sperm donor— he might still be a sperm donor for all I know."

"Was it through a clinic?"

"Not on this occasion. It was someone we knew at university— when we were students." He felt it best to clarify, seeing as they were still 'at university', albeit a different institution. "She wanted a baby but didn't want a partner."

"Jess went to your university, didn't she?"

"She's not Phee's mum."

"I bet Sean told her, though."

"He might've done. Actually, Phee's mum probably told Jess. They were very close, or they were at uni." For all the hours they'd spent talking, Josh had known next to nothing about Jess's social life beyond their mutual circle of friends. It was sad but likely intentional on Jess's part to obscure her less savoury endeavours.

"I wish I'd got to meet her," Libby said.

Josh nodded and said, "Me too," but he was secretly glad Jess would never have an influence over his daughter.

"Shaunna showed me photos of her. She was beautiful."

"She was." *On the outside.*

"And successf—oh! I've got it! Jess used to come to your surgery, didn't she?"

Josh groaned. "All the time, and no, I don't think she's haunting it. Ghosts aren't real."

"You can't disprove their existence."

"On balance—"

"And if it is Jess, then—"

"I don't want to have this discussion."

"—we could…" Libby trailed off as she processed what he'd said. Her face fell and she lowered her eyes. "Sorry. I didn't mean to upset you."

"I'm not upset."

"Would you rather talk about Sean?"

That made Josh laugh. "Yes. Curiously, I would."

"OK." She perked up. "He's not really, like, a proper dad, if you know what I mean. I mean, not like you and George, or Poppy's dad."

"He's not involved in Phee's life," Josh confirmed, "although she's always known who he is, and he sends her a birthday card every year."

"Wow! That's amazing."

"Why?"

"He forgot his own birthday last year."

"What I should have said is, he sends her a birthday card when I tell him to."

"Which means she didn't get a card for fourteen years or however long it was you weren't talking," Libby reasoned.

Josh laughed, which was a bit foolish with the cup to his mouth. Milk foam sprayed his face, and through her giggling, Libby fetched him a paper napkin. He carefully set his cup down again—the coffee was too hot anyway—and wiped his face dry. It was true, what she'd said about the birthday cards, or it would've been if Josh hadn't sent Sean an email annually to remind him, irrespective of whether they were talking to each other. He also wondered—briefly, before concluding it was yet another Sean–Shaunna confidence—how Libby knew about their long-term estrangement.

"You're gonna have to get used to sharing an office with him again," she said. "Or it might be another fourteen years."

"We've never shared an office, only a house—I say *only*. Sharing a house with Sean was no easy feat, and I imagine he felt much the same about sharing with me. He's having the storeroom."

Libby gaped at him in horror. "He can't go in that storeroom. It's too small!"

Josh was joking, but she was right again. The dimensions in his head had been wildly inaccurate: the storeroom was too small and his ex-consultation room was too big, as was the hallway at the top of the stairs. Even without converting the loft into a group therapy space, which Andy assured him could be completed within a couple of weeks, it would take some serious construction work to turn the first floor into two or maybe even three similarly sized consultation rooms. And there he'd been thinking with a lick of paint they'd be ready to open to the public in the summer, when their university contracts terminated. It was disappointing to say the least.

"I could be your receptionist," Libby said, for the time being thwarting his growing despondency.

"Only in the school holidays," he pointed out. She might be in her last year of high school, but then there was sixth form, and university after that. If Josh had any say in the matter, Libby would be in education for the next ten years.

"Whatever." She sounded flippant even though she loved school and wouldn't need coercing into staying on, not that he'd ever do that. "So should I call them?" she suggested.

"The Ghostbusters or Jeffries and Associates?" Josh asked with a grin that belied how spooked he was by the mysterious noises, which—typically—had come soon after he'd acknowledged his happiness at moving back into his surgery. Could the explanation be that simple? Subconscious sabotage? "I think we imagined it, Lib."

"But we both heard it."

"We can explain that through the power of suggestion. Maybe I acted as if I'd heard something, or as if I expected to hear something."

"If you say so."

She sounded as convinced as he was, which was not at all, but he liked the alternative even less.

***

"Hi. You both home?"

A mini gust whipped along the hall from the open front door, lifting the practice exam papers Libby had spread across the kitchen table. Two took flight; Libby caught one, Josh the other.

George appeared in the doorway, rubbing his hands. "Yes, then," he confirmed with a frown. "*More* practice papers?"

"I'm done now." Libby took the one Josh was clutching and gathered the rest into a pile. "My exam's in—"

"Four weeks and three days," Josh and George finished in unison.

Scooping up her pile, Libby stuck out her tongue at George and squished past him. "Your dinner's in the microwave. Sausages and mash. Two minutes."

"Thanks, Lib."

She continued on her way, calling down as she reached the top of the stairs, "Josh has something to tell you."

George looked up the stairs. "What?" Libby didn't answer. "Do you?" he asked Josh.

"Erm...not really?" Heat shot up his cheeks so fast he went into an immediate sweat and attempted a surreptitious beeline for the microwave to avoid George's scrutiny. "Two minutes. Let's see..." He fussed with the timer—

"Joshua..."

—and pushed the start button. "It's nothing important. How was art therapy?" He turned to George but didn't dare meet his gaze.

"Good," George answered, still watching suspiciously. "We talked about Jess."

"Oh. That's...interesting." Josh focused on the seconds counting down. A coincidence? It wasn't as if they never spoke about her, but twice in the same afternoon in two completely different settings and conversations?

"Yeah. Gabby was shocked to hear she had topless photos."

"Was she?" Josh attempted indifference.

"I thought they were mates at uni—Gabby and Jess," George went on as if he were oblivious to Josh's inner war. "Didn't they live in the same halls?"

"Not for long. Gabby moved to our halls when she defected from law to psychology."

"That's right. She told me that." George joined Josh in watching the countdown. "So they weren't friends?"

"They were...friendly. More than acquaintances."

"Uh-huh?" George nodded. The microwave pinged, but he made no move to open the door.

Several agonising seconds passed before Josh relented and opened it for him. "Would you get to the point, please?"

"I don't have one." George grabbed the plate and moved to the table, tucking in right away and fanning his mouth. "Hot."

"You should leave it to stand."

"Too hungry." George scooped up another forkful of mashed potato and blew on it. "Jess didn't chase boys at uni, then?"

And let it go, Josh thought but didn't say. "A bit, I suppose. After Simon, she mostly gave up and kept her nose to the grindstone."

"Who?"

"One of the law students. Jess and Simon were an item for the first couple of weeks. He wasn't good for her work ethic."

"Hmm." George shovelled in more mashed potato, following up with half a sausage. "What did Sean think of that?"

"I couldn't say." Josh handed him a knife. "You're so uncouth sometimes. I'd blame your mother, but I know better." Any poor table manners George had developed came from borderline living rough at uni and then on the ranch. To his credit, he cut a more sensible-sized chunk off the sausage the next time, and while he ate, Josh finished clearing the kitchen around him, hoping but not believing for a second that they were done with the Jess conversation.

"So," George said, rinsing his plate and handing it to Josh to put in the dishwasher, "in conclusion—"

"George…"

"OK, OK. One question."

"Go on."

"D'you think…Simon, was it?"

"Yes."

"D'you think he was responsible for the things Jess did?"

"No."

"You said he wasn't good for her work ethic."

"He was filthy rich by birth and bone idle, but he didn't have the brains for the kind of con Jess pulled off."

"Is that why they broke up?"

"You said *one* question."

"Same question, part b." George grinned hopefully.

Josh huffed. "No. They broke up because Simon was gay and asked Jess to marry him so he could keep his inheritance. She persuaded him to tell his parents the truth."

"Then he might not be filthy rich anymore," George reasoned.

"Who knows? And who cares? I don't." Josh's overplayed shrug fooled no-one. He grabbed the dishcloth and started wiping the kitchen counters. "What else did you and Gabby cover today?"

"You first. What was it you had to tell me?"

"Libby thinks the surgery needs bright colours. I said it was bright enough, but we're a long way off decorating. My room's too big for one thing, and—"

"Josh." George's hand landed on top of his, stilling the swish of the cloth over the already spotless surface. "It can't be that bad. Come on. Talk to me."

Josh shook his head. No. It wasn't bad. It was nothing. *Nothing.* But that nothingness spun and spun and became a vortex, stretching twenty-two and a half years into the past, and it was taking all of Josh's strength to not cross the event horizon, stay in the present.

They'd broken in, taken down his blinds, hung them up again, stolen his shoes, cut the power to his light…insisted his room was haunted, and then, when it was all over, when he and Sean had finally dug down to the bottom of it and proved it was a hoax, the inexplicable had happened, that single incident neither of them could dismiss as part of some ill-thought-out research project. A group hallucination derived from suggestion? Josh was not, nor had he ever been, suggestible; for the most part, he'd have vouched for Sean in that regard too. *And there's no such thing as ghosts.* Not then, not now.

"Come again?" George said.

"What?" Josh hung the dishcloth back on the drainer. "I didn't say a word."

"You said something about ghosts."

Sometimes life seemed little more than one big, elaborate praxinoscope because they'd had exactly the same conversation last time he thought he was being haunted. "Just imaginations in overdrive."

"Yep. I *imagined* you said something about ghosts."

"That's not what I meant, George."

"Then what did you mean?"

As if she'd spontaneously transported from her room to the kitchen, Libby appeared, minus the exam papers, in their place a tower of textbooks. "He means…" She struggled across to the table, dumped the books, turned and, with an apologetic glance at Josh, said, "There's a ghost in his surgery, and he doesn't know what to do about it."

4: Most Haunted

Sandison-Morley Residence
Present Day
Monday, 15ᵗʰ April

F OR REAL?" GEORGE stared at Libby, then at Josh, who held eye contact for as long as he could but had to abort when he admitted—to himself only—that what Libby had said was true. While she'd been occupied with her past papers, he'd mentally worked through every theory he knew, and not one of them explained to his satisfaction their experiences that afternoon.

"What the hell happened?" George asked.

"Nothing—" Josh started at the same time as Libby launched into a full account, which he punctuated with the same unconvincing arguments he'd given her earlier. By the time she was done, George's eyes were as wide as if he'd witnessed the incident firsthand.

"Whoa. That's unbelievable."

"Precisely," Josh said, "which is how we can be sure our minds were playing tricks on us."

"But we were both there!" Libby argued. "I heard what you heard!"

"Or, like I said, you were susceptible to my suggestions."

"Or, like *I* said, Jess is trying to tell you something and—"

"Enough!" Josh snapped.

Libby gasped in surprise, then her face crumpled and she fled the kitchen, swift feet thundering up the stairs into the bathroom. The door slammed shut, followed by the sharp click of the bolt driving home.

Josh stared after her, guilt and frustration waging war on his anger, although it was more like a sizzling wet cloth thrown over a pan of burning oil. He was vaguely aware of George saying, "Hey," and asking if he wanted a hug. Josh shook his head, or thought he had but couldn't be sure.

"No," he answered for good measure. Above him came the muffled honk of their daughter blowing her nose. He shifted his gaze upward. "But someone else could do with one, by the sound of it."

"She gave you a hard time today, huh?"

"She's been fine, mostly. She wanted to know about Sean's daughter, of course, so I had the Spanish Inquisition for a while, then she critiqued the surgery. She'd be sketching the redesign now if she wasn't so fixated on her exams and..." He couldn't bring himself to say it.

"The ghost?" George finished for him, adding before Josh could argue 'not a ghost', "You used the word first."

"As part of the statement 'there is no such thing as'. Do you think I'm wrong?"

"No, but something's got you rattled, and if it's not a ghost, what is it?"

"I don't know, which is why, first thing tomorrow, I'm going to call Dan and ask him to look at the electrics. Meanwhile—" Josh grimaced at a second bang of the bathroom door. "I have an apology to make." He moved to leave, but George stopped him with a hand on his arm.

"Give her some space."

"I shouldn't have shouted. None of this is her fault."

"If you try talking to her now, you'll end up having a row, and I don't want to get caught in the middle."

"I see." Josh advanced, lifting George's arms and positioning them into the hug he'd offered. "Saving your own neck, Morley?"

"Can you blame me?" George pulled back so that Josh's kiss missed on the first attempt. On the second, Josh gripped him by the ears and kept hold until the deed was done. It was no more than a peck, but it was enough to ease Josh's frazzled nerves.

After that, they moved to the living room, on George's recommendation, and chatted about his therapy session—an excuse to play with paint, as his mum called it. Last time, Gabby had asked him to sketch a house that wasn't modelled on a real-world location, which, given that George's paintings were artistic interpretations of people, animals and places he knew, had been a tough assignment. Today, he'd begun filling in the details, and he'd found it easier, he said, although he still couldn't see how it would help his dissociative disorder. As per usual, Josh offered to explain, and—as per usual—George rejected that offer.

"I'd be happy if I could get the door to look right," he grumbled. "And the roof. And the windows."

"And the walls and chimney stack..." Josh tormented.

"Yeah," George agreed ruefully. "It's all a bit askew right now."

"That's a matter of perspective, surely."

"Joshua..."

"Well, it is. Capturing a three-dimensional representation through a two-dimensional medium..."

George grunted and turned, head only, toward the TV. Josh smiled to himself, perpetually amused both by George's resistance to understanding the theory behind his therapy and by how, when they'd bought a sofa large enough to seat three, he was squashed up at one end while George was stretched full length with his head in Josh's lap. Still, it was a comforting normality, and he felt ready to deliver his apology, but it seemed he'd left it too long, as Libby was on her way down the stairs. Josh tapped George's shoulder to get him to sit up, which he did, and Josh drew breath, words at the ready. *I'm sorry I shouted. I was being unreasonable.*

"Where d'you think you're going?" was what he said instead, and that *was* reasonable at eight-thirty in the evening. Her coat and the enormous bag dangling from her side had already given him his answer, but he waited for her to say it.

"I'm going to stay at Shaunna's."

"Are you now." Not a question.

"If it's OK with you." And that was an afterthought.

"How are you getting there?"

"Andy's picking me up."

"You couldn't ask us for a lift?"

"Shaunna said he's just left the Red Lion, so he's coming past here anyway."

Josh glanced at George, who shrugged, leaving it to Josh. George would support him, whatever he decided, but he wasn't sure how to handle this. If it were a simple case of Libby being upset by his outburst, he'd have told her to go and have fun and to call him if she needed a lift home in the morning.

Or maybe it was that simple.

"Did you tell her what happened?"

"That you bit my head off, you mean?"

"No. The reason why I…bit your head off." He'd always hated that phrase—more so now when the cap fitted him so snugly.

Libby's expression was grim bordering on tearful. "I said we'd had an argument. Am I not allowed to tell her?"

That was a hell of a question. He trusted her enough to know that if he asked her not to share what had happened, she'd abide by that. *Ask a childhood abuse survivor to keep a shared secret?*

"You can tell her if you want to."

"Thanks."

"No problem." *Huge* problem. There was also a car with a huge engine idling outside their house.

Hearing it too, Libby scurried over to the sofa and leaned down to hug George, then Josh. Her bag slipped, knocking Josh's glasses onto the floor. "Oops!" She picked them up and put them back on his face. "Thank you for letting me go to Shaunna's."

He didn't say 'you're welcome' or anything of that ilk. She was sixteen years old and could leave any time she wanted. "Have a good evening."

"You too." Libby straightened and hoisted her bag back onto her shoulder. "It might not even come up."

It would. "Call when you're ready to come home. I'll come and get you."

"OK. Bye!" The front door opened and closed. The Mustang's purr became a growl, became a distant rumble.

For a few minutes after she'd gone, Josh watched the TV screen, and he could hear accompanying voices, but they didn't register as more than an annoying buzz.

"You did good," George said at last and got up from the sofa. "Coffee?"

"Are you having one?"

"Nope. I'm having hot chocolate."

"I'll join you, then."

"OK." George shook his head and sauntered from the room, muttering, "Strange man."

"Married you," Josh called after him.

"Yep," George called back.

Josh repositioned his glasses and unlocked his phone to send Shaunna a message, purportedly to thank her for always leaving her door open for Libby, but he was aware also of his desire to tell his side of the story. Not the argument part, although it dawned on him that they'd somehow bypassed his apology; he rectified that with a quick call to Libby, and it really was quick.

"Hey, Lib. I'm sorry I shouted."

"It's OK. I'm sorry I kept going on about it. Gotta go. Love you!" A blast of rock music was the last thing Josh heard as Libby ended the call.

If he hadn't known better, he'd have thought she was in the car of some irresponsible teenage boy. Well, he had the 'car' and 'irresponsible' bits right. He opened a text message to Shaunna and managed to type *'Hey. Thanks for this evening. I just…'* before an incoming call cut him off. He didn't recognise the number and almost dismissed it, but curiosity was, as usual, his worst enemy, so he hit answer.

"Hello?"

Silence.

"Hello?"

Still nothing.

George returned with the hot chocolates.

Josh quickly hung up and backspaced his message to Shaunna to the full stop, finishing off with '*You're a star. x*'. He took one of the mugs from George, who re-joined him on the sofa but stayed upright with legs crossed, his mug balanced on one knee.

"Who were you talking to?"

"Nobody. They didn't speak."

"Or they'd accidentally muted themselves. I do that all the time."

"All the time? You don't even look at your phone, never mind use it."

George grinned but offered no defence.

Josh sipped his hot chocolate, the sweet heat gradually working its magic, releasing the tension in his neck and shoulders until he was saggy as an old cardigan. Laughter from the TV drew his attention to the two guys ad-libbing a client–therapist scene, predictably featuring a chaise-longue. It bore little resemblance to a real modern-day therapy session—there would be no chaise-longues in his new surgery, just as there had been none in his old one—but the skit was quite funny in places.

"Like parenting, isn't it?" George nodded at the screen. "Completely made up on the spot."

Josh laughed. "All my experience, all those adolescents I've counselled, yet I've never been so out of my depth as I have this past year. I feel terrible about today."

"That's the first time you've raised your voice to her," George pointed out. "And she does push it."

"She hit a sore spot. A few, actually. She thought Sean might be playing a practical joke."

"Unlikely. Did you tell her what they did to you at uni?"

"No. We were rudely interrupted by a self-propelled toilet roll. I will tell her at some point, though, but there's more." Josh swirled the mug between his palms, even now struggling to talk about it, and this was the man with whom he had shared every facet of himself, the good and the bad, the brightest and the darkest. "Remember the night after Jess died, when I went back to her house?"

"Did you?"

"Yes! How do you not…" Josh's mind fast-forwarded through the days following Jess's passing and his grief-triggered hypomanic episode, during which he'd done a few things he'd rather not have George remember. "Never mind. I mustn't have told you, but that was when Jess's mum asked Shaunna and me if we'd scatter the ashes."

"I always wondered about that. So they were both at Jess's place too?"

"Her mum was. Shaunna turned up a bit later. I was sitting in the garden. I couldn't bring myself to go inside the house." He felt it best to skip that he'd had a packet of cigarettes in his hand and had almost started smoking again. "I'd been crying, I think, and I could see next to nothing, but I heard a noise. A door closing. It came from the house, and the lights were off, although the sky was brightening, so it must've been around five-thirty, six o'clock by then."

"How long were you there?"

"I left here just after midnight."

"Six hours? You sat in Jess's garden for *six hours*?"

"Yes, and it was bloody cold and wet, I can tell you. But that's by the by. Someone called my name, and because, clearly, I was not in a rational state of mind, I thought it was Jess." He chewed his cheek, elaborated. "Her ghost."

"But it was Jess's mum."

"They sounded so alike. I told Jess that once, right back when we first became friends. She disputed it—vehemently. She'd bring it up at seemingly random moments, citing examples of words she and her mum pronounced differently, or her mum would say some phrase or other, and Jess would insist, 'You'll never hear me saying that,' then catch herself doing exactly that."

"Yeah. I know that feeling," George muttered, which, in spite of the topic, made Josh smile. It didn't happen often, but there were certain things George said and did that he'd picked up from his mum, although he didn't swear half as much as she did. There were dockers who swore less than Iris Morley. "So it wasn't Jess's ghost?" George asked jokingly—a gentle push for Josh to keep going.

"Obviously not, but the thing is, George, when I heard my name, I wanted so much for it to be her that even after I'd followed her mum into the house, in my mind, it *was* Jess, and I'd have given anything for it to be her. This afternoon, after we adjourned to the coffee shop—that sounds so calm and casual. We *fled* to the coffee shop, which was when Libby suggested Jess could be haunting my surgery. She wasn't serious, or I hope she wasn't, but it threw me back to that night in the garden."

"You wanted it to be true again."

"I did, but at the same time, I was afraid. I couldn't tell you if that was more for the possibility of it being a practical joke or for the whole situation kicking off another cycle after I've been stable for so long. Libby was good, though. She realised what she'd said bothered me, and she quickly switched the subject back to Sean and Phee, which wasn't a vast improvement, but it kept me from ruminating."

"Yeah, right," George said with a knowing sideways glance.

"OK. From ruminating too deeply," Josh conceded. He noticed again the hot chocolate in his hands and took a long drink. He was ready to admit it now but didn't rush to move the mug away from his mouth. "In conclusion…" He swallowed the last powdery dregs with a shudder. "I wish I knew another grief counsellor I could trust the way I do Sean. I can't work through this on my own."

"That's a first!"

Josh elbowed George lightly in the side. "Watch it, or I'll be booking couples sessions with Gabby." George acted horrified by the idea, but that emerald twinkle in his eye said he wouldn't mind if Josh were serious, which he wasn't.

"Why not Sean?"

"Because of the way he felt about Jess. He was in love with her, but he was too scared to tell her."

"She could be scary."

"I don't disagree. Of course, Sean's never outright admitted it was fear that stopped him. They were both too busy with their careers, or at different points in their lives, or married in his case, and on and on—and he has the audacity to advise me on how I should be handling *my* grief." Josh gesticulated his annoyance, flinging the dregs from his mug over the back of the sofa.

George disarmed him and set the mug on the coffee table. "Sean's broken heart aside—"

"Not aside."

"You don't know what I was gonna say."

"What's your wager?" Josh asked, smugly confident.

"Hmm…I'll make the coffee for the next month."

"And if you win?"

"I never win this game."

"Perhaps this is a night of firsts."

"Perhaps you could get on with it and tell me what I was gonna say."

"You were going to ask if I think bereavement counselling will exorcise my ghost."

"Damn you, smarty-pants."

Josh grinned.

"So do you?" George asked.

"I think it's worth a shot—for Sean as well as me, but that's a fight for another time. He has enough to contend with."

"His secret love child…"

"She's not."

"And yet no-one knows about her."

Josh patted his lap, inviting George to resume his usual position. George obliged and blinked up at him expectantly.

"Fine," Josh relented. "The potted version—when we were at uni, Sean registered as a sperm donor because he needed the money. One of the law students asked him to make a direct deposit. Imogen Rowan. She was really rather beautiful, and uncommonly nice for a law undergrad." An image came to mind of Imogen sneaking out of Sean's room early one Sunday morning, shoes in hand and false eyelashes stuck to her cheek. She was halfway down the first flight of stairs before Josh drummed up the courage to tell her about the eyelashes, and he chased after her, then pointed mutely at her face. He blushed at the memory; he'd been so shy back then, but he could laugh about it now.

George was eyeing him curiously, so he finished off with, "Phoenix is, shall we say, the interest on Sean's investment."

"Right. That makes sense. Sort of."

"Which part doesn't?"

"If he was just a sperm donor, why is she here?"

"That, ma moitié, is a very good question."

5: Uneventful Vigil

GENIE HISSED AND clamped a palm to the back of her head, hardly daring to breathe. The jolt of pain dulled to a throb, and she tried again, a gentle bend of the knees, searching with fingertips for the last piece of music, which had drifted under the sofa during the madness of the previous evening. The rest was in a heap on the piano; Margaret must have tidied around post calling an ambulance. Xander had remained with Genie until the doorbell rang announcing the paramedics' arrival, when he'd bolted faster than a spooked colt. She'd neither heard from nor seen him since.

Treading gingerly so as not to further jar her brain, she carried the sheet music to the piano and set it with the rest, much of it crumpled from the scuffle with the poltergeist—or whatever she was supposed to call it. Genie knew a smattering of French but no German whatsoever, although the internet reliably informed her *poltergeist* translated literally into 'knocking spirit', which was on the nose from her perspective. From Xander's, who knew? He'd acted as if the term were a supernatural slur and had yet to satisfactorily explain why.

Still, the knock on the head had supplanted yesterday's sheer terror that had seen her calling him 'out of the blue' after two decades of avoiding contact with her peers. Or not them specifically; she'd avoided her family and anyone closely connected to them, including Xander, his cousins Gabby and Andrew, and *darling* Simon. She missed them dreadfully—even Simon—but like her privilege, she'd left their friendships behind to start anew.

For all of that, she didn't regret calling Xander, despite the high chance of him and her father running into each other at Westminster, which was why she'd pressed the issue of confidentiality. She'd not endured all these years out of her father's reach to present him with an excuse for re-establishing his hold over her life—and Phee's—and he would take it if it were offered.

A quiet *ahem* sounded from the doorway. "Sorry to disturb you, my lady."

"It's all right, Margaret. I was…" Genie blinked a couple of times, bringing the music score and her thoughts back into focus. She'd been on the cusp of playing out an entire imagined scenario that began with finding her father and sister on her doorstep and heartily embracing them both. Now that *had* to be due to the concussion. "Sorry, Margaret. What do you need?"

"If you recall, I have an appointment this morning, so I'm preparing lunch now. Should I cater for His Lordship and Jonathan?"

"I'd say so. Have you seen either of them this morning?"

"I haven't, but I'll make sandwiches so the lunch doesn't spoil, if that's acceptable?"

"Yes, that's perfect."

"Can I get anything for you now, my lady? Some fruit and yoghurt, perhaps?"

"Good Lord, no, but thank you."

"A cup of coffee then?"

Genie's stomach clenched at the prospect. "I'd say yes, but I don't think I'll keep one down. Is it usual to feel so queasy after a concussion?" Queasy, dizzy, and an intermittent sensation that her head was shrinking, but before she could voice her concern at being left to fend for herself for half a day, Margaret interjected.

"I've asked Victor to come and take a look at the dishwasher," which was to say, Margaret had asked her partner to look after Genie in her absence.

Tempting as it was to protest, Genie could only muster a smile of gratitude as, with a nod, Margaret retreated to the kitchen.

Genie gathered the pile of music and stooped to open the stool—not her wisest move, resulting only in a sharp inhalation and cramp in her neck. She paused and tensed; the cramp intensified. Eyes shut to stave off the whirling of the room, she turned her head ever so slowly to the right until the cramp eased and, when she felt safe to move again, lowered herself onto the stool with little regard for the possibility that a ghost child had sat there the previous evening. May well still be sitting there for all she knew.

Xander would have been able to tell her, of course, and she wondered if she should wake him, but perhaps that was a task best left to Jonathan, assuming the two hadn't fled Rowan Mews in the night. It was awfully strange that the men were still sleeping. Granted, the day was young, but new house guests generally rose early then loitered like…well, like unwelcome ghosts until someone tended their needs. They'd brought all that equipment, so in all probability they'd had a late night—should she instruct Margaret to forget about preparing lunch in favour of a hearty dinner? Were there any foods Xander wouldn't eat? She couldn't recall.

"I'm off now, my lady." Margaret stood in the doorway, fastening the buttons down the front of her wine-red mackintosh. "The sandwiches are in a Tupperware box on the island, and there's a jug of orange juice in the fridge. I should be back by two."

"Take your time, Margaret, and thank you again."

Margaret nodded to acknowledge she'd heard, but where usually she'd have departed, she remained where she was, fussing with her collar and adjusting her cuffs.

It occurred to Genie that if she asked what the appointment was, her assistant would tell her out of a sense of duty, but beyond her concern for Margaret's well-being, it was none of her business. Still, the woman seemed reluctant to leave.

"Is there something else?" Genie asked.

"No…I don't think so, my lady. Why do you ask?"

"You seem a little out of sorts, and I don't wish to pry, but… are you unwell?"

"Oh!" Margaret laughed uncomfortably and turned pink. "I'm in good health, I can assure you. It is not a medical matter."

She cleared her throat and took a step forward. "I have an interview." She surrendered the information as if under interrogation.

Genie reeled, taken completely by surprise. What could she say to that? She could hardly demand to know why Margaret hadn't told her she was looking for another job. Was she unhappy? Did she want more money? More time off? Those matters could be resolved easily, if only Margaret had said something before. An interview didn't necessarily mean she would be leaving her post, but it spoke of her desire to do so.

"I'll write you a reference, of course," Genie said diplomatically but couldn't help adding, "I wish you'd told me."

"I'm sorry, my lady. I didn't feel I could."

"I understand. I do hope it goes well for you."

"Thank you." Margaret backed out of the room, and Genie was glad. The conversation was becoming more excruciating by the second. A moment later, the front door closed.

"Well," Genie said, endeavouring to wear a brave face. "That's that, I suppose." Talking to herself helped, she'd found, and she continued to do so as she returned the music scores to the stool and set off for the kitchen, where she eyed the Tupperware box in dismay. It was absurd to feel so betrayed by Margaret's secrecy, but it wasn't just that. She'd had no inkling Margaret was looking for another job, and after twelve years, she'd imagined she knew the woman well enough to pick up on something being off.

She wondered, too, how their relationship would fare should Margaret's interview prove unsuccessful when the mere fact of it was already a stubborn tarnish that even the very best replacement would have trouble polishing away. When Margaret had asked for reviews of her salary in the past, Genie had always obliged and had given her a substantial pay rise after Jess passed. Not once had she refused to grant Margaret leave, irrespective of whether it coincided with the end of the tax year or the festive season, both of which times Genie needed help the most. In all matters of managing the house, Margaret was forthright, and she seemed satisfied by her work.

What was left? A complete change of career? Personal conflict?

Before Genie could further tie herself in knots, there came the sound of footsteps and male voices descending the staircase, and Xander then Jonathan appeared before her. Jonathan was showered and clean-shaven and carrying a leather Filofax-type organiser clamped to his chest as if it were the Bible; Xander was empty-handed and had the appearance of a drunk who had spent the night in a police cell.

"Good morning, gentlemen," Genie greeted them cheerfully. "How was your vigil?"

Jonathan opened his mouth, but Xander answered.

"It was not a *vigil*."

"Oh. Sorry. Then what—"

"How's the head?" Jonathan asked, and Genie smiled in gratitude at his intervention. Xander was pricklier than usual this morning, which was saying something.

"Sore but bearable. Can I offer you both breakfast?" She turned away and checked how much coffee was in the jug, discovering there was none. "I'll put on some—"

"No more for me, thank you," Xander said, thereby explaining the empty jug.

"Something else? A glass of juice or milk? A cup of tea?"

"No, thank you."

"Perhaps I could make the coffee, Your Ladyship?" Jonathan suggested. "Sorry, *Genie*," he added solemnly as if he hadn't done it deliberately to highlight the inappropriateness of a lady serving a staffer. It was a very long time since Genie had cared about that kind of nonsense etiquette, though she could imagine Xander being quite a stickler for it, so for the sake of peace, she bowed out, left Jonathan to perform his duty and took a seat on a stool at the island.

"What are your plans for today?" she asked generally, unsure who was most likely to answer. She'd have tried a more specific query, but she was a novice whose vocabulary on spiritual matters was derived from TV ghost-hunting, and every faux pas not only patently irritated Xander but also served to prove how far out of her wheelhouse she was.

"Excuse me. I must take this call." Extracting his phone from his organiser, Jonathan strode from the kitchen and out of the side door.

Genie eyed the dormant coffee machine, contemplating her role and Jonathan's and whether he'd forgive her if she did what she'd planned to in the first place, but her defiance drive was lower than usual—another consequence of the conk on the head?—so she decided to give it another minute. Then she realised how ridiculous that was in her own house and acted decisively.

Several minutes later and with no sign of Jonathan, Xander said, "Collecting more data."

"That's handy, having someone to do the legwork for you."

Xander pulled a small notebook from his inside pocket, set it down on the island and unfastened the elastic band holding it shut. The book sprang open at a place marked by a nub of a pencil. "You asked what my plans are for today. I plan to collect more data. Would you like to read it?" He briskly tapped the page.

"You don't mind?" Genie asked.

"I wouldn't make the offer if I did." He nudged the book in her direction.

Resuming her seat, Genie glanced down at the book, but she had a question about the previous evening. "You said we had to leave."

"Yes."

"Why?"

"The boy." Xander stared at her, the effect intensified by his glasses, strong-lensed and round with tortoiseshell frames. She'd never known him to wear any other design. He blinked twice, and she found herself blinking twice back, but if it were some kind of signalling system, she was clueless to its meaning.

"You say the boy…"

"He was screaming. A horrible noise. Gurgling…perhaps he drowned." Xander's gaze turned inward, his features harrowed in palpable distress. Genie felt selfish for thinking it, but she was glad she didn't share his gift.

"I'm sorry."

"Why?"

"I brought you here."

Xander bobbed his head in agreement. "I have heard and seen more awful things. Are you going to read now?"

"Yes." Genie focused again on the book, expecting a struggle to read without her glasses but having no such problem. Dark, bold numbers were pencilled down the left margins of both pages, each denoting a time at thirty-minute intervals from 22:30 through to 08:30. Next to 02:30 was a series of abbreviations and the time 02:42.

"What's this?" she asked.

"You have mice."

"They're a permanent fixture," Genie said ruefully. Such was the country life.

"You should use humane traps."

"Phee says that too. They're kinder, I know."

"And quieter," Xander said. He tapped the page again. "The snap of the spring sets off the microphone sensor."

"Oops. Sorry about that." Guiltily, Genie pushed the book back. "I'll make sure the traps are gone before you begin again tonight."

"Ghosts don't wait for nightfall. Those *vigils* you mention are for entertainment, the séances of the twenty-first century. Ghosts are imprints of human energy, which persists with no respect for the hour, or else they'd all be asleep when those TV shows film their vigils."

"That would be an improvement," Genie muttered dryly.

"I've had no cause to watch them." Xander closed the notebook and returned it to his pocket. "The traps can stay where they are. We're not trying to catch ghosts. We're ruling out physical causes, and I worry the equipment is malfunctioning. Then a rodent assures me it's working perfectly well. They're fascinating creatures, rats."

"Rats?!" Genie's nausea, which had abated somewhat, returned in full force.

"Not here," Xander said, matter of fact. Genie let out half a sigh of relief before he added, "Or none that I saw."

"Xander, please stop!" Genie implored, at which his lips twitched in amusement. He was terrorising her. That was new, or at least, she'd never picked up on it before. Xander behaved differently in company, both less talkative and more brusque when he did speak. Perhaps she was different too, as when Jonathan returned, the conversation ground to a halt until he gave it a jumpstart.

"You made the coffee," he accused.

"You were…occupied," Genie explained, then gave herself a ticking off. This was her house, and she'd make the coffee if she damn well pleased.

"For which I can only apologise. Perhaps I could pour for us?"

"Now look, Jonathan. You're my guests—both of you. If Margaret were here, I'd still pour the coffee. I can't abide standing on ceremony, especially so early in the day, so please, sit down and shut up!"

Jonathan's eyebrows formed a harried 'M' across his forehead, though the rest of his face remained remarkably stoic as he inclined towards Xander, who gave him a nod of permission, and finally, Jonathan sat.

"Good!" One small victory. "How do you take it?"

"As it comes, Your—Genie."

"You're incorrigible!"

"I try."

"No doubt! Xander, are you sure you don't want one?"

"Positive." He was already on his way out of the kitchen. "May I take another look at the piano?"

"You carry on."

He left. Genie poured herself and Jonathan coffee and carried both over to the island.

"Thank you." He picked up his cup right away, but barely had it touched his lips before Xander called his name.

Genie offered him a sympathetic smile. "Take it with you."

"I shall."

Soon after, the drawing room door closed with Xander and Jonathan on the inside, followed by the sound of someone—Xander, she could but hope—playing the piano. She didn't recognise the piece, but it was light and melodic and afforded her a few minutes of normality with her coffee and the daily newspaper. Indeed, considerably longer than a few minutes had passed when a light rap on the window signalled Margaret's partner had arrived.

"Good morning, Vic."

"Morning, Missus," he greeted as he stepped in the back door, plonked down his tool bag and wiped his feet thoroughly on the mat, which wasn't overkill on his part. Whenever he came here, he did so via the woods, drifting in on a blast of air so fresh and natural it was enough to lure even an indoorsy type like Genie out into the Shropshire wilds. Boots clean, Victor toed them off before he came in proper, his heavy steps muted by itchy-looking woollen socks.

"Coffee?" Genie offered.

"No, ta. I've had a pot of tea already this morning. Besides, shouldn't you be resting?"

"I'm fine, Vic. Really."

"Right, well. I said I'd take a look at that dishwasher of yours. Marg says it's not emptying fast enough, so likely a blockage in the waste pipe. I'll keep the noise down. Mind you…" He paused to listen. "That a CD I hear?"

"No. My friend Xander."

Victor's nod was approving yet also managed to convey 'not my kind of music'. Genie chuckled.

"I prefer something a little rockier myself." For which she had her alumni to thank. Sean had introduced her to political folksy rock, Jess to the heavier, dirtier stuff she'd listened to because Andy did. Genie's entire social life at university could be mapped out by a soundtrack she'd been trying to rebuild since graduation, some songs bare snatches of memory, a few notes or a hook line that was impossible to pin down, others she'd listened to until, as the saying went, she'd worn them out.

Victor had wasted no time getting started, but he was slow and steady, each plod back and forth between the utility room and his tool bag an opportunity to check on Genie's well-being.

That was Margaret all over. If the hospital decreed that Genie needed someone with her for twenty-four hours, then that was what she would jolly well have.

"God, I'll miss her." The sentiment escaped aloud, fortunately between Victor's walk-throughs, but she couldn't just let Margaret go like that. She had to try to fix it.

Typically, now she'd decided to act, Victor didn't come back for some time, and she almost lost her nerve, knowing what she was about to do was unfair on him *and* Margaret.

"Vic, may I ask you a question?"

He crouched over his tool bag but glanced her way. "I know that tone." And back into his bag. "If it's about Marg…"

"It is, and I hate to put you on the spot, but I need to understand. Have I upset her in some way? Could I make it right?"

Tools clanged together out of sight, and he chewed on nothing. She couldn't decide if he was giving her a chance to retract her request or figuring out how to respond. Either way, she was about to apologise and tell him to forget she'd said anything when he finally straightened, a large screwdriver in his hand.

"It's not my business how you keep order in your house, Missus, but it's nothing *you* did. Now, if you wouldn't mind…" He waved the screwdriver and made a speedy plod towards the utility room before she could interrogate him further.

Nothing I did? Then who? Phee was hardly ever home, and it worked to Margaret's advantage, as she took her annual leave during Phee's school holidays and got far more than she would with any other employer. If not Phee, then it had to be Paul, but that seemed equally unlikely. True, he was terribly messy, but he was polite and always expressed his thanks for his ironed, folded and put-away laundry. Genie couldn't imagine him ever doing anything bad enough for Margaret to resign; still, she'd ask him when he came home at the end of the week. Until then, she had no choice but to let the matter rest.

6: Another Morning

Tierney Residence
Present Day
Tuesday, 16ᵗʰ April

A NOTHER FAILED NIGHT of intimacy. Sean didn't even need to open his eyes to confirm he had the bed to himself. There'd be a message somewhere—on his phone, maybe, or on the pillows next to his—telling him she didn't want to wake him as if she were doing it for his benefit only. He understood. It would have resulted in yet another post-mortem of his making, and those were getting them nowhere.

Of course, he'd awoken with an erection, and it was comforting to have the physical confirmation of what his GP had told him: there was no medical reason for his lack of sexual appetite nor his inability to sustain an erection when an opportunity for love-making presented itself. If Sophie hadn't already left, they'd have made the most of the involuntary bodily response, which was fine by him, but eighteen months without release, Sean was past any attempt at self-pleasure when the thought alone had deflated what little interest his body had shown.

The alarm clock got in two bleeps before he silenced it and heaved himself to the side of the bed with a sigh. Tuesday morning, three hours of clinic, followed by—

"Ha-ha! It's Tuesday morning!" Sean bounced to his feet as his thoughts about the day ahead finally coalesced with the realisation that this particular Tuesday morning would be his last marred by three hours of appointments too short and prescriptive to be of use to him or his patients. He whisked the curtains open and grinned out at the dreary April showers tumbling from a leaden grey sky. None of it could darken the sunny feeling within.

He grabbed his dressing gown from the hook on the door and exited, peering in on Dylan as he passed. "Wake him now? No. I'll sort me out first—" on to the bathroom, a pee, shower running "—breakfast, daycare, clinic—" toilet flushed, under the water "—Jesus!—" and out of the scalding spray while the cistern refilled. "Did I ask Melanie to send that referral? God, I hope so…" And on and on with the mental list of things to do, things that should have been done, things that might need to be done, all of which would be forgotten before he left the house… until Sean was back in his room, dressed and running a comb through his hair.

"Daddy, Daddy, Daddy, Daddy."

"Hold on. I'm coming." Sean threw the comb down on the windowsill and kicked his dressing gown aside on his way out of the room. "Good morning, fella."

"Up, up, up!" The tiny prisoner in a saggy-bottomed teddy jumpsuit gripped his cot bars with both fists and shook, releasing only when Sean lifted him to liberation. "Toast!"

Sean laughed. "Shall we get you dressed first?"

"Toast. Please."

It was as broad as it was long, so Sean relented and carried Dylan down the stairs, setting him on the ground to close the safety gate.

"Finx," Dylan shouted, and he was off to the kitchen, where Sphinx was cleaning his paws in a play of indifference when he'd be wanting his breakfast as urgently as Dylan. Sean was undecided on the best order to tackle the hungry beasts.

"Don't—"

With a half-hearted hiss of protest, Sphinx jumped onto the coffee machine and out of reach of grabby toddler fingers that could never resist a snatch at that bushy tail. Sean hoisted Dylan up and into his high chair, strapped him in and inspected his hand. "Let me see that. Oh, you're fine. Right, tea…toast…"

The usual breakfast routine ensued: kettle filled, bread in the toaster, cat food in the bowl. Sean marvelled at how accomplished he felt now that it was second nature to him when not so long ago it was a mammoth effort to get just himself up and out the door in one decently assembled piece, and by quarter past eight, Tierney and son were both standing outside the house with their respective bags, waiting for the taxi to arrive.

Twenty-five past eight, they were *still* standing outside the house. Sean called the taxi firm.

"Busy morning. Should be with you within ten minutes."

"OK. Thanks."

Twenty-five to nine...

"Good morning, Sean."

"Morning, Victoria," Sean greeted his next-door neighbour.

"Still waiting for your taxi?"

"Aye." Sean took out his phone and called the firm again as his neighbour drove away towards her shop, which was in the opposite direction from the university and hospital. They'd had the discussion before.

"It's on its way," the taxi firm claimed.

"From where? Birmingham?" Sean did his best to sound jovial, though his patience was wearing very thin indeed.

Quarter to nine...

"Come on, Tierney." Josh clicked his key fob, remotely unlocking his car, and got in before there was any argument, although Sean could see a taxi—potentially theirs—in the distance and getting Dylan's car seat into the back of Josh's three-door hatchback was a pain in the neck. Deciding it was safer to risk upsetting the taxi firm, Sean secured Dylan, pushed the front seat back into position and climbed in beside Josh.

"Thanks very much."

"No problem. I need to see personnel." Josh signalled and pulled away from the kerb.

Sean looked him over. "You're not dressed for a meeting."

"I'm hoping they'll get the message once and for all."

"They might at that."

Josh was wearing what for him passed as scruffs: a light-blue and white rugby shirt with iron-creased sleeves, washed-out jeans and navy suede loafers. A self-conscious smile flickered across his lips when he sensed Sean's continued perusal of his attire.

"I'm going straight to the surgery," he explained.

"Ah, right." Sean was about to say he'd go there after he was done with clinic, but his thoughts skimmed over 'more faffing with taxis' straight to a decision made with no need to think. "I'm going to get a car."

"Good idea," Josh said. "No offence intended."

Sean laughed. "Liar."

"All right, I won't dally around it. I don't mind giving you a lift from time to time, but this is getting ridiculous."

"You don't have to tell me that, but you won't be doing it for much longer, will ye?"

Josh stopped at the traffic lights and brushed a speck of dust from the dashboard. "What will you get? Something flash?"

"God, no. Just a runaround like this."

"Hm." The traffic lights changed, and Josh pulled off again.

"You're not taking that as an insult, I hope."

"No."

Sean wasn't sure if he was imagining it or the radio was getting steadily louder.

"Yes, actually, I am," Josh said. "I've had this car for six years, and whilst I appreciate it's not exactly top-of-the-range, it more than suffices for my needs. Yet people insist on passing comment. What would you have me drive? One of those low-chassis sports models? Have you seen the potholes in the university car park? Never mind that I *won't be doing it much longer.* The roads are just as bad. Sunken grids and speed bumps and—"

"Hey!" Sean interrupted. "I didn't say anything other than implying—"

"Stating."

"All right, *stating* it's a runaround, which, by the car industry's standards, it is. And there's nothing wrong with that. Not at all. Christ, Joshy."

The radio volume returned to where it had started, and the journey quietly continued for several minutes. They were not good early morning travel companions, even though they'd been car-sharing for the past two years. But where Sean normally sat back out of the way of Josh's sniped complaints and knew better than to engage him, he was frustrated—with the taxi firm, the lack of transport, the three hours of clinic ahead of him, Sophie, Phee—

"I'm sorry if I overreacted," Josh mumbled.

"Aye, you did." Sean was out of gracious acceptance, and they were already at the university, so he saw no reason to put on an act.

"Do you need a lift to the hospital?" Josh asked as he stopped the car outside the day-care nursery's one-storey building. It had once borne an enormous, rainbow-coloured sign that shouted UNITOTS across the campus, but it had been removed for safety reasons.

"Thanks for the offer, but I'll walk." Sean got out and collected Dylan and their bags but left the child seat, slamming the door with a "See you later" that cut off Josh's "Are you—" The car was still idling after Sean had pressed the buzzer and been admitted into the building.

"Hello, Dylan," one of the nursery nurses greeted with an exuberant smile. Dylan's feet touched the ground, and he was immediately away to play.

"Oh, right, bye, then," Sean called after him, more disgruntled than he should've been.

With a laugh, the nursery nurse took Dylan's bag. "He's claiming the sandpit before Alicia gets here," she said. "He's here for the day, isn't he?"

"Yes, if that's all right with you?"

"Absolutely. I'm just putting the lunch orders together."

"Fair enough. I should be back around…" Sean took out his phone and activated the screen, ignoring the new message from Sophie in favour of opening his diary, such use as that was. He scratched his head. "I don't know, to be honest. Before five, though."

"No problem." The nursery nurse frowned. "Are you all right?"

"What, me?" Sean tapped his chest with his finger and pulled up a grin. "I don't know me backside from me elbow this morning, but I'm fine." He was touched—and worried—she'd noticed he was out of sorts. "Thank you for asking. See you later."

Once he was outside, Sean paused to gather his thoughts, tempted to stop by the university café for a shot of something, but there was a good chance he'd bump into Josh. There'd be questions asked that Sean didn't want to answer, so he forwent the coffee and set off for the campus exit, keeping a brisk pace until his shins ached from the effort, at which point he slowed and took out his phone to read Sophie's message.

He hadn't told her about his visitor the previous afternoon, which wasn't to say it was a secret. He'd told Sophie he'd been a sperm donor, and about this particular 'donation', back when they were new. Seeing as it hadn't come up in conversation since—not even when they were expecting Dylan—he could safely assume it was of no concern. However, there was a stark difference between 'anonymous donor to a clinic' and 'direct donation as a favour for a friend', and it was one which he and Genie, in their youthful naivety, had overlooked. All kids, angelic or otherwise, inevitably fell out with their parents and sought allegiances with those they believed would be most sympathetic and easiest persuaded to fight their corner.

It was a hell of a corner to fight, too, and none of Sean's business, or it shouldn't have been.

"One problem at a time," he advised himself and reactivated his phone screen.

Didn't go to London. Worried about you. Working at home today – be over this evening. x

He called her. "Soph?"

"Hi. Did you get my message?"

"I did. That's why I'm calling. I'm all right."

Sophie's silence told him she didn't believe it for a second.

"All right, I'm…not all right. I've got clinic in five minutes, and…" Sean stopped outside the convenience store on the run up to the hospital. It sold alcohol, and while he was long past cracking open the whiskey at nine in the morning, he was seriously contemplating buying a half-bottle for later.

"Sean?" Sophie prompted.

"Yeah, sorry. Will you be busy at lunchtime?"

"I can take a break."

"If you could come up to the clinic for twelve, I'd be very grateful."

"OK," Sophie agreed. She'd have caught the gist of his request. A staff member's last day usually meant a bit of a celebration.

"Thanks, Soph."

"Step away from the off-licence, Sean."

He managed a laugh at her canny knack and did as he was told. "I'll see you at twelve."

"You will. Bye."

At the bleep in his ear, he moved his phone away, using the last few minutes' walk to check for email or any other messages. There were none. For the time being, he was happy to accept it was a good thing.

"Good morning, Melanie," he greeted the psych admin as he breezed through the doors, pretending he hadn't spent the past half an hour on the brink of a relapse. "How are you this fine day?"

She snorted in disbelief. "I'd wait till you see your appointments list before calling it a fine day."

"Busy?"

"Tristan's out this afternoon."

"Where?"

"Like anyone tells me."

Sean rubbed his chin in thought and realised he hadn't shaved. Well, if that was the only casualty of his absent-minded dash from the house, he wasn't doing so badly at all. If he got five minutes, he'd pop to his office and dig out his electric shaver, but for now, he needed to make a decision.

When Sean had dropped to part-time so he could set up the counselling diploma at the university, the hospital trust had taken on Tristan Morris to share the clinical post. Back then, Sean's intention had been to stick it out for another year and then resign, but in the end, he'd kept both, plus his day at the hospice, and then introduced the Master's course at the university. His reasons for not resigning were many, not least that his counterpart was young and ambitious: were it not for cutbacks across the NHS, Sean was sure Tristan would've moved onwards and upwards already.

Sean was glad of the extra work, and not for the money, although it had enabled him to drink without ever getting in debt, and he'd paid off his mum's mortgage along the way. His work was still what he loved most—clinic notwithstanding—and in which he excelled, no matter what else was going on in his life.

All of that meant, in the normal course of events, he would have volunteered off the bat to cover Tristan's clinic hours, but it would be enough of a trial getting through to lunchtime, and that was without taking into consideration that he'd promised to spend a few hours with Josh sometime this week. They still needed to finalise building adjustments and flesh out their business plan. Sean couldn't help thinking the obstacles to them doing so might be an omen.

With some reluctance, he asked, "Have you cancelled Tristan's appointments, Mel?"

She shook her head. "Not yet. I was waiting for you to come in."

"How many would you say are urgent?"

Melanie scrolled with her mouse, studying the screen. "A couple, but they're late afternoon. I can call the unit, see if someone else can stand in?"

"Don't worry about it, lovely. I'll stay."

"Are you sure?"

Sean nodded swiftly and held out his hand for the first set of patient notes. Melanie placed the folder on his upturned palm but kept hold of it. "What?" he asked.

She shrugged. "I'll miss you, Sean."

"I bet you won't miss my shocking paperwork."

"You're not too bad these days."

"Only because you've trained me so well."

"And now I'll have to train someone new." She made a sad face, although she seemed to quite enjoy bending newbies into shape. "Right, Doctor Tierney, hop to it. You're already five minutes behind." She mimed cracking a whip, and Sean jumped sideways as if to avoid it. He was still grinning as he called his first patient's name.

The morning flew by once he was into the swing of it, and it was almost eleven-thirty before he had a chance to call Josh and break the news, although he went around the houses first.

"How did you get on with personnel?"

"They sent me to the dean, who offered me another incremental rise. No-one would believe the faculty's short of money."

"They'll have even less of the stuff if their performance drops."

"I'm one of twenty-five staff, Sean. My impact is minimal."

"Tell me again how many passed your Lifestyle Behaviour module."

Josh mumbled unintelligibly.

"What was that? A hundred percent? And how many dropped out?"

"That's just one module, and it's not even mine."

"Then there's the Methods mod—"

"Anyway," Josh cut in. "Is that all you called for?"

"Ah, no. I'm not going to make it this afternoon, I'm afraid."

"Did you say you would?"

"On the way to—shite. No, I didn't get that far." He wasn't about to rehash their discussion of whether Josh's car classed as a runaround to explain the sidetrack they'd taken.

"Is there something you're not telling me, Sean?"

"There's plenty, but none of it's to do with us setting up shop. My accomplice is off again."

"Why haven't they fired him yet?"

"He's a suck-up. But now I think on, I should be done by three-thirty. Will you still be there?"

"More than likely. Dan's coming to have a look at the electrics."

"All right. I'll head straight over once I'm done here. Do you need me to bring anything?"

"A packet of cigarettes and a bottle of whiskey?" Josh suggested.

Sean laughed. "Starting as we mean to go on?"

7: The Only Way is…

"THE WIRING'S FINE, as far as I can tell. It's a new consumer unit, and nothing's tripping." Dan switched off the multimeter and set it down on the worktop in the surgery's kitchenette.

Josh vented a sigh of frustration at another potential explanation struck off the list. "Thanks, anyway."

"No problem. Are you sure it was an electrical bang?"

"No. I'm just trying to narrow down the possibilities." Josh walked over to the cubicle of a room that housed the toilet and pretended he wasn't reluctant to open the door. "One of the bangs came from in here." He stepped aside and gestured with a wave of the hand, then froze, breath held. *Cold spot? Oh, good grief. Get a grip, Joshua.*

Dan edged past, his muscular shoulders almost the width of the small room, and peered up at the ceiling, tracing what Josh presumed was the route the wiring took. "Is there a loft hatch?"

"In my—the big room." Josh led the way back through.

"Has it got a retracting ladder?"

"I couldn't say, but there's a set of stepladders in the storeroom. Do you want me to…"

Dan was already out of the door.

"It can wait, you know," Josh called after him.

"I might as well do it while I'm here." He returned with the ladders and positioned them under the loft hatch.

"You'll get dirty."

With a quick smile in Josh's direction, Dan ascended and pushed the square cover up and out of the way. "No light up here. Can you grab my meter?"

Obediently, Josh went and fetched it from the kitchenette, panic already mounting. He managed the first rung before Dan reached down and took the meter from him.

"Cheers." Back up he went. A moment later, the black void overhead filled with pale blue light.

"That's handy," Josh said.

"Yeah." Dan grunted. "Not bright enough, unfortunately. Is this your stuff?"

"No. I've never ventured up there." The mere thought made Josh queasy, but sooner or later he'd have to if they were going to convert the loft into a useable space. In the meantime, he was happy to leave the investigating to someone else, even if it was Dan, who wouldn't hesitate to use his willing assistance as leverage at a later date and was, by now, balanced on the very top of the ladder. Josh swooned and shut his eyes. When he opened them again, Dan's head had disappeared from view.

"Whoa. There's some weird…"

Silence. Josh waited.

"Dan?"

Still no response, but Josh could see Dan's shoulder muscles flexing under the fabric of his shirt, so he didn't imagine he'd been decapitated by The Loft Monster or anything equally gruesome but more believable. A couple more minutes passed, followed by a scuffing sound above before Dan descended the ladder without holding on, meter in one hand, in the other a dusty board-game box, which he held out for Josh to take.

"What's… Oh!" Josh stared down at the printed lid.

"There's loads more stuff like that up there. Are you all right, mate?"

Josh nodded dumbly and took the box, brushing some of the dust from the lid. It caked and darkened on his clammy palm. "By *more stuff like this*, what do you mean, exactly?"

"Tarot cards, tipping tables, crystal ball, pendulum, a gong—before you ask, I only recognise it because Adele's into all that psychic crap. You want me to bring any of it down?"

Josh was starting to feel like one of those nodding bulldogs. He finally shook himself out of it. "Erm, no. Not now." He offered Dan a smile, hoping it looked less feeble than it felt. Unexplained noises, objects moving by themselves...and a whole stash of spiritualist's tools in his loft, the most worrisome of them all in his hand: the Ouija board.

"I'll put these away, then," Dan said and collapsed the ladders. "How long are you here?"

"Not sure. I'm waiting for Sean." Who had consistently been on time for the past three months, but it would take far longer than that to overwrite years of Tierney tardiness.

"If you're here over the weekend, I'll come down with Andy sometime, and I'll give him a nudge about the architect."

"Thank you."

Dan took the ladders away, calling, "See you Friday."

"You will," Josh confirmed half a minute later as the outside door closed, leaving him on his own.

With the Ouija board.

Focus not on its alleged purpose...

It was hard to gauge how old it was when such things were always made to look antiquated, although the box's design was similar to those stored in the spare room at home—his grandma's old board games, with printed labels covering the top face. Some were pre-WWII, like *Jeu de L'Oie*—Game of the Goose. Ludo—his favourite—was a 1940s edition, and the box containing the Ouija board—he assumed; he had yet to look inside—was very similar to that. However, the rest of what Dan had described was the paraphernalia of so-called mediums in the Victorian era. Could it have been up in the loft all that time? Perhaps not, but Josh's researcher brain caught the scent of a puzzle and pawed the ground.

Until fifteen years ago, when the building's use changed from residential to commercial, it had been two self-contained flats. Josh knew that much from what his former landlord had told him, a fact confirmed in the deeds, and on the balance of probability, the loft's contents belonged to a previous residential tenant. He wasn't sure of the legalities, whether he was required to notify the owner, or attempt to, and give them the opportunity to collect their property. In the past, he'd have sought Jess's advice and was moderately amused by the thought that if a Ouija board did as purported, he still could have.

Given the amount of time that had passed, he could probably safely dispose of the loft's contents; nonetheless, he sent a text message to his former landlord asking if he had any contact information for the previous tenants, and then set it aside in his mind—or tried to. His priorities were the party on Friday and getting the renovation underway. He didn't need to know who owned the stuff in the loft or where it had come from.

"I don't," Josh told himself, but his curiosity was overriding his prior fears of heights and hauntings and practical jokes—on reflection, the latter scared him most—and left him wondering if he was brave enough or, more to the point, foolish enough, to take a look in the loft for himself.

"Bugger it." Leaving the Ouija board on the kitchenette counter, he collected the ladders and positioned them under the loft hatch. The ceiling was higher than the one at home, but not by much.

"I can do this," he whispered as he began his ascent, slowly, carefully, keeping his sights on his goal. Three rungs from the top, he was high enough to push the hatch cover out of the way but not quite able to see inside. He stepped up again and took a moment to make sure he was steady before he pulled his phone from his pocket and activated the LED.

Dan was right: the light barely penetrated the darkness at all, but he could see a ramshackle heap of the accoutrements of mediumship immediately to his right, extending past the cast of the LED's misty white-blue beam. Beyond those were shapeless dark masses large enough to be furniture. They could almost have been bodies, although even if people didn't notice someone's absence, they'd be hard pushed to ignore the distinctly horrendous stench of decomposition.

By now driven only by his need to uncover the mystery—not that he really thought there were dead bodies up there—Josh climbed the final two steps and hoisted himself up onto the lip of the hatch, soon after establishing two facts. Firstly, there were no boards for him to walk on, so he couldn't explore further. Secondly, and more importantly, it wasn't the going up that bothered him.

***

Fifteen years ago
February

"THIS KITCHEN IS very…small." Josh turned slowly in the narrow walkway between the two shallow counters lining either side of the square space. If he'd extended his arms, he could have touched both walls, although the room's diminutive size was its least offensive feature. To his left was a heavily scratched two-ring induction stove; to his right, hanging at an angle of around ten degrees, was an eye-level cupboard deep enough to hold two rows of mugs. On the external wall, beneath the disproportionately large window adorned with orangey-red gingham curtains and vallance, was a chipped, off-white enamel sink and draining board.

Gordon Baines, owner of this 'competitively priced, highly desirable property' and Josh's prospective landlord, waited for him to complete his rotation before saying, "You certainly wouldn't get any purchase in the proverbial swing of a cat, and it's in need of substantial modernising, which is why I switched it to commercial use." Plucking a short pencil from behind his ear and a tiny notepad from his shirt pocket, Gordon jotted something. "I've done nothing to it, as you can see."

"Yes, I can see that." Josh eyed the threadbare curtains that lifted each time the old sash window rattled with the wind. "So if I were to take on the lease…"

"Those windows would be sorted, and we could refit the kitchenette or repurpose the space."

"I'd need somewhere to make drinks for my clients."

Gordon hummed, scribbled on his pad again and gestured for Josh to follow him as they continued their viewing. "Toilet."

Josh nodded. *Fairly self-explanatory.* It was in only marginally better shape than the sink in the kitchenette.

"I'll stick in a new one," Gordon said, pushing open the next door along. "Bedroom."

Josh peeked in and was surprised to discover an ancient wash basin and clawfoot bathtub, both covered in dust but fully intact and taking up half the room. The remaining space didn't look big enough to house a bolster pillow, let alone an entire bed. "You did say this was a bedroom, didn't you?"

"I did. Keep in mind this went up in the 1850s—no inside plumbing, a shared privy out the back. I've seen worse workarounds. The dentist who's taking on downstairs is keeping the equivalent space as his wash-up room, but I don't imagine you'd need one in your line of work."

"No."

"In which case, I'll be reclaiming the bath and sink, and we can put in partition walls to give you an office, storeroom—whatever suits."

"Great!" Finally, Josh was getting a sense of what the property would look like once the work had been done, and he was cautiously optimistic. One more room to go: this would be make-or-break.

"And the sitting room or whatchamacallit."

"Consultation room," Josh said, walking ahead. "Oh, yes. This is better." It was smaller than the bedroom, and the décor was awful—curling floral wallpaper and hole-ridden lino—but he hardly saw it, his mind overlaying the view with neutral, refreshing cream-coloured walls, beige carpet, light ash desk, matching chair and bookshelves—

"What is it you do again? Hypnotist?"

"Psychotherapist."

"That's the one." The man clearly had no idea what that meant, and Josh was tired of explaining, so he didn't. A year since he'd qualified, he'd already lost count of how many times people had misidentified his career as hypnotist, astrologer, psychiatrist— at least that one was on the right lines. That or they thought he was a psychic. It was frustrating. There again, a good fifty percent of Josh's uni cohort had been clueless about what they were studying, so perhaps it was asking too much of a layperson like Gordon Baines, who, aside from not understanding what Josh did for a living, was straightforward and honest, and the rent was very reasonable for the first floor of a building so close to the town centre. It would be a stretch until he was fully established, but it would be worth it to have his house to himself.

"What d'you reckon?" Gordon asked. "Does it suit?"

"I'd say so." Josh went over and looked out the window, down into the yard at the back of the building, beyond it an alleyway accessible by a gate. "The yard's part of the ground-floor lease, I presume?"

"No. The leases relate to the building only, but you have access rights for refuse disposal and use of the fire escape."

On tiptoes, Josh could make out the thin black metal steps at the bottom of the fire escape, which was as rickety and terrifying as any he'd seen and—he reminded himself—never had to use. He turned back and surveyed the length of the room, noticing the square hatch in the ceiling. "What about the loft?"

"Also not part of the lease. Will that be a problem?"

"Not at all." With or without partition walls, there was more than enough storage space for Josh's needs. "How soon will it be ready, realistically?"

"I only do realistically, Mr. Sandison. None of that promising it'll be done in a week when there's a good month's work here. To be safe, let's say six weeks at the outside. The electrician and heating engineer will be in and out within a couple of weeks, plasterer after that. Your downstairs neighbour has already paid his deposit, so we can tackle both floors at the same time, pending your name on the dotted line, of course. No rush, Mr. Sandison. I'd rather you be sure you want it."

Josh took out his cheque book and unclipped his pen from his shirt pocket. "I want it."

***

Exactly one month later, on a bright but chilly Saturday morning, with keys in hand and a good deal of trepidation that he put down to waking in the early hours from a bizarre but not especially frightening dream about a water park, Josh locked his car and approached the two newly double-glazed front doors. The one on the right offered a dim glimpse of the dark stairs up to the first floor—his renovated, remodelled surgery, which he had yet to see in its completed state. Gordon Baines had told him he could pop in anytime to see how it was going, and Josh had hinted heavily to his friends that he wanted to show off his new acquisition, fearing he'd made a huge mistake. All he'd received in return was vague reassurance from George and complete disinterest from everyone else. In retrospect, he could have been less opaque and admitted he needed someone to come with him, thereby avoiding this paralysing anxiety about entering the building.

To give himself a moment, he studied the door on the left. In the building's shadow, it shone tungsten yellow, illuminating the words etched into the glass—*D. Giles, Dentist*—Josh's downstairs neighbour, whom he could see in the reception area, laughing and joking with a female colleague. Within seconds, the man spotted Josh and strode towards him, his beaming white smile both greeting and testament to expertise in his trade as he swung the door open and thrust out a hand.

"Good morning! It's *very good* to meet you. I'm Giles. Donald Giles, for my sins. Everyone calls me Giles."

"Morning." Josh shook the offered hand, thrown somewhat by the man's ebullience. "Sandison. Josh."

"Josh." Giles released him from the very vigorous handshake not a moment too soon. "A psychotherapist, I believe?"

That was a major point in Giles's favour. "Yes, and you're a dentist."

Giles read his door sign and grinned lopsidedly. "So I'm told. When you have a mo, we should have a quick conflab about the internet and whatnot, but I'll leave you to settle in first. Why don't you pop down when you're ready, or I can come up to you if you prefer?"

"Erm, yes, OK. I'll just go and..." Josh waved his keys at his door, hoping it was explanation enough.

"I'll see you shortly!" With that, Giles about-turned and marched back to his colleague, leaving the door to slow-close in Josh's face, for which he was thankful. It was a bit too much interaction for his first day in his new surgery.

Alas, that was only the beginning. He'd barely made it to the top of the stairs when he heard the door at the bottom click open again, followed by swift, light footsteps heading upwards. Expecting to be met with Mr. Giles's dazzling grin, Josh turned and did a double-take. Not Giles.

"Jess. What—"

"Coffee?" Shaking the jar of instant granules like maracas, she did some kind of samba move up onto the landing, following with her own double-take. "Wowzer! When you said it was 'quite spacious', I thought you were being generous. This is *massive*! Where's the kettle?" She was off exploring before Josh could respond, which meant she also found the kitchenette—"OK, not so spacious in here"—and the kettle all by herself. "You should buy a filter coffee maker," she shouted over the gushing of a tap.

There was certainly nothing wrong with the water pressure. "I'll buy you one."

"I don't need a coffee maker," Josh protested, raising his voice to be heard and then having to quickly lower it again when Jess turned off the tap. "Even if I did, where the hell would I put it?"

Jess noisily opened and closed drawers until she found the teaspoons and then jabbed one through the paper membrane covering the jar. The *pop* was disproportionately explosive. "They're quite compact, you know."

"So? There's a café about two minutes along the street."

Jess rolled her eyes. "That goes without saying. In fact, scratch the coffee maker. We should look into some kind of intravenous delivery system."

"I really don't drink that much coffee."

"Oh, you really do." Jess found the mugs and spooned coffee into two, asking on the way to the fridge, "Presumably, you bought milk—yes, you did." He hadn't, but a quick check of the date confirmed it was fresh. She left the carton next to the mugs and brushed her hands together. "So you were about to give me the guided tour."

"I was?"

"Of course! You know what they say about a watched kettle? Come on." With her arm hooked through his, she gave him little choice, although he was secretly thrilled she'd sprung a surprise visit on him.

It didn't take long to show her around, given 'quite spacious' applied only to the landing—now the reception-cum-waiting room, complete with several low chairs and coffee table, for which he'd brought a small stack of back issues of *National Geographic* and *Psychology Today*. Jess gave the storeroom, broom cupboard and toilet a cursory glance, likewise Josh's consultation room on the premise they'd be drinking their coffee in there so she could critique it at her leisure; they were back at the kettle before it had boiled.

"I am allowed to sit on here, aren't I?" Jess called pointlessly, seeing as she'd made the coffee and headed straight for the brand-new sofa in the consultation room. Josh traipsed in after her, blushing when she wriggled down into the deep cushions and moaned indecently. "This is so comfy!"

Oh, good, she approves. At last, something to put a smile on his face. "It is, isn't it?" He sat at the other end and smoothed the sofa arm, transforming the short pile from mid to light blue and back again. He'd half considered asking Gordon Baines to install a chaise-longue, but it seemed too stuffy…too Freudian, which, contrary to the teasing he'd endured since completing his undergraduate dissertation entitled 'A Neo-Freudian Analysis of Friendship', he was not. That aside, the sofa was much more welcoming and would help put his clients at ease. "So what do you think?" he asked. "Idiotic or…?"

"The sofa or the whole shebang? Because the sofa is upholstered heaven."

"And the whole shebang?"

Peering up and around the room, Jess hummed thoughtfully but gave nothing away until she finally made eye contact with him and must have picked up on his anxiety, as she reached across to squeeze his hand.

"It's amazing. I love it! I think we're going to be very happy here."

"*We?*" Josh repeated.

Jess grinned. "I'm not giving up this sofa for anyone."

8: Clocking Out

Adult Mental Health Outpatients Clinic
Present Day
Tuesday 16th April

"YOU DO KNOW I've been here since twelve?" Sophie asked as Sean emerged into the waiting room, wiping his face with a length of blue paper towel.

"Aye, tell me about it," he grumbled. He'd overrun by forty minutes, leaving him with twenty minutes to grab lunch and buy an emergency deodorant from the hospital shop. For some unfathomable reason, the radiator was on full in the consulting room, and he'd sweated buckets in there. "Do I stink?" he asked.

Wrinkling her nose, Sophie hesitantly leaned in and took a cautious sniff. "Hmm...not stink, as such."

"Terrific. I'll see if I can cadge some scrubs."

"You do that, and I'll grab us a sandwich and drink."

"Thanks, Soph. See you at my office."

Sophie left for the cafeteria. Sean delayed a moment or so, contemplating which of his colleagues was around his size and most likely to have a spare tunic, and set off for the main corridor. He didn't even make it out of the clinic.

"Doctor Tierney!" Melanie called.

Sean glanced over his shoulder but kept moving.

"Where do you think you're going?"

"To borrow some scrubs. I'm sweating like a nun in a—" Sean stopped before the punchline. "Be right back," he said instead and made a dash for it. No more than ten steps along the corridor, he heard the *clip-clip-clip-clip* of fast-moving heeled shoes coming up from behind. Melanie rounded him and stopped with arms held wide, blocking his route.

"Mel—"

"Just five minutes. Please, Sean?" She gave him a *how could you deny me this much after all I've done for you* doe-eyed blink.

"I need to get out of this shirt."

"I can help you with that." Now, where some of the female staff may have turned the offer into a jokey flirtation, Melanie wasn't one of them, and she blushed crimson at her words. "I mean, I'll find you a tunic. I'll even give you an extra fifteen minutes before this afternoon's clinic."

Accepting he wasn't going to win, Sean relented with a sighed-out, "Fine," and followed her back into clinic, where—as he'd expected—quite a few members of the mental health team had gathered around the desk, all of them armed with disposable plastic cups, which they raised as he approached. He hated goodbyes. He was going to sob like a toddler with banged-up knees, but he donned his widest smile and hoped to God his armpits didn't kill anyone.

"Alright, team?"

"Sean." Francesca Marks, the unit manager, took a step towards him. "I know you didn't want a fuss, but we couldn't let you leave at the end of today as if you'd be back tomorrow."

"I'm not in of a Wednesday," Sean reminded her with a wink. They'd been having the same conversation for four years—since he went part-time—with Francesca convinced he changed his schedule every week. More like she was so busy she had no idea what the hell the day was.

Francesca's smile held, though she was quite emotional. "We started here the same year, as you know," she said. Sean nodded. Within a week of each other, in fact. Francesca—never Fran, she'd made that *very* clear—had beaten him to the bigger of the two offices in the then brand-new Parkwood Unit. "We've witnessed a lot of change, very little of it for the better. Remember when there were sixty permanent staff?"

"I do," Sean agreed nostalgically, noticing some of those standing behind Francesca shake their heads in disbelief. True, they had only two-thirds the patient intake of fourteen years ago, as long-term admissions had been transferred to specialist units, but they'd lost more than half of the permanent posts, mostly higher-band nurses, and those brought in to replace them were newly qualified, with healthcare assistants and agency staff filling the gaps. In the last inspection, the unit had been judged ineffective and not well led—a particularly heavy burden on poor Francesca's shoulders when she was doing the best she could with the limited resources at her disposal.

Those gathered in clinic for Sean's final embarrassment were a mix of permanent and agency staff, many of the latter as good as permanent—if one set aside the lack of employment benefits. When they were assigned good ones, Francesca was sure to ask the agency to send the same people again. Then there were the likes of Melanie the administrator and Janice the Modern Matron, both of whom had been there long before Sean and Francesca arrived like the young upstarts they were, thinking they could change the world and soon discovering Melanie and Janice had already made it as perfect a place as it could be.

Looking around the faces of the wonderful people in front of him, Sean was overwhelmed, remembering the countless kindnesses they had shown him over the years, so many incredible memories, not all of them happy, but they'd pulled together as a team—his team—and he was going to miss them very much. He was done for already, and Francesca hadn't even started.

"Come on, Ms. Marks. Put me out of me misery, will ye?" He laughed through his tears, and the team made sympathetic noises, for both him and Francesca, who was in no better a state.

"All right, Doctor Tierney. I wouldn't want to give you *a reason* to be late now, would I? Particularly as I hear your new co-pilot is even less tolerant of your tardiness than I am."

Sean laughed. "Aye, you could say that."

"We've all chipped in for a little leaving gift that might help."

"You're giving me Melanie? That's very generous of you."

Melanie muttered, "Ha, in your dreams," and gave him a sickly grin, followed by a real smile that melted into tears.

"Hey, don't you go falling apart on me. We've afternoon clinic to get through yet." Sean spotted Sophie loitering across the way and beckoned to her, hoping to take some of the heat off himself, but she stayed where she was and pointed past Sean to Francesca, who had moved while his attention was elsewhere and was now directly in front of him, holding out a large, flat package wrapped in bright-green shiny paper. Through a series of nods, raised eyebrows and rolled eyes, Francesca persuaded Sean to take the gift from her. He stared at the wrapping, letting the reflections of the lights overhead dazzle him.

"Five past one," Melanie warned.

"All right, I'm opening it already." Setting the box on the counter, he peeled away the tape and ripped the paper open, revealing plain brown cardboard with no clues as to what was contained within. He shoved the paper aside—ever-efficient Melanie immediately whisked it away—and flipped the box.

It was a wall clock, circular and around eighteen inches in diameter, green, of course. For an Irishman in England, everything was, but Sean was perfectly fine with that, and in any case was laughing so hard at the clock's set-up it could've been any colour at all. It only had an hour hand and four numbers: 12-ish, 3-ish, 6-ish and 9-ish, each approximately in the correct location. In the middle was what Sean now realised had become his catchphrase: *I'm not late, you're all early.*

"This is fantastic. Truly." Sean looked around his colleagues, nodding. "Thanks, all, so much. I'll miss yous, more than you could know."

"Even Doctor Morris?" Melanie asked wryly.

"Oh, especially Doctor Morris." They were like passing ships, and Sean begrudged having to give up his office to the man, but he supposed he would miss him in a way.

"We'll miss you too, Sean," Francesca said, advancing with her arms outstretched. He was well into the hug before he remembered he'd been sweating all morning.

"Ten past…"

"OK, Mel. Can you get me those scrub—oh, you've got them already." Sean didn't even bother asking her when on earth she'd managed to do that. She was nothing short of a miracle worker, although the tunic in question was from Paediatrics—intentionally, he envisaged—bright yellow and decorated with monkeys variously lounging on, jumping over and riding giant bananas. "Right. I'll get changed and scoff some lunch. Thank you again, you amazing people." Clutching his clock and his vibrant scrubs, he back-stepped away, bowing, and then quickly marched off towards Sophie, calling, "How long, Mel?"

"Ten minutes."

"Ten minutes, right…" Sean smiled at Sophie. "Have you seen this?" He held up the clock. Sophie lifted it so she could read the words and laughed. "It's going in my new consultation room," he said as the two of them set off at a good pace for Sean's office. It was a couple of minutes away, and by the time he made it there, changed and ate, it would be time to come back again, but he was desperate for a bit of peace away from his watchful, soon-to-be ex-colleagues.

"How's this morning been?" Sophie asked.

"Not too bad. Francesca asked me not to tell the patients I was leaving, which I wasn't happy about."

"Why did she do that?"

"I don't know. It's not like the majority could afford private treatment."

"Maybe she's hoping you'll change your mind," Sophie speculated.

"I doubt it." More likely, she'd be asking him to cover clinic on a casual basis if Tristan Morris kept getting up to his tricks, although Sean had been in on the interviews for his replacement, and he was satisfied they'd made a good decision.

As soon as he and Sophie were inside his office, Sean unbuttoned his shirt and then bashed his forehead. "Damn, I was going to buy—"

A can of deodorant materialised in front of him.

"Soph, you're a wonder." Off came the shirt. He sprayed generously into both armpits and all across his chest, turning the dark hairs white where the powder collected on them. "What's it smell like?"

"Deodorant," Sophie said, twitching her nose. "You should stop now." She opened and closed her mouth to dispel the taste. Sean put the lid back on the can and pulled on his yellow tunic, flexing his arms in a muscleman pose. Sophie laughed. "That's a good look for you."

"D'you think so? It's a wee bit like the Hawaiian shirts I used to wear before I came to work here." Sean smiled at the memory and the realisation he was almost free of the NHS again, though he doubted he'd get away with the arty attire of his younger days, certainly not without Josh passing comment.

Sophie handed him his sandwich and sat in his chair. "So, what happened?"

She was asking about his minor meltdown first thing. "I'm not sure. A bit wobbly because of the change, maybe?"

"It wasn't about last night?"

Sean nibbled at his sandwich. "No, I don't think so. It's not like it was different to any other time, is it? But there's something I need to talk to you about." He perched on the corner of his desk so he was partly facing her. "I had a visit yesterday from the daughter of an old friend. Biologically, she's my daughter too."

"Phoenix?"

"Aye, in the ashes phase, I'd say."

"I didn't realise you were in touch."

"We're not in general. She's always known who I am, and I've seen her a few times. She's sent me a couple of letters over the years, and she knew I worked at the uni, as she called my office.

Genie—her mum—and I haven't spoken in a good long while, but I got the impression Phee's giving her a hard time."

"Is Genie on her own?"

"No, and therein lies the problem. She's been with this guy Paul for about six years. I met him once, when they first got together. He must've only been twenty."

Sophie pushed a bottle of water across the desk to him. "I think I know where this is going." Sean could see from her expression that she was on the right track. "How bad is it?"

"Phee's pregnant."

"Oops!"

Sean chuckled ruefully. "You could say that."

"How old is Phee?"

"Coming up on eighteen. She's sitting her A' Levels, and she's adamant she's having the baby."

"Does Paul know? Or Genie?"

"No. That's where we got to yesterday. I told her to go home and talk to them—either of them. She had no intention of doing so and was expecting me to let her stay for a while. I did my best to talk her round, but…" Sean shrugged. He'd tried everything he could to get Phee to go home, short of borrowing a car and driving her there himself.

"Where is she now?"

"I booked her into a hotel for the night. She asked if she could stay at my place, and I'd have offered to sleep on the couch and let her have my bed, but it didn't feel right, you know? So I told her I didn't have the space."

"You don't," Sophie said.

"I didn't like leaving her to fend for herself, not with what she's going through. Of course, if I'd known she was coming, I'd have cleared out the attic for her. She could stay as long as she liked then."

"Next time, eh?"

"If there is one." Sean was undecided whether he wanted there to be. "We swapped mobile numbers, but I haven't heard a peep from her, and she's ignoring my calls and messages. Before you ask, I know she's OK—she's been online and she's still up here, even though she said she'd be getting the train back today. I don't know what to do for the best."

Sophie blew out a long breath and then offered Sean a sympathetic smile. "I can understand why you're struggling. Why didn't you tell me last night?"

"No real reason other than it's not something we've talked about in the past, and it shouldn't be an issue now."

"That makes sense."

Sean was grateful as ever for their down-to-earth, no-nonsense relationship. So much of it was good and healthy because they rarely became caught up in jealousy or comparing themselves to other partners, past or—theoretically—present. Sean hadn't been involved with anyone else, although he was fairly sure Sophie and her PhD supervisor had something going on. They'd been an item a few years back, and Sean had told Sophie he didn't want to know or, rather, he didn't expect her to tell him.

"When you say she's almost eighteen…?" Sophie asked.

"Her birthday's next month, which means she'll be free to do as she pleases—or it would if she were a commoner. Her grandfather is a marquess."

Sophie gave a weary eye-roll. "What's with all the nobility all of a sudden? Isn't George's art therapist a viscountess or something?"

"She will be. She and her younger brother asked permission for the two of them to share the title when their father dies. It caused a bit of a hoo-ha."

"Tell me again how you're not an Oxbridge graduate," Sophie joked, not for the first time. She'd always said Josh was too snooty to have studied at a commoners' university. Quite where a scruffy Irishman like Sean fitted into that picture, he had no idea.

"Our uni was redbrick—one of the best for law, I'll have you know." He wasn't sure why he was defending the institution or its faculty of law; the law undergraduates were some of the rudest, least considerate people he'd ever come into contact with—bullies, really—with one or two notable exceptions only. "Gabby and Genie were quite close back then," he intentionally mused aloud, smiling at the vivid images called to mind of the halls-warming party on his inaugural weekend when Gabby had introduced him and Genie, and the night the two girls had stayed over at his and Josh's place after an entirely innocent evening of Trivial Pursuit, and the far less innocent ones he and Genie had shared with Jess when Josh was in hospital. There had been a few more occasions of just him and Genie after she'd moved to London, the last of those being when she'd told him she was pregnant with Phee.

His recollection arrived at the morning-after fry-up— or throw-up in poor Genie's case—and his belly rumbled, prompting him to do something about the sandwich in his hand. He took a big bite and mumbled around it, "They might still be close, I suppose." It hadn't come up in conversation with Gabby, and he hadn't spoken to Genie in five years, although there was every likelihood they'd be catching up soon.

His mind drifted back to his present dilemma but got stuck in a loop that offered no solutions. He finished off the first half of the sandwich and swigged his water. "What do I do, Soph?"

"How long has it been going on between Phee and Paul?"

"Only a few months, she says."

"So she was seventeen when it started, and he's…twenty-six?"

"Somewhere around there."

Sophie unscrewed the cap from her bottle of water, took a mouthful and swallowed. Sean waited. "You want to know what I'd do in your situation, don't you?" she said. Sean nodded. She stared into the mid-distance, absently tapping the bottle against her teeth. The sound set him on edge. Still, he kept his mouth shut. "OK. Well, you don't have parental responsibility, so on that score, you'd be justified in keeping out of it. You could even argue the case for practitioner-client privilege. That said, she's a minor, so you might have to disclose—"

"Right, I know all this, Soph."

"I was getting it straight in my head."

"Fair enough."

"I think what I'd do…" Sophie leaned back in Sean's chair and twisted a few inches from side to side.

"That chair's a bit rickety," Sean warned at the same time as the back-adjustment spring dislodged. Sophie gripped the lip of the desk and sat forward. The chair sprang upright, hitting her in the back.

"Gee whizz, this thing's lethal."

"Why d'you think I let you sit in it?" Sean said mischievously, not that he could've stopped her.

"Have you reported it? The chair, I mean."

"Probably?" He couldn't remember if it was on the two-page list of faulty and broken equipment he'd given to site maintenance, seeing as it was six months ago and everything else was still faulty or broken. "You were saying…" he prompted.

"Yeah. I don't know Phee, obviously, but at her age, I had my head screwed on, and from what you've said, she has too. Did she swear you to secrecy?"

"Not at all."

"Or ask you not to tell her mum?"

"No."

"Hmm. Maybe she's hoping you will, which could be because she's scared—and maybe the boyfriend is culpable—or she's trying to stir trouble to break up the relationship." Sophie met his gaze. "You need to talk to her again, make a risk assessment."

"Treat her as if she's a patient? Is that what you're saying?"

Sophie nodded. "Do you want me to tag along?"

"Haven't you got to get back to London?"

"Not this week. I'll let Grant know something's come up."

"You don't have to—"

Sophie raised her hand to stop him. "Lunch break's over. I'll give Grant a call when I get home. You call Phee after clinic and make the arrangements." Sophie got up and put her sandwich wrapper in the bin on her way to the door. "You can have the car for the rest of the week too, if you're OK keeping hold of Dylan so I can still get some work done."

"Sure!" Sean agreed. Sometimes he wondered what he'd do without her.

"Come on," she encouraged in the same tone she used to get Dylan into his pushchair.

Sean removed the other half of sandwich from the plastic wrapper, threw the wrapper away and obediently followed her over to the door. "Thank you," he said sincerely.

She reached up and affectionately rubbed his stubbled cheek. No words needed, she opened the door, waited for him to close and lock it behind them, then accompanied him back to clinic, where she left him in Melanie's capable hands for his final stint.

9: Best Behaviour

Off Campus
Twenty-one years ago
November

WAKEY, WAKEY! RISE and shine!"

The curtains whisked open, spilling distressingly bright sunlight across the bed. Genie pulled the duvet over her face, but it didn't stay there.

"Oh my god, Jessica!" She grabbed her pillows, covering her bared boobs with one and flinging the other at Jess, who grinned and skipped from the room.

"Get up, Genie. It'll be worth your while, I guarantee it."

"I'm going to kill you, I swear!" She launched the second pillow after Jess. It hit the doorpost and plumped soundlessly on the floor next to the stolen duvet. "Bitch," Genie muttered. Already shivering, she swung her legs off the bed and sat, swaying and woozy. The night before had ended at four a.m., and it was Friday, therefore no lecture until the afternoon, although the way she was feeling, she wasn't sure she'd be sober enough to attend. Like she had the luxury of choice with Jess in full-of-beans mood. She'd drag Genie to the lecture theatre by her hair if that was what it took, never mind that they'd been as drunk as each other five hours ago, so said the alarm clock's faint, blurry numbers caught in the brash, low sun. It was a commendable effort for a November morning but did nothing to warm the biting chill of their crappy rented house with its non-existent insulation and next-to-useless central heating.

"Are you having a shower?" Jess shouted unnecessarily from the small landing.

"Are you asking or telling me?"

Jess reappeared in the doorway. "Actually, I was warning you that I'm about to do the dishes so you don't freeze your tits off."

"*You're* doing the dishes? Let me guess... Josh is coming over."

"On a Friday? You've got to be kidding. He'll probably meet up with us over the weekend, though."

"Ah! So your mum and dad are visiting." That gave Genie the impetus to get up off the bed. She liked Jess's parents, more so her mum than her dad, who wasn't creepy and had never looked at her the way most men did, but he was still a man, and experience made her cautious.

Jess unhooked the bathrobe from the door and held it open while Genie slid into it, then reached around her to fasten the belt. "Wrong again."

"About...?"

"Not my parents."

"I love how you waited until you had me where you wanted me."

Jess giggled, kissed Genie's cheek and released her. "Any time, any place, anywhere—except for here, this weekend." She followed up with a hopeful smile.

"Oh, Jess, don't make me leave. I feel like shit." Genie made a sad face, at which Jess rolled her eyes. They had a standing arrangement to keep out of the way if either of them had a hot date staying over, and killer hangover or not, Genie would abide by it. Still, it begged the question. "Anyone I know?"

"Nope. Someone from home. I might've mentioned him, though. He's just bought a new car, and he wants to take her on a good run."

"*Her.*"

"According to Andy—"

"Ha! 'I *might've* mentioned him,' she says..."

"OK, so I *have* mentioned him."

"Only once or twice—every bloody day."

"Not true!"

"Let's see, now. This *is* Andy with the massive—"

"If I may interrupt, Your Honour, my learned friend is referring to hearsay."

"Interesting name for it. What else? Hmm. Oh, yeah. Andy's into grunge like he's still fourteen or something but at least he eventually remembered what soap is."

"I did not say that!"

"Might I remind the defendant she is under oath?"

"OK. Fine," Jess relented. "Maybe you *should* stay somewhere else this weekend. You'll tell him I talk about him all the time, and he's already full of himself."

"What if I promise to keep my mouth shut?"

Jess folded her arms. "I'll believe that when I see it."

Genie sighed and squidged through the narrow gap between Jess's elbow and the doorpost, fake muttering, "Guess I'm bunking in with Gabby," but she was getting no sympathy here, not even when she added, "It's like being back at school," as she pushed the bathroom door shut and plonked down on the loo.

"You could always go stay with Sean. Isn't that what you usually do?"

"When you're not staying with him, you mean?"

"And there's another reason to kick you out," Jess said. Her footsteps receded down the stairs. "I'll vacuum now and do the dishes when you're finished in there."

"OK." Genie wiped and flushed and turned on the shower, all with one eye shut. She was getting a headache, which was maybe for the best. She might be past the hangover in time to spend the night squashed up in a single bed with Gabby or Sean. Neither option appealed, but it was fair when it was usually Genie asking Jess to make herself scarce. It was also infinitely preferable to watching Jess get up close and personal with some guy who supposedly meant nothing to her yet genuinely did come up in conversation on an almost daily basis.

Genie's thoughts spiralled further as she stood under the lukewarm water that had her washing so vigorously she grazed her belly—with a sponge! How was that even possible?—and with shampoo in her eyes, she managed to slash both shins speed-shaving. No matter that she kept telling herself it was only for the weekend; if Andy now owned a car, there was nothing to stop him coming to visit any time he liked, which would put an end to their girls-only fun.

And that, really, was the heart of it. Somewhere along the line, it had become more than 'fun' for Genie. Jess was still adamant there was no space in her life plan for a relationship, however much she loved Genie. When Genie pointed out they were too young to be thinking long term, Jess had shushed her and told her not to ruin the good thing they had before poking the shushing finger between Genie's lips, in and out, and into her own mouth as she slid onto Genie's knee, astride, hips rocking, back arched to push her breasts into Genie's face, impossible to see past or ignore.

There was only one place they could go from there, and all the while, Genie weighed up whether she could settle for keeping what they had, the gentle morning kisses and easy love-making on tap, or if she should move out and hope they stayed on speaking terms for the remainder of their studies—a miserable eternity or a glorious flash in the pan.

Satiated and without reaching resolution, Genie had fallen asleep in the middle of that balmy late-spring afternoon; when she awoke, sunlight draped silken gold across the room and Jess's supine, perfect, naked form, and she decided not to decide, but to wait until the decision was made for her.

So sure that time was nigh, Genie dressed in a hurry, relishing the wet, stinging chafe of her jeans against her wounds and pulling on a sleeveless top as, still barefoot, she descended the stairs under the cover of the vacuum cleaner's one-note song and swept a hand across Jess's back to startling effect. The note changed pitch. Jess stopped staring at Genie and held the hose between them. Genie tugged a spotty sock from the end and carried it through to the kitchen, laying it on the counter delicately, as if it were made of that same silken gold in which Jess was swathed in the image Genie's mind had captured and which she revisited so often it would reside within her for as long as she had breath. The vacuum cleaner powered down; the plug clattered as Jess rewound the cable. Abandoning the precious sock, Genie filled the kettle and switched it on, turning with a light-hearted smile and a question.

"Will he be jealous?"

"Who?" Jess's counter-question came with gaze averted and a bloom of pink across her cheekbones. "Oh! Andy, you mean?" She affected a laugh. "Jealous of what? Us? He'll think it's hot."

"What about the others?" Genie pressed. "The boys you've slept with since you've been here?"

"Yes, he'll be jealous." Jess glanced up, eyes narrowed in a challenge. "Are you planning to sabotage my weekend?"

Genie laughed as if it were a joke, as if she wasn't astonished Jess had asked. "Yeah." As if she wasn't the one who was jealous. "Cup of tea?"

"Please." The word carried a stealth sigh of relief, and as Jess turned and went back upstairs, muttering something about straightening her hair, it dawned on Genie that Jess really was afraid she would somehow ruin this weekend for her.

"Actually, you'll have to make it yourself." Genie overtook her on the landing. "Sorry."

"Where are you going?"

"Meeting with my personal tutor. Just remembered." It was the first excuse she'd thought of and an easy one to prove false, but she'd worry about that later. Right then, she needed to get away from the house and from Jess. Socks, boots, jacket on, she threw her books into her bag and dashed from her room, holding her breath as she passed Jess's slightly open door lest the tantalising warm-hair smell gripped her in its tendrils, down the stairs and from the house, not slowing until she reached the high street. That was when the whole muddled mess of emotions hit her, yet she kept walking, through her jealousy and rejection and anger and arousal because it *would* have been hot, the two of them and Andy. She'd never even seen a photo of him, but he would be a looker. They always were, and sharing Jess—with her career or other lovers—was never the issue. Losing her was.

It wasn't so much autopilot as self-preservation that steered Genie towards Cassandra's café and the promise of respite from cold sweats and nausea. There were only two customers, sitting at different tables, and Sean was working. She hadn't known he would be. In the drinking and laughter of the previous evening/ early hours, it hadn't come up in conversation, and she hated him a little for his cheery-as-ever grin. Was she the only one suffering?

His grin faltered as Genie approached the counter, and she pulled on her reserves, offering a contained, demure smile.

"Good morning, Sean."

"Morning, lovely. Are you all right?" He wiped his hands on his apron and adjusted the 'today's special' miniature sandwich board on top of the display cabinet. *Chocolate fudge cake.* Genie suppressed a shudder.

"A little hungover," she said. "You?"

"Dead on my feet," he admitted. "How's Jess?"

"Unscathed, apparently."

Sean's eyebrows disappeared beneath his copious dark-chocolate curls. "Have you had a fight?"

"Oh, nothing like that. But I do need to ask a favour."

"Ask away."

"Can I stay at your place this weekend?"

"Sure you can!"

"Josh won't mind, will he?"

"To be honest, I doubt he'll even notice. Half the time he forgets I live there, and then he'll spot me and look at me like he's thinking, 'Who are ye and what're you doing in me kitchen?'" Sean winked, but added, "I'll ask him when I'm done here for the day. How's that?"

"Thank you, Sean. I owe you one."

He tapped his temple. "Logged for later. Now, can I get you anything? Tea? Coffee? A bit of cake?"

Genie's oesophagus gave a pre-emptive clench. "No, thank you, but I ought to buy something." She surveyed the contents of the glass counter—fruit scones, butterfly cakes, strawberry tarts, decadent three-layered fudge cake with a piece missing…

"How about a round of buttered toast?" Sean suggested.

Her stomach offered a small growl of reluctant agreement, and Genie nodded carefully. "I'll give it a try."

"Go take a seat, and I'll bring it over. I might join you if that's all right?"

Genie shrugged her consent and selected a table butted against the mutely yellow side wall, her gaze drawn to the watercolour print closest to her. It was of a lone house on a dark, desolate clifftop, the backdrop a choppy, grey sea and overcast skies, a perfect summation of her present state of mind, from which she was briefly lured by the plate of toast that appeared on the table in front of her.

"Miserable, isn't it?" Sean said, taking the seat opposite. "Though I may have persuaded Cass to brighten the place up a bit."

Genie picked up half a slice of toast, taking a small bite from the corner. The salty smoothness of the melted butter coated her taste buds, comforting, soothing. She swallowed and took another, slightly bigger bite, chewed, swallowed and sagged gratefully when it stayed down with no ill effects. "She should keep the yellow walls."

"Do you think so?" Sean looked around the small café, prompting Genie to do the same. It was a bit off the beaten path and not the kind of place that catered for students, but on the two previous occasions she'd been in there, she'd stayed for hours, reading, oblivious to the world beyond the steamy windows that obscured the peaceful, homey atmosphere of this pocket of the past.

"Those odd little animals." She indicated the high, narrow shelves, eight in total, each holding three miniature porcelain figurines of dogs, cats, rabbits and so on, all eyeless or too small and far away for their eyes to be visible, making them pretty ghastly despite their small stature. "Those need to go. The paintings…" She was again captivated by the foreboding seascape over their table.

"Right. I have an idea about that," Sean said. "I was chatting with one of the art students who's after exhibiting his work with a view to selling a few pieces. He's in the same boat as me, you see."

"He's Irish?" Genie guessed.

"I mean he's skint."

"Oh!" That brought her back to reality with a jolt.

"So here's how it'd work…" Sean continued, and as he did, she reappraised her perception of him. The slightly too long hair, beard scruff, faded T-shirt and threadbare jeans, she'd assumed were stylistic choices. After all, everyone had one or two of those relatives who lived as if they were on their uppers when in reality they were sitting on a fortune. Not that she'd ever thought Sean was minted, but she hadn't realised until now that he was, in fact, destitute.

She tuned back in as he came to the end of his explanation, but she'd caught the gist.

"What d'you reckon?" he asked. He looked so earnest, even if she'd thought it was a terrible idea she couldn't have told him so, but she didn't think that.

"It's brilliant, Sean."

"Thanks. That means a lot coming from yourself."

"Me? What do I know? I'm a cossetted aristocrat."

"You're more savvy than you let on, Genie. So, we still need to figure out how much to stick on the price tags, and there's no guarantee Cass'll go for it."

"Well, *when* she does, tell her I'll take this picture off her hands."

Sean leaned back and studied it for a moment. "You like that?"

"Today, I do."

"Ah." He straightened up and looked her in the eye. "Want to share?"

"Not really," she said, then spilled everything, from Jess's attempt at being casual about Andy's visit right down to the fantasy image that lived in Genie's head, which was, she realised as she talked, what she was in love with. At first, it was mortifying, as if the words were being leached from her without her conscious permission, yet the longer Sean listened without judgement or comment, the less vulnerable and disheartened she became. The hangover was easing too, she noticed as the rambling stream slowed to a trickle, which was as well. There were customers waiting to be served. The lunchtime rush had begun, it seemed.

"Oh my goodness! Look at the time. I'm so sorry, Sean." Genie rose, as did he.

"No need, lovely." He beckoned her into a hug. "I offered you my ear, so I did."

"So you did." She kissed his cheek.

"How are you feeling?"

"Better. Thank you." She clung to him a moment longer, wishing she didn't have to go, but he had work to do. She stepped away and raised her hand in a wave, turning to leave.

"Hold on." Sean fished in his pocket and pulled out his keys, freeing one from the rest of the bunch. "I'm going straight to uni from here, and Josh'll already be at the library, so if you want to make yourself at home, no problem."

He held out the key, and Genie stared at it, not sure what to do. On the one hand, it felt like taking liberties. On the other, it meant she could avoid seeing Jess until lover boy had gone home.

Sean pressed the key into her hand and closed her fingers around it. "I'll see you later, OK?"

Genie nodded, pushing out a husky "See you later" on her way to the door. His kindness had left her tearful.

From the café, she went straight to Sean and Josh's house and waited until after the law lecture had started before she called home and left a message on the answering machine so Jess wouldn't worry where she'd gone. Assuming Jess gave it any thought at all.

***

Genie didn't know Josh well, this in spite of having mutual friends in Sean and Jess. What she did know was Josh wasn't one to hold his tongue, which made it all the more surprising he managed to do so until Saturday morning, when they crossed paths outside the bathroom.

"Sorry if this is a rude question, but how long are you intending to stay?"

"Only tonight—if that's OK with you, of course."

"Of course." Josh's tight-lipped smile told a different story, and he marched back into his room before she could tell him she'd make other arrangements. She hated when people cut her off like that and advanced on his door, fist raised to knock, but then lowered her hand. He had a right to be miffed, and she could afford a night in a hotel instead of imposing further on him or anyone else.

She returned to Sean's bedroom, her intention to grab her things and go before he awoke, but one look at him curled around the crumpled space in which she'd lain and she changed her mind and got back into bed. He draped his arm over her, awake or in his sleep, she couldn't tell and didn't care. Here with him, she was warm, safe and wanted, and her mind drifted into a daydream-like state, alert to every sound in this strange house—Josh clomping down the stairs, taps running, crockery landing heavily, cutlery jangling…a knock at the front door and an interchange that burned all hope of pretending, if only for a bit longer, that she was OK.

The conversation downstairs was loud and joyous, and it was clear from the way Jess spoke that she didn't know Genie was there. Or perhaps she did know and that was why she was spelling out her and Andy's plans for the day—just the two of them, unless Josh wanted to join them? Genie didn't hear his reply, and she didn't need to. Plainly, she had become an unwelcome obstacle in Jess's single life. She moved to get out of the bed, but Sean tensed his arm, clamping her to him.

"Stay here," he murmured.

"I can't." She fought him half-heartedly, and he lifted his arm away so she could leave if she wanted to, but she didn't want to. She wanted to hide forever in this dim room filled with his scent and his things and no trace of Jess.

"What are you going to do if you go down there now?"

"Have it out with her." Tears were coming. She swung her legs around and sat on the edge of the bed, but it made no difference. "What am I supposed to do, Sean?" He moved to sit next to her, and she leaned against him and swallowed, the tension in her throat turning it into a raw gulp.

"Ah, Christ, Genie. Come here."

Then she was back in his arms, sobbing into his chest hair in anger and frustration with herself because Jess hadn't led her on and none of this was her fault. An awful and somewhat conceited thought occurred to her, and she sniffed and cleared her throat as best she could to ask, "I'm not making you suffer like this, am I?"

"How d'you mean?"

"Like with Jess and me. For her, it's just friends with benefits, for me…"

"Ah, right. I get you now. No, other than drowning me, you're not—"

From bad to worse, Sean's assurance was cut off by a familiar series of three short raps and Jess's voice. "Sean? Are you awake? Can I come in?"

He mouthed *shite* and got up, signalling for Genie to keep quiet. "Hold on, Jessie. I'm…er…coming."

"Ugh. I didn't need to know that. I'll be downstairs when you're done. I'd like you to meet a friend of mine."

Sean scrambled into his jeans and bolted from the room. Genie crawled back under the duvet and pulled it right up to her chin, listening like a terrified teenager in a scary movie. Sean must have caught Jess on the landing, but his voice was a deep rumble, and Genie couldn't make out the words. Whatever they were, Jess said, "OK. Seven o'clock then?" Sean repeated the time and Jess went downstairs. The bedroom door opened, and Sean stepped in, leaning back against it and running his fingers through his dark mess of hair. "How're you doing there?" he asked.

"Better," Genie said and threw back the covers. "Bloody wonderful, in fact!" She snatched up her clothes from the floor and dressed in a frenzy. "So it's just me she's ashamed of."

"I don't think that's—"

"She brought him round to see Josh. She wants to introduce him to you. But I'm supposed to fuck off for the weekend?"

"Why does that mean she's ashamed of you? Maybe she's worried you'll unknowingly drop her in it."

"And you won't? No. It's bullshit, and what was that thing about seven o'clock?"

"She wants to meet at the SU. And—"

"Great. Well, I hope she's not expecting a peaceful evening."

"I'm not going, Genie."

"Of course you're going. You're *always* in the SU on a Saturday evening."

"Not this Saturday. I have plans." Sean pushed off from the door, into Genie's space. "Plans with you." He lightly grasped her arms, but she shook him off.

"I need to have it out with her."

"You need to cool off, not go in with guns blazing. Unless I'm reading you wrong and you don't want to salvage your friendship when this has blown over?"

"If there's a friendship to salvage..." Genie was breathless, and her heart was doing some sort of steeplechase, but it was hard to sustain her anger in the face of Sean's logic. She was raring for a screaming row, which would end everything—their friendship, their house share, Genie's time at university. It was a lot to lose, and she owed it to herself to do as Sean said and cool down, even if, in the end, there was nothing worth salvaging.

10: To-Do

A T HOME, IN a box in the spare room, was the keypad which had secured the external door at the bottom of the stairs that led to Josh's surgery, or what *had been* Josh's surgery before he gave up the lease. Now he owned the building, it was, in effect, his 'surgery' again. The idiomatic term had been the source of much unnecessary commentary the first time around, and he was loath to repeat that nonsense, but he had yet to come up with a more suitable name, and in any case, he had a business partner to consider this time.

Of course, whether they called it a surgery, therapy suite or something trendy and modern—*Wellness Centre? Perhaps not*—was something he should consider once he'd addressed his current situation.

Without the aid of the keypad.

Dan had installed it and later uninstalled it as per the 'return the building to its original state' term of the lease. Asking Dan to reinstall it was on Josh's to-do list—a seemingly ever-expanding entity, each subsequent addition shoving down further the redecorating he'd naively believed would have seen his surgery back in operation posthaste.

That was both the benefit and drawback of contracting Jeffries and Associates: they could do everything. A brief mention to Dan that he was thinking of remodelling was all it took to set the wheels in motion: the architect would be in touch in due course, and from his 'vantage point', Josh had no trouble visualising which walls should be demolished and where new walls should be erected to create three similarly sized consultation rooms.

As for the loft conversion…Josh was a one-to-one therapist all the way, and while he could see the benefit of having a space large enough for group therapy sessions, he was doing it for Shaunna. Well, not Shaunna per se, for the Daisy Foundation, but she was also the reason he'd agreed to become a trustee. Irrespective of the foundation being named after Jess's deceased baby sister, were it not for Shaunna, it wouldn't exist, and it was still without a base of operations.

So, at Josh's first trustees meeting, he'd offered the surgery's loft space, and Shaunna had hugged the breath out of him. Sean and Eleanor had been less effusive, but they'd been looking at property for months and hadn't found anywhere suitable, so the motion had carried unanimously.

Josh switched his phone to LED again and shone the feeble glow into the lumpy gloom. There was enough junk to fill a skip, maybe two, although some of it had if not financial value, certainly intrigue.

"No. Absolutely not," Josh admonished and switched off the LED. There were far more important things to worry about than the origins of the spiritualist stockpile in his loft, like, for instance, how he was going to get down from said loft with the minimum of fuss and embarrassment when the external door was locked and both sets of keys were in his jacket pocket.

Or perhaps the door wasn't locked after all.

Josh held his breath, listening hard. *There.* Thuds at regular intervals, so quiet he had to strain to hear them, but he was sure of it. Someone was coming up the stairs.

"Sean?"

The thudding stopped, but he received no response. Truthfully, he hadn't expected one.

"Not the wiring or plumbing," he recalled, given Dan had checked both less than an hour ago. "The building cooling down?" The day was wet and not especially warm, but he hadn't turned on the heating. With the residual heat rising from the dental practice downstairs, he'd rarely needed to. "It really is very warm up here...no cold spots." Quite why he was voicing his thoughts, he didn't know. Or, rather, he did know, but he'd be keeping that part to himself because—

The thudding started again.

Cold dread fought his mortification at being discovered, and won, sending a shiver of victory right through him.

"Is someone there?"

There wasn't, he already knew. The door *was* locked, and it was Tuesday—half-day for the dental practice—so Giles and his staff were long gone. There was no-one else in the building.

He was imagining it. He had to be. If not...

"I'm being ridiculous. There is no such thing as ghosts." Rationally, he believed it, but there was no getting away from the fact that yesterday, both he *and* Libby had heard the noises and seen the toilet roll unfurl, and he wasn't imagining that dull *thud, thud, thud.*

"Come on, Joshua, keep it together." He was nine feet up with only a flimsy set of stepladders beneath him, and he was acrophobic, so of course his pulse was racing.

Breathe in, two...three...four...

Out, two...three...four...

In— "Good God!" His phone's ring could've woken the dead, had they still been sleeping. "Tierney, you..." Taking one more deep breath for good measure, he answered the incoming call. "Yes?"

"Like that, is it?"

"Like what, Sean?"

"Never mind. Are you still at the surgery?"

"Erm...no." The lie was automatic, much like the regret that followed it.

"That's good. I know I said I was coming over, and I still can do, but if you don't need me—"

"I don't."

"Don't beat about the bush, will ye?"

"Sorry, I'm preoccupied. Is everything OK?"

"I'll come back to you on that one. I'm meeting up with Phee."

"Oh? How long's she here for?"

"I'll come back to you on that one too. How are you fixed for tomorrow?"

"Tomorrow…" *A good question.* "Yes, that's fine." He hoped.

"I'll be heading over straight from the hospice, so I'll see you about four."

"I'll be here." *Still be here.*

"Great stuff. Bye for now."

"Yes, bye."

Sean left it to Josh to end the call, and he wavered briefly, almost blurting it out before his thumb tapped the red button. Even then, he contemplated calling back, but no. They'd been here before, or not *here* precisely.

Josh replayed their interchange, brief as it was and with none of the usual Tierney gush of superfluous detail. Now he thought about it, Sean hadn't been himself earlier either, which Josh had put down to a tough last morning at the clinic. There was evidently more to it, but Sean wasn't telling. There again, Josh hadn't exactly been forthcoming, and not for the same reason he was reluctant to ask anyone else for help. That incident in their university halls of residence still defied rational explanation, and trying to find one had almost driven Josh insane—may well have contributed to his clinically diagnosed insanity.

He'd only stopped when they moved out of halls into a shared house, or not stopped. Redirected his fixation away from 'the paranormal' and toward the study of topics that would help him achieve his qualifications, but the unanswered questions, always somewhere in the back of his mind, were once more rising to the fore.

That would certainly explain why he'd lied on the phone: the last thing he needed was Sean egging him on, although the call had given him a much-needed distraction, and he felt calmer for it. Well, he was still stuck nine feet in the air, but his pulse wasn't beating retreat. He considered his options.

He could try calling George again, but it would be a waste of his phone's sorely depleted battery when he'd already sent two text messages, the first a vague *'When you're done at Ellie's, I could do with a hand at the surgery. x'*, the second a slightly more to the point *'SOS. I really need you to come now. x'*; for shame, he couldn't bring himself to type the words *I'm stuck in the loft.* He had to wonder whether there was any purpose to George having a phone for emergencies when it was never to hand in an actual emergency. OK, this wasn't one, technically, and as far as he knew, George was still at Eleanor's, so in theory, he could just call Eleanor and ask to speak to George. However, there was one *tiny* problem with that strategy.

He should never have told her their trip up the Eiffel Tower had cured his phobia. Her desensitisation programme, which consisted of dragging Josh to the top of increasingly tall structures, hadn't worked, largely because he'd refused to let it. First, there had been the dome of St. Paul's Cathedral, which, because it was interesting and despite the deathly spiral steps, had been bearable. Then there had been the ride in the cable car in Conway, which had scared the living daylights out of him. He thought he may even have passed out at one point. Finally, the Eiffel Tower—step three and...success! Or not, as getting drunk first was not a coping mechanism he'd endorse, but he would rather be stuck up in a loft for all eternity than admit to Eleanor he'd been lying all along.

So, not Eleanor, and not George.

Josh opened his contacts list and scrolled. *Adele...no. If she sets eyes on this lot*—he glowered at the loft stash—*she'll think all her Christmases have come at once. Andy...he'll have me abseiling my way out. Would that be so bad?* A quick downwards glance assured him it would. *Baines Property Services...potentially.* He mentally bookmarked Gordon Baines and continued scrolling through friends and business contacts, imagining the scenario for each, all of them horrific, leaving him with a shortlist of two, neither of whom he was eager to try.

Dan or Gordon Baines. Dan. Gordon Baines. He'd have flipped a coin if he'd had one to hand. *Lesser of two evils? Hard to say, but probably Gordon.* Embarrassing as it was to have his ex-landlord come and rescue him from the top of a stepladder of only moderate height, Josh could no longer feel his legs. He made the call.

"Good afternoon, Baines Property."

"Good afternoon. Would it be possible to speak to Gordon, please?"

"Who's calling?"

"Josh Sandison."

"One moment, please." He was put on hold—no music, mercifully—and then the same voice came back on the line. "Mr. Baines is in a meeting and asked me to tell you he'll call back shortly."

Josh held in his cry of anguish. "OK. Thank you. Please do tell him it's rather urgent."

"I'll be sure to let him know."

There was a bleep in Josh's ear. He moved his phone away and stared in dismay at the call-ended notification. The fingers of his other hand were stuck in claw formation and aching from clinging to the lip of the loft hatch, and he had cramp in his buttocks from keeping them tensed for so long because if he tumbled backwards...

"Now there's an idea." Crashing through the ceiling would certainly get him down quickly, but before he could give it serious consideration, his phone started ringing, and he nearly dropped it in his haste to answer it one-handed.

"Mr. Sandison. Gordon Baines here."

Oh, thank all that is... "Hey, Gordon. I appreciate you returning my call."

"No problem. I saw your message earlier, concerning the previous tenant, but haven't had chance to reply. Any information I had on them I passed on to your solicitor with the deeds and what-have-you."

"Right, that's useful, thanks. I was also wondering if, perchance, you still have a set of keys to the building?"

"Keys to the building…" Gordon sucked his teeth, the noise crackly and distorted. Josh moved the phone away and continued listening via the speaker. "I might be wrong, but I think I only had the two sets I gave to you. Have you lost them?"

"Erm… Not lost them, as such, more…I'm locked in."

"Oh? I had the locks checked before I put the building on the market."

"Yes, and I'm sure they're all working fine."

"Then how have you locked yourself in?"

"I, erm… It's complicated." It always worked when George said it. "Can you help me or not?" Josh was being bolshy, but he'd apologise later. *Anything* to get him out of his predicament.

"If I've got them, they'll be in the safe. I'll pop and have a look and call you straight back."

"It's OK, I'll wait on the—agh! The bloody bleep again! Please, please have another set."

Josh wasn't optimistic—about anything, ever, but particularly on this occasion—thus he had no justification for being so utterly disappointed when Gordon called back and confirmed the only two sets of keys to the first floor of the building were, as he'd said, in Josh's possession. Or, in fact, several feet down and to the left of his possession.

"Damn it!"

Back to his contacts, no more horsing around. He hit the call button. It didn't even ring out once.

"Alright, mate?"

"Dan. I need your help."

"Sounds urgent. Where are you?"

"Still at my surgery." *Yes, SURGERY. To hell with them all.*

"On my way."

"Thanks, Dan. Bring—"

It was probably as well he'd hung up. He'd know better than Josh what tools were needed to break in and then…what? Fireman's-lift him down? *The shame of it!* No, that wouldn't do at all.

Time for one last try.

He'd obviously turned around when he'd come up the ladder or he wouldn't be sitting the way he was and using it as a footrest. It couldn't be any harder to do that in reverse, or it shouldn't be, but lifting one foot without seeing what he was doing was a step into the unknown, and suddenly it wasn't a nine-foot drop; it was a bottomless chasm.

With one arm braced in front, the other behind, feet facing opposite directions, his body refused to comply, and his so-called-genius-level higher cognitive functions were thoroughly overridden by fear. He couldn't complete the turn, nor could he turn back. Or so he'd thought until the swift creak of hinges followed by a loud slam startled him. He jumped, jarring his back, and somehow—even afterwards he had no idea how—caught his toes under the top rung of the ladder, pulled it upwards and set it swaying from side to side. Scrabbling frantically, he made it back onto the lip—again, he had no idea how—startling a second time when the ladder toppled and clattered down onto the floor below.

"Oh," Josh said in the tiniest voice through almost-closed lips, terrified to move so much as a cheek muscle or blink as he cast his eyes along the ladder's length, a giant, wooden arrow pointing to the previously open, now closed kitchenette door, beyond it the box containing, according to its label, the Ouija board.

Mere parlour tricks of the Victorian nouveau riche, he reminded himself, though it mattered not what he believed. With the ladder horizontal and far beneath his freely dangling feet, he was absolutely, unequivocally buggered.

11: Privilege Is as Privilege Does

High Street
Present Day
Tuesday, 16th April

"WHAT D'YOU FANCY? Pizza? Cheeseburgers?" Sean opened the front passenger-side door of Sophie's car, offering the seat to Phee, but she cut him dead.

"Do *you* like junk food?"

"I love it. I'm not supposed to eat it, mind, but I'm happy to go wherever you want to go."

Phee ducked her head and glanced past Sean, eyeing Sophie—behind the wheel. "What does *she* want to do?"

"Sophie," Sean provided as if it had been an innocent oversight. He had a good idea what Phee was doing. She'd been perfectly pleasant the previous day—when she'd defined the terms of engagement and had his undivided attention—and he wanted her to feel safe, but he wasn't about to let her get the upper hand. "Soph? Any thoughts?"

"Oh, you know me. I'm easy. But if you're after suggestions, how about the Chinese place along the high street? Their menu is quite—"

"Look, I don't care, all right? Just…" Phee shut her eyes and exhaled loudly.

Sean took a step back and watched her face, waiting for her to open her eyes again before he asked coolly, "Are you done?"

Whether in response to his offhandedness, he couldn't say, but she finally got in the car, closing the door harder than was necessary—not quite a slam. Sean delayed a few seconds before he climbed in behind her, focusing on fastening his seat belt and reminding himself she was under duress. Meanwhile, she sat with arms crossed, staring out of the front window. Sean cleared his throat, about to prompt her to buckle in, but apparently that was enough for her to get the message. Sophie waited for her to finish before she put the car in gear and pulled away from the kerb.

Several minutes of silence later, Phee mumbled, "I'm not actually hungry."

"All right, so…shall we go to a pub?" Sean suggested.

"And drink orange juice all night? If this is the best you can do, you might as well give up now."

"The best we can do?" Sean queried. Phee had inherited her mother's talent for biting sarcasm, but there was a playfulness to it. He might get a smile out of her yet.

"You're obviously taking me out to dinner for a reason."

"We thought you'd want to get out of that hotel room for a few."

"Yeah, of course that's all there is to it."

Sophie briefly met Sean's gaze in the mirror, and he gave her a nod, happy to hand over to the expert.

"What have you eaten today, Phee?" she asked.

"Breakfast at the hotel. Continental. Just the smell of the Full English made me vomit."

Sophie hummed, sympathetic but noncommittal.

"You've told her, I take it?" Phee peered over her shoulder, addressing Sean.

"Aye. Is that all right?"

"It'll have to be, won't it?" She turned to face front again. "And what do you think I should do, Sophie?"

"About what?"

"Being pregnant, obviously."

"What do you want to do?"

"Keep the baby."

"Uh-huh." Sophie signalled right. Sean frowned. He'd figured out where she was taking them, and it was a good choice but not one he'd have made.

A few minutes passed without further conversation and with Phee itching to speak. Perhaps they were doing her a disservice by not giving the lecture she was clearly expecting and instead taking a professional stance, leaving the way open for her to say as much or as little as she wanted.

Sophie pulled up to the kerb and turned to Phee with a smile. "Here we are."

"Here being?"

"My house."

"Yours?" Phee eyed the building in disbelief. It was a detached house, quite large and well-kept, but unimpressive to someone of Phee's social standing. "Aren't you a student?"

"Postgrad, yes," Sophie confirmed. "I live with my parents."

"But…" Phee wagged her finger between Sean and Sophie. "You have a child."

"Yes."

"You don't live together?"

"No."

"And you're still a couple? How does that work?"

Sophie turned off the engine and unfastened her seat belt. "Come in and see for yourself." She opened the car door, asking as she got out, "Who wants tea and toast?"

"Wh…?" The door closed on Phee's unfinished question.

"Soph's tea and toast is fantastic," Sean said.

"I'm sure it is, but what the hell?" Her anger was a defence mechanism and not an easy one to break down, but Sean would have to work with it.

"All right." He sat forward and casually leaned his elbows on the back rests. He'd give her like for like. "What were you hoping to achieve?"

"I don't know what you're asking. By getting pregnant? It was an accident. I didn't—"

"By coming all the way up here to see me." He wouldn't normally interrupt a patient, but, he reminded himself, Phee wasn't one.

She pursed her lips, letting the air escape in a series of little pops as she thought about her answer. Sean detected the very short moment she considered lying before she shrugged and relented. "I don't know, honestly. I think...I just needed to tell someone?"

Sean nodded to show she had his attention while giving her the opportunity to elaborate. Instead, she opened the glove box, which contained the manual for the car stereo and a baby-blue waffle blanket, right now the most fascinating objects in the world. She wasn't going to get there on her own.

"Did it matter who?" Sean asked.

"Kind of. I wanted to talk to a grown-up. Yes, I know I'm nearly eighteen. I mean a proper grown-up, someone...older. Sorry. I don't wish to be insulting."

"Well, I am getting on a bit."

A whisper of a smile sneaked past Phee's guarded resistance. "Mum says you're older than her."

"By about three years, aye." It had seemed a much greater difference when they were at university. Now they were in their forties, it was nothing, especially compared to the near decade between Phee and Paul.

"She talks about you a lot," Phee said.

"Does she now?" He was pleasantly surprised to hear that, and it must've shown because Phee gave him a wary but amused smirk.

"Usually when she's pissed off with me."

"That's not so great."

"And sometimes when she's not," Phee modified. "Apparently, I inherited your cheeky charm." From the way she was reading him, his 'cheeky charm' wasn't all he'd passed on.

"I suppose there are worse things."

Phee's eyebrows rose. "Such as?"

Too many to count, and maybe she had a right to know about some of them, but this wasn't the time. "I'll write you a list," he said. Now she was a little more at ease, Sean steered them back on track. "You said you needed to tell someone, and I'm glad to be that person, but, well, you told me and then you shut yourself away in your hotel room."

"Because you freaked out."

"I did, that's true. Which is why Sophie offered to accompany us this evening. She's not so easily scared."

"Of course she's not. She's a woman."

"You're on to something there, for sure, but there's another reason." He needed to take care with his words. "I don't know what the situation is with you and Paul—"

"It was consensual." Phee's defences went straight back up.

"I'm not saying he pushed you into anything, but he is your mother's boyfriend...your stepdad."

"No!" She swivelled in her seat and glared, less with fury than determination. "He's never been my *stepdad*. He's only eight years older than me!"

"It doesn't matter. You're not yet eighteen, and he's an adult in a position of trust. Do you understand what that means?"

"It's child abuse? I'm not a child!"

"As far as the law's concerned—"

"You're wrong."

"No, Phee, I'm not—"

"Yes, *Sean*, you are." Yanking her bag open, she pulled out her phone and poked the button, to no effect. "Shit. Can I borrow yours?"

"To do what?"

"Prove I'm right."

Sean's phone was in his pocket, but he hesitated in handing it over. What she wanted to show him might put him in an even more difficult position.

"Forget it. I'll ask Sophie." She was out of the car and away towards the house before Sean registered what she'd said.

He heard the bell ring and held back to give Sophie time to answer. She knew how to handle Phee, and it was nothing to do with her being a woman, or maybe it was, to an extent. She might only be at the start of her PhD, but Sophie had already earned herself a reputation as an excellent children's and young people's counsellor and was a better psychologist than Sean would ever be.

A brief interchange took place on the doorstep before Phee, with chin jutting defiantly to cover her uncertainty, went inside. Sophie frowned at Sean by way of asking if he was coming in. He supposed he ought, though she'd find more use in a chocolate fireguard. At least she had the decency to not laugh when he caught his foot in the seat belt and near fell flat on his face exiting the car. Miraculously, he made it inside the house without further substantiating his ineptitude, and she squeezed his arm in reassurance as she leaned around him to point her key fob at the car. *Good old Soph.* He hadn't intended to offload his troubles onto her, but he was glad she'd let him do so.

"How about that tea and toast?" She led the way up the stairs to her and Dylan's quarters. "Or I can make you something else?"

"Tea and toast is fine, thanks," Phee replied, a little fazed. "This is an apartment?"

"Kind of." Sophie directed Phee—and Sean, who'd been there countless times and knew the way but was a little fazed himself— into her living room. "My mum and dad live downstairs, Dylan and I live up here, and we share the kitchen. Make yourselves comfy. I won't be long."

"I'll make it if you like," Sean offered—reluctantly. He didn't mind doing it, and would rather that than be turned to stone by Phee's dark gaze, but he'd meant what he'd said about Sophie's toast being fantastic. She claimed it was mere luck at happening upon a decent toaster that consistently popped out beautiful squares of even golden brown. Sean remained convinced the soft yet crispy, hot but not too hot, generously buttered and ultimately delicious toast was the product of a sorcery to which only a select few were privy.

Sophie dismissed his offer with a stern, "Sit," and pointed him at the sofa. What else could he do but as he was told?

Phee loitered until Sophie had gone and then wandered the perimeter of the room, examining the photos on the mantelpiece and the certificates that hung in the alcoves to either side.

"Dylan's," she murmured, leaning closer to read his *Star of the Week* award for 'helping other children' and then brushing her fingertips over the glass covering his green-paint handprints. "I've just realised…" she said, moving on to the other alcove without finishing the sentence. She studied Sophie's certificates for a while before she asked, "Were you her lecturer?"

"For her counselling diploma and Master's degree, I was," Sean confirmed, then added, in case she was collecting ammunition, "after we got together."

Phee nodded and continued her perusal along the bookshelves on the next wall. She took her time, only finishing as Sophie came back upstairs, though Sean imagined Phee would have been hard pushed to name one title on those shelves.

Sophie set the tray she'd brought on the long, low table in the centre of the room and handed out small plates. "Help yourselves," she invited. "And say if you want more, OK?"

"Thank you." Phee collected the top-most slice of toast from the plate on the tray and took it to the armchair next to the empty fireplace.

"Thanks, Soph." Sean waited until she was settled beside him before he grabbed a piece for himself. He was gagging for a cup of tea, but the pot needed to stand a bit longer, so he sat back and picked at his toast, watching Phee, who appeared to be staring into the dark grate, lost in thought, but her eyes were turned to her left—Dylan's alcove—lending credence to Sean's interpretation of what she'd 'just realised'.

"So, Phee, how are things with your mum and grandparents these days?"

Phee shrugged and took another bite of her toast, eyes averted. "They're still not speaking."

"And your aunt…what's her name again?"

"Isla."

"That's right. I never met her."

"Neither have I." Her shudder cut off Sean's reading of how she felt about not knowing her aunt. She put the uneaten half of her toast on the plate. "I'm sorry. It's delicious and everything, but I can't decide if it's making me feel more sick or less. Is that normal?" She looked to Sophie for an answer.

"Well, they say every pregnancy is different, but it got me like that too."

"Please tell me it goes away soon." She'd become very pale.

"Mine stopped around fourteen weeks."

"Fourteen weeks?" She closed her eyes and breathed slowly and deeply.

Watching her battle the nausea hotwired Sean's brain, setting off an irrepressible surge of emotion and a need to ease her suffering, the same as he felt for Dylan.

"He's your half-brother," he said.

Phee gave a weak smile. "Yeah. It hit me before." She looked up at the green handprints. "Is he with a babysitter tonight?"

"No. He's downstairs with my parents," Sophie said. "I don't know if he's still awake. Should I go and see?"

"I'd like to meet him."

"OK." Sophie popped the last of her toast into her mouth and used gestures to instruct Sean to pour the tea on her way out of the room. He did the honours.

"If you're going to eat that, you'd be wise to do it before Dylan gets here. He likes his food, he does."

Phee took another bite and chewed carefully, making a bitter-pill face as she swallowed. She shuddered again. "Where's the bathroom?" She put her plate on the table and stood.

"Door at the end of the landing."

"Thanks." She didn't move an inch. "I think it's going away again. God, it's awful. They should tell you about this in sex ed. No-one would ever get pregnant again."

Sean laughed quietly at her joke. By his female colleagues' accounts, morning sickness was but the first trial of many in pregnancy. Somehow, he didn't think Phee would appreciate hearing that. "You have sugar in your tea, don't you?"

"Two, please."

She sat again, this time settling back into the chair with her feet underneath her. Some of the colour had returned to her cheeks. Sean finished stirring her tea and handed it to her.

"Thanks." She smiled up at him. "And thank you for not putting me straight back on the train."

"I'd never have done that."

"Or calling my mum."

"Ah, well, that's another matter."

"If you have to…"

"Legally—" Sean began, but she cut him off as she had in the car.

"I told you. Paul didn't break any laws. Does Sophie have a computer?"

"In her bedroom. Look, I don't need to see proof, Phee."

"Why? Because you *know* I'm wrong?"

"Tell me why you're not," Sean challenged.

"Paul isn't my legal guardian, is he?"

"He's still an adult with a duty of care towards you."

"No, he's Mum's boyfriend. You know? Like you're the sperm donor?"

She'd made Sean more than that the moment she'd confided in him, but he understood what she was saying. Legally, he had no parental responsibility. Genie had insisted on it, even when she was alone with a small child, no job and nowhere to live. It hadn't stopped Sean sending money when he could afford to and offering support as a friend, but his obligation was to Genie, not Phee, and maintaining Phee's confidence jeopardised that friendship. Even so, she was right about Paul; irrespective of the immorality of taking up with his girlfriend's seventeen-year-old daughter, he hadn't committed a crime.

For now, Sean was satisfied that Phee wasn't at risk, and Genie thought she was staying with a friend. There was no real urgency to act, and he could justify keeping what he knew to himself, but he was optimistic he could at least persuade Phee to tell her mum where she was and was big enough to admit it was, in part, self-serving. Of course, unless Phee planned on doing the same kind of moonlight flit her mother had, Genie would find out soon enough about the pregnancy. As for the rest—that, too, would have to wait, as Sophie had returned with their very sleepy son.

"Look, Dylan." She stopped in the doorway to give him a chance to assess the situation. His smile at seeing his daddy evaporated when he noticed Phee, and he snuggled into Sophie's neck, alternately closing his eyes and then peeping to see if the stranger was still there. "That's Phee," Sophie said. "Are you going to say hello?"

Dylan shook his head.

"Hi, Dylan." Phee's cheery tone was slightly higher than her husky speaking voice—another thing she'd inherited from her mother. Dylan scowled, unimpressed.

"It's not you," Sophie assured her. "He's always like this with new people."

Phee smiled. "It's OK. Margaret who works for my mum brought her granddaughter with her last Christmas, and she was the same at first."

Sophie came in and sat on the sofa, Dylan clinging to her like a baby macaque. He didn't even let go when she tore off a finger of toast and offered it to him.

"Must be shattered, poor little fella," Sean said, using the statement to cover that he was checking the time. It had been a long, stressful day, but he didn't want to put additional pressure on Phee. All the while, her eyes hadn't strayed from Dylan, nor his from her.

"You're a cutie," she cooed. He buried his face in Sophie's shirt. Phee sighed. "I'm going to tell Mum," she said, still watching Dylan. "But I need to talk to Paul first." Sean and Sophie gave each other a sideways glance. When Sean looked back at Phee, she met his gaze and held it. "I know what you think, but the only abuse here is of Mum's trust. I wish we'd waited until they'd officially broken it off."

"Is it on the cards?" Sophie asked.

Phee nodded. "They hardly spend any time together. Paul's got a place in London. I think they're just too lazy to—" She grimaced. "Sorry. Never mind."

Again, Sean and Sophie glanced at each other but with knowing smiles. It wasn't the first time someone had passed that same judgement on their relationship. People usually assumed they were separated and had joint custody, but they were happy living apart. They shared the burden when Dylan was giving them merry hell; they both continued to develop their careers; it was right for them.

"Don't worry," Sean comforted, as Phee was still mortified by what she'd said. She'd yet to learn to moderate her thoughts before they reached her mouth—some people never mastered it— but in the ways that mattered, she was mature and understood the consequences of her actions. Facing those consequences was another thing entirely, and Sean was reminded of what Sophie had said in his office earlier that afternoon about Phee's reasons for coming to him. "Would you like me to talk to your mum for you, or come with you?"

"No—thanks—but if she kicks me out…"

"You are always welcome, lovely."

Sophie nodded. "Yes, you are."

Dylan trumped in his nappy.

"See?" Sean said with a wink. "Even your wee half-brother agrees."

12: In Front of Every Good Man…

The Surgery
Present Day
Tuesday, 16th April

A SERIES OF THUMPS, dull, deep and likely emanating from a fist, echoed up the stairwell while a torrent of foul language poured out of Josh's phone.

"I can't pick this…stupid…bloody…" Another bang was followed by a muted roar. "That's it," Dan said. "I'm calling the locksmith."

"No!" The word was out before Josh could check himself. "I don't want a locksmith."

"The guy's not cheap, but he's good," Dan argued, no doubt mistaking Josh's petulance for miserliness, but the cost was irrelevant; he simply could not take more ridicule, even if that which he'd endured so far had been his own. His curiosity had made a fool of him, and his pride had ensured he'd had plenty of time to reflect.

"Have you tried shouldering it?" Josh suggested, bravado courtesy of desperation.

"Are you having a laugh? They've got flimsier doors on Fort Knox."

It was a very sturdy door, Josh had to agree. In retrospect, insisting Dan had a few more details before he came a-charging to the rescue would have been wiser, because why would he carry a lock pick or a ladder either in or on his trusty steed?

"Just call the locksmith," Josh relented.

"No need. I've got a plan."

"What kind of plan?"

"Breaking and entering with the owner's permission."

"Don't you dare involve the police in this."

"Who said anything about involving the police? No, I'm gonna…"

Dan went on, but Josh was no longer listening, his brain providing documentary-style footage of half a dozen uniformed officers arriving with a big metal rammer, battering his door down and charging up the stairs. *Hello, hello, hello, what's all this then?* Oh, how they'd laugh.

"…replace the window, but it'll be cheaper than a new lock. Won't be long."

"Wait!" Josh shouted. "Wait! Dan! Where are you going? Don't leave me here!" If he sounded panicked…well, he was, but there was the bleep of Dan's car alarm deactivating and he ended the call. He'd gone, presumably to fetch a ladder, and all Josh could do was wait.

He stared at his phone screen, his mood darkening with it, and added 'fix broken window' to his mental list. It would have to be one on the front of the building too, seeing as the gate leading from the alley into the backyard was locked, and the key was on the same bunch as the rest. *Unless I call Mr. Giles… No.* Josh was his landlord and before that shared business premises with him for fourteen years, yet he barely knew the man, which was entirely on Josh, given Giles had made every effort to befriend him.

"A front window it is. There can't be *that* many people around at this time, can there?" Josh checked: the middle of rush hour. "Just bloody perfect—actually, *how* is he going to bring a ladder here?" He was thinking aloud. "Or maybe I'm talking to you, *oh source of unexplained phenomena.*"

Structural or imagined audience notwithstanding, the fact remained: Dan's convertible lacked a roof to which a rack could be affixed. No rack, thus no means to transport a ladder, therefore a further delay in the proceedings, and Josh's need for the loo was threatening to surpass his other concerns.

There was no purpose whatsoever to constantly waking his phone. Indeed, it was counter-productive with eleven percent battery life remaining when he and Dan may need to coordinate their efforts. It was a tremendous test of his willpower, but Josh deactivated the screen and tried to think of something else—anything but his full bladder and the mute throb in his lower legs. He gingerly shifted position and searched his brain for inspiration.

I wonder what's for dinner. George and Libby would have eaten already, having assumed—entirely reasonably—that Josh had lost track of the time, and George still wouldn't have seen the messages and missed calls. Josh thought about calling Libby, an option he'd rejected outright earlier because she'd been with Shaunna and, painful as it was to admit it, he no longer trusted Shaunna to keep his confidence with Sean. Josh would tell Sean himself when he was ready.

Disliking the path his thoughts had taken, he checked his phone again—ten percent—and searched the vicinity for distractions. A few feet away, almost in arm's reach, there was a small mahogany box, an eight-inch cube. From Dan's earlier inventory of 'all that psychic crap', Josh surmised the box contained a crystal ball, and if he shuffled a little to his right, he was sure he could reach it—that or fall through the ceiling, and there was no predicting the outcome, which struck him as suitably ironic.

That was as far as his contemplation of more foolish pursuits went, his attention caught by the clangs of an aluminium ladder being placed and extended. Dan had made it back far quicker than Josh had anticipated. He couldn't see any of the front windows from where he was but listened hard, trying to discern what was going on from the type and proximity of each clang. By the sound of it, Dan was ascending the ladder; Josh counted the steps—twenty in all—with breath held, but still jumped when he heard a loud rap on the window. *This is it.* Pressing his fingers to his ears and closing his eyes, he waited for the smash.

It didn't come.

Plastic creaked as the window frame was prised apart; a tool scraped along the resultant gap. Two short, sharp clicks suggested the safety hinges had popped off their rivets, followed by the thud of something landing on the floor, or *someone*, because there were footsteps, and then—

"Hiya!"

Josh's eyes sprang open and he peered down in astonishment at his grinning rescuer. "Adele! Hey! Where's Dan?"

"Holding the ladder, or he was. D'you want me to help you down first or go and let him in?"

"I would very much like to get down."

"OK," Adele agreed cheerfully and bent to pick up the stepladder, backing up as she lifted it into a vertical position. "Aren't you scared of heights?"

"Yes. But clearly, you're not. You just climbed through an upstairs window."

"Oh, I used to do it all the time. Usually drunk." Her tone was dismissive, but then she frowned and hummed quietly, as if the danger had only now dawned on her. She shrugged it off. "What are you doing up there, by the way?"

"I came up to look at—" Josh remembered who he was talking to. "Never mind. Can we just…"

"Get you down," Adele finished for him.

"Please."

"Hmm. Let's think." Steadying the ladder with one hand and tapping her teeth with the vibrant pink index fingernail of the other, Adele studied the loft hatch for ten seconds or more, or probably less, but Josh's patience had departed some time ago. As he reached the point where leaping to freedom and using Adele to cushion his landing seemed his best chance of escape, she said, "I've got it."

"Good stuff." He sounded positively jovial, but his pulse was accelerating and threatening to blow out his eardrums. Desperate as he was to get down, he still had to do exactly that, and he was terrified. Rather than give in to it, he focused on Adele, who was calm and in control, and in that moment, when he was depending on her to save his neck, he realised, for the first time in their thirty-six-year acquaintance, he trusted her with his life.

"Now, Josh, if you can move your feet back a teeny, tiny bit," she instructed as she extended the ladder and secured the two halves, not in their usual A-formation but in one perpendicular length, which she angled towards the opposite side of the hatch to where Josh perched, stiff-legged, as if he were sitting on a chair, but still managed to do as she said. He kept his eyes fixed on hers as she lifted, tipped and pulled the ladder back. She glanced up and smiled. "Nearly there." Josh heard the quiet buzz of a vibrating phone. "Dan," she said and huffed. "Thinks I've forgotten him. D'you know, he was going to take out the entire window? Idiot." She gave the ladder another tug. "Is it resting securely?"

"I think so?" Josh's impression was that she'd only asked him so he wouldn't feel quite so useless, and he appreciated her efforts but was more than happy to defer.

"Fab. Now, you need to lean forward and put your feet on the closest rung."

"OK." Josh took a big breath...and didn't move. "I can't."

"You can."

"I can't."

"'No such word as can't,' my dad used to say, which is silly because there is. But whatever, you can. I know you can. Remember the first time you came down your loft stairs at home?"

"Yes." He could still see it in his mind's eye—staring down those steep, metal stairs, thinking if he ever made it to the bottom, he would never, ever go up there again. But everyone had gone to so much trouble on his behalf, he'd had to try. Same as tonight. In fact, this was easier. He didn't have to step into thin air.

He could do this. He was already almost on the ladder. And then he was on the ladder. And, finally, he was at the bottom of the ladder, stepping onto terra firma, or not, but there was floor beneath his feet and that was good enough.

"See?" Adele gave him a big beaming, ever so slightly smug grin, and then squeaked under the pressure of his hug.

"Adele, my saviour! I love you. Thank you," he gushed. "Sorry. Got to go." He released her and fled the room, accompanied by her giggles.

"I'll go and let in pain-in-the-ass, if that's OK?" she called.

"Sure." He didn't care about anything other than the pure, glorious relief of making it to the toilet, and he positively relished the pins and needles in his bottom. So, he now had a method for getting down from a loft as well as getting up, but he had no plans to test it anytime soon. Or ever again. Once Dan and Andy's contractors had installed the stairs and lift, there would be no need. In the meantime, he'd ask someone else to empty the loft, but it could wait.

By the time Josh emerged, Dan was almost done reattaching the window vent through which Adele had crawled. "Thanks." Josh met her gaze as he said it; after all, she'd done the hard work.

"No worries." Dan carefully pulled the vent shut. "It's secure, but the hinges will need replacing."

"OK. I'll deal with that in the morning." It was a small price to pay and much cheaper than having to replace the entire unit.

"Our Andy could probably sort that for you. I'd volunteer myself, but I'm in Wales for the next couple of days."

"If he wouldn't mind." It would save adding it to the list, such as it made a difference by this point.

"Where do these go?" Adele asked, holding the stepladders, which she'd already collapsed.

"In the—not in there!" Josh watched, statue-like, as Adele swung the kitchenette door open.

"Sorry!" She shut the door again and turned towards him for further instruction, but he didn't get as far as issuing it and saw the moment her brain processed the visual data from the room. She turned back, quite slowly, but Josh was dumbfounded so let her prop the ladders against the wall and open the door a second time. Reverently, she advanced and picked up the Ouija board box with both hands. "Where did this come from? Is it yours?"

Josh's laughter was equal parts incredulity and hysteria. "What do you think?"

"Then whose is it?"

"I don't know, but..." Maybe she could help him. "There's more."

"Really?" She was almost hyperventilating in excitement.

Dan shook his head. "Mental. I'm gonna take our Mike's van and ladder back. See you in twenty."

"OK. Tell him thanks," Josh said. He watched until Dan was no longer in sight and then looked back at Adele. "Would you like to do me a favour?"

Adele peered up at the open hatch and back at Josh, blinking in query. He nodded. She jigged up and down—"Yay!"—and wasted no time in returning the Ouija board to its prior location and putting the ladder back in situ. Up and down she went, spritely, confident, providing a running commentary on her progress. It wasn't until she descended with the last load that Josh noticed she was wearing running shoes rather than her usual high heels. Adele was petite—five foot two in stockinged feet—but tonight she was a giant of admirable strength.

"This stuff is amazing!" She leaned a folded table against the wall and dug in her pocket. "Look at these." She walked over to Josh and handed him a pack of tarot cards. "I'll shut the hatch," she said and verily flew back up to do so.

Josh held the cards away from him as if they might explode and offloaded them as soon as Adele had put the ladders away. She hadn't laughed at him for getting stuck in the loft, but she was definitely amused by his reaction to the items she'd brought down.

"Can I open them?" she asked.

"If you must."

She pulled out the tab, carefully tipping the box so the cards slid against her palm. "Wow... Do they look hand-painted to you?"

Josh squinted at the pictures on the cards. They were highly detailed with fine lines and lots of colour, but he couldn't see them well enough without his glasses. "If they are hand-painted, that would make them valuable, wouldn't it?"

"I'd say so." Adele flipped through the pack, pausing to study a card here and there. "What are you gonna do with it all?"

"Sell it, I suppose." Until that point, the only thing he'd cared about was getting it all out of his surgery, and it was still his primary consideration, but sell it?

"I'll buy it from you." Adele fed the tarot cards back into their packet and carefully set them down on top of the pile. She pirouetted to face him, stopping before she completed the spin, her mouth a tiny, surprised 'o'.

Josh sandwiched his lips between his teeth, clamping them tightly, attempting to clear his mind of all thoughts associated with tarot cards and Ouija boards and doors slamming and self-powered toilet rolls. He almost succeeded too, but Adele wasn't fooled. She took a couple of tiptoed steps towards him, all the while with her gaze locked on his face—by now a good shade pinker than her nails.

"You don't want to sell, do you?"

"It's not that..." he began, but he couldn't do it. He couldn't bare-faced lie to Adele even if he had done so many times before, back in the days when he'd believed she lacked the level of awareness required to know he was lying to her or talking down to her or any of the other frankly dreadful ways he'd treated her and everyone else. *Josh Sandison, therapist* had not been a very nice person. Keeping the emotional dam in place had been a job in itself, and it was an unparalleled relief to not have to do that anymore. But could he trust Adele with this?

"I want to know whose it is, or was, and return it to them if I can."

Adele's perfect pencilled eyebrows rose, along with the corners of her mouth. She fought both, to no avail. She didn't believe him, and rightly so. In spite of his mini-epiphany, he was still lying through his teeth.

"Why don't you have Botox injections?" Josh asked and then gasped, horrified he'd thought it out loud.

"Pardon?" Adele blinked in astonishment.

"I just...well, I noticed..." Josh sighed. "You can frown. That's all I meant."

Back to being amused, Adele scratched her head for show. "Actually, I do have Botox, but the techniques are very advanced these days. I can frown—" she did so "—scowl—" it was a rubbish scowl but nonetheless demonstrated full control of her facial muscles "—grin like a chimpanzee—" and that was just hilarious.

"Yes, I've got it now, thank you." Josh snorted, pleased Adele was laughing too. "I'm sorry."

"Why?"

"That was really rude of me."

"I've always liked your honesty," she said, which brought him up short. All those years of avoiding him in one-to-one situations suggested otherwise. "I just don't like you looking into my head," she qualified.

Ah, yes. That. He tried not to, he really did, but it was like trying to hold back the tide, particularly with Adele. Still, she continued to surprise him.

"If you're thinking about injections for yourself—"

"God, no," Josh dismissed quickly, but then... "Do you think it's something I should consider?" He took out his phone, using the dark screen as a mirror, and made some exaggerated facial expressions. *Not too wrinkly yet.*

Adele shrugged. "It's up to you, sweetie." She hardly ever called him 'sweetie'—only when she had the upper hand. "But if you do decide to go for it, I can put you in touch with just the right person."

"Thanks." Josh was glad for the tangent their conversation had taken. He was ready to address other matters now and eyed the stash from the loft. "I *do* want to return it to its rightful owner—or descendant thereof, perhaps—but not yet. I want to research what all these props—"

"Tools," Adele corrected.

"I want to know how they work, what they're supposed to do."

"I can tell you what they *do*," Adele corrected him again.

"All of them?"

She gave the pile a cursory glance. "Yep."

"Wow. OK, well, erm…"

"Would you like me to store them for you?"

Josh nodded slowly, not a 'yes' yet; he was considering…or trying to make himself consider because he'd decided already. "Do you have room for them?"

Adele grinned. "I have a very big house."

Josh laughed at her brag. He'd yet to visit Adele and Dan's new house, but he'd seen photos, and she wasn't exaggerating. "Yes, please. I'd rather no-one knew about this."

"I won't breathe a word," she promised, even though she was forever letting secrets slip, but it was the best she had. "If we hurry, we'll get it all in your car before Dan gets back."

"Good thinking." Josh retrieved his keys from his jacket, took the cards and pendulum, left Adele with the runes and crystal ball, and went ahead to unlock the car. A second trip saw the lamps and tables brought down.

"Only the Ouija board and the gong to go," she said, poking two large, ugly brass lamps into what was left of Josh's boot space before they went back up for the last of it. "Which do you want?"

"Gong," Josh answered without hesitation. Just the thought of touching the box containing the Ouija board gave him the heebie-jeebies. He picked up the very light gong; it reverberated with each step as he followed Adele downstairs.

"Have you ever played with a Ouija board?" he asked.

"Used, yes, because it's not a toy," Adele said. "Too many times to count." They reached the bottom of the stairs, and she held the door open for him, then ushered him out.

"Why that rather than something else?"

"Well, with the tables and pendulum, you can only ask yes/no questions. The Ouija board's sort of a bit like text messaging the Spirit World."

"The original SMS," Josh mused. He waited for Adele to load the Ouija board into his car and then laid the gong on top, quickly shutting the boot when he heard the smooth, low growl of Dan's convertible approaching.

Dan drew up at the kerb and lowered his window. "All done?"

Adele looked at Josh rather than answer.

"All done," he confirmed.

She hugged him and whispered, "Come over Thursday evening. He'll still be in Cardiff."

"OK," Josh whispered back.

Adele released him and dashed around to the passenger side of Dan's car, offering a little wave before she climbed in.

"See you Friday," Dan said.

"And not before." Josh saw them off and went back inside to collect his jacket, well and truly ready for home. He was so exhausted he didn't even bother going around to check if all the lights were off and the doors and windows were shut.

But he wasn't so exhausted he missed the dark square in the ceiling formed by the open loft hatch.

13: One Man's Treasure

"N OW, ARE YOU sure about this?" Sean pulled on the handbrake and switched off the ignition, ducking to take in the façade of the train station beyond the windscreen. Liverpool Lime Street had undergone a few face lifts since he first laid eyes on it all those years ago. As a naïve young Irish fella newly arrived in England, it had signified the beginning of an amazing journey, and he'd relished the adventure of travelling solo, striking up conversations with every stranger who'd stay still long enough to chat. As a forty-three-year-old father about to put his seventeen-year-old progeny on an intercity train, the enormous automatic doors may as well have been the gaping maw of hell itself.

No answer forthcoming, he looked to his passenger. "Are you all right?" A daft question whenever it was asked but especially at this ungodly hour and asked of a woman running the gauntlet with morning sickness. Nevertheless, Phee deigned to give him an answer, in the form of a short nod and hum in the affirmative through clamped lips. "If you'd let me drive you, we could stop for a break whenever you want."

"Thanks, but no."

He'd hoped to wear her down, having offered the same several times since last night, after she'd sent him the text to say she'd booked onto the first train to London Euston, but she was sticking to her guns in a spectacular demonstration of *what goes around comes around.* Now he knew how his mother had felt, watching her youngest son leave for a strange new land, and it was damned difficult to stop himself making the same demand of Phee. *Promise you won't go to London. Go home to your mum where I know you're safe and loved.* But she was going, and he could like it or lump it.

"Did you get a hold of Paul in the end?"

A short head shake.

"So he doesn't know you're coming. What if he's not there?"

"He will be, don't worry."

Sean chuckled ruefully. "There's no chance of that, young Phee. Well, come on, then. Let's get you safely on that there train." He was out of the car before she could protest that he didn't need to accompany her onto the platform. Just as he couldn't change her mind, she wouldn't change his.

The doors swished open to admit them, and Phee strode confidently ahead, her eyes on the Departures board. She slowed to read it, then turned on the spot, scanning the platform numbers until she found hers, sparing a scowl for Sean as she set off again. "You can leave me here. I know where to go, and I'm sure you have a lot to do."

"That I do." He strolled along beside her, pretending he wasn't getting the measure of the other folks heading for the London train, mostly commuters dashing, heads down, single-minded and oblivious. "But I won't be doing it until I've seen you on your way."

"Is it a private clinic, where you work?"

"No. A hospice."

"Won't they mind if you arrive late?"

"I'm not in until ten, but I'm hoping to put in a couple of hours at home first, sorting out the junk in my attic, just in case."

"In case you want to buy more junk?"

Sean glanced sideways at her. "My door's always open to you, Phee."

"I bet you say that to all the girls."

"Honestly? I say it to everyone. And I mean it too." He held eye contact with her until she broke away.

"What do you do at the hospice?" she asked.

"I'm part of a team—doctors, nurses, carers, counsellors—who provide end-of-life care."

"Is it stressful?"

"It can be, but it's very fulfilling." He wished they'd started this conversation two days ago when there was time to do it properly. "Do you have any thoughts on a career yet, or are you leaving your options open?"

"Law."

"Following in your mum's footsteps."

"I am," Phee said, and she sounded proud to be doing so. "I've already learnt tons of useful stuff, not just from Mum. From her friend Jess. She's a family solicitor—or she was. She's dead now. That's what I want to be, but I don't know if I can anymore. I was supposed to start uni in September."

Sean's heart was still going like the clappers at the mention of Jess. Genie mustn't have told Phee that Jess had been one of his friends too, and a lot more than that. Were it not for Jess and Josh's friendship, Sean might never have met Genie, and Phee's conception wouldn't have happened. Sean would've liked to share that with her; he thought she'd appreciate the insight. But again, it wasn't the right time, so he returned to what she'd said about uni. "You still could go, you know. Sophie—"

"I don't want to." The abruptness of her interruption was startling but, as Sean had learned over the past two days, not out of character. She was a straight shooter when she chose to be, so he pushed a bit harder because a lot of younger people weren't aware that it was possible to be a parent and pursue a career at the same time.

"Can I ask why not?"

"I want to do it right—have the baby, study, then my career. I have it all planned out. Kind of."

"Is that so?" Sean wasn't sure what to make of that statement. Had she planned to get pregnant? It put a very different slant on things if she had, yet she'd been adamant it was an accident, so perhaps they were talking at cross-purposes. That was too deep and contentious a discussion to have in a train station, particularly as they'd reached the barrier, and it was more important they said goodbye on a positive note so Phee felt she could count on his support in future.

He glanced along the platform and consciously relaxed the deep frown that had him gozzy-eyed from trying to see past his eyebrows. Good, strong eyebrows they were too, which Shaunna was itching to attack with her wax strips—'just to tidy them up a little'. She'd have to strap him to a chair first. He'd tried plucking them once, way back, when he'd cared that he was a scruffy gorilla in contrast to his well-groomed peers. He'd still got the jobs and the women, though he'd never fully understood why, but his looks had mattered less to him as time went on. These days, he was mostly happy with his lot, bushy eyebrows and all.

He gestured to the snazzy new train Phee would be boarding imminently. "That's like Cinderella's carriage compared to the old steam locomotive I got from here when I came to study."

"Really?"

"Aye. Well, not the steam bit. It wasn't that long ago. Twenty-two and a half years…" On mornings like this, when the air was cool and dewy, with all the same sights and sounds, it felt like only yesterday. "I got shocking drunk on the overnight ferry and fell asleep just before we docked. If the crew hadn't woken me up, I'd have ended up back in Belfast."

Phee laughed and then shuddered. "There's no chance of that happening to me on this train."

"A good thing," Sean said. "So what's your plan?"

"Plan?" Her eyes went startle-wide, and Sean's gut clenched. He had an awful feeling he'd been right about it not being an accident, but he'd meant in the short-term and clarified as such.

"Today. You're going straight to see Paul, are you?"

"Oh! Yes. His offices are near Euston—a five-minute walk. I'll tell him about…" she rubbed lightly over her abdomen "…and that I'm giving him a chance to talk to Mum before I do."

"Right. So you'll be heading home after you've seen Paul, will you?"

"God, for a sperm donor, you're a seriously overbearing father."

Sean winked. "I'd do the same for anyone." It was true, but there were deeper motivations at work on this occasion. His commitment to Genie, for one.

The guard at the barrier gave a last call for passengers.

"I'd better go," Phee said.

"All right. Will you call me to let me know you've arrived safe and sound?"

"In London or back home?"

"Both."

"See? Overbearing." Phee's twinkly-eyed grin was one Sean knew well. He'd seen it in the mirror often enough.

"Cheeky, you." He wanted to hug her, but he settled for giving her a firm but hopefully not too businesslike nod and then grunted in surprise when she threw herself at him and squeezed fiercely.

"Thanks for everything," she said.

"You're welcome."

She released him and moved off, walking backwards. "Thank Sophie for me?"

"I will. You have a safe journey."

She nodded and smiled, a little tearfully, Sean thought. Within seconds, she was through the turnstile and hurrying along the train to her carriage. She waved as she boarded, and Sean waved back. He waited while the doors closed, the whistle blew and the train pulled away from the platform, then he returned to the car, using the drive home to mentally inventory what he thought was in his attic rather than worry about what Phee had got herself into.

***

It was a sad fact, but ruthlessness wasn't a quality Sean possessed, which was no bad thing. Who needed a ruthless psychologist, after all? However, when it came to tackling the abundance of boxes in his attic—by the looks of it two for each of the fourteen years he'd lived in the house—a small measure of the stuff would have gone a long way.

One positive: since he'd had the stairs and skylight put in, it was a lot easier to navigate than the last time he'd been up there, when he'd spent hours digging through old issues of BPS journals, searching for an article he'd co-authored with his PhD supervisor. He could've accessed it online, but it still meant something to see his name in print.

"I could dig out the copies I want and ditch the rest, maybe," he told Sphinx, who was presently inspecting every box on the lookout for one he could turn into a temporary penthouse suite. Sean opened the box closest to him and removed the contents— a couple of old belts, a pair of braces and what looked suspiciously like lederhosen, although he had no memory of ever owning any. "There y'are, old fella." He pushed the box Sphinx's way and knelt in the space it left. Sphinx gave it a swift and dismissive look-see and prowled on, weaving between the haphazard stacks that doubled in height for every row further they were from the hatch.

Sean opened the flaps of the box to his right and then sprang back as something slithered from it and over his knees. Now, he was the first to admit he wasn't the most agile of chaps, but by God, did he get to his feet fast. It took him a moment to collect his senses and brave a look at whatever he'd set free.

"Ah, Jesus." He laughed at himself and stooped to retrieve the black tie, clamping the slippery garment between his fingers as he recalled his frantic search of the house a few months back, knowing he had one somewhere, but he'd been running late, so he'd bought a new one in the airport for three times what it would've cost on the high street. Still, his dad's widow and kids seemed to appreciate Sean and his brother's grieving-sons act, and if nothing else, he had a spare black tie now, in case, God forbid, he wore one of them out.

Coiling it and poking it into his pocket, he pulled the box closer and peered inside, trawling his hand through the multitude of ties, like a pit of deflated snakes in an array of colours and patterns—paisley, striped, polka-dot, cartoon print. He rarely wore one at all these days, having transferred his love of mad shirts to mad ties when he took the job at the hospital and later ditched those too in favour of smart-but-casual shirts with a button undone at the collar.

Boring, sure, but comfort took precedence on long days in clinic or stuck behind a desk. He wouldn't miss any of that, although he was already missing his colleagues and he hadn't been gone twenty-four hours yet. It was in the little things—the fleeting thought to tell Melanie about something or other when he saw her because she'd find it amusing and then remembering he wouldn't see her, or calling Francesca on a convoluted pretext, knowing she'd see right through it. Well, he supposed he could still call Francesca. Divorce hadn't stopped him, so why should resigning his post? He might even dig out a few of those old shirts—they had to be somewhere in one of these boxes. Sean could just picture Josh's reaction to him turning up on day one of the new surgery in orange-and-green palm-tree print, and it set him off chortling to himself as he moved on from the ties and dug in to the next box in the row.

He wasn't sure how, but he knew before he untucked the flaps what he'd find inside, and his hands shook as he did so, withdrawing swiftly when he felt a sharp edge dig into his skin. Squeezing the resulting pinprick cut, he watched the blood bead before shoving his finger in his mouth and one-handedly flipping the box open. It contained decanters and whiskey tumblers— two coordinating sets in lead crystal of differing designs. Only one casualty, other than himself, which was something.

The decanters were gifts from postgrad students he'd supervised, one of whom he still saw at conferences from time to time. The other had joined the RAF, and while Sean was aware she'd made significant contributions to the current body of work on bereavement and attention, her research was classified and would remain so long after she'd retired from active service.

Sean was both touched and horrified that those two students had picked up on his love of whiskey. Neither had known him well enough to realise his relationship with hard liquor was not a healthy one—nobody had before Sophie, although he'd always thought Francesca had suspected, even before their brief but amicably dissolved sojourn into marriage. People said managers were those who were promoted out of the way because they couldn't do the job, but Francesca had been a fantastic psych nurse in her day. She just happened to be a better administrator.

Sean moved the decanters and surviving three glasses into the box he'd emptied for Sphinx and put it and the ties by the stairs, ready to take to the hospice's shop in town. Next box: his certificates. His colleagues, in particular the immodest Doctor Norris, displayed the originals on their office walls, but Sean's had been photocopies, since his GP's had been stolen during a break-in and the replacements had cost a fortune. Sean thumbed through the stack, glad they were individually stowed in plastic wallets, as his finger was still bleeding, smearing enough genetic matter to turn the box into a full false-identity kit: beneath his degree, diploma and fellowship certificates were his birth and marriage certificates and his first passport.

He'd been twenty-four before he'd needed a passport and even then had only used it twice. Flipping it open, he prepared for the misery of comparing his crinkled, greying self to the young, hopeful fella in the photo but was thoroughly waylaid by the other photos stowed within. A strip of four from a photo booth, taken directly after the one on his passport: Jess; Jess and Genie; Jess and him; the three of them. They looked drunk and more than likely had been. More importantly, they looked happy. Sean couldn't remember if that was also a true record, but when he thought back to that time, which he seemed to do often of late, he recalled only one dark spot. As enormous and pervasive as it had been, it had failed to blot out the good times, so yes, he could say with some certainty that with his two favourite women on his lap, his smile was the genuine article.

Three boxes down, another couple of dozen to go. Sean pushed the certificates box against the wall so he didn't accidentally send that to the charity shop and shuffled on his bottom towards the next row, stacked two high. As he was lifting one down onto his lap, from somewhere Sphinx emitted the low growl that meant he'd come face-to-face with an adversary, followed by a hiss and the sound of several boxes toppling as the cat skittered through the cardboard maze and shot past Sean and down the stairs. Sean's hand immediately went to his chest.

"Christ. That's not worrying at all," he muttered, hoping his plan to clear the attic wouldn't turn out to be the death of him because Sphinx's behaviour suggested he had company. The question was: what kind? A rat? Another cat?

Quietly, he rose to his knees so he could see over the cardboard fortress to where the scuffle had taken place. A couple of boxes were on their sides, but apart from that, there was no movement, no sound, no sign of anything that might've spooked Sphinx, leaving Sean more intrigued than he was afraid.

It took a bit of shuffling things around to reach the back wall, and in the process he located the box containing his Hawaiian shirts as well as another full of audio cassettes, but he made it to the toppled boxes at last. The one nearest was taped shut, the contents secure but pushing to escape. Sean righted it, cringing at the telltale tinkle of more breakages. And that was when he saw it. A flash of white fur that once again threw him backwards in surprise. By now, he was sweating buckets and leaving dark handprints on anything he touched. He was in half a mind to join Sphinx downstairs and call pest control before he went any further, but whatever was lurking behind the box was no longer moving.

"Come on, Tierney, get your head in the game." He took a moment to breathe and be realistic. Worst-case scenario, a neighbour's pet rabbit or similar had sneaked in when Sphinx was out hunting. Or perhaps a dove had come in through the roof and got stuck. Either way, Sean was in no danger. Still, he maintained a healthy caution as he nudged the box out of the way. The white creature moved with it. Sean stopped. The creature stopped. Sean nudged the box, and a little more. The creature matched him move for move. Not hiding. Stuck.

Taking decisive action, he grabbed the box and hoisted it into the air. The creature—which he had now identified—came with it, dangled briefly by a leg and then plopped down at Sean's feet.

A teddy bear and not so white as it had been, clutching a red embroidered heart. *Love You Always.*

"You…" Sean picked it up and looked it in the glassy black eyes. "Causing trouble again, are ye?" He smoothed the stitched message with his thumb—the same action he'd used to wipe away Genie's tears as she'd nursed that very same bear and Jess had packed up around them. "I don't know what you're playing at, turning up now, little man, or even how you got here." Sean carried the bear reverently, taking care not to drop it as he stepped over the boxes and headed downstairs. He was done for one morning and ready for a cup of tea, or was that a teddy bear's picnic?

14: Into the Light

Rowan Mews
Present Day
Wednesday, 17th April

GENIE SCUFFLED INTO the kitchen, each step across the tiles an unpleasant reminder that her mules were still beside her bed, but caffeine was more important, so she forged onwards to the coffee machine, filled it with beans and pressed the power button, all with eyes half-open. She'd had another of those nights trapped in semi-sleep limbo, unable to get comfortable with the stubborn, delicate egg on the back of her head and having too many people in the house—far more than she was aware of if she were to believe Xander.

Nothing else had happened since the sheet music and piano incident, and while she could stomach the company in the circumstances, she worried she was wasting time Xander could put to greater use elsewhere. He insisted she wasn't, and she had no reason to doubt him. Xander was nothing if not honest. Nevertheless, she'd called on him to investigate her poltergeist, and she felt as if she were retaining him under false pretences. Perhaps better that than the alternative.

At last, the grinder whirred to life, and she inhaled deeply, breathing in fresh coffee and the waft of cool, ionised air, the latter prompting her to fully open her eyes. If there was cool air, there had to be an open window or door; either her poltergeist had become claustrophobic or she wasn't the only one up early.

"Good morning, Xander," she greeted, one foot in, one out. The sun was below the treeline, yet oddly, the patio paving was warmer than the kitchen floor. "Would you like a cup of coffee? It's brewing now."

"I can smell it. I'd like a cup, thank you."

Genie nodded and began to retreat but changed her mind. The coffee would be a while yet, and she enjoyed the refreshing tingle of the misty morning air against her skin. It was also a rare chance for an open conversation with Xander without Jonathan's interruptions. He was evidently more than Xander's private secretary—his carer too, perhaps, although Xander hadn't needed help when they were younger.

"Is there something you wish to say?" Xander kept his back to her but turned his head as if glancing over his shoulder. Genie took it as an invitation to move closer and stopped on his left side, leaving a couple of feet between them.

"Not really, but we haven't talked forever."

"We had a conversation at Gabby's wedding."

"It was hardly a conversation, Xander. And that was what, twelve years ago?"

"Fourteen."

"Worse still!" Genie laughed lightly, which prompted a half-smile from Xander. "I feel awful, dragging you away from London like this."

"You didn't drag me. I came of my own free will."

"I requested your help knowing you wouldn't refuse," Genie amended. "You've been here for two days and worked nonstop."

"I like it."

"No doubt, but it's still good to catch up, isn't it?"

Xander didn't protest her claim.

"So, how have you been?"

"Very well, thank you for asking."

"Work keeping you busy?"

"It's Easter recess, but in general, I'm well occupied with research and committee meetings."

"Sounds…riveting," Genie murmured dryly, realising too late that Xander had taken her literally.

"It's not, I assure you. Still, I have my private commissions." His unease showed in the tension that drew his shoulders up towards his ears. He expected to be ridiculed. Genie's stomach lurched guiltily at the memory flashes of making fun, insisting it was all in Xander's imagination, refusing to entertain his nonsense stories of invisible inhabitants in his family's home. She was still sceptical, but she also recognised it would have been less cruel if they had left Xander to his 'flights of fancy' rather than insisting he join in their games. After all, what difference had it made to them?

Of course, they were children then—she, Gabby, Simon and Xander, not friends as such but fellow passengers through their formative years—and as they'd matured, they'd come to accept Xander's ghosts as just one of his many peculiarities. There was little point telling him they didn't exist when he believed absolutely. Out of common respect, he'd deserved better than that from his closest childhood acquaintances—those who had known him best.

"I'm sorry, Xander."

He frowned, and rightly so, as her apology had come apropos of nothing.

"I meant for not believing you."

"Do you believe me now?"

She weighed it up, still clinging to a vain hope that she'd hallucinated the entire thing. "I'm open to the possibility," she said and then nearly jumped out of her skin at Xander's single loud clap of the hands. Now he was smiling.

"Then we are ready to begin." With those words, he marched past her, back into the house, and poured himself the first cup of coffee from the jug.

Genie followed him in, surprised when he offered to pour coffee for her too. She nodded her agreement and perched on a stool next to the island, averting her eyes while Xander struggled to clamber onto the stool on the other side. He managed it, with a fair bit of grunting. Pushing a few straggling hairs from his eyes, he regained his composure and directed Genie to her coffee.

"Thanks." She took a lingering sip to give him time to settle before she asked her question. "Does my being open to the possibility of the existence of ghosts make a difference to your investigation here?"

"No."

"Oh." She waited. He didn't elaborate. "OK. Well…" She sighed, completely stumped. "You said we're ready to begin."

"Yes." Xander set aside his cup and slithered awkwardly from the stool he'd fought so hard to mount. "A test," he said.

"Of what?"

"Your openness." He stopped in front of the range and stayed entirely still other than his head and eyes, which seemed to track movement. It was like watching a mime artist whose intent Genie had yet to discern.

"Do you see her?" he asked.

"Who am I supposed to see?"

"I believe she's the housekeeper. Or a cook." He scanned the space in front of him, up and down, and shook his head. "Her attire is wrong."

"Why? What's she wearing?"

Xander paused his bizarre actions and cast a smug glance Genie's way. "I'm not telling you."

"Ah." So the test was whether her mind was open enough to pick up on the alleged presence of the spectral housekeeper. "I can't see anything at all." She hoped she sounded suitably apologetic.

"You're not trying."

She drew breath to protest but conceded. "No, you're quite right. Don't you have to be sensitive to these things in the first place? I mean, you've always seen ghosts. I've never seen one in my life."

"You said you saw your daughter's bedside lamp being thrown across the room."

"I saw it hit the mirror," Genie clarified. True, no-one else had been in the room at the time, but she hadn't seen where the lamp was beforehand, nor any sign of a potential thrower. It could've been balanced on top of the mirror for all she knew, though that, too, would have been odd.

"You dreamt of your grandmother the night after she died," Xander added.

"I...I..." Genie stammered but couldn't go on. Xander was the only person she'd told about the dream, knowing he wouldn't mock her for wondering if it held a deeper meaning than simply reflecting remorse for her defiance. Her parents had given her an ultimatum, so certain she'd do what was expected of her once she was penniless, and she may well have gone running back to them had it not been for that dream and already being pregnant with Phee.

Instead, she'd struggled on, a single mother in a flat that was little more than a bedsit, escorting wealthy men to make ends meet and refusing her father's offers of financial assistance, knowing it would come with more strings than a symphony orchestra. It had taken her five years, but she'd accrued sufficient savings to fulfil the dream's prophecy and buy her grandmother's house. Even then, her father couldn't let her be.

"My father bought the piano," she said. Half-aware of Xander's reaction—a mere nod—she continued, "We always had one—what is a manor house without?—though none of us played. My mother doesn't care for music, but my father..." Genie smiled to herself, remembering. "All he asked was that I try to learn, and I did. I tried so very hard, but I can barely sing a note in key never mind master 'Für Elise'.

"I knew what he'd done as soon as I saw the lorry at the gates. The piano came with a handwritten delivery note—a gift for his granddaughter, whom he was not permitted to meet, but perhaps I might allow her to learn what I had not."

"Has he ever met your daughter?" Xander asked.

Genie shook her head. "My parents would use any relationship they build with Phee to bring us home. My father largely seems to have given up, but my mother still tries her luck from time to time. Each birthday, Phee receives an abundance of cards from people she doesn't know—her grandparents, aunt, cousins, biological father—and I've explained as best I can.

"It's different now, of course. We have a little more say in whom we marry or whether we marry at all. I won't spoil the illusion for her, but the piano was not an innocent gift from grandfather to granddaughter. It's all the more tragic because my problem was never with my father. It was with the Hendersons. Even after Simon came out, both sets of parents insisted we should bury the hatchet."

"In each other?" Xander suggested, to Genie's surprise. He'd cracked a joke and was grinning from ear to ear. She didn't recall him ever doing either, which made it all the more hilarious. And so, despite the early hour, her myriad guests and lack of sleep, she found herself in pleats with laughter.

"Oh, Xander. I hadn't realised you're such a hoot."

"I have my moments," he said modestly.

"You certainly do," Genie agreed, settling down a little. "Now, I hope you'll forgive me leaving you to your own devices. I need to shower, and then later—assuming you're amenable—we should have breakfast while you give me a full roll call of the ghosts with whom I share my abode. What say you?"

"I'm amenable," Xander confirmed. He extracted his notebook from his shirt pocket and set it on the island, pressing it flat with his palm.

"Excellent. See you shortly." Genie stepped down from her stool, finishing her coffee on the move. She was almost at the staircase when Xander called after her.

"What should I tell Jonathan?"

"Whatever you think."

"I'll give him the morning off so you can speak freely."

Genie peered back into the kitchen, but Xander was already absorbed in his note-making. She continued on her way upstairs, stalwartly avoiding the querulous smirks common to all her female ancestors, captured in the four portraits leering down at her. The paintings had belonged to her grandmother, which was the only reason they stayed, and in fact, the only reason Genie had rehung them once Phee's night terrors subsided to a less disruptive loathing of the four pairs of eyes that watched her every step, as they were doing Genie's now.

On the two occasions Phee had taken a tumble on the stairs, she'd been convinced 'those ugly, nasty women' were to blame, and Genie had to agree—on the ugly nastiness. Bulbous noses, beady eyes, mealy mouths and nary a chin between them, her ancestors were, ironically, no oil paintings. They were also long dead and buried—in the case of her great-great-great-grandmother and namesake, Imogen Edwina Rowan nee Stewart, a hundred years ago.

Meanwhile, the portrait of her grandmother, whom Genie had adored more than anyone bar her daughter, had pride of place above the hearth. A beautiful, gregarious brunette to the day she died, Isabella Catherine Rowan—*Lady Bella*, everyone called her, Genie included—had entertained a host of beaus in her lifetime and had been a tremendous influence, encouraging Genie to 'be her own woman' and live every day to the fullest. Genie had done so, although perhaps not how her grandmother had envisaged. At university, she'd indulged in all that the student experience had to offer and dared say been a bit of a wild one, but what she'd wanted, more than the high life and a string of handsome suitors or a stoic, privileged existence in a loveless manor house, was to be a mother. No husband or tiresome civic duties; just a child and a chance to build and share a loving bond.

Largely to appease her parents, she'd graduated, but after that, she'd steered her own path. She'd become pregnant and given birth to the most beautiful girl in the world. Phoenix Isabella had brought purpose to Genie's life, and love, so much love.

Everything Genie had done since had been for Phee, and she regretted nothing, regardless of what her parents, grandmother or that sneering line of ugly, nasty women might have thought of her.

In her room, she undressed and stepped into the shower, twisting the dial so that the effect was a warm, gentle rain that did little to ease the stiffness in her neck and shoulders but, crucially, didn't aggravate her tender scalp. The past few weeks, she'd been on her own, which was quite usual with Phee at school and Paul away on business, but it was spring break, and she'd expected to see more of her daughter, though she couldn't blame Phee for choosing to spend it elsewhere. Close as they were, what kind of young woman wanted to waste her best years keeping her mother company? Genie certainly hadn't, and she didn't expect it of Phee, but she hoped her daughter was staying safe, taking precautions and above all having fun.

In truth, neither was she surprised Paul had stayed away longer than usual. Their relationship had been stagnating for a while and seemed only to continue because breaking up was an inconvenience. She couldn't say she missed him particularly, though she'd have taken some solace from his presence over the past few days.

Perhaps it wasn't remarkable that she'd found it instead in Xander and his confidence that he could get to the bottom of whatever was going on with the house. And if it all proved to be a figment of her lonely imagination, Xander would have no problem telling her so, just as he'd recognised her discomfort in talking about the alleged poltergeist in front of Jonathan or anyone other than Xander himself.

As she dried off and dressed, she interrogated her feelings. Was her willingness to open up to Xander a sign she didn't care what he thought of her? No. Unlikely as it would seem to their mutual acquaintances, all of whom were aware of Xander's accidental—and frank—exposés, she trusted him to keep her confidences.

Satisfied her trust in Xander was the genuine article, Genie gave her wet hair a quick finger ruffle and admired her reflection, pleased with what she saw. A few greys shone amidst the browns; her smile deepened the lines and expanded the roundness of her cheeks, but on the whole, she was doing all right for forty-one.

She was still smiling as she exited her room, ready to give her best efforts to seeing Xander's ghosts, but the smile quickly turned to horror as she reached the top of the stairs. All four portraits had tipped sideways; the one immediately to her left—her great-great-great-grandmother's—continued to sway until, before her eyes, it lifted free of its hook and slid down the wall. The frame broke apart on impact with the step, one half staying where it fell, the other still attached to the painting, which bounced, end over end, all the way to the bottom of the stairs. A further noise had Genie grabbing for the banister: the familiar tinkle of a small bunch of keys dropped onto the bureau.

"Hey, Mum. I'm home. Where are you?"

***

"There." Phee firmly patted the sticking plaster. Genie withdrew her hand with a hiss. "All done."

"Thank you, darling." The gash across her palm wasn't particularly deep, but it had bled profusely and continued to sting and throb even now it was clean and dressed.

Phee tidied away the first-aid kit, her mouth tiny, lips cinched like a tightly clenched bum hole. She kicked Genie's mules out from under the table and slid her feet into them, briefly meeting her mother's gaze before disappearing into the utility room. "I'm going to check you didn't miss any glass."

"Be careful," Genie warned.

Phee reappeared, dustpan in hand.

"Mother, you look like someone beat the shit out of you."

Genie managed a small laugh at that. It aptly described how she felt. "All the more reason for you to take care."

"Yeah, right." Phee exited with an eye-roll, calling back, "You still haven't told me where Margaret is—or why those weirdos are here."

"She's taking the rest of the week off, and a little respect, please." Genie heard Phee's huff over the shoosh of the brush and the scrape of more glass splinters digging into the floor—who knew a tiny fluorescent tube could cause so much carnage?—followed by the *click-click* of muled feet returning.

Phee left the dustpan on the side and held up the half-framed, bent portrait. "What do you want me to do with this? Burn it?"

"If only…" Genie murmured wistfully. "Leave it in the hall. I'll ask Margaret to take it to the shop next week." That was assuming she came back once she'd taken the requested time off to consider her options.

Phee stood the portrait, face against the wall. "That's an improvement." She came back into the kitchen grinning, although there was still a faraway glaze to her eyes, and she was terribly pale.

"Much better," Genie agreed. "Too many Jägerbombs?"

"What?"

"Have you been partying hard?"

"Oh! Yeah. I need sleep."

"How's Sarah?"

"Fine." Phee nodded. She wasn't meeting Genie's gaze now. "Why is Xander here, Mum?"

"I invited him. We haven't seen each other since you were small. You probably won't remember. We went to his cousin Gabrielle's wedding."

"I remember," Phee said.

"You do? Well, Xander was in the area, so—"

"The house is haunted, isn't it?"

"What? Where… Why on earth would you think that? Of course it's not!"

"That portrait flew off the wall, Mum. I mean, *literally* flew."

"I must've caught it with my arm."

"Right. That's totally what I saw. And the black eyes are from walking into a door or something?"

"I slipped and hit my— Hang on. I do not have black eyes!"

Shaking her head, Phee dug a compact mirror from her bag and held it in front of Genie's face. In irritation, Genie snatched it from her and moved it to a suitable viewing distance.

"Oh, hell's bells." Her eyes were ringed in black and purple, turning yellow at the edges, so she couldn't even pass it off as the result of insomnia. It didn't stop her trying, though. "I've had a couple of late nights, that's all."

"Those are bruises, Mum."

"All right, let's say they are. Why would it have anything to do with the house being haunted?"

"So you're admitting it is?"

"No! For all you know, we could've been burgled, or maybe I was mugged—"

"Or got into a fight with Xander?" Phee finished, laughing at the ridiculousness of it. "He's a ghost hunter, and there are so many cameras in my room it looks like someone's shooting a porno."

"Phoenix Rowan!"

"Come on, Mother. I'm not a child! Just tell me the truth. Have we got a poltergeist?"

"A malevolent entity," Xander said, startling Genie and Phee with his sudden appearance. "Hello, Phoenix." He took a step towards her but remained out of arm's reach. "I'm Xander, a friend of your mother's."

"I know!" Phee shrieked. "We've met before." She side-stepped around him and stomped, still wearing Genie's mules, down the hall. "Am I allowed in my room without an exorcist?"

Genie looked to Xander in panic. He gave a small, supercilious chuckle.

"Demons don't exist."

"How about vampires?" Phee shouted from upstairs. "Or werewolves?" The slam of her bedroom door sent a percussive shudder through the wall. Another painting fell. Genie burst into tears.

"Oh God. I don't know what's going on anymore." She shut her eyes against the sight of Xander's bemused stare.

"It's all right," he said in what he probably thought was a soothing tone. "Vampires and werewolves are the stuff of fiction."

"I know that!" Genie wailed. Until four days ago, she'd thought ghosts were the stuff of fiction too.

"You don't need to worry for your daughter's safety."

"Because demons and vampires and werewolves don't exist? Xander, look at me!" She held up her cut palm, indicating with her other hand her black eyes and foolishly jabbing a finger at the bump on her crown. "How can you say Phee is safe?"

"Your...poltergeist...is afraid of her." He peered up towards the heavy thud of bass now coming from Phee's room. "And with just cause."

In a tearful mess of sobs and laughter, Genie tugged a length off the roll of paper towel and blew her nose. "Are you sure she's safe?" she asked, addressing the underside of Xander's chin, seeing as he was still staring at the ceiling.

"I am." At last, he looked her in the eye. "I would like to take you and Phoenix out for lunch."

"You would?"

"Yes. It will be easier to explain what I have established and how I will solve your problem."

Genie blew her nose again. "Where do you have in mind?"

"The—"

A scream from upstairs stopped Xander mid-flow.

Genie ran, barely registering the sharp prick of a missed glass splinter slicing into her left heel as she raced up the stairs, unaware that Xander was hot on her tail until he bumped into her when she came to a halt on the landing.

Before her stood Jonathan, one hand over his eyes, the other clutching a camera, statuesque in the face of Phee's gorgon glare.

His demise would have been a relief, perhaps even comical, were it not for the realisation that crawled over Genie as she took in her daughter's underwear-clad form, framed by her open bedroom door. The babe she had nursed at her breast, the child she had bathed and dressed, the thirteen-year-old who had clung to her for strength during her first menstrual cycle, endured spots and growing pains to emerge victorious in pre-holiday bikini fashion shows...was pregnant.

15: Too Much

Sandison-Morley Residence
Present Day
Wednesday, 17ᵗʰ April

"COFFEE?" JOSH ASKED and departed back along his hall, leaving Sean on the doorstep.

"Err…yeah. Why not?" Nonplussed, Sean stepped in, shutting the door behind him, and followed Josh to the kitchen. It wasn't as if they usually stood on ceremony, but some kind of explanation for the terse '*change of plan – we'll meet at my place*' text message seemed in order.

"You were out early this morning," Josh remarked casually.

"I dropped Phee at the train station."

"That was a short visit."

"Aye." Sean wasn't in the mood for sharing, considering his first workable state of arousal in almost two years had coincided with finding the 'Love You Always' bear, a bizarre stimulus that doubled as bromide to his poor, beleaguered libido. Now he thought on, it was probably more to do with the photo memento of those sultry three-in-a-bed nights with his beautiful girls. It was stirring again. Maybe there was hope for him yet, although, with Josh's owl eyes on him, it wilted as fast as it had sprouted. Sean locked away the accompanying mental images and concentrated on the present puzzle. "Why aren't we doing this at your surgery?"

"*Our* surgery—what do you think of 'wellness centre' as a name?"

Sean shrugged. "Not much. And again, why are we here and not there?"

"No furniture."

"Right." It wasn't news and was a half-explanation at best. "So we're...what?" Sean made a face behind Josh's back when he abandoned him a second time then reappeared a moment later with his open laptop balanced on his arm.

"We're what?" Josh repeated.

Sean laughed at their ludicrous non-conversation. "Weren't we going to sketch out a floor plan?"

"Yes, which we can do here—whilst sitting on furniture." One-handed, Josh typed something, paused, frowned and handed over his laptop. "Can't we?"

"We can, I suppose, but..." Sean trailed off and squinted at the diagram on the screen. "What's this?" He indicated the 'CR1' label in the middle of a large rectangle.

"My former consultation room. The small numbers are the dimensions in metres."

From that, Sean extrapolated the rest of the abbreviations and the rooms they referred to, but he was a visualiser and he'd only been to Josh's surgery a handful of times—while sober. He didn't care to count how many times he'd staggered up to the building, intent on having it out with him once and for all, only to find it locked up and empty because it was late into the evening, which had perhaps been as well.

The flash of the coffee machine's 'ready' light caught Sean's eye, reminding him he was supposed to be looking over Josh's measurements. "I'll take your word for it that these are accurate."

Josh extracted the full cup and exchanged it for his laptop so Sean could carry his drink. "My office?"

"Sure." Sean followed him upstairs, wondering what was going on. Josh seemed stable, but Sean couldn't get a decent read on him. It was a long time since he'd had that problem.

"Of course—" Josh directed Sean to the beanbag chair, which he loved sitting in...until it came to getting out of the thing. "—we don't yet know where the lift and loft stairs are going."

"I imagine—ooph!" The chair was always closer to the floor than Sean thought, and he lost about a third of his coffee on impact. He put down his cup while he shuffled into a more upright position and took the handful of tissues Josh dangled over him to mop up his mess. "There'll be structural constraints." He dropped the soggy mass into the wastepaper basket. "Remind me to empty that for you."

With a grunt, Josh handed the laptop back to Sean and woke his desktop computer. "Switch to the other document," he instructed.

Sean did so. "I'd have brought my laptop if I'd known we were working like this. I could still go and get it."

"No need."

Josh typed, and the text on the laptop screen changed along with his keystrokes. That got Sean's attention for real, and his eyes widened until the muscles strained. "Spooky!"

Josh sighed in overplayed exasperation. "It's mirrored, the same as the monitors and projector screens in the lecture theatre."

"I didn't mean that." Sean scratched his head as if it would alleviate the itch on the inside. "Did I send you an email in the early hours?"

"No," Josh answered and then, doubting himself, opened his email software. "Did you?"

Sean switched his attention between the laptop and desktop screens. "That's not showing up here."

"I'm only sharing the document." Josh had always been the more tech-savvy of the two, which, when it came to teaching materials and research reports, served their mutual benefit while also giving Sean a complex, not of inferiority; more that he wasn't pulling his weight.

Conscious of sticking his 'big Irish nose' where it wasn't wanted, Sean went back to the document in front of him, less reading it than playing 'spot the difference'. It could be a prank, he supposed, but Josh had an aggressive aversion to practical jokes, and this would have been a terrible one.

"No emails from you," Josh confirmed.

"Good to know." Sean leaned to the side until he could wriggle his phone free from his pocket. "It's only a rough draft—not even spellchecked—but I had a lousy night. Woke up Christ knows how many times, convinced we were at the surgery with a massive blueprint laid out on the floor." No dreams about Phee, though, or none he could recall. Plenty of awake time worrying, which was why he'd wondered if he'd sent the email in his sleep—he'd done that before—but it was still in his drafts folder. Checking he had the right recipient, he tapped 'send'. "There you go."

Josh refreshed his inbox and clicked on the new message.

"Great minds, eh?" Sean said jovially, making light, even though Josh hadn't had time to take in what was on his screen. There was some truth to that: they'd studied together, worked in the same field for over a decade and taught at the same institution for the past four years. They shared the same ethos on what an 'ideal' therapy service looked like, which was how they'd ended up resigning from their salaried posts and embarking on this business venture with little to no discussion beforehand.

There wasn't much text in Sean's email, but several minutes on, Josh was still staring at it, as dumbfounded as Sean was himself. The bullet-pointed list Josh had shared, displayed on the laptop at Sean's side, was, verbatim, identical to the one in Sean's email displayed on Josh's screen.

"So we're agreed, then," Josh said and quit his email app. "About putting the group therapy room in the loft space." He spun his chair in Sean's direction. Josh was pale at the best of times, but despite his undisguised attempt to act as if all was well, he looked ready to pass out.

"Are you OK?" Sean asked.

He half-nodded. "Andy said all we need to do at this stage is put together a rough pen sketch of our essentials and desirables, and he'll pass it on to the architect when they go in to measure up properly. I gave him a set of keys—"

"Hang on," Sean interrupted, still toying with the idea of pressing Josh on the matter of the identical lists but ultimately opting for the safer challenge. "When's Andy meeting with the architect?" He unlocked his phone and opened his diary. It was desolate without all the hospital stuff.

"I don't know. Jeffries and Associates has it all under control."

"You don't want to talk to the architect yourself?" Sean was baffled, bordering on incredulous. He was confident Andy and Dan Jeffries would do an outstanding job—they wouldn't dare give Josh less than their best—but Sean feared his future was slipping through his fingers, and if he was feeling that way, Josh should have been up the wall. It was, after all, his money behind the project. More to the point, Sean had only known him to hand over the reins once, and even then he'd put up a hell of a fight.

"Do you think we should talk to the architect?" Josh asked.

"Yeah, I do," Sean said gruffly, also thinking it was as well he hadn't burnt his NHS bridges. "What's going on, mate?"

Josh's nostrils flared as they always did when Sean called him 'mate'. He hadn't done it on purpose but refused to get waylaid in an apology.

"Are you having second thoughts?"

"Of course not!" Josh laughed, and there was an underlying note of hysteria, to Sean's relief. Like working a screwdriver under the lid of a paint tin, all the while praying it wouldn't explode in his face, he could find a way in with that.

"Is this about sharing your space?"

"If it were, I'd be in trouble. I can't afford to do this on my own, Sean. Perhaps I should be asking—are *you* having second thoughts?"

"Not at all! Sure, I'm nervous. This is new for me, the private practice, but I'm excited for the challenge. Or I was. But there's something going on, isn't there? I'm not imagining it."

For a long time, Josh sat motionless, ankles crossed, hands clasped in his lap, blinks the only break in eye contact. He looked a better colour now, a little pink returning to his cheeks, and the tension in his jaw gradually eased. Finally, he nodded. "The surgery—" he swallowed, sniffed in a breath "—appears to be—" picked up his coffee "—haunted." He lifted the cup to his mouth and hid behind it.

Haunted. Sean shouldn't have been surprised. After all these years, he could predict Josh's reaction to most situations, and he'd picked up on the attempt to relinquish control, but he hadn't expected it to be for the same reason as last time. There was, according to Josh, no afterlife, no heaven, hell or purgatory, no souls to pass beyond the veil. Ghosts were 'the products of compromised minds', and he'd accepted his subsequent diagnosis of bipolar disorder as proof, or as close to proof as a psychologist could get.

"I'm not hypo, Sean."

"Did I say a word?"

"You thought it."

He shrugged. "True enough, but let's talk about it this time around, shall we? What makes you say it's haunted?"

"Same as last time, and I didn't say it *was* haunted. I said it *appears* to be. Come on. I need to show you something." Abandoning coffee, computer and beanbag-hobbled comrade, Josh left the room.

"Hang on!' Sean called after him. "Can you give me a…shite."

He tried rocking back and forth a few times, but that was getting him nowhere fast, so he resorted to a roll sideways onto his hands and knees and heaved to his feet. It was slightly easier than trying to stand straight from sitting but still an almighty effort, and he was sweating by the time he made it downstairs to the hallway, where Josh was at the front door, car keys in hand.

"What took you so long?"

"Funny," Sean muttered, glad Josh was more his usual self. Rather than ask more questions, he followed Josh outside and stood by as he remotely unlocked his car and stepped behind it, hand poised on the boot catch.

"To clarify, in the event I need to, I still don't believe in an afterlife."

"OK," Sean accepted, even though he sensed doubt in Josh's once-solid conviction.

"On Monday, after we left you with Phee, Libby and I went to the surgery. We witnessed some…mundane incidents that defied explanation."

"Such as?"

"Doors slamming, bangs with no observable cause, a toilet roll unfurling itself."

"Right, so should I give you the stupid list? An open window? An electrical fault? Subsidence?"

"None of the above. Dan checked the electrics and plumbing— all in good working order. But while he was there, he went up into the loft, which was where he found…" A catch clicked; Josh hoisted the boot open and gestured to the objects within.

Even from a few feet away, Sean had no problem identifying what he was looking at. He couldn't decide if the fact Josh had brought it home with him rather than ditching it at the recycling centre at the first opportunity was more or less surprising than his claim that the surgery 'appeared' to be haunted.

"May I?" he asked.

Josh shrugged his consent and moved around to the side of the car from where he presided distractedly over Sean's exploration.

Sean leaned in and tilted the enormous gong out of the way to get a good look at the rest of the haul. The tarot cards, crystal ball and Ouija board he recognised, the rest not so much, but it was safe to assume it was more of the same.

"It was up there fifteen years minimum," Josh said, answering what would have been Sean's next question. "When I took on the lease, the landlord said something about needing access to the loft to disconnect the old water tank, but I don't recall him ever going up there. In any case, some of this stuff is much older."

"Don't they make it look that way for authenticity's sake?"

"I thought that too initially, but look at that box." Josh directed Sean to the Ouija board. "It's 1940s' construction, not just made to look old."

Sean lifted it out and examined it more closely. It was sturdy, thin plywood rather than cardboard, held together with panel pins, and the labels were faded for real. On first inspection, Sean had to concur: the box was decades old. "Whose is it? Any idea?"

"None whatsoever. Gordon Baines had a 999-year lease on the entire row, which entitled him to compulsorily purchase the freehold on my building when the previous owner died in 1982, but he didn't change it over to commercial use until fifteen years ago. My guess is the stuff in the loft belonged to the last residential tenant."

"Are you going to ask Baines about it?"

"I already did. He said he'd passed on all the information to my solicitor."

"And?"

"And…?"

"What did your solicitor say?"

"I haven't spoken to them yet, but I will." A car passed by; Josh followed its progress into the distance. He was on edge, and Sean was curious but didn't probe. All in good time. He put the box back and shut the boot.

They returned inside, where Josh went straight to the coffee machine while Sean diverted towards the stairs with a call of, "I'll go get the cups."

"Leave them. I'll use clean ones."

"If you say so." Sean stood in the kitchen doorway, watching Josh toil intently or give the impression of doing so to avoid eye contact. There was more to this than a few unexplained noises and finding a load of spiritualist tat in the loft, and it bothered Sean that after all this time and everything they'd been through, Josh still couldn't be honest with him.

"So are you planning to sell it or dump it or…?"

"Adele offered to look after it until I track down the owner."

"You might need to use it to find them if it's as old as you say."

Josh shot Sean a look that was not of appreciation for his joke. "If I can find out who they were, I should be able to locate their descendants—assuming they have any."

"And if they don't?"

"I'll decide later."

"Maybe Adele will buy it from you."

"If it comes to that, I'll let her have it."

"All right, so…" Sean had spotted the shift from haunted surgery to the spiritualist haul when it happened—a natural one for anyone else. "Let's backtrack a bit. The things that happened when you and Libby were there—are we talking pranksters again?"

"Well, it's rather convenient, don't you think? Unexplained phenomena one day and the next I happen upon all that junk? Maybe someone else knew it was there and decided to have a bit of fun at my expense."

"Who? An ex-client?"

"No." The machine bleeped; Josh extracted the first cup and placed a second under the spout, then wiped everything down and rinsed the cloth. "Tony Baines."

"I'd swear you called him Gordon earlier."

"Tony is Gordon's son. He was there when I negotiated the purchase, and it was clear he thought he'd be taking over the business when his dad retired."

"Surely it's too late now for Tony to do anything about your place. You bought it outright, didn't you?"

"For well under market value. He could buy it back from me for more than I paid and still make a profit, and if that's his game, I'm tempted, I must admit."

Now they were getting somewhere. "You don't submit to pranksters, remember?" Sean said.

"This is different. Last time, I'd have lost out. This time, I stand to gain."

"Then you *are* having second thoughts."

"Not second thoughts, but it's risky, and I have a family to provide for. Have you any idea how much teenage daughters cost?" Josh must've realised the insensitivity of what he'd said, as he turned lead-poisoning pink.

"Not really." Sean patted Josh's arm amicably, having learned long ago not to take his tactlessness to heart. Josh only said what everyone thought, and while a few days of keeping tabs on Phee had given Sean some insight into how quickly teenage daughters could chomp through money, he didn't have to worry about her school supplies, clothing and feeding her or ensuring she had a social life.

"I'm sorry."

"No need, Joshy. You're right, I don't have much idea, and I will tell you what's going on with Phee, but let's get this sorted out first, all right?"

"OK." Josh's agreement was tentative, suspicious. He'd opened up a little and seemed willing to listen. Still, Sean would need to tread carefully.

"I have a suggestion, but before I make it, I must be frank with you, and you're free to tell me if I'm way off here. Now, you and George may well have been talking about it for months beforehand, but from my perspective, it looked like you rushed into buying the building."

Josh's expression didn't change—a blank mask but for the occasional attentive blink. Sean pressed on.

"Whether it was down to hypomania or that you couldn't stand the idea of someone else taking it on? Doesn't matter. All I'm saying is it wasn't your usual well-considered approach." Sean paused again. Still no argument.

"Then there was your most recent brush with death. I won't insult you with lessons in egg-sucking. You know the psychological impact. We tell our clients to hold off on big decisions, and sure, you'd already made it, but somebody shot you, for Christ's sake. No-one would think less of you for changing your mind. You could have put the building straight back on the market or become a landlord yourself and leased the space to someone else. You still could, and if that's what you want to do, if I'm the reason you haven't, then don't let me stop you. My house is paid for. I only have Dylan's and my day-to-day living expenses to think about, and if push came to shove, I'm sure I could talk Francesca into giving me a few hours in clinic.

"But if you're wanting to see it through…well, I know you don't want to lose the momentum, but we can slow up a wee bit. We've time on our side here. What I'm suggesting is we give ourselves six months, longer if need be, to get up and running. Any new clients come our way in the meantime, we can see them at my place or even rent an office somewhere. That way, the Jeffries lads can get on with the work without it being a rush job. We can tout for business, and when we're ready, we'll have an official opening. And if you're not wanting to deal with the architect, I'll happily take that on."

Sean gave a nod to indicate he was done and got on with drinking his coffee, leaving Josh to mull it over, play out every feasible outcome. It wouldn't take him long and ultimately might not make any difference because Josh's decisions were black and white, all or nothing. He didn't compromise; he didn't know how. But that was what Sean was offering: something between charge ahead at full speed and run like hell in the opposite direction.

Over the rim of his cup, Sean watched and waited. He was a patient man, so people said, and he had plenty for his oldest, dearest friend, whose posture had changed, a slight twitch in his cheek signifying his deliberations were complete.

Patient or otherwise, right then, mere seconds away from the verdict, Sean could gladly have wrung the neck of whoever was on the other end of that call.

As perplexed as if he'd never seen one before, Josh pulled his phone from his pocket and hit the 'answer' button.

"Hello?" He met Sean's gaze. "Hello?" He moved his phone away and checked the screen—"Still connected"—and put it back to his ear. "*Hello?*" After a few seconds of saying no more, Josh ended the call.

"Wrong number?"

"Who knows? They didn't say anything. So, I've considered what you said, and—"

"That's strange."

"It happens. As I was—"

"You get a lot of silent calls, do you?"

"Don't we all?" Josh held up his hand, stopping Sean from interrupting again, and he would've done, having convinced himself Josh was going to turn him down and sell the building from right under them, uni resignations be damned. "Yes," Josh said. "But we need to agree on a completion date."

"So we're still game on? I don't have to go cap-in-hand to Francesca?"

"Only if you want to."

"Christ, no." Sean took out his phone and unlocked it. "All right, let's see…exorcists…" He ducked and narrowly avoided a flying teaspoon.

16: The Wrong Side

H IYA."
Josh looked up—eyes only—from his third attempt to fit everything from his desk's top drawer into the plastic crate. "Hey, Shaunna. Fancy seeing you here!"

"How's it going?" She remained in the doorway, her hand curled around the edge of the door.

"Oh...*fine*." Josh slammed the drawer shut and sat back. "I'm sick of it—I've half a mind to chuck the lot." He glared at the crate, overflowing despite his Tetris-style packing, which he'd regret later when he couldn't get any of it out again, and turned his attention to Shaunna. "Are you waiting for Sean?"

"No. Why?"

"Just wondering why you haven't come in."

"Oh!" Shaunna came a couple of steps closer but left the door open. "Can we... Is now a good time to talk Daisy Foundation business?"

"That depends."

"On?"

"How long it'll take." Josh already had a good idea which Daisy Foundation business Shaunna wanted to talk about, and the trial of *too-much-to-do vs friend-in-need* waged in his mind. For the plaintiff, this was the third interruption of the morning. *Did you or did you not waste the past thirty minutes arranging desk sundries on a desk which, as of five p.m. next Friday, will no longer be yours?*

"Not to worry." Shaunna pursed her lips and turned away from him.

Mr. Sandison-Morley, did you or—

"Wait!" If he didn't relent, she'd use his unwillingness against him in future. No, that wasn't a fair judgement. *He'd* use his unwillingness against himself and project it onto her. "What do you want to talk about?"

"Doesn't matter." She was still heading—slowly—for the door.

"Shaunna…"

"If you're too busy."

"I'm busy, but not *too* busy." He sighed. "You came all the way here."

"I was already here."

"I'm not even doing anything useful. Come in. Please?"

At last, she shut the door and turned back with a cheeky grin. He folded his arms. Of course she'd known he'd relent.

"Sean's off-site, isn't he?" he asked.

"Yep. I didn't come to see him. Guess who's been accepted for the counselling diploma!"

"Really? I wasn't aware you'd applied."

"To four different institutions. I'm sure I told you."

"I mean I didn't know you'd applied here."

"Well, I wasn't going to, with you and Sean being the course leaders, but he talked me into it."

"He's a bugger. He's still leading the course."

"And he'll still be teaching me, but he won't do my observations or mark my assignments. Your replacement will. I just had my first supervision meeting with her."

"How did that go?"

"OK. She's a bit…"

"Eccentric?" Josh suggested.

"I was going with bonkers myself."

Josh laughed. "That too." He could hardly believe it when Zara Kaminsky-Lederman's job application arrived in his inbox; by the time Sean had not only shortlisted her but also offered her the position, Josh was quite convinced he'd passed into some parallel universe where Sean and Zara didn't hate each other's guts.

Perversely, Josh liked Zsa Zsa—the nickname he'd given her way back when she'd waltzed into his new surgery, flung herself on his sofa and called him 'daahling'. She was every bit as glamorous and dramatic as the Hollywood star and no doubt would get on the nerves of some students and faculty. However, she was the most successful and longest-serving psychotherapist in their town, and since she'd taken so many of their former students on placement, she had an excellent knowledge of the course requirements. Eccentric and bonkers, yes, but absolutely the right person for the job, and she was already in post, so Josh couldn't have rescinded his resignation had his meeting with Sean gone differently.

"So you wanted—oh! Congratulations on getting onto the course." He'd almost forgotten to offer them. "And thanks again for having Libby over the other night."

"Thank you," Shaunna accepted graciously, followed by, "And we love having her over, so no thanks needed," then, "Lawyers."

"Lawyers?" That wasn't the Daisy Foundation business he'd anticipated.

"Don't worry, hun. The drop-in centre's still kind of wish-list territory. No rush." That *was*, however. "We haven't even looked at how much it will cost to run yet, and we can hold off doing anything about it for the time being."

"Bloody Tierney and his big mouth."

"Sorry?"

"It was his idea to postpone, not mine."

"I've no idea what you're talking about," Shaunna said.

"In that case, forget I said anything. At least, forget I blamed Sean. So you know, we're postponing the official opening of the surgery, but I meant what I said. I'm converting the loft for the Daisy Foundation—unless you've found a better venue?"

"No, of course not. But…" Shaunna's nose wrinkled, and she sighed. "After what happened on Monday at your surgery—"

"Electrical fault," Josh interrupted, hoping only he could see the rapid flutter of his shirt front. He usually had no trouble lying convincingly, although he couldn't recall having lied to Shaunna before. "So lawyers then," he said, reassured that his poker face was holding when she stopped giving him that patient, confide-in-me look and nodded. "Haven't we found one yet?"

"*We* haven't, no," Shaunna answered, which was a forewarning rather than a jab—he hoped, even if he'd have deserved it. His question was only marginally better than her bringing up his and Libby's ghostly adventures, and he should already have known the answer. In his defence, he was, by consensus, more a 'sleeping trustee' of the foundation, there to make up numbers and cast his vote when called upon to do so.

"Look, Josh, I know you don't want to deal with the interviews…"

"You didn't ask me," he pointed out.

"Because you're still working here and trying to get the surgery fixed up, and then there's Libby's exams and…I wouldn't be asking now if there was anyone else available."

"You don't want me involved in the interviews, do you?"

Shaunna's cheeks turned the colour of cherry blossom. She came over and sat with her bag in her lap, strap still on her shoulder. "Please try not to take this the wrong way. I love your straight talk. I value your opinion above almost anyone else's. But—"

"You don't want me to scare off your candidates."

"Yeah." She grimaced. "I'm sorry."

Josh shrugged, a little hurt, but he couldn't argue when her point was valid. "What do you need me to do?" he asked, counter to the childish impulse to sulk.

"Would you mind sitting in on an interview this afternoon?"

"Can't Eleanor make it?"

"No childcare."

"Sean?"

"Probably, but I need someone sensible on my side, and—"

"He's not someone sensible?"

Shaunna faked weighing it up. "He can be."

"Except if it relates to—"

"It's not about Jess," Shaunna interjected.

"It's *always* about Jess." The Charity Commission had recommended months ago that they appoint a legal expert to their board of trustees, and all four of them were acutely aware of the root of their difficulty in doing so.

"Not on this occasion. The thing is…" Shaunna pressed her lips together as if to spread an application of gloss. "OK, so, Sean's having…how to put it…"

"Say no more." For as much as Josh's curiosity was egging him on, he hated putting her in a position where she felt she had to breach Sean's confidence. "I'll do the interview."

"Thanks. You probably already know what's going on with him."

"Probably." The obvious issue was Phee turning up, but Sean seemed to be coping with that, which left only Jess and his as-yet-unresolved regret for what might have been but wasn't. "What's the problem with the lawyer we're interviewing this afternoon?"

"She's too cheap."

Josh laughed. "That's not something you hear often about lawyers."

"She has her reasons."

"Criminal record?" he speculated.

"No." Now Shaunna laughed—and rolled her eyes. "I bet she's never had so much as a parking ticket. She's one of those pure-as-the-driven-snow types. And recently widowed."

"How recently?"

"Last week."

"Wow. That *is* recent. Does Sean know?"

"Not yet, but it was the first thing she said after we'd done the hellos on the phone, and I know I bounce back quickly, but a week?" She shook her head. "I'm not happy about taking her on this soon after her husband died, and Sean and bereavement…"

"Is like a kid in a sweet shop," Josh finished.

"Exactly. I'm worried he'll offer her the job out of sympathy or as occupational therapy or something."

"No, he won't," Josh said with certainty.

"He's a softy."

"In his personal life. In fact, gullible springs to mind. But when he's wearing his professional hat…"

Shaunna put her hands together and fluttered her eyelashes.

"I already said I'd—ooph!" Her hug was sudden and enthusiastic. "What's this for?"

"A reward for not stamping your feet." She released him and grinned.

"As if I would!"

"As if you wouldn't!" This time, she moved off like she meant it, calling, "The interview's at one," on her way out.

***

Campion Trust Boardroom
One p.m.

"PLEASE COME THROUGH." Shaunna appeared in the doorway, gesturing with her hand and giving Josh a dubious, slightly manic smile. A woman in a mauve, A-line-skirt suit bustled past her into the Campion Trust boardroom, the Daisy Foundation's temporary—assuming Josh ever managed to set foot in his surgery again—HQ.

Josh rose from his seat to greet her. "Good morning, Mrs.—"

"Dorothy Lomax." Her face widened with her glossy-mauve smile, and a large, warm hand firmly gripped and near shook his arm out of its socket. Mauve nail varnish. Mauve shoes…

"Dorothy, this is Josh, one of our trustees," Shaunna explained on his stunned behalf. She shut the door and came around to his side of the table. "Thanks for coming in."

"That's quite all right. As I mentioned on the phone, my husband passed away recently, and I find I'm at something of a loose end. It's really no hardship."

"I understand," Shaunna said, yet her cynicism hadn't diminished. Josh, however, was intrigued; Dorothy Lomax was nothing like the grieving widow he'd envisaged.

"Perhaps it would help if I explained." She turned in her seat, directly facing Josh and once again treating him to that wide, mauve smile. "My husband had been unwell for a long time. Cancer, angina, diabetes, dementia—he had all kinds wrong with him, poor chap."

Beside Josh, Shaunna grew an inch with muscle tension.

"It's a long time since he was the strong, intelligent man I married—and a relief to be free of the responsibility, to be frank. He refused to go into a nursing home, back when he was still capable of expressing such wishes. Fortunately, his critical illness insurance covered his care at home, and we'd saved sufficient that I was able to give up work to oversee his nurses. They were marvellous, it's such a thankless task."

Shaunna nodded in agreement. "My dad has Alzheimer's."

Dorothy's forehead crinkled like crepe paper. "I'm sorry for you, pet." She stretched her stout arm as far across the table as it would reach and patted the wood comfortingly, her mauve fingernails vibrant against the polished pale beech.

"Thank you." Shaunna's voice was quiet and unsteady. She cleared her throat and sent a waft of almond breeze Josh's way as she flicked her hair over her shoulder. It was her trip switch back to business mode. "You mentioned you're a specialist in charities."

"That's correct, yes. Social enterprise more so than charities. Milton—my husband—was the expert on charity law."

"He was a lawyer too?"

"Yes, we all three were *solicitors*—Milton, my sister and myself. My sister's expertise was in inheritance law."

Josh glanced over the CV in front of him. It was on there—Lomax Barnes Solicitors, senior partner until six years ago, which matched what she'd told them, but there was something not right. Just a feeling, the kind he didn't often get because he researched in advance and was prepared for most eventualities. His failure on this occasion was nothing to do with taking shortcuts; he'd intentionally come to this interview with no preconceptions, or none beyond knowing Shaunna's opinion, and that Dorothy was a widow whose fees were substantially lower than they should have been.

"What's the catch?" Josh glanced up and caught her taken-aback blink.

"Begging your pardon?"

"Why are you charging so little?"

"The house is paid for, there's money in the bank, and no children. I have only myself to consider. And I'm bored, Mr…"

"Just Josh," he said. "May I ask, if you don't need the money—"

"Why am I charging at all?" she interrupted.

"Yes, that would've been my question, had I been allowed to finish it."

"My apologies. Do you realise how often men interrupt women?"

"Very, I imagine." It was a well-researched area of social psychology, and he'd read countless papers. Men interrupted, dominated discussions and frequently talked over their female counterparts. Josh was fully aware of the advantages of being a white middle-class man, and how poor his social etiquette could be, so he tried to be equally rude to everyone. Well, he didn't *try* to be rude at all, but he didn't think he discriminated when choosing whether to bite his tongue or say it how it was. "You still haven't answered my question."

"I don't believe anyone should work for free, irrespective of whether it's for a good cause, and supporting families after the demise of a little one is a truly worthy cause. But even trustees attract an honorarium, do you not?"

"No," Shaunna answered before Josh could get there. "We chose not to because it's a charity, and we need the money less than those we're helping."

"That's your prerogative, pet. My fees are open to negotiation, of course, but I stand by what I said. I won't work for free, nor do I think you should."

"Moving on..." Shaunna brusquely shuffled her papers, meeting Josh's gaze for a second before she looked over their list of questions, no doubt seeking out the trickiest. She was irritated and ready to give their interviewee the heave-ho, which was a shame. Josh rather liked Dorothy Lomax.

***

Three p.m.

"AND ANOTHER ONE bites the dust." Sean tossed his ring binder onto the table and leaned back, tipping his chair and sweeping his knuckles against the wall behind. "I'm sick of this feckin' boardroom. How many's that we've seen now? Twenty?"

Shaunna shut the door and returned to her seat next to his. "Hardly! That was number seven."

"Any more on the list?"

"Nope. You've successfully scared them all away."

"Hey now, I've been perfectly charming." He tried to make it sound light-hearted.

"I was joking."

"As that may be, my boss at the hospital said the same and ordered me to keep it shut when we were interviewing for my replacement. It's a good thing to keep these people on their toes— a test of resilience, you know? Are my expectations unrealistic?"

Shaunna patted his hand. "It's not you. Or not just you. Jess might not have been who we thought she was, but I don't remember her ever being as mercenary as that." She nodded after the departing applicant—a Basil Lawson who'd formerly worked for the prestigious 'This', 'That', and 'The Other' and demanded an hourly rate on a par with a professional footballer's salary. "Or not with us," Shaunna qualified.

"No, you're right. Lawyers are shockingly overpaid for what they do, but it's not so much about the money-grabbing. It's how they're presenting themselves."

"Yeah. With Jess, there was no pretence."

"Or not with us…"

At Sean's intentional borrowing of her words, Shaunna did a combined half-smile, shrug and sigh. "We never asked, did we?"

"I don't think she'd have lied to us if we had."

"Then I'm glad I didn't." She nodded as if confirming for herself the truth of her words. Whatever Jess had been, whatever she'd done, Shaunna had loved her as much as Sean had, though in a wholly different way. "I feel like we're measuring them all against someone who didn't exist," she said.

"Is that what we're doing?" Sean was interrogating his own judgement as much as hers.

"Trying to find someone Jess would've approved of makes no sense."

"Because she's not here, you mean?"

"Not even that. You know my beliefs, Sean. My mum's still a constant presence in my life—sometimes I forget only I can sense her. Well, Adele says she can too, but it's Adele, so I'm taking it with a pinch of salt."

"Isn't salt what you use to keep the ghosties away?" Sean tormented, which earned him a well-deserved toe in the shin. "Go on. What were you saying?"

"Even believing as I do that Jess is with us in spirit, she didn't set a good example, and she'd have told us that herself."

"All right." Sean flipped his binder shut with a sense of finality. "So what do we do?"

"Hand over to Josh?" Shaunna suggested.

"Tempting." Other than he had even less tolerance of lawyers than they did, although he'd been open to the possibility of giving their penultimate candidate a trial run. "You never did tell me why you brought him in for the interview earlier."

"He was free, you weren't."

"I popped out for lunch with Soph. If I'd known you had someone coming in, I'd have rescheduled."

"You didn't miss much." Shaunna fed her copies of the applications back into their plastic wallets—an evasive manoeuvre if ever Sean saw one. "But we can't afford to dismiss her purely because I don't like her."

"Why not? You're a damned good judge of character."

"Do you think?"

Sean shrugged, all faux humility. "You picked me as a friend. How much proof do you need?"

Shaunna shook her head, her hair an undulating tide of glossy red that crashed over her shoulders. Leaning in closer, she pinched his cheek to recapture his attention. "We could always readvertise."

"All right. Do you want to sort that out now, or—actually, I've a better idea."

Shaunna put her fingertip on her chin as if she were about to take a wild guess. "Take this to Milky's and get out of this feckin' boardroom?"

"You read my mind, for sure."

She shrugged and gave him a seductive smile. "It's a gift."

17: Lonely Women

Rowan Mews
Two years ago

I CAN'T FIND MY blue shirt."
Genie glanced up from her book as Paul came back into the bedroom holding a suit by a hanger, his attention on it rather than her.

"Try the hamper," she said and returned to her reading.

The bathroom light clicked on, followed by a few muffled thuds, then, "Damn it."

She sighed, awaiting the predictable outcome of his discovery—his own fault, always assuming someone else would unpack his case and launder his clothes, but also not *entirely* his fault. He was young with no responsibilities beyond his career, and routine bred expectation.

He stormed back into the bedroom. "It's not in there."

"You have other shirts, Paul." She didn't look up this time.

"They'll need ironing."

"Then ask Margaret."

With much grumbling, he hooked his suit hanger over the door and heaved his case onto the bed, the weight pinning Genie's legs under the duvet. She knew by his disgusted sneer the moment he'd found his blue shirt. "For God's sake." He threw it on the floor, followed by the rest of the dirty clothes and underwear that had been left in the case. "It reeks."

"Look on the bright side. You've only been home *a day.*"

"Meaning what, exactly?"

"Meaning it would've smelled far worse if it had been longer."

"I'll have to buy one on my way to the office." He stomped off again.

"Another one," Genie muttered. He didn't hear her. She flipped the page and continued to read while he thumped back and forth, dumping old underwear and whatever else he'd found lurking in his closet into the suitcase. Not a word of the book was going in, but she'd had a late night, so she stayed put, refusing to entertain his tantrum.

She wasn't angry with him, but lately, she'd become accustomed to her own company again, and his flouncing, which she'd found easy to ignore in the past, was getting on her nerves. Other factors were at play that were nothing to do with Paul, and she was trying her hardest to not take those out on him and make the most of their increasingly scarce time together. Since his promotion, he worked away four days out of seven, and more often than not, when he was home she was out with a client at some social event or other.

Their respective work was a double-edged sword, both keeping them apart and sustaining their relationship. Indeed, it was how they'd met—at a gala put on by the pharmaceutical company Paul worked for. The CEO had hired Genie to be his plus-one for the evening, at which Paul had been one of a handful of young, buff and obscenely beautiful reps paraded as eye candy for rich, randy directors and investors. Despite the difference in their ages and that he could've had his pick of the guests, an innocent coincidence of their trips to freshen up had sparked an instant, mutual attraction, and as soon as the CEO had dispensed with Genie's services, she and Paul had taken off for his hotel room.

Had she known at the time that Paul was still a teenager, she'd have pulled the brakes before their damned hot flirting went any further, but he'd looked older—she'd have put him at twenty-eight or nine, older than he was now—so she hadn't even thought to ask. Five years on, the fifteen-year age gap should have felt less of a chasm, not more, yet every day, something rammed it home—her fortieth birthday looming on the horizon,

Phee starting her A' Levels in a few months' time, Paul's inability to deal with his laundry when all he had to do was move it from his case to the hamper and Margaret would take care of it.

Once again, Genie reminded herself that none of this was Paul's fault, or at least, he was acting no differently than usual. Excellent sales rep and lover that he was, he lacked many of the most basic yet essential life skills—skills which Genie wouldn't have acquired either, had she, like he, continued to live at home during her undergraduate years. Granted, she'd have become a stinking recluse were it not for Jess coming to her rescue whenever she ran out of clean clothes, toiletries or cosmetics. Such were the trials for one who had never had to worry where these things came from, as was Paul's lot now, but it wasn't her duty to mollycoddle him.

It was only when the front door slammed she noticed his suitcase was gone from the bed and he'd left without saying goodbye. Or had he? She'd been so engrossed in her thoughts she didn't know, and she fleetingly imagined how awful it would be if something were to happen to him and she had to live with *our last conversation was an argument.* Much as she regretted that he'd left on a sour note, it was a relief to have the house to herself again for the next thirty-six hours, when Phee would arrive home for spring break.

Oddly, that was something she didn't regret, even though she hadn't wanted Phee to go to boarding school. It had been Phee's choice, which Genie had tried not to take to heart. The independent streak was in Phee's genes, inherited from both parents, and she needed space and freedom to be herself. If Genie were ever to try to curtail that, as had been done to her, she expected Phee would treat her with the same contempt Genie felt for her parents. But she didn't want to think about them today, or any day, so she dog-eared the page and cast aside her book in favour of a leisurely shower followed by breakfast on the patio.

She was almost finished when Margaret arrived at eight-thirty with the newspaper and her customary refusal to sit and share a pot of tea with the lady of the house. Dear Margaret and her observance of custom. She had come to Genie with only three years of service behind her but with an exceptional reference from an elderly baroness whose only complaint was that Margaret was 'remarkably staid for one so young': she was only a little older than Genie yet had borne the outlook of a sixty-year-old woman from the beginning. Still, theirs was a good working relationship, which Genie had no desire to disrupt by impetuously seeking Margaret's agreement that Paul was a selfish slob, thus she settled for mentioning the heap of dirty laundry in the bedroom and let her assistant do what she was paid to do, then perused the newspaper to pass the remaining few minutes until nine o'clock.

No need for scrolling her contacts list; the number she'd called every day for twenty years never left the top of the screen. She tapped the name and put her phone to her ear.

"Hello?"

"Hi, Steph, it's Genie."

"Hi, Genie. How are you?"

"I'm well, thank you. How was your holiday?" It was a touchy subject, but better that than put Jess's mum in a position where she felt compelled to answer 'I'm fine' when she absolutely wouldn't be.

"Lovely. The weather was stunning—not *too* hot, which it can be in Florida—and I have a smashing tan. All over!"

"Oh, I say!" Genie laughed, reminded again of where Jess's sassiness came from. She and her mum were so alike. "And how's Madam?"

"Better now she's back in her own house. When did you last speak to her?"

"Yesterday morning."

"Ah. So you'll have heard all about last week's chemo then."

"Yes." Genie matched Steph's weary tone but doubted Jess had subjected her mother to the same rant about how she wished she was dead already. Somehow, Genie had staved off the tears long enough to say what she hoped were all the right, supportive things before she'd hung up, sent Phee a text that simply said '*I love you. Mum x*', then sobbed her heart out until Paul distracted her with sex, wine and dinner.

"Is she up yet?" she asked.

"She's still in bed, but she's awake. I'm just taking the phone up to her. One sec."

There was crackling on the line and muffled voices, then Jess's feeble, "Hey."

"Hey, gorgeous. I didn't wake you, did I?"

She heard Jess's mum say, "I'll leave you in peace," followed by a few seconds' silence before Jess spoke again.

"I've been awake all night, Genie. It's *awful*. I can hear her crying in the room next door."

"Oh, Jess. I'm sorry."

"I even tried listening to music, but how does anyone sleep with music playing?"

"Depends on what it is. I found those meditation CDs we used to listen to very relaxing."

"Because you were always stoned."

"I was not!" Although she'd admit to having dabbled from time to time, considerably more than that after they'd graduated. "Maybe you could try the sound of the ocean or something."

"Ugh, no. I feel nauseous as it is. On the plus side, I don't have to put up with it for long."

A prickle of something—fear, sadness, anger—crept over Genie's scalp as she clamped her teeth to trap *I wish you'd stop saying things like that*. She'd promised she'd treat Jess the same as always, but those words carried the danger of subjecting her to more 'awful tears', so she went with, "Morbid but true."

"Well, hopefully. I haven't—"

"I thought you wanted to go to your friends' wedding."

"I do. That's not—"

"And didn't the oncologist say staying positive would—"

"Imogen, please shut up a minute. You misunderstood me, as per usual."

"But…" Genie folded the newspaper and pressed it flat. She'd only ever misunderstood Jess once. Catastrophically so. "Sorry. What *did* you mean?"

"Andy's moving back in with me."

"That's a drastic measure to get your mum to leave," Genie joked, hoping pithy humour would shield her loathing from Jess's ears because it was *always* Andy.

"It's not like that, and she isn't leaving. Not permanently. Unfortunately."

"Jess…"

"I know. I'm an ungrateful cow. But how is this helping me, Genie? She talks to me like we're strangers in the street, then goes off and has a cry. It's like Daisy dying all over again."

"For her, it's *exactly* like Daisy dying all over again." That was downright mean to say, but it was the truth.

"It's not about her, though, is it?"

Genie drew breath, but Jess ploughed on.

"I'm not denying she's hurting. I just mean she needs to stop pretending she's staying here for my benefit when clearly it's for hers."

"Clearly," Genie muttered. Jess's answering annoyance came in the form of noisy huffing and puffing on the phone mic, but she didn't challenge what Genie had said. Nor did Genie expect her to understand. She wasn't a mother. "Anyway, Jessica, this isn't a purely social call. The package arrived."

"Oh, good. Did you open it?"

"Was I supposed to?"

"Not necessarily, but you can if you like. You know about everything that's in there."

"OK. Well, it's in the vault, so unless you really need me to open it…" Genie crossed her fingers, hoping the answer was no. Not that it was a crypt-type vault; more a walk-in safe at the back of the wine cellar, but there was so much old junk in there and the concomitant dust, it left her wheezy and itchy-eyed for hours after each visit.

"No, it's fine," Jess said. "Oh! There is one thing in there you don't know about, but I'll tell you another time."

"You can't leave me dangling like that!"

Jess laughed, but she wasn't telling.

"Damn you, Jessica. I'm going to have to break out the antihistamines again."

"I'll text you when we get off the phone. How about that?"

"In that case, I'm hanging up."

"Don't you dare!"

Now Genie laughed. "I was joking, although I do need to go soon. Phee's home tomorrow, and I promised we'd go away somewhere—pick up a last-minute deal."

"You'll get a better deal if you leave it till the day you want to go."

"It's too risky."

"That's what I'd do."

"I'm not you."

"Lucky for you."

Genie sighed. "I could slap you sometimes. Or hug you. I'm never sure which."

"Then lucky for me, too, that this is only a phone call."

"Actually..." Between school fees, Margaret's wages and the usual bills, she couldn't afford more than a few days away, and she'd said they'd go somewhere hot with a pool, which they would, but life was undeniably short. "Are you well enough for visitors?"

"You and Phee?"

"Yeah. It'll be the week after next."

"I'll be here."

"Great. I'll call you later and figure out hotels and whatnot."

"Andy's the man to talk to for that. He'll get you a hefty discount."

"Even better. That's what I love about you."

"I have hot friends who get you stuff on the cheap?"

"Too right!" The less said about the hot friends part, the better, although they'd never talked about what had happened. It was a long time ago, in another life, really, when Genie still had access to her inheritance and Jess wasn't terminally ill. Perhaps that was why she kept mentioning Andy now. "I'm going, Jess. Don't forget to send me that text."

"Hang on!"

Genie waited, listening for clues over the too-quiet line.

"OK," Jess said at last. "She's gone outside for a cigarette, so I can tell you now. Andy and I are getting married."

"You're *what*?"

"Two words."

"True love?" Genie sniped but again managed to inflect it as a joke. Jess falling in love was even less likely than Paul unpacking his case without prompting.

"Inheritance tax."

"Thank God! You had me worried there."

"Ha. What about you and Paul? Any danger of you tying—"

"None at all. And I'm definitely going now. I'll talk to you later, OK? I love you."

"Love you too."

"And don't forget to give your mum my love."

"Will it stop her whinging?"

"Has it stopped you?"

"I'm not your friend anymore. Bye."

Genie's phone beeped in her ear, and she laughed. Jess had hung up on her. Same as usual.

***

Present Day
Thursday, 18th April

GENIE DROPPED THE package, still sealed, back into the crate where it slid into the gap between the deeds to Rowan Mews and her parents' wills. After Jess passed, Andy had told Genie to incinerate it, but she had so little of Jess left, she couldn't. And, of course, Andy being Andy, he hadn't come back to her to check it had been destroyed. If he had, she'd have lied, despite knowing that the documents inside the thick brown paper were an incriminating fiction she'd helped create.

That familiar prickle started on the back of her neck, raced over her scalp, down her face, arms and torso, leaving goosebumps in its wake and her nipples resembling the knobbed lids of humbug jars. It was a feeling she now recognised as grief and disillusionment—that Jess had thought it necessary to offer bribes to secure Genie's assistance. That her love and their friendship had never been enough. The irony was laughable; the contacts she'd made through her work as an escort were what made it possible for her to do what Jess asked, in return for never having to deal with those men again. Her fortune had been restored, or that was how Jess had sold it, as if she were the croupier of some ethereal roulette wheel, fixing wins in favour of the neediest and most deserving.

Genie was now a woman of independent means, and in the year and a half since Jess's death, the money had passed through so many accounts and fund managers, charity projects and property developments, it was as stain-free as a newly laundered tablecloth. She would never again have to worry about school fees or first cars or lavish holidays, all those things she had wanted to provide for her daughter without saddling them both with familial obligation, and the only way of tracing it back to Jess's transgressions was through the contents of that package, which could be ashes in an instant.

All that money and she still hadn't been able to stop Phee throwing her life away for a few minutes' pleasure with some boy.

There were photos in the vault. Old photos of her baby girl, shiny dark-chocolate curls like Sean's, the rosiest cheeks and that sweet little smile captured on camera, the accompanying giggles as clear in Genie's mind as if she were hearing them all over again. But there had been no giggles since Phee came home. No laughter, tears, arguments, recriminations. Just the daily confirmation of nausea and fatigue and a refusal to leave her Liquorice Allsorts room until Xander and Jonathan 'pack up their shit and go'.

With the folder containing Margaret's references in her hand, Genie locked the vault and returned to the main house, snagging a pinot noir on her way through the cellar, which needed a restock; like most things of late, it was too much trouble. Writing this reference, for instance: Margaret hadn't yet given notice, but if she were asking for references, it was surely a foregone conclusion, and Genie had never written one before, hence she was taking her lead from the one provided by Margaret's former employer. Perhaps she shouldn't have agreed so easily, or so readily kowtowed to Phee's demand, as once Xander caught wind of it, he couldn't have 'packed his shit' any quicker. Well, he hadn't actually packed it; Jonathan had, but the net result was the same. Come the end of spring break when Phee returned to school, Genie would be rattling around this old house on her own. Of course, Paul would be home some of the time, but that thought brought her less solace with every passing day. Perhaps she should come to an agreement with the poltergeist now: *you stick to your rooms, I'll stick to mine, and we'll get along just fine.*

Genie opened the wine and filled a glass, raising it to her unseen housemate, gulped it down as if were mere grape juice and then filled the glass again, not a care for whether it was at its best when her options were quite starkly that she could either embrace a life of solitude or she could have it out with Phee.

Alas, the decision was ripped from her hands along with the glass when the music scores that she would have sworn on her daughter's life had been in the piano stool erupted from the music stand as if propelled by an industrial fan. They were still fluttering to the floor as Phee appeared in Genie's peripheral vision. All bar one, which came to a rest in the puddle of wine around Genie's feet.

"I'm going out," Phee said, then, "Agh. Mother!"

The song played, beginner's fingers bashing at the keys, a rhythmless accompaniment to drunken voices...

Alouette, gentille alouette
Alouette, je te plumerai

...and laughter.

"Mum?"

Je te plumerai la tête
Je te plumerai la tête
Et la tête, et la tête
Alouette, Alouette
Oh, oh, oh, oh

"Fine. Ignore me then! But you'll have to deal with that cut yourself. I'll see you tomorrow."

"It's not even the right piece." Half aware of the front door opening, Genie bent and peeled the wet paper from the floor, holding it out on her upturned palm as she straightened. "See? 'L'Alouette', not 'Alouette'."

The front door closed again, but Phee hadn't left.

"Mum?" She came into the room. "What are you on?"

"The music. Listen." Genie sang along. "*Alouette, gentille alouette, Alouette, je te plumerai.*" She felt the bottle slipping from her hand and tightened her grasp as Phee tried to take it from her.

"Let go, Mum. You're drunk."

Genie laughed. "But I've only had one glass!" And yet... she did *feel* drunk. She stared at the half-full bottle. "Maybe I should eat." She shifted her gaze to her daughter's eyes, ringed with exhaustion and bushbaby wide. "And so should you."

"Mum, please—"

"I know you're pregnant."

Genie's arm sprang back with the force of Phee's sudden release of the bottle. The music stopped.

"How…?"

"How do I know? I'm your mum." Genie brushed her knuckles over Phee's peach-soft cheek, wine dripping from the music score scrunched in her hand. "Come and sit with me."

"I can't. I'm going out."

"Where?"

"I'm meeting Sarah at the pub."

"Are you really?"

"For God's sake, Mum. Yes. At the Hare and Hounds. Here." Phee yanked her phone from her pocket and jabbed the screen. "Shit. Line busy. But I swear that's where I'm going. If you don't believe me, come with me."

"I *do* believe you," Genie said.

"I've never lied to you."

"Never?"

"No. And I never would!"

"Where were you last weekend?"

Phee pursed her lips.

"Ah, a loophole. All right, then tell me this. Is he your boyfriend or someone you met at a party or…?"

Phee shook her head, pleading. "Don't, Mum."

"It's OK. You're not in trouble, darling."

"I've *got to go*." Phee pecked Genie's cheek and made a dash for the door, but not quickly enough to hide the crumple of her sweet face from her mother.

"You can tell me anything. You know that, don't you?" Genie called after her desperately. Phee left without looking back.

18: To Love and Friendship

"A NOTHER?" SEAN NODDED at Shaunna's glass, empty but for the last dregs of a cherry yoghurt-not-smoothie that looked disturbingly like coagulated blood.

Shaunna gulped and shuddered. "No, thank you. I'm driving."

"You don't drive."

"I don't have a car either."

"So the Mustang's all Andy's then?"

"Ha. What do you think?"

"I think you're very generous to let him chauffeur you around."

"Generous, you say…"

"I wouldn't say no to having you in my passenger seat."

Shaunna's eyebrows arched, and her lashes swooped low. "There's more room in the back."

"You'd know better than me."

She shook her head. "I've never done it in a car."

"Really?"

"Really. Have you?"

"No. Nor does it appeal. All those sticky-out bits to work around, and there's the chance you'll get caught by some poor old lady walking her poodle."

"That's what makes it so much of a turn-on."

"The old lady and the poodle?"

Shaunna rolled her eyes, always a dramatic display, but she was hamming it up today, as if to hide how she was really

189

feeling. On the whole, though, she seemed her usual happy self. "You knew what I meant," she said. "It's the illicitness of it, like being a horny teenager again."

Sean sat back and watched her thoughts take hold—saucy ones, by the looks of it, as her cheeks had taken on a rosy hue and she was biting her lower lip. What a joy it would have been to see inside her mind right now, to be a voyeur to the memories that had her shifting in her seat. But for all their flirting and open conversations about their sex lives—or lack of one in Sean's case—Shaunna kept her teenage antics to herself, and he didn't want to ask, fearing she'd misunderstand his intent because he knew how it would sound. Even now, with her seemingly in a mental tryst with some teen dreamboat, when he pictured her in his head—calling it 'fantasising' made it seem sordid and unsavoury—she appeared just as she was: a voluptuous, magnificent redhead in her forties.

He was no dirty old man. Not like that cheating scumbag Paul. Sean had met a few like him over the years, and he'd done what he had to, mechanically going through the motions of impartial assessment and treatment, all the while with his sights on the drink at the end that would purge his disgust. Why had he accepted Phee's word that it was consensual? Did she know herself well enough to make that kind of informed decision, especially when it affected the rest of her life?

That was what he'd have asked Shaunna if he could. She'd been through teen pregnancy and motherhood. The little he did know was that she'd put her life on hold, much as Phee planned to, until her daughter started school. Did she regret it? Would she do it differently if she could go back?

He'd stared too long, and Shaunna had escaped her thoughts before he had. Now he was in trouble. After all, her openness wasn't the only reason he'd encouraged her when she'd said she wanted to become a sex therapist. It hadn't been part of the equation at all. She could read minds as adeptly as any psychotherapist worth their salt, himself and Josh included, and the tables had turned.

She waited, giving him a chance to speak. Feebly, he came up with, "Are you sure you don't want another drink?"

"I'm sure," she said. She trapped him with her gaze—blue-eyed today, which he had a feeling was her natural eye colour. He considered asking, to shift the focus back to her, but she was on to him and jumped in first. "What's up, Sean?"

"Why d'you ask?"

"In case you want to share, but you don't have to tell me."

"That's not how this works," he said.

"How what works?"

"Us."

"Oh, there's an 'us' now, is there?" She gave him a flash of that tantalising smile, the one where her lips parted a little and the tip of her tongue rested between her teeth. Sometimes it was a deliberate play in her flirting repertoire; sometimes it spontaneously manifested. In this instance, it was deliberate, and flirtatious, but with a different goal in mind.

"All right," he said, averting his eyes. "You can stop now. I'm at ease already."

"Hmm-hmm. If your shoulders were any tenser, your arms would stick out like windmill sails."

He hadn't realised until she said it, and he tried to loosen up. On top of being stressed, lugging all those boxes down from the attic had done him no favours, and his blood pressure was probably sky high. "Will you be offering massage once your sex clinic's up and running?"

She folded her arms. The overhead light reflected off her glossy pout. "I'm not answering that until you're straight with me and tell me what's wrong. You keep offering me drinks, so you clearly want me to stay."

"Can I not just enjoy your company?"

"If you were actually enjoying it…"

He held up his hands in surrender. "Fine. You got me." Could he say it? As he knew far too well, sometimes the will was there but the flesh was having none of it. He gave it a go. "My friend's daughter is pregnant. She's only seventeen."

Her response was non-verbal, and rich. A slight arch of the eyebrows, a relaxing of the lips, eye movement down, then up, no blinking. She sat forward, elbows resting on the table, arms still folded, and looked him dead in the eye. "And?"

"And…" He didn't know where to begin, and once again he took too long figuring it out for himself.

"You're worried she's thrown her life away," Shaunna said.

"No! God, not at all. I mean, if I hadn't met you, I'd be pulling my hair out over it, but look at you. You're setting up to embark on your second career, and you excel at your first. You're shacked up with a damn good-looking successful fella. Your eldest daughter is an amazing young woman, and all three of them are beautiful—a credit to you. You're brilliant."

Shaunna's answering laughter was bashful but brittle. "You make me sound superhuman."

"I'm not ruling it out," he joked, then asked seriously, "Do you not think you're successful?"

She thought about it for a while before she answered. "I don't know. Maybe I am, but it's not as if any of it was planned, or not planned in the way they get you to write down your targets and what you need to do to achieve them."

"'They' being?"

"Huh?"

"Who had you writing down targets?"

"Oh! Doctor Lederman. We had our first supervision meeting this morning."

"Did it go all right?"

"It went fine, thank you for asking, *aaaaand* back to you." Finally, she unfolded her arms and raised a finger. "I need to pee, but I'm not done with you." She dashed off, leaving him alone at the table.

For a moment, he thought he was alone in the milk bar, but then a member of staff popped up from behind the counter and smiled at him. She was new, and while he always made the effort to learn people's names and use them, he didn't know hers yet and she was too far away for him to read her nametag.

"Are you waiting to shut up shop?" he asked.

"Not yet." She glanced at the giant clock on the milk bar's back wall and frowned.

"It's always wrong," Sean said, taking out his phone, curious himself now. Time spent in Shaunna's company whizzed by, and beyond 'the duration of three yoghurt-not-smoothies', he couldn't have said with any accuracy how long they'd been sitting there. "It's six-thirty…" He stumbled again over not knowing her name.

"Thanks," she said, still scowling at the useless clock. "We're open for another half an hour."

"Grand. If you need us to clear out, just say, all right?"

She nodded and bobbed out of sight again, continuing with whatever she'd been doing under the counter.

"So…" Shaunna said as she resumed her seat across the table. "I was thinking in the loo. I need to ask you something." She adjusted her hairclip and tucked a loose curl behind her ear. It was the low-key equivalent of the *hair down, flick over the shoulder, I mean business* Shaunna. "I think I already know the answer, and if I'm right, you're gonna hit the roof, but I still need to ask, to be sure. I've never seen you so worked up before."

She hadn't even asked whatever it was and already she'd got Sean's back up, but he could see it was both difficult and important to her, so he nodded. "Go on."

Deep breath, hold. "Did you sleep with one of your undergrads and get her pregnant?"

"What the—" A roar of fury pushed its way up his throat, and the pressure in his head was unbearable. Hit the roof? He could've blown the thing to outer space. But his defences were holding— so far—and there had to be a reason for her asking. A good one. However it seemed, this was not an accusation that he would do something so abhorrent made by someone he loved, respected and trusted and of whom he had believed those sentiments were reciprocal.

He managed to push out a gruff, "No," at more or less normal volume but didn't dare say anything else.

"OK," she said. "I'm sorry I had to ask."

"So am I." He reached behind him for his coat, intending to get out of there before he exploded or fell apart, it could go either way, but she grabbed his arm, stopping him. He shot her a warning glance, and she flinched but didn't back down.

"Hear me out, Sean. Please?"

He didn't move, and she released him, tentatively, her expression beseeching him to stay. He nodded, no promises.

She was quiet for a few minutes, weighing her words and taking great care to not offend him further. He wasn't sure that was a possibility when he was beyond offended and the only bolster against the utter devastation of his self-esteem was his rapidly diminishing anger. There was still enough in the reserve for him to tell her to get on with it, but he gave her the benefit of the doubt and waited until, finally, she was ready.

"You think I'm this powerful, intuitive goddess-like being, Sean, but I'm not. I'm an ordinary woman. A mum. A hairdresser. Yes, I'm trying to be something more, but those psychology courses I did—it was so hard for me because I'm not like you and Josh and Ellie and Jess. I'm not naturally clever. I struggle with every word. I mean, you've no idea how long it took me to get my head around Piaget. You and Josh—that's how you talk all the time, but it's like a foreign language to me.

"And it's not just that. I remember you saying I'm kind of doing therapy on my salon clients already, but sometimes I get it so wrong. Like this woman came in a few weeks ago with an awful cut, and I felt sorry for her, so I made her a cuppa and let her cry on my shoulder. She said she'd been to the big salon on the high street and one of their trainees had done the hack job, so I thought the least I could do was tidy it up, stick a tint on it, turn it into something she could stand seeing in the mirror. I only charged her for a cut.

"Then last week, one of the salons across town called to say someone had been in asking them to fix her hair because a trainee in our shop had messed up her colour. We don't even have a trainee! Thank God Hayley's an understanding boss. The woman was a con artist, and I fell for it."

"We all make mistakes," Sean said, and if the words sounded harsh, then what of it? He'd thought they knew each other better than this. Better than she knew a walk-in client.

"I'm not explaining this well."

"No?"

"No!" She reached for his hand, and he was too slow to dodge. She squeezed. "I assume the best of you, Sean. Always. I've never doubted you."

"That's not how it feels—comparing what's happening here to some woman you met the one time. How—ah." His higher reasoning skills must have been reconnecting by increments. "You doubted your own judgement."

"Right!" She relaxed her grip on him, palpably relieved that he understood where she was coming from, although there was a way to go yet. "Believe it or not, I asked because I'm trying to be a good friend."

"Yeah, I'm not seeing that. Can you explain it to me?"

"I'm trying to. The thing is, I can usually see right through you. I'm not saying you're shallow or anything like that. You're wide open to me. Intentionally, I think. But this week, especially today, you're closed off somehow, and I was trying to figure it out in the loo. Why would you be so worried about this friend's daughter when you say what I've achieved reassures you she still has a future—unless you feel culpable? Why would you care that much unless you're involved with the girl in some way?

"I'm not saying you only care about people you have a connection with. I saw how you were with Libby when she first came here, but this is different. It's deep inside you, like you're burying it, and it's dark—worry and shame and regret and disgust. So…I thought maybe you were trying to confess something awful to me, and I talked myself into being sympathetic and understanding, even though I'd have wanted to rip your balls off and choke you with them if you'd admitted what I accused you of. I'm so, so glad I was wrong."

"You and me both, lovely." The sentiment wasn't there yet, but Sean was no longer seething. "Well, what can I say? Other than it's no wonder you get it wrong from time to time. How the hell do you cope with that level of empathy?"

"I got it *really* wrong, though, didn't I? I feel awful."

"Don't. All right, you maybe went about it badly, and I can't say I'm pleased you hit me with that, but you're dead on with everything except the motivation. To tell you the truth, I'm in awe."

"In awe…of me?"

"Aye." The menu board behind the counter darkened, and the coffee machine powered down. Sean met the server's gaze and nodded to indicate 'message received'. To Shaunna, he said, "We should go."

"Yeah. I was just thinking if I stay here much longer, Andy'll send out the search and rescue. I hadn't realised it was so late." She stood to put on her coat.

Sean did the same and then walked ahead of her, holding the door open as they both said good night to the server and stepped out into the light but cool evening.

"I'll give you a lift home," Sean said.

"I can walk."

"I know, but you took the time to explain to me. It's only fair I do the same." He unlocked Sophie's car and opened the passenger door.

Shaunna stared at it for a few seconds before relenting and climbing in. "Thank you for the lift, but like I said, you don't have to tell me—unless you want to."

"It might help me shed light on some of that darkness you picked up on."

"In that case..." Shaunna fastened her seat belt. "You may begin."

And so he did, and he didn't stop until he'd told her everything—about Phee and Paul and how desperate he was to check in with Genie, at the same time wanting to give Phee time to tell her mum what was going on. By then, they'd stopped outside Shaunna and Andy's place, and they watched, in silence, the outline of Andy carrying the twins across the room and up the stairs.

"He'll be giving them a bath," Shaunna said.

"I'm fine, you know. You don't have to stay with me."

"That's not what I'm doing." She inhaled slowly, exhaled twice as long, unclipped her seat belt and opened the door. "Remember what I said about your balls? If you see him—Paul—that's what you need to do, and if you can't do it, bring him to me." And with those words and a kiss on his cheek, she was gone.

19: Unsettling Symmetry

"DOROTHY LOMAX?" ADELE repeated with a frown as she grabbed half the stuff from Josh's boot and waited for him to shut it. "I know that name."

"You do?"

"I think so. I wonder where from." She led the way inside the house. "What does she look like?"

"Mauve," Josh said, his surroundings a blur as he followed Adele up the stairs and into one of the bedrooms—or not a bedroom, he discovered when she said, "Closet light on," and the dark space transformed into a veritable boutique of women's clothing and accessories. Josh uttered a breathless "Wow!" which had Adele beaming as brightly as the many, many LEDs in the ceiling and around the mirror that took up an entire wall.

"I'll put this lot up there," she said, looking upwards yet tapping her toe against a deep drawer at floor level. The drawer slow-opened, revealing itself to be a step, onto which she climbed, permitting her to reach the passenger-plane-style overhead lockers.

"Adele, this is…fabulous!" Josh gushed, openly covetous of the gadgets.

"Thanks!" With a grin, she took the rest of the items from him, stacking the lot in the locker. She jumped down off her step, a perfect landing in high heels, said, "Secure closet"—counting in a whisper through doors one to three—"four," and the locker door swung shut. "There. All safe and sound. How about a coffee? I'll give you the tour later."

"OK. And thanks." In a daze, Josh followed her back down the stairs.

"She left an impression?" Adele said.

"Hmm?"

"Dorothy."

"Oh! More a purple haze, I'd say. She even smelled mauve."

Adele giggled, glancing at him over her shoulder. "I know exactly what you mean. Like all those perfumes we used to wear back in school. Well, us girls, at any rate. You can still buy them in the department store."

"A heavy, fruity scent, I recall."

"Yep. And always in purple bottles. It makes sense, though, doesn't it? Purple's the colour of success and creativity—maybe that's why women my age are doing so well for ourselves."

"Maybe," Josh said diplomatically. Adele was heavily into pop psychology—dream interpretation, reading body language, feng shui, self-help, neuro-linguistic programming, parapsychology— and on occasion, he'd indulge her, but he was already under pressure from Libby to deploy some 'colour psychology' in the surgery. If she ever discovered she had an ally in Adele, they'd gang up on him, and they'd win. He dreaded to think what colour the walls would end up then.

Adele deposited him outside a partly open door and continued on her way, calling, "Go in, make yourself at home."

Josh peeked in before entering and muttered, "Bloody hell." Were it not for all the soft furnishings, he'd have heard an echo. It was a hangar of a room that diminished the two four-seater sofas and cinema-worthy TV down to normal-people size. The décor was presumably the result of compromise, as the walls were plain white, but the sofas were a deep teal, and the prints on the two walls not taken up by a TV and a double door also had teal accents. It was so tidy it was almost unlived in, but what struck Josh more than the size, the formality or the colour coordination, was the perfect 180° symmetry, as if the room were half the width and reflected in a mirror even more enormous than the one in Adele's closet. It wasn't. He'd checked.

As Josh finished his sightseeing rotation, Adele appeared at his side and handed him one of the two lattes in glasses she'd brought with her. "What do you think? Do you love it, or…?" She braced in advance of his answer.

Josh gave it another look. He'd always admired Adele and Dan for their stylishness. Between Adele's interest in fashion and Dan's love of tech, they were early adopters, often months ahead of the trends, and there was nothing wrong with the room. Yet there was something very wrong, and he couldn't work out what, beyond knowing he really didn't like it.

"I love it, Adele."

"Yay! I thought you would. The sofas are amazingly comfy." She beckoned to him, and once again, he followed in her wake, sitting where she told him—he could agree the sofa lived up to her description—and sipping his somewhat feeble latte while she explained where she had procured each item and the theory behind its placement. Symmetry was the latest fad, apparently. At least there was a sound psychological basis for that.

She reached the end of her sales pitch as Josh swallowed down the last of his beige warm milk, which was when it dawned on him that it wasn't only Dan missing from the house. They were completely alone.

"Where are Shu and Robbie this evening?"

The buzz of Josh's phone vibrating sounded before Adele could reply, and she tilted her head in query, but Josh couldn't have appeased her curiosity if he'd wanted to. He didn't recognise the number, although it was a mobile this time, not the landline that had silently called him twice this week.

He hit the answer button and accidentally put the call on speaker. "Hello?"

"Good evening. Sorry to trouble you. Am I speaking with Josh Sandison?"

"You are." He made eye contact with Adele and mouthed *I recognise his voice. Do you?* She shook her head but pursed her lips in appreciation. The guy's voice was exquisite, with a rich, round tone and a very expensive accent.

"Hi, Josh," that exquisite voice continued. "You probably don't remember me. The name's Simon Henderson. We—"

"The inbred Adonis," Josh said and immediately shoved his fist in his mouth. Adele spluttered into her latte.

"Sorry?"

"Never mind." Josh could've slapped himself. He hadn't been intentionally insulting, just *very* surprised. "Yes, I remember you. How are you?"

"Well, thanks. And you?"

"Yes, I'm well too. How can I help you, Simon?"

"We share some acquaintances."

Josh knew that. "Whom specifically in relation to this call?"

"Gabby Bowes. Or Porter-Bowes these days. I met up with her at a gallery showing a couple of days ago, and she…ah, how to put it? She mentioned you were shopping around for a legal specialist in charity work?"

Josh was quietly astonished, which was to say rendered speechless. He muted the phone and stared at Adele, not that he expected her to know what he should say.

"Who is he?" she asked.

"A guy from uni. He studied law with Jess. I hadn't realised George had said anything."

"George knows him?"

"No, I meant to Gabby."

"Who?"

"George's art therapist."

"George has an art therapist?"

"Are you still there?" Simon asked.

"Yes. Oh!" Josh scrabbled to unmute the phone. "Sorry, I was wondering why Gabby mentioned it to you."

"If I have the wrong impression, I apologise."

"Not at all. This is probably a silly question, but *do* you specialise in charity work?"

"Ah." Simon chuckled. "Had I not been fully briefed in advance, I may have been inclined to say yes."

Josh shook his head, perpetually exasperated—and perhaps a little proud—that he had the kind of reputation that preceded him. "So if you're not a charity specialist…"

"I'm a commercial barrister, mostly largescale property acquisition, but I have worked with several charitable organisations."

"Which ones?"

Simon's laughter was like an air-clearing thunderstorm rumbling into the distance. "Gabby said you'd ask a lot of questions."

"I'm not about to divulge our requirements to a cold caller."

Adele covered her mouth but still snorted a giggle.

"Of course you're not," Simon said good-naturedly. "Perhaps if I could have your email address and send my CV, you can check my credentials at your leisure."

"Yes. That's acceptable. I'll send it to you in a text message."

"Great. I'll put my offer in writing, and if you're interested in discussing the matter further, I'd be happy to meet with you face-to-face."

"I'll be in touch," Josh said, then added, "Thanks for calling, Simon."

"Thanks for answering. Take care, now."

Josh ended the call and put his phone away. "That was Simon Henderson," he said. "The guy Jess had the hots for in her first week at uni."

"The rich one?"

Josh wrinkled his nose. "The first of many rich ones, I'd say. He's landed gentry. He asked her to marry him."

"Yes! And she told him she wasn't the marrying kind."

Josh coughed, attempting to cover his amusement. "Something like that."

Adele pouted. "She told me all about it, you know."

"Did she?"

"Yes. She wasn't high enough class for his family, but they didn't get that far because he told them he was gay even though he could've lost his inheritance."

"Wow, Jess really did tell you everything!" That or Adele had overheard a conversation she shouldn't have.

"Are you considering his offer?"

"Honestly, Adele, I have no idea." A week of Shaunna et al. interviewing lawyers and still without one, Josh couldn't justify turning Simon away without good reason, but the phone call alone had agitated the stew of emotions that had been accumulating since Monday's unexplained events.

"I know what'll help with that decision," Adele said. Josh waited for her to embellish. "I'll read your tarot."

"Absolutely not."

"Or we could use my rune—"

"Seriously. Enough of the hocus-pocus."

She tittered. "I'm teasing. I know you're confident in making decisions without asking Spirit for help."

"I wouldn't say confident..." Josh argued, but what he lacked in that regard couldn't be found in 'Spirit'.

"But you don't believe in *all that spiritualist crap*." Adele smiled to sweeten her sarcasm and then gasped. "Oh! D'you remember Gavrilovich?"

"Gary the Russian medium? Yes," Josh said suspiciously, seeing as Gavrilovich call-me-Gary Ovsianikov had done a number on him at what should've been an evening of fun entertainment. "Why?"

"He passed over last Christmas. And no, he didn't see it coming." She covered her mouth, horrified by her joke, and then fell into a fit of giggles. Despite his best efforts, Josh fell with her.

"Oh, Adele. That's hilarious! Not that he died." He wiped his eyes with his thumb. "Was it sudden?"

"I'm not sure. I read about it online."

"Not in your cards?"

She lightly smacked his arm, her giggles silenced by his mockery. "I'm sorry," he said. "I can't help it."

"I know." She swirled the last inch of her coffee and lifted it to her mouth but then moved it away again. "I don't get it. You don't think any of that stuff from your loft works and don't believe Gary could communicate with the spirits, yet you freaked out when he told you he was in contact with your mum."

"Because he manipulated my feelings and the feelings of everyone else who was there. I'm certain he wasn't talking to the dead, but it still affected me."

"Why, if you're so sure he was a fake?"

"How do you feel when I look into your head, as you put it?"

"Really uncomfortable, like you know all my secrets."

"That's how I felt at the psychic night. Gary took his cues from my reactions. It's similar to what I do—reading people's expressions and behaviour—although I try not to do it without their consent."

"But you gave Gary your consent by being there."

"Yes, that's true." Like he'd given the psychology department his consent by becoming one of their undergraduates. Sometimes his naivety dismayed him. "The thing is, it should be informed consent, and I admit I didn't know what a psychic night entailed. Suffice to say, I hadn't foreseen him telling a room full of strangers that I'm an orphan."

"Oh." Adele looked stricken. "I'm so sorry."

"Why?"

"I invited you."

"Yes, you *invited* me. And I accepted. You didn't force me to go. It's not your fault curiosity got the better of me and I let Gary cold read me. Because that's all it is, Adele. No psychic ability required."

"But even if Gary was doing that cold-reading thing, it doesn't mean it's not real. There are lots of other mediums out there."

"OK, but so far, psychologists haven't found much evidence to suggest it *is* real." Josh was conveniently overlooking the other thing Gary had said to him. Even if taken in conjunction with Monday's strangeness and what had happened in his halls of residence all those years ago, it was of no significance in scientific terms. However, it *was* significant to him, so profoundly so he'd hardly slept in days and could now hear Gary's words echoing in his memory as clearly as two years ago.

Whether you choose to believe what I say or not, your friend needs to see a doctor. It won't make any difference in the end, of course.

Josh had never told anyone about it. Or no-one but George, who wasn't sceptical as such but had inherited his mother's take-no-crap attitude and had reminded Josh that digging dirt on people wasn't his exclusive domain. If that was how Gary had gleaned the information, then he should have been working for the Secret Service because Jess's terminal prognosis hadn't been confirmed until the day after the so-called psychic night.

Still, Josh had accepted George's reasoning. Gary *could* have accessed Josh's GPS data and the oncology department's records and established he hadn't been attending an appointment himself. That would be sufficient for a starting point; the rest could be gleaned from Josh's responses on the night. It seemed a lot of effort to go to for just one audience member and impractical to do it for all sixty in attendance. Then again, clairvoyance was a lucrative business. Perhaps good old Gary had a team of minimum-wage research monkeys tapping away behind the scenes. In a just world, that would be what happened to parapsychology graduates caught with their ethical pants around their ankles, like Ali, Josh's torturer in the name of empirical study.

A polite cough at his side brought Josh out of his thoughts and alerted him that a certain blonde friend with a passion for all things psychic was doing some cold reading of her own. He met her ponderous, sideways-tilted gaze, and she smiled.

"Shall I make more lattes?"

"Yes," he answered for some unfathomable reason. The first latte had been palatable but largely devoid of caffeine, and he had work he should be getting on with, but he couldn't say he wasn't enjoying her company this evening. Or he had been until she tottered across the room that made him uncomfortable and he realised why that was. "I'll come with you," he said.

"You don't have to."

He did have to, lest he break the symmetry again with his singular presence, but she was quick, and the hallway was already empty by the time he escaped. "Adele?"

"In here!"

There were four doors, all slightly ajar to the same extent, as had the living room door been earlier, and he couldn't discern where she was from the direction of her voice. He tried the two doors closest: the first was a WC; the second concealed a narrow staircase presumably leading to a cellar. "In where?"

The answering giggle came from behind him and gave him no clearer a sense of where she was, but before he could try a third door—which would also have been the wrong one—Adele's grinning face popped into view.

"Sorry." She didn't look or sound it. "I forgot you don't know where the kitchen is."

Josh snuffed his disgruntlement and followed her into the mercifully asymmetrical kitchen, although alien abductees had never faced such blinding brightness. It was so *white and shiny*! High-gloss cabinet doors, polished marble worktops, porcelain tiles on the walls and floor. He almost asked if Adele had modelled it on her plastic surgeon's operating theatre, but her expectant blinks saved them both from his thoughtlessness.

"This is incredible, Adele," he said instead, which wasn't a lie. He liked how clean and uncluttered it was, but perhaps Libby was on to something with incorporating a little colour into his surgery renovation.

As if she'd read his mind—and Josh was ruling out nothing—Adele asked, "Is green still your favourite colour?"

He smiled bashfully, delighted that she remembered whilst still not comfortable with her having figured it out in the first place. "Yes," he confirmed.

"Hm." She handed him a full latte glass, positioned a second one under the nozzle of the coffee machine—also white—and said, "Set kitchen to emerald green." And just like that, all that shiny white turned to a rich, vibrant green.

"Wow!" Josh stared around him in wonder. "How did you do that?"

Adele grinned. "It's magic. Do you love it?"

"I really do!" It was the truth this time.

"Would you like a go?"

"Can I?"

She nodded encouragingly.

"OK. Erm...so I just say, 'set kitchen to...sky blue' and—"

Adele clapped in glee at his surprise when on his command the green faded gently into a fetching pale azure. "You could have this in your kitchen," she said.

Josh nodded in distracted agreement.

"Or any room," she said. "We have it in the kids' rooms and the gym, and—"

Josh put down his latte and planted a noisy kiss on her forehead. "Adele, you are a genius!" She staggered slightly as he released her.

"I am?"

"You are. You've just solved my surgery colour dilemma."

"Yay!" She clapped again, applauding herself. "I'm a genius!"

"So." Josh pulled out a stool at the island, sat, latte in hand, and gestured for Adele to join him. "Teach me about colour psychology."

"F...for real?"

"Yes, please."

She did a mini jump up onto the other stool and considered him through narrowed eyes. "First, you have to be honest with me."

"OK." Josh prepared for a barrage of questions about his colour preferences, the kind of mood he wanted to create and so on. He should've known better.

"What is it you don't like about my living room?"

20: By One's Teeth

Rowan Mews
Present Day
Friday, 19ᵗʰ April

"MOORHAVEN NHS TRUST."

Damn it. "Hello...again!" Genie completed the gate doodle depicting her attempts thus far to make it past the hospital switchboard, although this operator, unlike the coarse Northerners before, had a throaty, Scottish accent that added a luscious curl to the 'r' and aspirated the 'h', reminding Genie of her old maths teacher, a slick-haired, sharp-featured little man who'd treated all of his charges with the same impatient contempt. As reminiscences went, it didn't bode well for a successful conclusion to her telephone quest. "I wonder if you could help me?"

"I'll certainly try," the operator replied blithely.

"I'm hoping to get through to Doctor Sean Tierney. He works on the Parkwood Wing. Before you ask, I know it's a big department, and no, I don't have an extension number."

"Ah. You've called already."

"Five times now," Genie sighed.

"All right, well, let's see if we can make this the last. I'm going to have a chat with the Parkwood admin office. I'll have to put you on hold for a minute, OK?"

"OK."

At least this operator hadn't connected her to a phantom extension with no phone at the end of it, although listening to the distorted 'hold' Muzak, Genie thought she might have preferred the dead-line tone. It took her a moment to realise the digital *beep-beep* wasn't part of the composition but was her incoming-call alert. Phee. *Damn.* They needed to talk, but the way Genie's luck was going, the operator would come back on the line and, deciding she'd given up, disconnect her. Placating herself that it would be better to speak to Phee face-to-face, Genie dismissed her call and went back to waiting.

Perhaps she wouldn't have been quite so irritated by this rigmarole if she could shake the feeling that Sean had intentionally withheld his new mobile number from her, but why would he? It wasn't as if she called him all the time. In fact, she couldn't remember when they'd last spoken, other than knowing for sure that whenever it was, she'd done the calling. In all the time they'd been friends, he'd never called her.

As the archived 'conversation' with a dud number showed, he'd sent texts from time to time—another trait Phee had inherited from him, it seemed, the difference being that Phee *would* call if her messages went unanswered. It had been tempting last night to not respond to Phee's apologetic '*I'm sorry I didn't tell you. I love you xx*' and force her hand, but Genie knew how to pick her battles, so she'd replied '*I love you so much – I'm here for you always xx*' and tried to get some sleep, securing a couple of hours at best.

The 'hold' music stopped without resolving, and the operator said, "Hello?"

"Hi."

"Bad news, I'm afraid. Doctor Tierney *did* work here, but he doesn't anymore."

Genie inhaled sharply in surprise—not because Sean had left the hospital, although that was surprising in itself. She coughed on the influx of suddenly cold, dry air, and then did it again when her breath misted in front of her. After the madness of the past few days, her thoughts went straight to more ghastly causes than British springtime weather, as if that weren't ghastly enough.

Unable to bring herself to move, she scanned the kitchen, shifting her eyes only, for signs of her invisible house guest, but aside from Xander's detection of a phantom housekeeper, nothing untoward had happened in there. If she really wanted to know—which she didn't—she'd have to go into the drawing room, where the piano was.

"Are you OK there?" her friendly Scots operator asked, which reinstated some reason, permitting her to consider that perhaps it was just a chilly morning, even if the sun's reflection off the tiles had been dazzling enough that she'd closed the blinds. She tweaked the cord, peeking out between the slats, and could have cried with relief at the steam rising from roofs half covered in light frost where the sun had yet to reach.

"Yes, thank you," she said. Her throat still a little tickly, she grabbed her upturned cup from the drainer and filled it from the sink tap, swallowing down a couple of mouthfuls of tepid, chlorine-heavy water before she attempted to say anything further. All the while, the operator waited: Genie could hear the hum of the busy hospital and their murmured words to someone else. When the murmuring came to a pause, she said, "My apologies. I don't suppose you have another number for Doctor Tierney?"

"I don't, but if you wouldn't mind giving me your details, I'll forward them to his colleague, who said she'd contact him on your behalf."

"Wonderful!" Genie gave her name and number and sincerely wished the operator a lovely day before they ended the call. Now she could only wait and hope Sean phoned back. Those few moments of interaction with a stranger had diminished the urgency of her need to talk to him to wanting simply to catch up and find out what he was doing if he no longer worked at the hospital. He'd given her the impression they'd have to carry him out of there in a body bag before he'd leave, but that was a long time ago.

Out of habit, Genie sipped from the cup in her hand, expecting coffee, and shuddered at the bleachy, filmy aftertaste. Tipping the water into the sink, she set off the coffee maker and popped to the loo, trying to pin down when, exactly, she'd last talked to Sean. Was it before or after Paul came on the scene? She thought she'd introduced them, but she may have merely rehearsed doing so. She knew it was before Jess became sick because Genie had been sworn to secrecy. It had been like carrying a tumour of her own, and she'd come within a hair's breadth of breaking her word, especially towards the end. No-one else knew what Jess had meant to her, nor would she have trusted anyone other than Sean to maintain the secret, but ultimately, sharing her burden with him would also have made it his, and so she'd kept it to herself, even when Jess cut contact a few weeks before she died.

She returned to the kitchen, where the coffee maker was still dripping, and she urged it on. Her reflections had taken a bleak turn, and a partisan one at that. So little of note happened in her life, often she felt as if she were on a horse trotting around the same paddock, day upon day, with loss the only, mercifully rare variation. First her grandmother, then Jess, and now she feared her relationship with Paul was in countdown. Even her daughter, whose very existence gave Genie's meaning, was causing more heartache than she thought she could withstand. Of course, she'd been there before, when Phee, aged eight, had fractured her shoulder performing a complex gymnastic manoeuvre, and again when, aged twelve, she'd shown symptoms of meningitis. Like all mothers, Genie had made it through both scares because what else could she do? She'd chosen lone parenthood and in general felt she coped perfectly well, but at times like these she wished there were someone to help carry the load.

With that acknowledgement, it came to her, clear as crystal. The last time she'd spoken to Sean was when Phee was admitted to hospital. There was no practical reason he should be any more invested than Paul in Phee's well-being, yet he'd arrived at the hospital before the blood test results were back—not meningitis, thank God, but an acute sinus infection that nonetheless needed aggressive antibiotics to send it on its way. Once Phee had settled for the night, Sean had taken Genie home and slept on the sofa until Paul rudely disturbed him the following morning.

Genie's anger had quickly dissolved into a hurt that had endured, but she refused to let Paul see it, and not because he was a poor stepfather. He was no stepfather at all. As with Sean, she'd been adamant from the start that her relationship with Paul was separate from her life with Phee, irrespective of the three of them sharing a house. It was no hardship, considering how rare it was for them all to be home at once. She'd also made it clear to Phee that Paul was not to be involved in their battles.

Genie was aware she was being contrary. The meningitis scare came when she and Paul were still fairly new, but she didn't think it was too much to expect his emotional support when her daughter had a life-threatening illness. Granted, it hadn't been what they feared, but Paul hadn't known that until he arrived home, fresh-faced and casting filthy glances in Sean's direction while asking chirpily how Phee was faring as if she'd gone to bed with the sniffles. He worked for the company who'd developed the pneumococcal vaccine, for goodness' sake. He *knew* the danger.

That was why, now, she was going to such lengths to get hold of Sean instead of calling Paul, and her actions spoke volumes. Their relationship was as dead as Xander's ghosts, and she should do the decent thing and end it. It was better to push people away—her parents, her sister, her old friends, Sean—than to let a relationship fester into something rotten, in Genie's experience. Her grandmother and Jess were the only ones she'd fought to keep in her life, and they'd left her.

The coffee had stopped dripping some time ago, replaced by the steady drip of tears she'd left unattended until her phone rang, which was timely and might just have saved her from cracking open a wine bottle before noon. Alas, it was not the call she'd hoped for. It was from Xander's office. Genie wiped her eyes and gave her nose a quick blow before she answered.

"Hello?"

"Hello, Your Ladyship, it's Jonathan Reardon, calling on behalf of Lord Etherington-Bowes."

"Genie," she reminded him. "How can I help you, Jonathan?"

"His Lordship has suggested—" He stopped when Xander spoke in the background, his voice suddenly becoming clearer, presumably now on speaker phone.

"We will come back once your daughter has returned to school."

"If that is all right with you, of course," Jonathan added.

"It should be." Between morning sickness and the emotional upheaval, Genie wasn't sure if Phee would be returning to school, but she needed to give Xander a firmer answer. "May I call you back later?"

"Ask her what time," Xander said.

"By five o'clock this afternoon," Genie answered and heard Xander grunt in the affirmative. "Sorry to dash, but I'm waiting for an important call."

"My apologies, Your—Genie. Goodbye for now."

"Bye," Genie replied, but Jonathan had already cut her off, and a good thing that was too, as her screen lit up with another incoming call. Still not Sean.

"Hello, darling."

"Why didn't you answer my texts?" Phee demanded.

"I didn't see them."

"No surprise there! You're a phone demon this morning. I've been trying to call you for hours."

"Hardly hours."

"Hours!"

Genie glanced at the clock, confirming it had been no more than twenty minutes, although a further glance at her call log also confirmed two further missed calls from her daughter.

"You *never* use your phone," Phee said, which was mostly true. Since Jess's passing, the only regular outgoing calls Genie made were to Phee. "Who were you talking to? Xander?"

"Yes. Well, briefly." Despite their text truce, Genie hesitated before she asked, "How are you feeling this morning?"

"I'm…all right. Are you?"

"Tired, but I'm fine. What time are you coming home?"

"Not sure yet. Why?" Phee was already on guard.

"I thought we could do something—go to the cinema?"

"The cinema."

"It doesn't have to be."

"Is there something you want to see?"

"I've no idea what's on."

"Knowing our luck, a rescreening of *Poltergeist*," Phee said dryly.

Whether it was because of nerves, fatigue, relief or perhaps a combination of all three, Phee's joke broke the stalemate, and they laughed as they volleyed titles of all the ghost films they'd seen together—something they'd always loved to do. A scary movie, complete with bucket of popcorn and massive drinks, was prime mother-and-daughter time when the only pressure was on their over-taxed bladders. No need to talk about difficult things.

"OK," Phee said, calling a ceasefire. "I'd really like that."

"Should I pick you up, or are you coming home first?"

"Can you come and get me now? I need to shower and change."

"Of course, darling. See you in..." Genie's phone beeped, and she moved it so she could see the screen. Another incoming call, this time from an unknown mobile number. She put the phone back to her ear. "A client's trying to call me. I'll leave as soon as I've spoken to them. Love you."

"OK, Mum. Love you too."

Genie wasn't quite quick enough to reach the answer button. She clicked on the missed call.

"Your call cannot be taken at the moment—"

She hung up and started counting, intending to call back in thirty seconds, but the caller was trying again.

"Genie?"

"Sean! Hi!"

"I got a message you'd called the hospital. Is everything all right?"

"Oh, yes! Everything's fine!" she declared bravely before, in an instant, all her false cheer dissolved into a wretched sob that rendered her incapable of further lies while at the other end of the line Sean offered quiet reassurances that he was still there. She could take her time, he said, and she did, through no choice of her own, as the emotions she'd held in, not just for the past few days but for years, rushed like whitewater rapids through her mind. It was, in the end, the realisation Phee would know she'd been crying that stemmed the flow, and still Sean waited as, for the second time that morning, she wiped her eyes and blew her nose into a rough paper towel.

"It's funny," she said. "According to Xander, people cry too loudly to hear those they miss."

Sean chuckled. "He might be on to something—if by that you mean you've missed me."

"I always do, Sean." She cleared her throat with some success. "You're no longer working at the hospital?"

"No, but I only finished there two days ago. I don't know if you remember Josh Sandison—one of the other psych students from uni?"

"Your old housemate?"

"The very fellow. We're setting up a private clinic."

"Wow. Excellent. Are you excited?"

"I am. What about you? Still looking after rich gentlemen?"

"God, no. I got out of that game a couple of years back, after—" Genie turned her abrupt cut-off into a cough, but there was no way she could bluff her way out, not with Sean. It would be unfair on them both if she tried. "Do you know Jess passed?"

"I do."

"Right. I wasn't sure you'd stayed in touch."

"We hadn't. I planned to, but you know me."

"Indeed, I do."

Sean grunted. "I'm sorry, Genie. I get caught up in work, and the time passes me by, and I think to myself, 'I should call,' but it's always too late at night, and then I forget the next day, and on it goes. But I have missed you. I really have."

"And Jess?"

"I miss her tremendously. We lived a few miles apart and worked in the same town for all those years, it's an awful shame. But we reconnected a little while before she passed."

"I'm glad, Sean." Genie carefully phrased her words. "I'm not telling you this to be cruel, but she never mentioned you."

"No, and likewise. You stayed in touch?"

"Almost to the end. That was when I gave up the escort business."

"It was a wake-up call," Sean said.

"Something like that."

"You saw the news reports, I'm sure."

"Yes." Genie had seen them, and she'd refused to read them. She'd had no need to.

"Were you surprised?" he asked.

"Not really. She was ambitious, a risk-taker."

"That she was."

"You don't seem surprised either," Genie noted.

"Not now I've made my peace with who she was and the way she kept everything compartmentalised. Like, when I think back to what you said about how mad she was when she found out you were expecting Phee…"

"Because it was with you." Genie nodded and smiled to herself. She'd taken some sordid satisfaction from getting a rise out of Jess—the closest she'd come to a display of possessiveness, except Genie knew now it was no such thing. Jess had been protecting her secrets, even back then, which was why she'd kicked Genie out of the house whenever Andy came to visit until it suited her needs not to. "Did you go to her funeral?" she asked.

"Yeah."

"Was it a good one?"

Sean laughed. "See, now, you could only say that to a Catholic boy. Aye, it was lovely, as funerals go. The wake was in a Chinese restaurant."

"That's…unusual."

"And a welcome change from where I'm standing. I've given up the booze, Genie."

"Really?" Too late, her astonishment was out there.

"Three years dry."

"Three years? Gosh! I can't imagine how hard that must be. Does it get easier?"

"I suppose it does, but I have rough days, you know?"

"I do." She was having a glut of them, and it felt like the right moment in their conversation to tell Sean why she'd made contact. "So, ah…" The right moment, but now it was here, she could barely bring herself to say it. "I've had an eventful week."

"OK." She could tell from his tone that he'd switched to 'psychologist' mode.

"Well… When… What…" Before she went through all the Ws, she paused, employing what she'd learnt long ago about constructing an argument. State the facts, then elaborate. "Two things," she said. "First, I have a poltergeist. Second, Phee's pregnant."

She waited for a response, and it was safe to say she'd received the one she'd have expected from anyone other than Sean. She'd never known him to be lost for words. Perhaps he was waiting for her to explain, or their call had disconnected.

"Are you still there, Sean?"

"I am. I'm…processing."

"OK. Sorry."

"No need. To recap, by poltergeist, are we talking stuff turning up someplace other than where you left it, or—"

"Lamps shattering mirrors, pictures falling off walls. That kind of thing."

"That kind of thing," Sean echoed. "The usual, then."

Genie's hysteria poked a finger into her side, eliciting a high-pitched titter.

"Now I understand why you mentioned Xander."

"He's looking into it for me."

"Good." Sean was still using a neutral but sympathetic tone that made it impossible to gauge his true thoughts or feelings. "And Phee—is it official or a suspicion?"

That was a good question because an '*I'm sorry I didn't tell you*' text message was no admission. "Somewhere between the two. I told her I knew. She has neither confirmed nor denied it."

"She'd make a fine politician."

"She'd make a fine anything she put her mind to," Genie said, adding in her head, *if she hasn't thrown it all away.*

"Just like her mum," Sean flattered as if he were privy to her thoughts. "All right. What d'you need from me?"

"A listening ear."

"Anytime."

"And a means to reach it."

"Are ye too posh for plastic cups and string in your neck of the woods?"

"Ha-ha. I've got your number now."

"You always did, Genie."

"Hmm." The conversation was taking a sentimental turn, and on another day, she'd have maybe indulged him, but her emotions were beyond frayed. "I need to go and collect Phee from her friend's place. We're going to the cinema."

"OK, lovely. It's been grand talking to you."

"Same here."

"And I mean it. You can call me anytime. Who knows, I might even call you again!"

"I've had more than my share of the unexpected this week."

"Next week, then," Sean said, his grin audible. "Take care, Genie."

"I will. You too." Genie ended the call and used her phone's camera to check her face. Slightly bloodshot eyes, a tinge of red around her nostrils. Better than she'd anticipated.

21: Abstinence

A Friend's House
Present Day
Friday, 19th April

A RE YOU STILL in there?" The bathroom door handle twisted a couple of times and sprang back. "Phee?"

"Hold on." She flushed the loo and took a tiny sip of mouthwash. Her gag reflex violently ejected it.

"OK, you're scaring me now," Sarah said from the other side of the door. "*Please* let me in."

Lips clamped in teeth, Phee crossed the dizzying checkerboard floor of the enormous bathroom and unlocked the door. "I'm fine." She saw how unconvincing her carefree smile was when Sarah mirrored it back with added irony.

"Your mum's outside."

"Good. I can't wait to go home, get a shower..." Phee made a small sobbing sound, but she could've cried for real. "We're going to the cinema."

"Shower and jim-jams is what you need," Sarah advised, watching over her in a motherly fashion while Phee went around the room gathering her make-up, phone charger and purse. "You didn't even drink that much, did you?"

"No. I had two vodkas." She'd stuck to water all night. Slinging her bag over her shoulder, she followed Sarah downstairs.

"Maybe you were right, then, about Dad's cooking."

"Shh! He'll hear you, and anyway, it wasn't his cooking."

"He's gone to work. But you said it tasted weird."

"It'll be a stomach bug or something." She hated lying to Sarah—hated even more that Sarah's dad was getting the blame for something he hadn't done. She'd always loved his chicken pasanda—until last night, when she'd swallowed one mouthful and had to sprint from the dining room.

They reached the front door and hugged.

"Thanks for letting me stay."

Sarah drew back and frowned. "Why are you thanking me?"

"It's polite."

"You don't usually thank me."

"I don't usually spend half the night throwing up in your bathroom."

"Hmm." Sarah wasn't buying it. In fact, Phee was sure the entire conversation, like the one they'd had after dinner the previous evening, was a fishing expedition. Sarah was in her final year of uni, so she didn't know Phee's sickness had begun weeks ago at school, but they'd been friends a long time. She'd have picked up that Phee was hiding something, but there was no way she could tell Sarah. No way.

"Talk over the weekend?" she said, closing off the discussion.

"OK, prin. Enjoy your movie."

"I'll try."

Sarah stepped aside, and Phee left, waving on her way out to the car.

"Hey, Mum." She shut the car door and turned to fasten her seat belt, coming almost nose-to-nose with her mother's harrowed face. "What?"

"You're terribly pale, darling."

"I didn't put any make-up on yet. No point before I shower, is there?" She tilted her head meaningfully to get her mother moving, and it worked, but it didn't stop her going on.

"Have you been throwing up?"

"Not really."

"What does that mean?"

"Mum…"

"And are you eating and drinking enough? Whatever you decide to do, you still need to look after yourself."

"I am. Look, can we talk about something else or, you know, not talk at all?"

"As you wish."

It wouldn't last. To prove it, Phee counted down from five in her head. She reached two.

"We can postpone the cinema trip."

"No."

If nothing else, it meant a couple of hours without the constant questioning, which was what had prompted her to flee to Sean five days ago. Had he given her the choice, she'd have still been there, avoiding the inevitable moment when she told her mum the truth and it ruined everything forever. So however crap she felt, she'd suck it up for an afternoon at the cinema with her mum because it might be the last one.

***

Tierney Residence

GETTING A WEEKDAY morning to himself, Sean felt like he was pulling a sicky. He'd been watching breakfast telly and enjoying hot, fresh tea while the rest of the world went off to work. Then Francesca's PA had called to pass on Genie's number, bringing his leisurely breakfast to a grinding halt.

The conversation with Genie could have gone a lot worse. She didn't cope well with anything that was out of her control, and her daughter's independent streak had tested her many times over the years, each eliciting a telephone counselling session where she ranted and Sean listened and took the genetic blame blows on the 'Irish' chin that was so much more endearing on his offspring.

Ignoring the meningitis scare, a terrifying night all round, the last time had been when Phee asked to go to boarding school, and Genie had lost the plot for a while, pouring out this whole mess of things that had happened to her at boarding school, any one of which would see most people in therapy for years. But on that, like almost every other occasion, all Genie required of Sean was that he listened. It was one of her greatest strengths: once she'd talked it out of her system, she moved on.

This pregnancy malarkey, though, was a whole new level of out of Genie's control, and Sean worried for them both. Phee hadn't told her mum who the father was; that much was clear from what Genie *hadn't* said, and now Sean was wondering whether as an ignorant bystander he'd have naturally asked if there was a boyfriend on the scene. Had he given himself away by not asking? Genie hadn't picked up on it, but she'd realise in time, he was sure of it. She was as astute as they came, and she'd want to know why he hadn't frogmarched Phee straight home and insisted she tell her mother what was going on, but that wasn't Sean's decision to make.

Honesty's a good thing. He said it so often it felt like a catchphrase, but experience told him it was almost always true. Not the little white lies or minor indiscretions. The kind of dishonesty that takes root and taints every thought, feeling and interaction. However brutal or painful, laying it all out in a safe, mediated space was a chance for those involved to truly understand each other and nurture a more meaningful relationship, regardless of how much or how little time they had left.

That was what had him stumped. For the first time in as long as he could remember, he wasn't sure honesty *was* the good or right thing for Phee and Genie, and he'd floundered, sent Phee packing when he should have offered to mediate, to be their safe space. It was cowardly and futile, like hiding under a flimsy sheet while the roof caved in, because whichever way he looked at it, the fallout would be devastating. If Phee told her mum about Paul, it would destroy Genie's trust; if she kept it a secret, it would hang over their relationship forever.

And God almighty, he needed a drink. Every night since Phee turned up, he'd gone to bed, relieved to have made it through another day without succumbing to the urge and with the hope that tomorrow he'd feel different, but it was still there when he awoke, and it clung on relentlessly, infiltrating his thoughts and crumbling his resolve.

He could do some baking, although he'd used up his quota of that distraction this week. "*More* soda bread?" Soph's mum had said. "How lovely!" He'd need to do some shopping first, however, and shops sold whiskey, so that was out of the question. Cleaning, maybe? Catch up on some reading? That appealed no more than cleaning.

Downing the dregs of his tea on the way to the kitchen, he weighed up the options. Baking always put his mind at ease, so he should at least check if it was possible.

"Right, let's see…" Opening all the cupboards, he stood back. "No eggs, no flour." He picked up a pot and shook it. "Got bicarb, a bit of sugar." He closed the cupboards and went to the fridge. "Not enough milk, no butter." The cat flap clicked. "Christ, it's like Old Mother Hubbard's here, Sphinx—oh, it's you again, is it?"

Jinja hopped up onto the counter and tucked into Sphinx's breakfast. Sean shook his head, laughing because what else could he do? Tell Josh to train his cat not to walk in uninvited? He'd have more success getting Jinja to train Josh, but it wasn't fair on Sphinx. Cantankerous, independent old so-and-so that he was, he picked battles he could win, and Jinja wasn't one of them.

"Come on, out you go." Ignoring the mewl of protest, Sean scooped up the big orange tom and put him outside, making a mental note to ask Josh later where he'd bought Jinja's microchip-programmed cat flap and maybe take back his claim that it was a faddy gadget.

Sadly, the interlude with Jinja wasn't enough to shake Sean's desire for drink, and he was in his coat with the front door half open when a tiny spark of willpower gave him pause. If he left the house, he'd buy whiskey, and he couldn't trust himself to stay put. Before he could think on it further, he shut the door and locked it, removed the key from the lock and did the same with the back door. Looping both onto the same ring, he opened the living room window and threw the keys as hard as he could.

"Ah, shite." His willpower might have been weaker than a newborn kitten, but apparently his throwing arm was in fine form, as the bunch of keys flew straight over the hedge and clattered onto the pavement beyond.

***

Rowan Mews

FOR ONCE, PHEE was in full agreement with her mum that they needed to make a move. She couldn't get into her clothes fast enough after she heard the bottle smash. The stench of wine was vile but not the reason why she'd raced out to the car, still no make-up, wet hair dripping down her top as she fought to fasten her seat belt on the move. No, the reason for her immediate compliance was that they'd both been upstairs when the bottle, which Phee had watched her mum put in the fridge, had somehow smashed into a thousand pieces all along the hall.

"Oh my God, that beep is driving me mental! Can you stop a minute?"

Without taking her eyes from the road, her mum indicated and pulled over. As soon as she did, Phee's seat belt clicked into place and the beeping stopped. Still facing forward, her mum indicated again and re-joined the flow of traffic.

"When are you going to call Xander?" Phee asked.

"Later."

"Before we get to the cinema?"

"You told me to send him away. Now you want him to come back?"

"No, I don't, but there's a ghost in our house. It could harm us."

"I don't think—"

"It threw a bottle!" Phee leaned forward and squeezed her hair over the footwell.

"Do you have to do that?"

"Well, have you got a towel?" She opened the glove compartment, as if there'd be one in there, and shut it hard.

"There's a roll of blue paper towel under the seat."

"Argh! You could've said!"

Her mum huffed and checked the rear-view mirror.

Phee reached under her seat and found the end of the roll, pulling a length from it and wrapping it turban-style around her head. "I could call him," she suggested.

"No."

"You're driving."

"It can wait until I've parked the car."

"But it's already injured you." Phee stared at the side of her mum's head, ready to argue if she claimed she'd 'just fallen' again. "You'll never forgive yourself if it hurts me…your only child."

Her mum laughed. "Fine. You can call him. Phone's in my bag."

Phee reached behind her for the enormous tapestry thing her mother insisted on filling with all kinds of junk, which had spilled across the back seat from being thrown into the car. The phone had slid onto the floor, out of reach. Phee unfastened her seat belt, setting off the beep again, and climbed through the gap.

"That is *so annoying*!" She picked up the phone and unlocked the screen.

"It really could've waited, darling."

"Do you think?"

"Whatever it is won't hurt you. Xander said it's scared of you."

"Wh…" Phee stared at the phone screen, immobilised. The adrenaline rush of their hasty escape had kept her nausea at bay; now it whooshed up her throat in a tidal wave that erupted before she had the window fully open. Vomit splattered down the glass and along the side of the car, and the sight of it brought more. Meanwhile, her mother switched from rambling about ghosts to parroting familiar soothing assurances. *It'll be better soon, I promise.*

Phee wanted to tell her to shut up, but still the vomit kept on coming. She couldn't believe she'd been such an idiot, thinking she could trust him. Of course he was going to tell her mother, who kept looking at her through the mirror, all soft-eyed and concerned like nothing had changed, but everything had, and it was never going to get better. Not with that call at the top of the log. Thirty-three minutes, incoming, from Sean Tierney.

***

Tierney Residence

IN THE END, Sean called Shaunna, and there was no logical reason for it. Josh was only two doors away, and his car was outside, so he was definitely home. Sophie would have been straight over in a taxi. He could rely on either of them to keep him sober, as they'd done countless times before, but talking to Genie had stirred something deeper, more complicated, a feeling Sean hadn't experienced in almost two years. Desire.

So he'd called Shaunna, who was at work in the salon five miles away with no transport. Would she ask Andy to drive her? Call a taxi? Catch a bus? If Sean claimed he hadn't considered the inconvenience beforehand, it would be an outright lie. It was a selfish, ill-conceived and dangerous move, and worst of all, he didn't care.

Alcohol briefly lost its salience again, leaving him free to admit that that was a lie too. He *did* care, and there was the rub—and also the outline of a certain redhead approaching the front door. Keys rattled; the lock clicked. Sean set aside his self-pity and smoothed his shirt, only now thinking to check whether it was clean enough for entertaining.

Like a flash fire, she was, marching past him with barely a glance, swinging open the door to the living room where she lingered briefly, then on to the kitchen and his wee office off to the side. Most houses in the terrace had knocked the two rooms through to make a bigger kitchen, and Sean had felt the lure to keep up with the Joneses—or the Sandison-Morleys at any rate—but what use was a family-size kitchen to a lone healthcare professional/academic one slip of the bottle away from losing his shared parenting rights?

Shaunna passed him by again, paused only to deposit her coat on the banister, then up the stairs she went, same performance: his bedroom, Dylan's bedroom, the bathroom. She was longer in there; the small part of him that clung naively to his self-respect reasoned she was using the loo but surrendered at the clanging of the stairs to the attic. A minute later, she was back downstairs and standing in front of him.

"It's clear," she said. "No booze anywhere."

"I could've told you that and saved you the trouble. More trouble."

"Right. And I would totally have taken you at your word after you called and said, 'I'm desperate here. Can you come over?'"

"I only called fifteen minutes ago. How did you get here so quickly?"

"Client with a motorbike."

Now she said it, Sean noticed her cheeks were rosier than usual, and her copious red curls were constrained by a thick plait, which she duly unravelled, setting them free. Like some lush beauty in a shampoo ad, she shook her head in a swirl of shiny spirals that cascaded over her shoulders and down her back. A few strands caught around the tag of her tunic's zip, which sat just below her collarbone, its asymmetrical placement drawing Sean's gaze down, following the contour of her left breast, until she gave a shrill whistle and his attention snapped back to her face.

"I'm sorry." He bowed his head, ashamed.

"For what? It's not as if we've never looked at each other in that way before, is it? And I'd soon let you know if you overstepped, believe me."

"That doesn't give me a right to objectify you."

Shaunna laughed. "Is that what you were doing?"

"Well…no. But…ah, hell." Managing to bypass her so he couldn't accidentally ogle her again, he stared up at the ceiling. His brain was a scramble of guilt and need and relief that it wasn't the need for alcohol anymore.

"What are you thinking about?" she asked.

What to say… The truth? That he'd wished often they were both single with this set-up specifically in mind? That he felt inadequate and unworthy in her presence? After all, here was he: out-of-shape, poorly recovering alcoholic with erectile dysfunction. And here was she: drop-dead gorgeous, sensual beauty.

"Sean?" She stepped towards him, into his space. He glanced down, instantly caught in the kaleidoscope of her eyes: greens, browns, hints of blue. Contact lenses today, he acknowledged as, from one hypnotic stimulus to another, he caught the motion of her tongue flicking across her lips and quickly averted his gaze upwards again.

"Wondering whether banging me head on this wall might knock some sense into me." He bumped back against the wall behind him.

"Don't do that." She stepped closer and tilted her chin up, which had the secondary effect of bringing their torsos together, touching at the points they protruded—her breasts, his paunch. God, that was an awful word, but it was how he felt—middle-aged spread, greying hair, pallid, crinkly skin…

"What about Andy?" he blurted as if this moment, this maddeningly erotic moment, were a prelude to some glorious love-making rather than his mind trying to process the myriad conflicting messages from his traitorous body.

"Andy thinks we've been doing it anyway," she said.

"He…what?" No conflicting messages now. His mind and body were in agreement, and it was flight all the way, but that he could escape. "Andy thinks…we're having an affair?"

"An affair?" Her lips curved, not quite a smile, but certainly amused. "An affair is a secret. Behind people's backs."

"Right, so…this… This…is…" God, if he could string together a whole sentence, it'd be grand. "This, if we continued, that is…" He vented a breath and some of his tension. "What I mean is—" He laughed at himself. "Jaysus, someone help me out here."

"Are you trying to find a way to tell me you don't want this?"

"Oh, I want this, all right," Sean confirmed.

Shaunna laughed, a little breathless, it seemed, and relieved. Had she honestly believed he didn't?

But that was the thing. What Andy must've picked up on was the wanting, which was not the same as doing and was all well and good for those in a healthy relationship. There was also nothing wrong with admiring from afar, or even up close. A bit of innocent flirting could be good for the self-esteem of all involved, assuming they'd all consented.

"Do you always do this?" Shaunna asked. At Sean's puzzled frown, she explained, "Weigh up the pros and cons."

"I'm not…well, all right, I am, and maybe? I don't know. It's been a while since I've been in this situation of wanting and knowing I stand a good chance of getting somewhere. But here's the pr—" Shaunna's lips muffled the rest of the word, and he lost any that might have followed to passion.

It was a funny thing, a kiss. The fantasising of soft lips and warm breath, always perfectly fragrant, and noses didn't get in the way. Hours, he'd spent, watching her lips while she talked; she'd notice and reward his attentiveness with a seductive smile or a slow swish of tongue. Andy's descriptor of red hot was dead on; it was astonishing the plastic straw in her milkshake didn't just melt away.

The real deal was more, better than everything he'd imagined, and his mind had set the bar impossibly high. As she eased her lips from his, he inhaled deeply, sighing out the air in relief that she wasn't taking it further. All the while they'd been kissing, sex had been on his horizon and coming at him faster by the second.

"What are you thinking about now?" she asked.

"What a spectacular kisser y'are," he answered with a wink.

"Hmm…" Shaunna pulled back so she could look at him but kept her arms around his neck, her body pressed to his. "You're worried about your lack of erection."

He considered lying, but why bother when she could feel its absence between them?

"Sometimes I get it up just fine, but that's as far as it goes. Other times, like now, I'm so turned on, but I've nothing to work with, if you catch my drift."

Tenderly, Shaunna smoothed his hair back from his forehead. He hadn't noticed he was sweating. "Do you remember the conversation we had about sex therapy?" she asked.

In spite of his self-consciousness, Sean smiled. "Aye. And d'you remember I told you it didn't involve the thing itself?"

She gave him a wry grin. "I knew that, wise-ass. What I'm getting at is we can deal with that side of it, for real."

"Ah, right, so this was an intervention?" Sean said, play-pushing her away.

"Well, duh! You called me!" She laughed, as did he. "I did it to get your mind off alcohol, although don't think I wouldn't be interested."

"If I didn't have Soph and you didn't have Andy?"

"You said it."

The sexual attraction was still there, in the background as usual, but the intensity, which would inevitably have ended in the bedroom if Sean had been capable, was over.

"Look, hun, maybe I'm not the right person to talk to about this, but you do need to talk to someone. How long has it been, did you say? Two years?"

"It could be a fair bit longer than that, honestly. Between drinking and Dylan coming along and losing Jessie, I don't remember the last time both me and little Sean had our heads in the game."

"What about your relationship before Sophie?"

"Francesca?" His memories of their short, mutually unsatisfying marriage were shamefully sketchy, none of them involving sex. It might have been a different story if they'd ditched work for a week and gone on a honeymoon. They used to joke that they were bigamists, married to the hospital as well as each other, and agreed to a no-fault divorce, but that hadn't stopped Sean admonishing himself for failing to put in the effort.

"Shall I make us a cuppa?" Shaunna suggested. She must have noticed him sliding.

"That'd be smashing."

"All right." She moved to leave, but he caught her hand and brought it to his lips in a courtly rather than erotic gesture.

"Thank you."

"No thanks needed. You did the same for me when I flipped out after Jess passed. Besides..." She leaned close, her breath hot in his ear as she murmured, "One day, you'll choose sex over a cup of tea." She drew back again and blew him a kiss as she headed for the kettle. "Therapy goals."

22: Party

Shaunna and Andy's Garden
Present Day
Friday, 19th April

ONCE, MANY YEARS ago, under a moderately ancient oak tree, Josh and Gabby had a conversation. Like most of those he'd had in university, it was a one-off and all the more significant for it. He recalled with vivid clarity the skeletal dark branches creaking overhead, the damp chill of the bench soaking through his trousers, the familiar, much missed catch of cigarette smoke in his throat and, of course, every last word he and Gabby had shared that day.

He could think of no reason why that particular conversation should come to mind upon opening the gate to Shaunna and Andy's garden where in excess of thirty people had gathered, by invitation, to celebrate his and George's birthdays. Granted, Gabby was among that number, although Josh had yet to spot her, and in his endeavour to do so, everything became clear.

That day, under the oak tree, if Gabby had asked Josh what his life would look like at forty, his answer would've been long, detailed and wholly inaccurate. At seventeen, Josh had foreseen a single life, his academic career taking precedence, evenings spent reading papers, a wealth of qualifications in disciplines pursued for pleasure—a second Master's in English literature, history or mathematics, perhaps all three, and a doctorate. Had that been his lot, he would have been content, fulfilled, accomplished. But the seventeen-year-old Joshua Sandison who had, that day under the oak tree, shared a secret and in his youthful arrogance doled out advice he was not yet qualified to give, was a blueprint for a different life.

He still doubted the wisdom of the advice he'd offered, yet it had shown him an alternative path, one which meant, when mental illness intersected his planned route, he was faced not with a dead end but a fork in the road. To the left lay academia, a precarious highway beset by diversions, any one of which might have led to his final destination; to the right, psychotherapy, a life-giving bypass under heavy construction but flowing with potential. And he, a young man who loathed change and thrived on routine, stepped into the unknown, onto a path he would not have taken without that conversation twenty-two and a half years ago, a path which had safely carried him into his future and made it possible for him to be here, now, celebrating his fortieth birthday with his husband, adopted daughter and all of these people, who were indeed his friends.

"Here they are. The men of the hour!" Dan raised his beer bottle—a signal to all those in hearing range to follow his lead. Adele rushed over and hugged the breath out of George, squealing "Happy Birthday" so loudly he blinked with each syllable and once more for good measure as she deposited a big, shiny, pink kiss on his cheek.

"Thanks, Adele." He staggered upon release only to be accosted by seemingly every other woman in attendance, while Josh sneaked past. He didn't get far, brought to a halt by the realisation he was walking into a marquee so large it encompassed everyone and everything—the pagoda, Jacuzzi, pots of shrubs, even trees—transforming Shaunna and Andy's garden into a fragrant arboretum. Amid the cherry and apple blossom shone tiny pearls of creamy light; blue sparkles flittered through the water dome of the miniature fountain beneath the Japanese maple; discs like cat's eyes flanked the meandering path from the house to the rustic wall at the far end, where a banner—no, make that a mural—hung. Were it not for being so utterly overwhelmed by everything, Josh might have laughed, for it declared in oversized glittery blue and green letters:

HAPPY
18th + 21st + 40th
BIRTHDAY
GEORGE & JOSH

"Hiya!" Adele popped up in front of him, lipstick refreshed on her broad, confident smile, and well it should be. The moment he'd sent her the requested list of guests to invite, he'd essentially given her carte blanche on this party, and he'd had no qualms doing so. After all, she'd organised their wedding, and it had been perfect. Still, he couldn't help teasing her a little.

"You do know George is forty-one today, don't you?"

She tutted and lightly slapped his arm. "Do you like it?"

"I do, Adele. I love it." He glanced back towards the gate, where George had made it a few inches further under the canvas if that. The women might have been done with him, but the children were not. Oliver—almost seven and dressed identically to his CEO father—gave George a very business-like handshake while the smaller ones clung to his legs and hung off his arms. He was utterly in his element.

Birthday greeting delivered, Oliver turned and strode a few feet along the path before breaking into a dash and dodging between the adults, a young man on a mission; it took only a few seconds to figure out what that mission was.

Adele went up on tiptoes and cupped her hand around Josh's ear, although the music prohibited whispering. "Isn't he a little young to be going steady?"

Josh leaned away so he could act incredulous to her face. "Says the woman whose children's father she's gone steady with—"

"On and off..."

"—since reception class, to the man who married the boy he fell in love with when he was seven." As he said it, Oliver emerged from the crowd, a hand clasped in his, and advanced on Josh and Adele.

"Hey, Ollie. Hey, Shabina. Thanks for coming."

"We wouldn't miss it for the world," Oliver said.

"The whole, whole world?" Josh asked and was rewarded with a shy grin from Oliver and a giggle from Shabina—Oliver's best friend *in the whole, whole world.* "You look very smart." At that, the children put their shoulders back and chins up proudly. They made a beautiful couple. "I love your suit, Shabina."

"Thanks. My mum made it." She held out the hem of the top to show off to full effect the soft peach fabric with its slightly darker edges.

"Wow!" Adele said. "It's gorgeous! Is your mum a designer?"

"No. She just makes our clothes."

"She's super talented. Look at that pleating!"

Shabina gave a little twirl that sent the fabric swirling around her like the copious, delicate petals of a rose. "And she teaches the ladies in the refuge how to sew too."

"Your mum's amazing!" Josh gushed, glancing around to see if Anu was there, but no. Shabina must've come with James and Oliver, which was a shame, as the reminder of Anu's talents set Josh off thinking of all the potential, even among his immediate friends and acquaintances, for a whole host of creative therapies, but perhaps the middle of his long-anticipated birthday party wasn't the best time to explore that idea. He made a mental note to talk to Anu later and turned his attention back to Oliver and Shabina. "I hope you both have lots of fun this evening."

"We will," Oliver said, reinstating his grip on Shabina's hand, adding as something of an afterthought, "We hope you do too," before the pair traipsed off whence they came.

"All the Browns must be born middle-aged," Adele remarked, and Josh laughed. It was a fair observation, given Oliver's younger brother was slumped on Eleanor's knee, his face old-man wrinkly and grumpy from having recently woken from a nap. "Your phone's ringing, by the way."

Frowning, Josh fished it out of his pocket in time to see 'call ended'. "How on earth did you hear that?" With or without the music playing from speakers discreetly positioned in the shrubbery, Adele shouldn't have heard a thing. His phone was set to silent.

"I told you! I'm sensitive to vibrations." She grinned mischievously. "Who was it?"

"No idea." It was that same number again, and other than it having their area code, he didn't recognise it. He put his phone away. "In any case, everyone I know is here. On which note, I suppose I ought to do the rounds."

Adele shrugged. "It's *your* party—"

"And I'll cry if I want to?"

Adele looked aghast.

"It's a song," Josh explained.

"I knew that! But you can do what you want. I don't care as long as you're happy..."

"I am," Josh assured her sincerely.

"Then my work here is done." With a wave of her fingertips producing a blur of pink that matched her lips, off she went, still somehow managing to stride with purpose in six-inch wedged heels. She passed Gabby and her husband, who were heading Josh's way.

"Good evening, both."

"Good evening, Josh."

"I'm so glad you could come," Josh said as he and Gabby embraced, the only reluctance this time in releasing each other.

"Thank you for the invitation. I'm afraid Howard was called away on family business."

"Oh?" *Not her husband then.* Josh reappraised Gabby's companion over her shoulder.

"I hope you don't mind," she murmured, stepping back and gesturing stiffly. "Josh, this is my agent and very good friend Dustin."

"Hello." Dustin leaned in for a warmish, formal hand shake.

"Agent?" Josh questioned.

"He arranges my gallery shows and sales," Gabby answered.

"I see." Josh was still getting the measure of the man but offered him a quick smile. "Thanks for accompanying her this evening."

"She almost didn't make it," Dustin said.

"How so?"

"Nothing to worry about," Gabby interjected. "It's been an... unusual week. That's all." She diverted her attention to their surroundings. "This is marvellous, isn't it?"

"Unusual in what way?" Josh pressed.

"Really, it's nothing. Do you need a drink or..." She met Josh's gaze and trailed off.

"Simon Henderson called me," he said. It was a shot into the twilight rather than the dark because something—maybe the side effects of Adele's vibrational sensitivity—was telling him Gabby's 'unusual' week and his shared some common features.

"I thought he might."

"He said he'd spoken to you."

"Yes. I hope it was all right to pass on your details. It seemed serendipitous that he should attend one of my exhibitions on the same day George mentioned you were having trouble finding legal representation."

"He's the wrong kind of barrister, unfortunately," Josh said, at which Gabby's face fell. "But thank you for thinking of me. Well, of the Daisy Foundation."

She reached out and squeezed his forearm. "I know you didn't like him, but you should give him a chance. He's changed a good deal since our university days, and he loved Jess very much."

Josh clamped his teeth. 'Didn't like him' was putting it mildly. Nor had he ever seen any indication that Simon cared for anyone other than himself. However, tonight was neither the time nor place for exercises in pedantry, so Josh nodded, smiled blandly, and said, "I'll keep that in mind. Now, I really must say hello to a few more people and get that drink you mentioned—do either of you need a top-up?"

Gabby and Dustin waved away his offer and found a quiet corner to hide out under the canopy of cherry blossom. Gabby barely knew anyone at the party, and Josh didn't like leaving her to her own devices, but she smiled and nodded, which he took as reassurance that she was fine and prepared to welcome the rest of his guests.

It took little effort on his part, as mostly they came to him. First Kris and Ade regaled him with their latest chat show adventure—a forewarning that they'd given the British viewing public a potted biography of *Josh Sandison-Morley, Psychotherapist, Mind Reader and Offender Profiler* and that one of the producers seemed *very* interested in talking to him about an idea they had for a crime show. Josh was flattered and, he realised with some surprise, not averse to the idea now he was free of his university work, so he agreed to Kris passing his number on to the producer.

Next, Sean and Sophie brought him a bottle of beer and an official invitation to Dylan's baptism in six weeks' time. Josh was a 'godparent' and didn't need a bit of paper to tell him where and when it was, but he accepted the fancy card and made a show of saving the date to his diary.

After that came Krissi, Wotto, Jay and Hadyn, none of whom he'd expected to turn out for a fortieth birthday party on a Friday evening when they were young, wild and free, by comparison. Krissi was already beyond tipsy, but as always, her three companions—her fiancé, BFF and BFF's right-hand man respectively—were looking after her.

No sooner had they departed than Shaunna crept up behind Josh and murmured, "Hiya, hun," in his ear. He nearly dropped his beer.

"Sorry." She hugged him and kissed his cheek. "Are you OK?"

"Yes, astonishingly."

"Who knew you had so many friends?"

"Not me, that's for sure!" He raised his hands, gesturing to the marquee, the tables and chairs along the sides, all the lights twinkling among the foliage. "This is incredible, Shaunna."

"I'd love to take credit for it, but those Jeffries boys, you know?"

"Ha. Yes." No job too small to turn into something extravagant. "Mind you, it would be nothing without Adele's event-planning expertise or those magical green fingers of yours."

"Thanks." Shaunna looked up and around her, smiling at what she saw. A year ago, when she and Andy had bought the house, the garden was an overgrown mess, and they'd worked like Trojans through sun, wind, hail and rain to transform it into this enchanting outdoor room.

"Speaking of magic," she said, looping Josh's arm, "have you seen your cake?" She spun him 180° so he was once more facing the wall at the end of the garden.

"Not yet—oh! *Wow!*" Now he had, he didn't know how he'd missed it before. It was huge, and it was dessert rather than cake, chilling in a solid ice bowl the size of a satellite dish. Specifically, it was a super-size version of George's favourite dessert— orange sorbet and white chocolate ice cream, topped with orange liqueur syrup and flaked dark chocolate—Wotto's now infamous *Pure Bliss*. "Quick! Get me a spoon before George sees it!"

Shaunna laughed. "There's plenty more in the freezer. Actually, where is George?"

Both turned back and located him, no trouble at all, courtesy of his current swarm of fans, this time in the form of those present who were part of the Lions football team.

"I'm glad Rob made it this evening," Josh said.

"Me too. Adele wasn't going to invite him."

Josh sighed. He'd known when he gave Adele his guest list that putting Rob Simpson-Stone's name on it would cause trouble.

Like most of those at the party, Rob was Josh and George's high school alumni, and Adele had never got on with him. Over the past couple of years, her minor dislike had turned to outright scorn; that he'd been working undercover made no difference, nor that he had been hurt the most by Jess's con. As far as Adele was concerned, Rob was a liar who'd abused their trust, and once she made up her mind about someone, there was more chance of reversing the Earth's spin than changing her opinion.

"You invited him, didn't you?" Josh said.

"Yeah, I did."

"Thank you."

"Welcome. Oh, look! I can actually see your husband!"

A few of the footballers peeled away to replenish their beers, and George looked over, meeting Josh's gaze, holding it for a few seconds, perhaps as many as five, before the guys from the farm stepped in, breaking the connection.

"What did he say?" Shaunna asked.

"Hm?" Still entranced, Josh processed the question after the fact and frowned. "Who? George?"

"Yeah. That whole 'my mind to your mind' thing you and he do?"

"Neither of us have the ears for that."

"Obviously, you wouldn't be able to hear him from all the way over here."

"I mean we're not Vulcans."

"Eh?"

"Star Trek?"

Shaunna gave a few ultra-long-lashed blinks of confusion.

"Never mind," Josh said. "He was checking I was OK with fending for myself while he plays to his adoring fans."

"Hmm. Yep. I bet that's the real reason Kris dumped him in high school."

"Spotlight too small for two?"

"Exactly!"

It had been considerably more complicated, as is the way of adolescent love, but Shaunna's theory had some merit. Aside from on the football pitch, George wasn't a show-off, yet he didn't shy away from attention or admiration when it came his way, and it was doing so in abundance.

That was how it continued for most of the evening. George garnered crowds and kept them entertained, always with a drink in hand despite never making it more than a few feet from the gate. Josh wondered—but also acknowledged it was ridiculous—if their guests were conspiring to keep them apart. It seemed whenever he made any move to re-join George, someone intercepted, and so he eventually gave up and resorted to people-watching. It was no great hardship.

Of course, he'd have liked to do a good deal more than watching because he had questions, such as who Rob's date was. A police officer or soldier maybe? She had the confident, slightly pugnacious stance to be either of those. Whoever she was and whatever her reasons for being there, it was good to see Rob enjoying her company in his usual stoic way. Undercover work had cost him dearly, and there was no overlooking that Jess had been to blame for that.

There was also something going on with Krissi. Murmurings and furtive finger-pointing resolved into her storming off with Wotto in pursuit, while Jay and Hadyn loitered and then...

Josh missed what happened next when two Jeffries brothers lumbered into his line of sight. His phone was also vibrating again.

"Alright, mate?" Andy began but paused for Josh to take the call. He needn't have bothered.

"Wrong number?" Dan asked.

"I presume so." Another hang-up, same number.

"What d'you reckon, then?" Dan tilted his head, only the vaguest indication he was asking about the party set-up.

"It's awesome."

"Not *all* our doing, of course."

"No." On another day, Josh might've challenged Dan to give credit where it was due, but with Simon's re-emergence on top of what had happened at the surgery and now these mystery phone calls, his grip on rationality was slipping. It had to be Tony Baines. Had to be.

"You look spooked, mate. Are you all right?"

Josh tuned back in and tried to discern which brother had spoken. He didn't usually have that problem, but both were eyeing him like he was a misfiring engine they were trying to fix.

"I'm fine." He backed up his claim with a smile that prompted matching raised eyebrows from the not-twins.

"Can we talk shop?" Dan asked. It would have been a tactless question from anyone other than a fellow workaholic.

"Sure."

"I was telling him—" Dan thumbed in his brother's direction "—about your electrical fault that isn't."

"OK?"

"Yeah, so," Andy picked up from Dan, "I'm gonna have a gander at the timber—if it's all right with you."

"Why wouldn't it be?"

"I might have to take down some of the ceiling."

"Ah." Josh was beginning to understand why building contracts rarely completed on time. "How much of the ceiling?"

"Depends what I find."

"Deathwatch beetle," Dan said with a ponderous, slightly smug nod.

"Pardon?"

Andy's lip curled at his brother.

"They can make a hell of a racket," Dan added.

Andy squared up to him. "Who's the CSTDB around here?"

"All right, smart arse. What d'you reckon it is?"

"I won't know until I've looked into it."

Intent on deciphering the abbreviation—*Chartered Slayer of the Deathwatch Beetle?*—Josh let them bicker for a while, but they were loud and dangerously close to fisticuffs, so in the end he had to step in.

"They're not anything to do with death, are they? The beetles."

"Nah." Andy shrugged the tension out of his shoulders and backed down, but not without a killing glare at Dan. "Old superstition, that is."

Josh didn't imagine for one minute that the presence of alarmingly named insects could explain unfurling toilet rolls, but still. It was better than no explanation at all.

"OK," he said. "You have my permission to do what you need to."

"Great. I'll get in there first thing Monday. The architect's coming at noon, so—"

"Actually..." Josh interrupted, but fear hijacked his thoughts before he could follow through on Sean's advice and volunteer to tag along. He didn't need to talk to the architect. It would all be fine. "I'll send you my notes via email."

"Good stuff." Andy said, and there the discussion ended, with him sniffing the air like an overgrown Bisto kid as a delectable waft of cheesy, yeasty goodness came their way.

It turned out Krissi hadn't stormed off in a huff. She and Wotto had returned with freshly baked pizza and garlic bread, an excellent choice, to Josh's mind, and all conversations ceased as the guests descended en masse to have their fill of the delicious party food—a welcome change from cold sausage rolls and curly-crusted sandwiches—followed by a bowl of birthday dessert for those who wanted it, and most did.

It wasn't long after that when Krissi and the gang packed their equipment into a van and left. George's farm colleagues weren't far behind them, followed by most of the children.

In the midst of all the coming and going and eating, Josh's phone vibrated thrice more. The first time, he'd returned the call, ready to blast Tony Baines or whoever it was, and was miffed when all he got was the continuous dead-line beep. After the third call, he turned off his phone. Even if he hadn't promised

George he'd stop chasing mysteries, he had no real desire to go to war with a hoax caller. Not this evening when the guests had dwindled until only their closest friends remained.

The Circle. Nine friends from high school, give or take a swindling lawyer and a smug Irish psychologist. Friends who had promised long ago to give him and George the perfect birthday party, and as the two of them joined the rest around the giant ice bowl to tuck into what was left of the Perfect Bliss dessert/birthday cake, each armed with a spoon, it was safe to say they'd delivered on that promise.

23: Spa Partners

"STOP DOING THE soft-eyes thing on me, Mother. I'm *fine!*" To emphasise, Phee took a large bite of her cheeseburger, but what some insultingly called the Rowan women's 'mealy mouths' was as much about what went into them as came out. With no room to chew, Phee's cheeks ballooned and she spat the chunk of cheeseburger into a paper napkin.

"It is terribly dry," Genie justified, though she had not yet touched her burger. Perhaps fast food hadn't been the wisest choice, but she'd wanted so much to stick to the usual routine of their cinema trips, hoping that doing so would act like a reset button and delete the past few weeks. The plan had fallen at the first hurdle, the evidence in clear sight, courtesy of the restaurant's glass front overlooking the leisure complex car park. The three-hour turnaround the mobile car-cleaning company had quoted was almost up, but the two young men who'd arrived following Genie's call were still hard at it, lugging industrial machinery in and out of their van and clambering all over the car.

"Mum? Hel-lo?"

"Hmm?" Genie turned away from the window and smiled at her daughter. "Sorry. What did you say?"

"Try it without the bun." Phee waved her half-eaten naked burger in demonstration.

"Ah. Yes, a good idea." Genie followed her example and dismantled her burger, then picked at the warmish brown patty, no appetite whatsoever. "What did you think of the film? Awful?"

"So bad! And how was that a rom com, please? I mean, her high heels breaking wasn't funny the first time."

"It *was* romantic, though," Genie argued.

"Yeah, whatever, Mother." Phee shook her head in light-hearted disparagement of Genie's soft spot for snappily dressed, blonde-haired 'totty', in this instance the female lead who had, in a modern and—as Genie knew from bitter experience—unlikely twist in the trope, got her man *and* held on to her high-powered corporate career. Of course, she and Phee would have enjoyed it more had they been rom com fans rather than two people escaping a real-life horror movie, on which note...

"I need to return Jonathan's call."

"Yes, you do."

"I know you don't like them being in the house—"

"I don't care as long as Xander gets that ghost out."

"I'm sure he will, but I think we should stay away until he has."

"Where? A hotel?"

"Yes."

"Please not the Travel Inn."

"Goodness, no!" Genie laughed. "I thought we could make a little holiday of it, drive up to Wharton Hall."

"Where?" Phee already had her phone out, researching.

"Staffordshire, not far from where I went to uni."

"Got it. Wharton Hall Hotel and Spa. 'A peaceful haven surrounded by acres of rich landscape, this Georgian mansion was home to the—'" Phee stopped reading and looked up. "The *Rowan* family?" Genie nodded. "As in *our* family?" Genie nodded again. Phee read on. "'...was home to the Rowan family until the late 1980s, when Grange Estate Management PLC renovated the property, transforming it into a highly popular retreat. Relax in our natural spa pools, saunas and Roman baths, detox in our aromatherapy, massage and beauty therapy suite or simply enjoy a walk in the fresh, open air.'" Phee scrolled. "Daily yoga in the Japanese gardens—do they have those Zen gardens where you rake patterns in sand?"

"I've no idea," Genie said. "I've never been."

"Didn't you live there in the eighties?"

"No. We've always lived in Shropshire. Your great-great-uncle Edward lived there before the Second World War, but he was killed on the battlefield as it were, and he never married or had children, so it stood empty for forty years, derelict, actually, before Grange took over managing the estate. They've made an excellent job of it, too, according to your grandfather, and he's a notoriously difficult man to please."

"Wait—it still belongs to our family?"

"Yes. Well, to your grandfather."

"And when he dies—"

"It will go to your aunt," Genie said, nodding with each word, although Phee hadn't brought up the non-inheritance in a while. She'd had no cause to since Jess died.

"We still get to stay there for free, right?" Phee asked with a conniving smirk and returned to perusing the website.

"Sadly not." Or not without Genie backing down, and that wasn't an option while Phee was still young enough for her grandparents to meddle in her life.

"Sucks. Should I fill in this online booking form?"

"Yes. Do that, and I'll phone Jonathan." Scooping up the paper burger wrapper and her largely uneaten meal, Genie dropped it in the closest bin and headed outside, her mission interrupted by an incoming call. Paul.

"Genie?"

"Hello, darling. Are you home?"

"Yes. I've been back half an hour. Where are you? Shopping?"

"No. Phee and I went to see a film. Listen, we're going away for a few days—make the most of the spring break and whatnot."

"I can't come with you. I'm flying to Germany tomorrow, remember?" Paul's tone was brusque, and it riled Genie, but she played it cool.

"Yes, I do remember, and I meant Phee and me."

"When did you plan this?"

"Spur of the moment."

"So I'm eating dinner alone. *Again.*"

"I'm sorry, darling."

"It's fine." He was still snippy, but she sensed he was trying to be reasonable. "Have a good time."

"Thank you." Genie paused, not ready to sign off on the call yet. "When you get back, we should chat."

"About us?" The lack of delay and accuracy of his guess was telling.

"Yes, but I don't want you fretting over it while you're away."

"Too busy for that!"

"A good thing, too. I'll let you go."

"OK. See you in two weeks."

"You will. Bye, darling."

"Bye." No click as he hung up, the silent moment marking another step closer to the end, and Genie hadn't thought to ask about the shattered wine bottle. Margaret must have been in and cleaned it up or Paul would have mentioned it. Hoping it meant she intended to stay rather than having returned to work her notice, Genie sent a quick message of thanks to her assistant and finally got around to calling Jonathan, who must surely have had the phone in his hand, as he picked up right away.

"Hello, *Genie.*"

She sniffed back her pointless annoyance. "Hello, Jonathan. Sorry I couldn't talk earlier. I'm taking my daughter away for the week, so if you can let Xander know you'll have the place to yourselves…"

"Jolly good."

"When should I tell Margaret to expect you?"

"On Monday. We have a prior engagement this weekend."

"Wonderful. I'll let her know. Thank you, both—again—for being so patient with us."

"That's quite all right. I'll update you daily—"

"No need. Just tell me when it's over."

"As you wish. Is there anything else?"

"No, that's all."

"Then do have a pleasant trip."

"We will. Bye for now."

That done, Genie turned to go back inside the fast-food restaurant and walked straight into Phee.

"Oops! Sorry, darling."

"You've been out here forever."

"Yes. Paul called. He's pissed off we're not at home."

"He's got a nerve when he's left you to deal with the poltergeist on your own."

"He doesn't know we have a poltergeist."

"He might by now."

Genie chuckled. "That he might. Are we all booked in?"

"Yep. What are we going to do about clothes? Go back to the house?"

"I thought we could pick up some underwear, maybe a couple of outfits on the way."

"Where? By the time they're done with the car, all the shops will be shut." As Phee spoke, the car cleaners closed the back doors of their van, and the one Genie had spoken to earlier looked around the car park, waving when he spotted them. Genie and Phee started to walk over.

"How about the supermarket?" Genie suggested.

"For clothes or toiletries?"

"Both. It might not be high fashion, but—"

"We'll be wearing bathrobes for the next week," Phee finished.

"Quite." Genie smiled as they met up with the car cleaner.

"All done," he said, beckoning for her to follow him on a tour of their work, and Genie was impressed by how thorough they'd been. The car hadn't been so clean and shiny since she'd bought it.

"Upholstery's still slightly damp in the back." He gestured to the paper cover on the seat. "I'd avoid sitting there until tomorrow if you can. You paid online, didn't you?"

"I did, yes, and I'll be leaving a glowing review. Thank you so much!"

"No problem." He handed over the keys and with a swift smile climbed into his van.

"Are you ready?" Genie asked.

"Yep. Let's do this. Ooh! One sec." Phone in hand, Phee leaned close and pressed her cheek to Genie's. "Smile!" They both made faces half smile, half pout; Phee took the photo, tagged it *#roadtrip with mama* and shared it on her profile.

Genie hadn't even started the car before her phone pinged. Phee's friend Sarah had liked the photo and left a comment: *Gorgeous! Could be sisters! x*

"Is she saying I look young or you look old?" Genie wondered aloud, although with her wrinkles filtered out, it was something of a glimpse into the past.

"You're beautiful, Mother. Get over it."

"As are you, darling girl."

"Hmph. I wish I had your nose. Mine's too…squidgy."

"Squidgy?"

"Boneless. Like Sean's. I'm glad I got his hair, though. No offence."

"Oh, I'm with you on that." Genie's hair was dark too but fine and straight, not thick and wavy like Sean's and Phee's. She studied the photo a moment longer, seeing more of Sean than herself in Phee's features—strong eyebrows, in Phee's case tamed to frame her brown eyes, the slight dimples in her cheeks and that cute bobble chin—as well as a serendipitous opportunity to come clean about their trip. Before she did, however, she put her phone away and got them on the road.

"Can I put on some music?" Phee asked.

"Absolutely." Genie left a beat, then said, casually, "Funnily enough, I had a good natter with Sean this morning."

Phee hummed, confirming she'd heard, but she was—Genie hoped—distracted by finding something they'd both want to listen to and didn't say anything.

"I told him about our poltergeist."

"OK."

Genie waited. Music started coming through the car's speakers, too quietly to make out the song, and Phee made no move to turn it up. Still, Genie waited, and then, at the point where it seemed Phee was expecting her to continue unprompted, Phee asked, "What did he say?"

"About the poltergeist, very little. Mostly, we talked about Jess."

"Sticking with the ghost theme, then."

A chill rushed up Genie's back, and she tightened her grip on the steering wheel to conceal the shiver. The connection hadn't escaped her, despite what she'd told Xander. She'd registered it the moment she'd picked up the score and seen the title 'L'Alouette', an entirely different composition from 'Alouette', yet it had planted the children's song in her head and with it a wisp of something—a feeling rather than a memory—that she hadn't yet placed beyond knowing it was to do with Jess.

"Her funeral was lovely, Sean said."

"Yeah, I've never really got that."

"I suppose he meant it was a celebration of her life rather than a gloomy affair."

"No, I mean…Jess was your bestie, right? And you were all at uni together."

"Hm?"

"Well, did you fall out or something? Because you talked to each other every day, but you didn't go to her funeral and Sean did. Is that weird, or it is me?"

"No, it's not you." Phee's observation hit the same nerve Sean had twanged earlier. Had Genie been the only one to abide by Jess's wishes, or the only one upon whom those wishes had been conferred? She'd spent much of the movie trying to convince herself it was the former. She'd failed, hence this trip. "You must understand, Jess was a very private person. And conscious of her appearance."

"Vain, you mean."

Genie laughed, thinking back over the hours of hair straightening and make-up perfecting and trying on a hundred different combinations of dresses and shoes before every night out. "She could be. She would've hated anyone seeing her so sick, especially towards the end."

"Oh, yeah. Like Sarah's mum." Phee became quiet, and Genie respected her silence, knowing she was thinking about Sarah's mother's battle with cancer. The girls were quite young when she died, and the four-year difference in their ages had been much starker, but they'd always been close, so Phee had witnessed the final stages of the disease, although she'd never talked about it, or not to Genie.

A few minutes passed. Genie was counting the time in miles, so she couldn't be sure how long, but she didn't want to miss her window of opportunity.

"I'd like to invite Sean to join us for dinner one evening. He's only an hour or so from Wharton Hall. Is that all right with you?"

"Sure!" Phee changed the song on the stereo and turned up the volume a notch or two—still too quiet for Genie's old ears. "He must be a good person to have around when you're sick. Like, you know, properly sick, how Sarah's mum and Jess were, not..." She trailed off and turned to look out the passenger window.

"Yes, he must," Genie agreed, glossing over Phee's avoidance and her own sudden tearfulness. How much her daughter had changed these past years. Some of it was natural development taking its course, the emotional roller coaster every adolescent must ride in the face of peer pressure, the stress of making big study decisions, choosing a career, proving they could be a grown-up. Gone were the days when Phee had trusted her mother with even the smallest of confidences—crushes on musicians and social media superstars, her often unpopular opinion of this perfume or that fashion. No more. Phee had become secretive and sullen and nothing like the gorgeous young woman who had pleaded for the most outlandish bedroom makeover not five months ago. Every part of Genie ached with maternal need to protect her daughter, to ease her pain and sadness, but what could she do when Phee, like Jess, was pushing her away?

"This is all I'm going to say, OK?"

"About what?"

"You know what. I just want you to know I support you whatever happens, whatever you decide. That's all."

"Hmm." Phee faced front again and turned up the stereo, making further conversation impossible, but Genie meant it. Unless Phee chose to open up to her, she would not mention it again.

***

Phee awoke, shivering and with the vilest taste in her mouth, but no nausea, which was an amazing feeling. It had been constant for weeks.

"We're here," her mum said.

"How long have I been asleep?"

"A couple of hours."

"Wow." That would be why she was so stiff then. She fished around for the bottle of water they'd bought when they'd stopped off at the supermarket—the last thing she remembered of their journey—and sipped, taking the time to figure out her surroundings. They were parked, along with about ten other cars, in a small car park with old-fashioned streetlamps and a tall hedge. That was about all she could see, even when she followed her mum to the back of the car to retrieve their basic carry-on bags, purchased to hold the small selection of toiletries and underwear, plus a bikini, T-shirt and pair of pyjamas each. Phee wished she'd bought a hoodie; she couldn't stop shivering.

"You'll feel better once you've had something to eat," her mum said as they set off in the direction indicated by an arrow on a stick at the car park's entrance; glowing windows were now also visible between the swaying branches of the big old trees up ahead.

"You weren't going to say anything else," Phee pointed out as they crunched their way along a narrow gravel path surrounded by disturbingly neat flower beds planted with rose bushes that glowed an even sicklier green than Phee did every morning. At least the roses could blame the rock-shaped solar LEDs; Phee's predicament was all her own doing.

"I'm not. We've only eaten popcorn and a cheeseburger all day, and we could both do with a decent meal." Her mum held open the door. "Let's be hoped it's not one of those places that thinks quinoa is a decent meal."

"What's quinoa ever done to you?" Phee stepped inside and immediately resorted to mouth-breathing. There were so many smells of food and coffee and perfumed oils and lotions, the pungent mixture turned her stomach, and she gritted her teeth, telling herself not to be sick, although maybe eating something would help. "Food would be good," she said.

"What d'you fancy?"

"Something quick so I can go to bed."

Her mum's eyes went all soft and sympathetic again. "I'll get us booked in and ask for room service. How about that?"

"Fine. Whatever." Phee flopped into one of the low chairs lined up against the wall and chanced another small sniff. Her mouth instantly filled with saliva, and she shot to her feet, scanning the various doors, all with signs, none of them a toilet. That left her one choice: she bolted outside and as far down the path as she could, then she spewed, somehow missing the rose bushes but catching another whiff of that horrible berries and coffee stink. She spewed again, and again, and thought *screw you, morning sickness* because it was nothing like being normally sick, when you felt better once you'd thrown up. This didn't go away, and she was so done with it when it wasn't even morning, *and* she had an audience. She wiped her mouth and sneaked a look, not surprised to discover her mum helicoptering with their bags dangling from her shoulder and that stupid face on her again.

"Can we go to our rooms yet?" Phee snapped out the question and hated herself for it, but her body and brain felt totally out of her control.

"Yes," her mum replied coolly, no soft mushiness now. "Someone's going to bring us a toaster, bread, butter and preserves."

"That's like hospital food. Did you tell them I'm sick?"

"You're vomiting in their flower bed."

A quick look through the window confirmed Phee was in plain sight of everyone in the reception area. "Well, that's just great."

"The toast will help. Come on. We're in rooms twenty-four and twenty-five—should I lose you along the way." Her mum didn't wait for her, which was fair enough. Phee was being a bitch.

***

The toast worked. For a little while, anyway—long enough to say sorry for being a bitch, take a shower and get into bed, all forgiven. Then she'd zonked out, oblivious, until she'd woken in the same position a minute or so ago, no clue how long she'd slept or what the time was. She felt around under her pillow for her phone and, not finding it, remembered it was still on top of the drawers across the room. But the bed was warm and comfy, and if she stayed absolutely still, she didn't feel sick…

"Darling, are you awake?"

…and she could pretend she was still asleep, except…

Except she didn't want to. She wanted more toast. And she wanted her mum.

"Yeah. What time is it?"

"A quarter past nine." The door between their rooms opened a few inches, and her mum's head poked through the gap. "May I come in?"

"Uh-huh." Phee shuffled up and over, leaving sitting space on the side of the bed. Her mum accepted.

"How did you sleep?"

"Like a log, apparently. Eleven hours?!"

"You did say you were tired."

"I did." Eleven hours was a *long* sleep. Still, she couldn't deny she felt tons better for it. "Did you sleep well?"

"Yes, I did, thank you, although I have been awake a while, enjoying the peace. It's such a relief to be away from all that nonsense at home, don't you think? And it's a gorgeous day out there."

Phee could see that from the yellow light sneaking around the edges of the window blinds. Her mum noticed her looking and got up to open them.

"Have you phoned Sean?" Phee asked.

"Not yet. I doubt he's up."

Phee opened her mouth, then clamped it shut again. She'd already slipped up once, when she'd said Sean would be a good person to have around if you were really ill, and it seemed she'd got away with it. But saying *If he's got Dylan today, he'll have been up for ages* would have been game over. Even not saying it, her mum was suspicious, and Phee hated the awkwardness between them. She wanted so much to tell her and kept trying, but she couldn't make the words come out. She watched her mum fuss with the cords on the blind, then straighten Phee's phone.

"Six percent battery."

"I forgot to plug it in. Have you had breakfast yet?"

"No. I was waiting for you. Do you feel up to it this morning?"

"I want to try." Breakfast and more.

"Where's your charger?"

"In my bag—front pocket. You can get it out, I don't mind."

Her mum opened the zip as if the bag's contents were explosive and fished around inside. "It's not here. Just a piece of paper. You can use mine for now."

"Take it out."

"The paper?"

Phee nodded.

Frowning, her mum extracted the folded square of paper and looked to Phee for instruction.

"Just look at it, Mum, please, because I can't…" She didn't need to say more. Her mum was holding the paper at arm's length and squinting.

"Twelve weeks."

"Thirteen now."

Much like Sean had been, her mum was transfixed, but everything else was so different. Seeing Sophie and Sean with Dylan, listening to Sarah's stories about uni, not being able to drink on a night out, the constant throwing up and tiredness— she'd been so sure that she was keeping this baby. Now, the only thing she was sure of was that she didn't want her mum to become attached to that ultrasound picture.

"I don't know what to do."

"Do you want to talk about it?"

"Maybe, but not yet."

"All right." Her mum folded the picture and returned it to Phee's bag. "So where is your charger?"

"In there somewhere." Phee sprang out of bed, only realising when the nausea caught up with her, and ran into her mum's arms. "I love you."

"I love you too." Her mum squeezed gently and released, while Phee clung on, ready to make up for all the months she'd gone without and *maybe* feeling a little less sick than before.

24: Runaround

Heading to the University
Present Day
Monday, 22ⁿᵈ April

Y OU LOT MAKE my time-keeping look good," Sean said jovially,
hoping to get his point across and avoid confrontation as he
secured Dylan in the back of the taxi. Via the rear-view mirror,
the cabbie offered a wan smile and held it until his passengers
were safely strapped in, then indicated and pulled away from
the kerb.

"We're short of drivers," he said, no apology, and proceeded
with a lengthy explanation about soaring fuel and insurance costs
and how they made peanuts out of these short daytime fares,
especially in rush hour, conveniently overlooking that there were
not enough other vehicles on the road to count as traffic let alone
a traffic jam. Sean nodded and threw in an occasional 'ah, right',
half-listening to the man's waffle and planning his day, comforted
by the knowledge it would be the last that began with a thirty-
minute wait for a prebooked taxi because one way another, he'd
have his own car by the end of it.

It hadn't originally been on today's agenda. It hadn't been
in Sean's immediate plans at all, not that he'd been spouting
nonsense when he told Josh he was thinking about getting
a car. With the university winding down for the summer and the
therapy centre still very much in the development phase, he'd
mostly be working from home or parenting Dylan, and it was
daft getting a car and having it sit outside the house for the next
six months. Or that had been true until yesterday. Two phone

calls changed all that. Not even a week away from the NHS and Francesca was begging him to cover for Doctor Morris. So that was tomorrow morning gone for a Burton. As for today…

Typical, when he'd taken Genie's point on board about her always calling him and had vowed to do something about it, that she'd jumped in first, and what a nice surprise it was to hear her voice for the second time in three days. Did he want to join her and Phee for dinner? Absolutely! Was he worried she'd realise they were hiding something? Was his mother a Catholic?

With Sophie back in London, Sean considered asking her parents if they could mind Dylan. It would be a late night for the wee fella, although he'd be a handy distraction, and he did enjoy visiting new places. Of course, he was a smasher in the car and would sleep all the way home. So that was that then. Drop Dylan off at the nursery, get this meeting with Zara out the way, and—

"…pound eighty, ta." The cabbie's demand for cash alerted Sean that they'd stopped outside Unitots. He handed over a couple of notes, told the cabbie to keep the change and carted both son and toddler seat into the building where, as always, a young smiling nursery nurse stood ready to greet them.

"Good morning, Dylan! Good morning, Dylan's dad!"

"Good morning, lovely. Can I trouble you to store this car seat for me? Hopefully, it'll be the last time."

"You're not leaving us, are you?" She followed Sean to the cubby hole reserved for parents' junk and lost property.

"Not at all." He offloaded the seat and turned to her with a grin. "I'm going car shopping."

"Oh! Cool! What are you getting?"

"Don't know yet. Just a runaround. Good on fuel economy. Electric maybe. Any recommendations?"

"I ride a bike everywhere, but my boyfriend works at the dealership on the high street, and he'll probably give you a discount. Hold on." She scurried away across the playroom and bent over one of the miniature tables, returning half a minute later with a large sheet of rough paper. "Sorry about the crayon."

Sean chuckled at the name and number scrawled in chunky, red characters. "The job has to have some perks. Thanks very much. I should be back by two. OK?"

"Yep. Dylan, your dad's going now." Dylan was already elbow deep in sand but waved his spade in goodbye.

"Be good," Sean said, in all probability to himself, and left for his office via the campus coffee shop. It was busy, the queue extending almost to the door, but they were quick to serve, and in any case, a vibrant swirl of turquoise and purple three people in front told him his colleague was running almost as late as he was. That was one point in Zara's favour. Josh would have already decided Sean was a no-show and cancelled the meeting.

Zara reached the front of the queue and ordered a chai latte, rummaging in her giant handbag and giving the server a running commentary on how she could never find her wallet, in the midst of it spotting Sean. "And breakfast tea too, zank you!"

Sean stepped out of the line and set aside his annoyance. He'd intended to have a coffee, but he could put up with tea for the sake of peace and a hasty getaway. Once they had their drinks in hands, they headed for Sean's office, both glancing through the open door of the one next to it, formerly Josh's, being cleaned for its next occupant, whoever that may be—not Zara. Her one-year, part-time contract didn't afford her the luxury of an office.

"Let me clear that chair for you." Sean found a speck on his desk for his cup and grabbed the pile of books from the seat, not sure where else to put them.

"It is fine. I prefer to stand when I can."

"Fair dos." Sean dumped the books on the floor, adding a few more to the pile to give him a corner of desk to perch on so he could maintain eye level with his new colleague. In the decade they'd known each other, their interactions had been minimal in quantity and terse in quality. Zara had told him the first time they'd met, when the ink was still wet on his doctorate, that she'd given up clinical psychology for the more worthwhile pursuit of private psychotherapy. Young and arrogant, he'd mistakenly assumed she saw him as competition, this grand, glamorous octogenarian who'd been in the profession longer than Sean had been alive. He'd later upgraded that delusion, recognising himself as an instrument of patriarchy, yet she took no issue with Josh. In fact, she seemed to like Josh, which was rare enough in itself, so maybe there was some classism involved. Zara and Josh were, after all, both born middle-class, whereas Sean, regardless of his qualifications and more than decent salary, would always be working class.

Whatever the cause—and it could come down to a basic clash of personality—there was something honest about his and Zara's mutual loathing. Sure, she rubbed him completely the wrong way, but he still had tremendous respect for her, and if nothing else, she respected his position as course leader. It was proving a good recipe for effective working too, as they were done within the hour, finalising the teaching, learning and assessment for the entire year. It put Sean well ahead of schedule, and he was glad. Now he'd set his mind to it, he couldn't wait to buy a car—his first since he'd given up driving in favour of drinking—and he booked a taxi as soon as Zara left his office. After the cabbie's spiel that morning, he'd prepared for a long wait and was pleasantly surprised when it arrived ten minutes later, even if Murphy's law had delivered the same driver, who was in no better a mood than he'd been first thing.

"Blimey, that was a short day."

"Aye. All those weeks' holiday too." Sean had heard all the teaching-related jabs before. When he was younger and angrier, he'd argued back—in defence of his faculty colleagues, as he was an education interloper—but the sentiment was endemic and stubborn as hell to change.

"Where to?"

"Do you know the car dealership on the high street?"

"The one with all the flash motors out front?"

"I wish."

"The other one, then." The cabbie negotiated his way around the myriad tiny hatchbacks owned by staff and students alike and headed for the town centre. "What d'you fancy? An SUV?"

"Can you imagine me trying to find a spot for one of them on campus?" Sean leaned to the side and squinted at the insignia on the steering wheel. "This seems a decent car."

"Yeah, it's not bad." Inspired by Sean's observation, the cabbie launched into another monologue, arguing with himself over the pros and cons of every possible variation in fuel type, engine size, transmission, interior trim and paint finish. It was tedious but relevant, so Sean paid attention. By the time they reached the dealership, he'd been talked out of a small hatchback. Apart from that, all bets were on.

With another handsome tip, he bade the man farewell and spent a moment eyeing the lines of shiny cars glinting on the forecourt, too many to choose from.

"Good morning, sir." A head popped up amid the sea of cars, soon after followed by the rest of a young man in a sharp grey suit, white shirt and burgundy tie. He stopped about a yard from Sean and tilted his head so he was looking side on. "Doctor Tierney! Hello!"

"Hello," Sean replied, trying and failing to place the salesman anywhere other than there and then.

"Carter O'Reilly. You won't remember me, but you gave a lecture to my BSc Psych cohort five years ago."

"You've a good memory."

"It was a good lecture."

"Thanks. I'm glad you think so." Sean took out the piece of paper from the nursery nurse and unfolded it. "You come highly recommended yourself."

Carter looked at the paper and laughed. "Red crayon. Gotta be my Katie. So how can I help you this morning, Doctor Tierney?"

"It's Sean, and I'm after a car."

"OK. Do you have any particular make or type in mind?"

"Maybe a mid-size hatchback or saloon."

"A family car?"

"Big enough for me and my son. And I need it today, so."

"We've got a few that've already been serviced and valeted. Depending on finance, they're drive-aways."

"I'm paying cash," Sean said.

"Do you want some time to browse?"

"That'd be grand, thanks."

"I'll be in the sales office." Carter retreated to the building at the back of the lot and left Sean to peruse at his leisure. There were around a dozen vehicles with 'Drive me away today' stickers, on the surface all in good shape and within Sean's budget. He wasn't flush by any means, and buying a car would wipe out a few years' savings, but better that than getting a loan. Before he'd gone to uni—back when he still lived in Derry—his old boss had been beaten and left for dead by his creditors, and it had given Sean a lifelong aversion to being in debt.

The only time he'd borrowed money was to finance his postgraduate studies, and they were paid off before his thirtieth birthday, thanks to Genie. He'd planned on making further sperm donations of the anonymous variety and had even passed the screening with a fertility clinic, but by then he'd realised he was more than a heavy drinker, so he'd ignored the clinic's phone calls and letters, and eventually they'd stopped trying to contact him. From time to time, he wondered if they'd taken him off the bank, as they should have done, or if they'd sold off his sample donation and he had a whole clutch of children he knew nothing about.

I might need one of these people carriers if they did. Sean walked around the silver seven-seater, admiring its smart leather interior before he moved on to the next car—the 'runaround' he'd said he'd get, and it was cheap, but he had other considerations now. Road presence, boot space, insurance premiums and Carter's commission. It was also the same model as Josh's, which was a recommendation in itself, but Sean wasn't persuaded.

The next car was the same as Sophie's, and again, it was a decent car at a good price, but they'd look like they were going for *his 'n' hers,* which shouldn't have mattered and wouldn't have done so now, except that thinking about the fertility clinic always reminded him that he'd misled Sophie, implying Phee was the result of one of many sperm donations and downplaying how important his and Genie's relationship was to him. He'd lied to Genie too, and perhaps it was taking the coward's route by withdrawing into his professional persona so he could justify keeping Phee's confidence, but he had no right to breach it. Not for the sake of self-preservation. As someone who was always telling folks to be honest, the hypocrisy was tasting particularly bitter on his tongue.

Sean reached the end of the forecourt and turned, looking back along the line of cars, none of them grabbing his attention, although a McLaren F1 would have struggled to penetrate the mental quagmire this morning. If he made an arbitrary choice, he'd be stuck with the consequences for at least a couple of years, so…

"Hello, Carter? I could do with your expertise out here."

"Sure!" Carter pretty much leapt over his desk and led the way back outside. "What would you like to know? Engine specs? Service history? MPG?"

"Which one would you buy?"

"Oh! Erm, well…I don't actually drive, but for you…we might have the perfect match." He strode past Sean and stood beside one of the cars, gesticulating proudly as he eschewed its technical specifications. "Two-litre turbo diesel eco engine, only twenty thousand on the clock, eighteen-inch gun-metal alloys—"

"Does it go?" Sean asked.

"Like shit off a shovel."

"That'll do me."

"Wouldn't you like to take it for a test drive first?"

"I trust you."

"You do?"

"Is there a reason I shouldn't?"

"Well…no, but you don't know me."

"Are you not wanting to sell me the car, Carter?"

"No. I mean, yeah."

Sean laughed. "Sorry. I've thrown you for a loop, haven't I? We'll do it your way—just tell me what you need me to do, then I'll buy the car and get out of your hair. How's that?"

"Great!" Carter nodded, much happier now they were back on the usual track. He snagged the keys from the office, and they took the car out for a short test drive. Sean played along, commenting on the handling, asking questions about the controls, insurance group, road tax and so on as they occurred to him, then promptly forgetting the answers.

"You can change your mind," Carter said as they turned back onto the high street and Sean eased the car to a stop outside the dealership.

"I'm happy to go ahead with my purchase."

"If you're sure."

"Would you just let me buy the feckin' car?"

For a moment, Carter stared at Sean in alarm, but then Sean winked and added, "You're in charge here, all right?"

"Well, I'm not. He is." Carter nodded to indicate the man casually moving across the forecourt, surreptitiously watching and swiping a chamois over the cars' bonnets as he passed them by. His suit and shoes looked very expensive.

"You're obviously putting that psychology degree to good use."

"How d'you mean?"

"You're earning your boss plenty of money by the looks of it."

"Oh!" Carter smiled and opened the passenger door. "Yeah, I suppose. I only got a third class." He got out and waited while Sean did likewise.

"It's still an honours degree."

"True." Carter held back a little longer, waiting for his boss to return inside. "I'll have a word with him, see what we can do for cash."

"No chance, matey. I'll pay the asking price."

"But—"

"But nothing. That's your commission, so it is." Sean took a chance and slung his arm around young Carter's shoulders. "I've got the money. If I don't give it to you, I'll only waste it on my pension. But if your Katie should ask, I'll tell her you were very accommodating."

Twenty minutes later, Sean walked off the forecourt, keys in hand, and slid into the driver's seat of his new-to-him car. It wasn't flash like Dan's convertible, or classic like Andy's Mustang. Nor was it a runaround hatchback like Josh's or Soph's. It was a bit on the heavy side and maybe a little unwieldy, but with its dark-green metallic finish and chrome trim, it had a distinguished look about it. Grinning to himself, Sean started the engine and set the radio to a local station. Carter's third-class psychology degree might not look much on paper, but the lad deserved a PhD for the way he applied self-extension theory to peddling his wares, and he'd read Sean like a pro.

25: Reflections

IT WAS AS well Sean hadn't opted for a basic runaround. The car park outside Wharton Hall was like something from a TV programme on the lifestyles of the rich and famous. Reverse-parking his fair-to-middling hatchback in a space at the end of a row of top-of-the-range Porsches, BMWs and Mercedes, along with a couple of Bentleys and a Rolls Royce, he turned off the ignition and unclipped Dylan's car seat. Dylan continued staring out of the passenger window at the vista of posh cars dappled orange by the low, early evening sun, the lush greenery and the vast mansion beyond.

"Are you ready, little man?"

"Dis?" Dylan pointed.

"A very big house. Want to go see?"

Receiving a nod of agreement, Sean walked around to Dylan's side of the car and lifted him out, letting Dylan grip his finger and walk, as was his preference, and he was enthralled.

"Dis?"

"Red roses."

"Fowas?"

"That's right."

"Dis?"

"Oak tree."

"Dis?"

"Squirrels."

Dylan broke free; Sean moved swiftly and caught his hand.

"We'll look at the squirrels later. Come on."

"Dis?"

"Doorbell." It was a loud one, too, and made Dylan jump.

The second they stepped inside and he spotted other people, he grabbed at Sean's trousers, asking to be carried. Sean obliged. It made it easier to navigate the enormous hallways, although it was nothing like the musty old stately home he'd been expecting. The walls were smooth and pale blue, the furniture was Swedish functional, and the signage was excellent. Within minutes, they reached the restaurant, and the maître d' accompanied them to a table for four in the centre of the room where Genie and Phee were already seated. Dylan shouted and pointed at Phee, who was facing them; thankfully, Genie was mid sip of wine or they'd have already given the game away.

The moment she saw Sean, Genie was on her feet and smiling broadly, sending Sean's heart into a wild flutter.

They hugged and kissed cheeks. "I'm so happy to see you!" she gushed.

"Likewise." Sean fended off the brief glimmer of regret that they'd left it so long and put on his poker face. "Young Phee! My goodness, look at you! How are ye?"

"Hello, Sean." She rose from her chair as he approached and they briefly hugged. "I'm well, thanks. Hello, Dylan."

While she wasn't entirely a stranger to him, it would take more than one meeting for him to get past his shyness, so for the time being, they were back on safe ground.

A member of the restaurant staff came over, took drinks orders—sparkling apple juice for both father and son—and switched one of the chairs for a high chair. Sean settled Dylan first and then sat and picked up the menu.

"My treat," Genie said quickly before he balked at the lack of prices—a sure sign that eating here cost anything between a week's and a month's pay, depending on how much one earned, not that any of the other patrons would be counting the pennies.

They were mostly dressed on the smart side of casual athletic, and it was all designer gear. Except for their table. Sean subtly took in Genie's and Phee's ordinary attire over the top of his menu. He didn't want to fight Genie over the bill, but he refused to let her pay if she was short.

"Is anything tickling your taste buds?" Genie asked.

"Maybe." He couldn't be sure it was her knee, but someone's definitely bumped his. "No kids' meals." He studied Dylan. "Fish or chicken, little man?"

"Fishhhh!"

"A sophisticated palate!" Genie remarked.

"Aye. He likes his food, don't you? Fishcake and peas is one of his favourites."

"Fishcake and…" Frowning, Genie scanned the menu and found the corresponding dish. "Ah! Fishcake and peas." Or, in fact, *'river-caught salmon cake, served with lemon-infused organic petits pois and jasmine rice'*.

"My entire life is a lie," Phee lamented.

Genie and Sean laughed and shared a knowing look. The Rowans would never be commoners, but Genie's choice to become pregnant and raise her child alone had guaranteed Phee a more grounded upbringing than her peers.

Sean didn't bother discussing starters with Dylan. He'd end up wearing most of the soup and treat the paté like Play-Doh, which left mixed melon as the only option. So, when the waiter returned, Sean ordered soup and rosemary-grilled chicken with sweet potato and asparagus for himself and melon and salmon cake for Dylan. Phee opted for the same as Sean, Genie for a mixed melon starter and a truffle risotto main course. The waiter left them alone again, giving Sean a chance to take a good look around. Other than the very high ceiling, he could have been in a restaurant anywhere in England. Bare French windows looked out onto a covered terrace where a few souls were braving the chilly spring evening in favour of dining al fresco.

The fresh air must have given them all an appetite, as their starters arrived and they descended on them like peasants at a banquet, which Sean supposed he and Dylan were. The food was tasty, although on the 'nouvelle cuisine' side, presentation-wise. Five silent minutes later, all four sat with empty plates or dishes before them.

"Excuse me," Phee said and pushed away from the table. Sean watched her scurry across the room and disappear through a door he guessed led to the Ladies'.

"Morning sickness," Genie explained, which Sean had already figured for himself.

"She's suffering, is she?"

"She is. Alas, she is her mother's daughter."

Sean couldn't comment on that. His memory of Genie's pregnancy was sketchy, and guilt reared its head for a second, but he reminded himself he wasn't at fault. For one thing, she'd been living in London by then, while he was part way through his PhD at Bristol. For another, he was tanked up most of the time. "How is she otherwise?"

Genie shrugged. "She doesn't talk to me anymore. I don't even know if there's a boyfriend or it was a one-night thing. She showed me a picture of the ultrasound and said she wanted to talk but not yet. I'm worried she's running out of time."

"An ultrasound's done at twelve weeks, isn't it?"

"Yes, and—"

"She's coming back," Sean interrupted.

Genie nodded her understanding and muttered, "Incidentally, I told her we'd spoken on Friday but not what about."

"Gotcha."

Fortunately, the waiter arrived at the same time as Phee, diverting her attention from them to the clearing of the table.

"So how are you enjoying your stay?" Sean asked, addressing both Genie and Phee but lingering on the latter, who was ghostly pale and looked ready to fall fast asleep in her dinner.

"It's OK," she said. "You do know we own this place, right?"

"You what now?"

Genie waved her hand. "*We* don't own it. My father does."

"Well, I never! Didn't Jessie used to come here?"

"She did," Genie confirmed, her expression turning dour. "With Andy."

"Ah."

"I liked Andy," Phee said. She was watching Dylan tap his spoon on the table so didn't notice her mother's dismay.

"You only met him once, darling."

"So? He looked after Jess when she was dying. He can't be that bad."

Dylan's spoon-tapping became louder.

"Yes, well, he didn't do it on his own, but *of course* he gets all the credit because he's a man."

"Du-du-du-du-du," Dylan sang along with his percussion solo, and not quietly. Several people at nearby tables muttered and cast disdainful glances their way.

"So, young Phee," Sean said, disarming his son and hoping to nip off the conversation, "how does it feel to have a little brother?"

She homed in on Sean with narrowed eyes. "I know what you're doing."

"I'm sure you do."

"Think I'll go and powder my nose," Genie said and departed faster than Phee had.

"You haven't told her," Sean accused.

"No."

"Did you talk to Paul?"

"No."

"Phee—"

"Don't lecture me."

"I'm not going to, I promise. But help me understand."

Phee lowered her head. "I feel awful. She's been amazing, so...patient and supportive. She's not just my mum. She's my best friend."

"And you slept with her boyfriend," Sean said, finally catching on to the dynamic he hadn't recognised before because he'd been stuck on the idea of Paul being a pervert. He was keeping that judgement in reserve, however. "Are you having doubts about seeing it through?"

"Keeping the baby?" Phee asked, then nodded, answering her own question.

"All right. So maybe you could take Paul out of the equation for now, just talk to your mum about the rest of it."

"She'll expect me to have an abortion."

"No. She'll expect you to do what's best for you."

Dylan reached for Phee's spoon, making a grabby-hand motion. Phee smiled and gave it to him. "I like it," she said. "Having a little brother."

"I'm glad."

"You and Sophie are such good parents."

"Thanks, although it's mostly Soph. Your mum's right, you know, about how men get extra credit for what women do all the time."

"I get that, but what's her problem with Andy?"

"Not my place to say. So will you talk to her?"

"Yes, when we go home. We're having a really good time here, and I don't want to ruin it, not if it's…" Phee's face crumpled.

"The last time you'll have fun together?" Sean said. Phee nodded and blinked hard, fighting back the tears. Sean leaned over and squeezed her hand. "It won't be, lovely. Don't you worry."

It seemed Genie had meant it about going to powder her nose, as she returned with her face freshly made up, and it was more rather than less obvious that she'd been crying. Realising it was on him to salvage the evening, Sean shifted modes slightly, directing their interactions as he would a family therapy session. If Genie and Phee were aware of what he was doing, they didn't let on, and gradually, the tension between them eased.

There were a few hairy moments, particularly when the conversation moved on to Sophie, and Phee asked if Sean had borrowed Sophie's car to come to Wharton Hall. Genie didn't seem to notice. She was distracted and restless and not at all herself but was startled out of her malady when Dylan pointed at the window and shouted, "Skrill!"

All three turned to look.

"You're very clever, Dylan," Phee praised.

"We saw lots of squirrels earlier, didn't we?" Sean said.

Dylan made grabby-hands again. "Get it."

"Would it be all right to take him outside?" Phee asked.

"Sure!"

"Come on, Dylan. Shall we go and see the squirrels?"

Dylan wriggled against his high chair straps, which Phee duly unfastened and lifted him clear. He gripped her fingers, and together, they departed.

"She's good with him," Genie said, watching them through the French windows.

"Aye, she is."

"I don't want her to have this baby, Sean."

"I know."

Phee picked up Dylan, and they descended the terrace steps, out of sight.

"It's so peaceful here," Genie said.

"It is."

"Easy to ignore the real world, put off difficult decisions... forget our house is haunted."

Sean beckoned to a passing waiter. "Could we have some coffee, please?"

The waiter nodded and departed.

"It's no bad thing you're taking a wee break from it all," Sean said.

"I suppose not." Genie didn't sound convinced. "I wonder how Xander is getting on."

"Have you spoken to him?"

"Not since this afternoon. Rather, I spoke to his assistant this afternoon. Xander doesn't do phones."

"How is he these days?"

"Same as ever. Less hair."

"He must be bald by now."

Genie laughed. "Almost!"

"I had a very interesting conversation with him once." The day in question expanded like magic before his mind's eye, the details filling out as the waiter deposited their coffees on the table.

Genie stirred cream into hers, barely taking her eyes off Sean, keen to hear the story, or perhaps there was more. She took a sip, hummed in pleasure, and set down the cup, still holding him in her glorious gaze. "You were saying?"

Sean added a dash of cream to his coffee as he continued. "We'd been invigilating an exam. Level one law, it was, or history maybe. Whatever, Xander was obligated to be there—they were sticklers for making sure we fulfilled our postgrad duties— and I needed the money, so I took on anything they'd give me, then we went to the SU afterwards. God knows what he was drinking, but once he started, he didn't shut up. He told me about the ghosts like it was a normal thing to admit that he saw them and they were as real to me as to him. His dad was sick. Dying, actually. Congestive heart failure. And Xander couldn't wait for it to happen. I mean, I didn't get on with my old fella, but I never wished him dead."

"Is your dad still alive?"

"No. He passed a few months back. Heart failure, would you believe? It's common in men of their generation. Bit of a leveller too. Nobody knew, did they? The dangers of smoking, drinking too much, all that saturated fat."

"Quite," Genie said, both of them glancing ruefully at the jug of cream they'd partaken of and then laughing. "My grandmother had heart disease, although that wasn't what killed her in the end. She overdosed on tranquillisers."

"I remember you telling me."

"I don't think she took her own life, but we'll never know. I miss her." Genie's gaze became distant for a moment, then she sighed and shrugged. "She had a good innings, as they say. As did Xander's father. We always thought him cruel, the way he kept his wife and son at arm's length, but perhaps he was wired the same way as Xander."

"There is a genetic component to autism, so it's possible."

"And I can see why Xander would've been glad to be rid of him. He could be a tyrant."

"Ah, well, I didn't get to the point."

"Because you ramble," Genie teased.

"True enough. What I was going to say was Xander couldn't wait to prove to his dad that he really did see ghosts."

"He thought he'd see his dad after he died."

"Yeah. I haven't spoken to him since, so I don't know if he ever did."

"He certainly hasn't mentioned it to me, and we've talked a lot of late. Have you ever seen a ghost, Sean?"

"No."

"Do you believe they're real?"

"I'm open to the possibility. How could I not be after what happened in our halls?"

"Why? What happened in your halls?"

"So I don't get accused of rambling again…" Sean paused to admire Genie's playful pout and felt a stir of interest down below. Fat lot of use it was tonight, with children present. He pushed on. "Things we couldn't explain, which was why Josh and I moved out. We were both special cases and could've stayed in halls for the duration, but not after what we witnessed."

"Poltergeist activity."

"For want of a better description. It was nothing too terrible or dramatic, but it doesn't need to be. Of course, Joshy was having none of it, then or now. We're having a similar situation with the building for our business, and he's convinced the previous owner's son—still alive, I should add—is trying to scare him into selling it back to him."

"What do *you* think?"

"I think Josh is worried he's taken on too much. That or our girl Jessie isn't yet at rest."

Hearing those words, Genie became rigid.

"What?" Sean asked.

"Does 'Alouette' mean anything to you?"

Sean thought about it, but nothing came to mind. "No. Why?"

"It was the only thing Jess could play on the piano. After we moved into my grandmother's house, she visited a couple of times and got absolutely hammered. She was straight on the piano, insisting we sang it in rounds." Despite how rattled she was, Genie managed a small smile. "It was a terrible racket, but it was fun. The day before I phoned you, I heard it, that song, the way she'd played it. It was so real, Sean."

"Is that why you invited me? You were after a rational explanation?"

"No. I wanted the company of someone who loved her as much as I did."

"Then you made the right call." He took Genie's hand and kissed her knuckles. "I need to head home soon. I'm sorry."

"Me too," she said, but they didn't get to dwell in the moment for long, as the intrepid squirrel hunters returned, fresh-faced and conspiratorial.

"Tell your dad what we saw, Dylan."

"Skrill!"

"And…" Phee prompted.

"Fock!"

Sean flinched, as did several of the remaining patrons, nosey so-and-sos that they were. "A what?"

"A fox. I'd love to take Dylan exploring in the morning. Is that OK?"

"It'd be grand, but I'm working tomorrow."

"Oh." Phee sagged into her seat with Dylan still in her arms.

Sean cursed himself for not making a clean break from the hospital, and Doctor Morris for making it impossible for him to do so.

***

One appointment, the rest no-shows. It was hardly worth getting out of bed for. Still, no hanging around for taxis took out some of the sting, and the rest of the day was Sean's own. Seeing Genie had settled his craving for drink somewhat, even if it had left space for a different kind of craving and a whole lot of wondering *what if…* that meant he got hardly any work done at all.

Wednesday morning, still delighting in the freedom of having his own transport, Sean dropped Dylan at Unitots and drove to the hospice, unprepared for the force of the flashback that hit him as he stopped the car in the same spot as the last time he'd driven there, almost two years ago.

"You're going to insist on a wheelchair, aren't you?"

"Not at all, lovely. You're a big girl. I'm sure if you need a chair, you'll ask for one."

She'd sneered at him, but he'd held fast. She'd neither wanted nor needed his sympathy.

"Shall we?" he'd asked.

She hadn't answered, and he hadn't wanted to rush her, so he'd let her take in the view. It was beautiful, the hospice, smaller but in many respects similar to Wharton Hall: a Victorian mansion set back from the road and accessible via a winding, private avenue beneath a canopy of blossom in spring, spectacular foliage in summer, horse-chestnut- and acorn-laden boughs in autumn and a raw, perfect starkness in winter. It had been summer when they'd come here, when the landscaped grounds were full of life and colour that distracted from the rising damp, missing roof tiles and crack-riddled walls. There lay the difference between the Rowans' former stately home turned lucrative health spa and this desperately underfunded sanctuary for those nearing the end of their lives.

"It must cost a lot to keep this place ticking over," she'd said.

"Yeah, it does. They're always fundraising."

Less so now than then.

"I suppose they receive quite a bit from legacies."

"Indeed they do."

Like a well-loved band T-shirt, the funds Jess bequeathed had faded with each laundering, leaving her beneficiaries in the clear, but her encore had been an extravagant display of cunning, not kindness. Sean had never doubted that. Like all those who had held her dear, Jess had betrayed and abandoned him, yet he had believed he was the exception, protected by distance and his hard-earned career in palliative care.

All those years of field research, instructing others, telling people how to grieve. His expertise had turned him into a fool. He hadn't accepted the truth of who Jess was; he wasn't moving forward. Granted, he'd never experienced the burning jealousy Genie felt towards Andy, nor Josh's overwhelming sense of failure for not seeing through Jess's lies, but Sean's balls were still in Jess's hands. The state his sex drive was in, that might as well have been literal.

Seeing Genie had dislodged something, wedged open a door to a past he'd dared not revisit. Daydreams of a life they never had, not the conventional fairy-tale wedded bliss but something a little more free-love, bohemian, where they were their own people yet part of a whole. That was the open relationship he craved, not just the one glorious week they'd lived and loved together; for always. If he hadn't been blind drunk for the entirety of his twenties, been any kind of catch at all, he'd have told Genie and Jess how he felt.

Could they have made it work? He didn't know, and now he never would.

26: Blueprints

Jeffries and Associates
Present Day
Friday, 26th April

"G OOD EVENING, GENTS." Dan pulled the front door wide open. "We're in my office—you haven't seen the house yet, have you?"

"No," Josh replied—too quickly, judging by Sean's frown.

"Not yet," Sean said. "It's rather grand, isn't it?"

"Bloody enormous, you mean?" Dan moved off. "That's not me bragging, by the way. Adele had the final say. You want the tour or shall we get straight down to business?"

Sean shrugged and deferred to Josh.

"Let's have the tour," Josh said, following Dan into the hall. No need to act lost: Josh had parked in the garage last time, and it was a very different space coming at it from the opposite direction.

"Living room." Dan indicated a door on the right and opened it with a flourish. Josh and Sean moved forward only as much as was necessary to see inside.

"Has Adele gone out for the evening?" Josh eyed the vast room, empty but for the two large black sofas and nest of tables that looked like doll's house furniture in comparison.

"She's taken Shu to ballet class. They're usually back around half seven, and Robbie's asleep, so we should get an hour without interruption."

Josh nodded and vented a relieved sigh. So far, it seemed Adele had done as he'd asked and not breathed a word to anyone about the Ouija board and other stuff she'd stowed for him, but he wasn't quite on top of his feelings, and Adele would have reacted had she been there. Then Sean would have noticed her reaction and plied her for information, not that it would take much for Adele to crack and spill everything, including Josh's phone call from Simon.

For the time being, the super-sized living room had Sean's full attention. "That TV's not far off the size of the front wall of my house."

Dan laughed. "Yeah, it's the biggest I could find or it'd be like sitting in the gods at the footy."

"Wouldn't it just?" Sean murmured, turning a little greener than the regular Irish.

"And the dining room..." Dan walked them through the living room to a set of double doors, beyond which was a slightly smaller space containing an oval table about the same size as the one in Campion Trust's boardroom, above it a chandelier that consisted of a wave formation of around sixty crystal balls suspended on barely visible cables from an oval of black glass.

"I love that." Josh hadn't seen the dining room on his previous visit, which was a shame. The seeming randomness of the light fitting's design compensated for the mind-bending symmetry in the adjacent living room.

"Not bad, is it? If you ever fancy getting one—or something similar, it's a one-off—let me know. We deliver for the designers, and they'd give you a hefty discount."

"I'll keep it in mind," Josh said. The drop from ceiling to tabletop in Dan and Adele's dining room was greater than from ceiling to floor in their modest terrace house—they'd have crystal balls dangling in their gravy.

Dan led them past the table and through another door, into the kitchen. As Josh had already seen, it was yet another enormous space with a show-home quality to it, and now he'd also seen the dining room, he noticed the oval theme was common across both spaces. The kitchen was in its default bright white tabula rasa state, with a splash of cool blue around the centre island.

"Is that done with LEDs?" Josh asked as if he didn't know.

"Smart LEDs, yep. Perfect if your *better* half insists on changing the décor every five minutes."

"*Or...*you need to switch the ambience of a space to suit the activity within it," Josh said, ignoring Dan's snipe at Adele for once because it suited his purpose. "Could we fit those in the surgery?"

"Yeah, no problem. A small recess around the top and bottom of the walls, paint everything white, and the job's a good'n."

"Excellent! What do you think, Sean?"

Sean nodded noncommittally. "Yours is a pet-free home, I take it?" he asked Dan.

"So far. Shu's going through the 'Can we get a puppy?' phase."

"Are you considering it?"

Dan shook his head. "We've got the space—Delta five three six, lights, garden one..."

Josh and Sean's attention snapped to the window as the evening twilight instantly became artificial daylight, illuminating the expansive garden behind the house.

Dan continued, "We're not animal lovers. Adele didn't have pets as a kid. I've only ever had fish, and she relegated them to the backyard."

Josh scanned the landscaping until he located the pond—or was that a swimming pool? No. There'd have been more bragging. Still, it was big enough for adults to swim in, never mind koi carp.

"So a kitten's out of the question," Sean said.

"There's a wire-mesh guard over the pond. It stops kids and heron. I'm guessing it'd stop cats too."

"For now." Sean waggled his thumbs. "We're all doomed when they get these."

Briefly, Dan looked alarmed but then smiled and said, "It might be worth thinking about if she keeps pestering. Shall we move on?" He already had. "You don't want to see upstairs, do you?"

Seeing as he'd already been up there, Josh gestured to Sean, who shrugged and said, "Seen one bedroom, seen 'em all."

"You're not wrong. We're down here." Dan disappeared around a corner. Having lost Adele in a matter of seconds the last time, Josh wasn't taking any chances and put on a bit of a sprint.

"Aye, aye, what's the hurry?" Sean muttered but kept up just the same as they followed Dan down a staircase to the basement.

"My office," Dan said, and what an office it was.

"Wow!" Josh came to a standstill, forgetting anyone was behind him until Sean shoved him out of the way.

"Good, eh?" Dan said.

Josh drifted forward, taking it all in. Against the wall to his right was a desk—gargantuan, of course—with a plush, high-backed swivel chair neatly tucked under one end, at the other end a fancy electronic gaming chair partly reclined and facing the wrong way. The desk's midsection was taken up by a computer with two monitors and gadgets galore, most connected to a spaghetti heap of charging cables. Two filing cabinets stood next to the desk, and next to those were four easy chairs grouped around a low, circular table.

The left side of the room was mostly occupied by some kind of weightlifting contraption with a seat and straps all over the place. At least, Josh assumed it was for weightlifting, given the Jeffries brothers' penchant for pumping iron. His gaze drifted back to the gadgets on and around the desk, no idea what most of them did, and he was desperate to ask, but that wasn't why they were here. He realised he hadn't answered Dan's question and quickly said, "Yes. Very good."

Dan thumbed at a closed door in the back wall. "Toilet, if you need it, although, I think... Bro?"

"Yeah?" came the response from the other side of the door.

"You'd best not be having a crap."

The toilet flushed. Thirty seconds later, the door opened on Andy zipping his jeans. "I wasn't. Oh, alright? Didn't know you were here." He extended his hand to Josh and then Sean to be shaken, which was uncharacteristically formal for Andy, and not pleasant. Andy's hands were still wet, hopefully from washing them. Josh saw the moment the same thought occurred to Sean and bit the inside of his cheek so he didn't laugh.

"Coffee?" Dan asked, already positioning a cup under the spout of a machine that looked a lot like the one Josh had at home, except newer, shinier...*bigger.*

"Yes, please." He didn't bother saying which kind. Dan would know, just as he knew what everyone drank on quiz night. He could even accurately gauge who was 'staying off the beer' for a night and substituted with their non-alcoholic beverage of choice. To most people, it was part of Dan's charm, but Josh found it infuriating, especially *that* coffee machine because Dan couldn't help himself; he always had to go one better.

"Here you go." He handed Josh a cup.

"Thanks." He took a sip, half-hoping it would be lousy, but it tasted as good as the cappuccinos from the machine at home.

Once everyone had a drink in their hand and had found somewhere to sit—the easy chairs were comfortable if not a little on the low side—Dan picked up one of the gadgets from his desk and stuck it on top of a filing cabinet, projecting a blurry square onto the wall opposite. He twiddled with the focus, and from the blur a blueprint emerged. Josh had to squint to make it out, given it was a scan of a scarred carbon-copy, but he soon established it matched the layout of his building.

"Andy," Dan prompted and exchanged places with his brother.

"Right...where's that pointer?" He rooted around the desk until he found it. "First-storey floor plan. The architect has a better copy—we figured she needed it more than we did."

She? Josh almost repeated it aloud, surprised that Jeffries and Associates were working with a female architect. Almost all of their 'associates' were male.

"These—" Andy shone the laser at the projection, moving the red dot along the bolder lines "—are structural walls. This is the west wall of the current consultation room, and these are the kitchen, toilet and storeroom."

It took Josh a few seconds to orientate himself: the wall in question divided his former waiting room from his consultation room, the two largest spaces. "Does that mean those walls have to stay?"

Andy shook his head. "We'll stick an RSJ in, but the kitchen wall's staying. You wanted three consultation rooms, correct?"

"Yes," Josh confirmed.

Andy clicked to the next slide, this time displaying a clean, modern architectural plan. "I'll show you the 3D in a sec, so you get a better idea of how it'll look. That wall I mentioned currently cuts across here." He moved the red dot up through the blank middle of the plan then along a thick black line. "This is the new wall, two metres to the west of the wall that's coming out, which'll leave you a little reception area and a wide corridor past consultation rooms one, two, three..." He traced each of the three spaces demarcated. "The larger, accessible wet room will go here—" currently the storeroom "—and the staircase to the loft will be here—" above the stairs from street level to the first floor. "The kitchen wall is staying, but we need to rebuild it. It's shifting."

"Shifting as in subsidence?" There'd been no mention of it in the surveyor's report when Josh bought the building.

"Nah. Just changes in temperature and humidity. I only noticed because the door wouldn't shut. Too much play on—"

"Wait," Josh interrupted. "Do you mean the toilet door?"

"The storeroom. You've had problems with the toilet door not shutting?"

"In a manner of speaking." More like flinging itself wide open.

"They're both in the same area, and the dentist's office is in that corner."

"Tech," Dan said as if it explained everything.

"Tech?" Josh queried.

"Computers give off a fair bit of heat."

"Oh! I see." Josh nodded, internally crying *Eureka!* Modern machines ran much cooler than the old ones, but it was as good a rational explanation as any for the self-propelled doors—it may even explain the flying toilet roll—so Josh had no desire to test Andy and Dan's theory, which had to be a first.

"Any questions?" Andy asked.

Josh shook his head but caught a glimpse of his companion's thoughtful pose. "Sean?"

"Nothing from me."

"Right, then. On to the 3D..." Andy switched the display. "So, this is the view from—"

"Hold up, bro," Dan stopped him. "Josh, did you have something to say?"

"No, but Sean does."

Sean's eyebrows rose. "I don't."

Josh tried to stare him into submission, but Sean kept up the pretence of being fully engaged with the presentation despite it currently consisting of the external view of the building dimmed out and partly obscured by a big white play button. Perhaps he really did have nothing to contribute at this stage, but Sean's reluctance to engage in critical discussion of the therapy suite had been there since the outset, and Josh was tremendously worried about it. No matter that he owned the building; it was a joint undertaking, and without Sean's input, the business plan and all this construction work could be for nought.

"Dudes?" Andy was still waiting for the go-ahead.

Josh left a further couple of seconds for Sean to break his peace before he gave up. "Sorry, Andy. Go on."

"OK. This should be a pretty familiar sight..." The play button disappeared, and the view focused on the external door, which opened. The virtual camera entered and panned upwards as if ascending the stairs to the first storey, turning left at the top into the new corridor. Door one: the first consultation room, furnished with a desk, a chair, a sofa and bookshelf, closer together but in roughly the same position as they'd been in Josh's former surgery. Door two: the second consultation room, which also had a desk, chair and sofa. The third had a sofa and two armchairs arranged around a circular coffee table. At the end of the corridor was the door to the kitchenette, which looked the same as always, to its right a small office and then another door that opened onto a narrow empty space. "Storeroom," Andy explained, panning ninety degrees to face a final door that swung open, revealing the wet room, double the size of the old toilet and fitted with rails, a changing bed and an emergency cord.

So far, it was along the lines Josh had envisaged the day he'd been stuck at the top of the loft ladder, and he had to keep reminding himself he was watching a 3D rendering because it was extraordinarily real. Indeed, it didn't properly register until the camera backed out of the wet room, retracing their virtual steps past the kitchenette, then consultation rooms three, two, one, and sent Josh's acrophobia into a tailspin. He scrunched his eyes shut.

"Where's the wall gone?"

"Ah, yeah." Andy chuckled. "That's where the lift's meant to be. There's a glitch. Hold on."

Josh cracked open one eye, ready to close it again if need be, and watched through his lashes as Andy switched to a different file and the corridor that had terminated in a sheer drop into the backyard was replaced with what had to still be his building but from an unfamiliar, external perspective.

"Rear view," Andy explained, "entering via the new gate from the alley. That's the lift shaft…" The red dot of the laser zoomed up and down the grey rectangle extending from the ground to the roof on the back left-hand end of the building. As the view angle changed, the grey rectangle morphed into a cuboid with a door in the bottom segment. The door opened, revealing a lift. The camera took them inside. Behind Josh, Dan cleared his throat.

"Another coffee?" he asked and dodged away to the machine, his back to the screen. Josh had hardly touched his first coffee.

"Yes, thanks," he said and quickly knocked it back. Once upon a time, he'd treated Dan's fear of lifts and, wickedly, was glad it had endured, a humbling flaw in the Perfect Man. On another day, Sean would have noticed Dan's ill ease, and his nosiness would have prompted a probing frown or, if he was feeling particularly empathetic, seen him following Josh's lead. Today, he was in a world of his own and carried on nursing his drink, staring through the image as the lift indicator lights signalled they were bypassing the first floor.

A moment later, the virtual lift door opened, although not the one through which they'd entered, and again the view was a novel one, for there was the loft, bright and spacious with vast skylights, smooth, plain walls and a solid floor. Josh was so excited, he took too large a gulp of his new coffee and coughed most of it back out, splattering it all over his face and down his front. Still no response from Sean, but Andy, playing the consummate professional, handed Josh a tissue and kept going, quickly pointing out various features—the control panel for the blinds, sound system and lights, all smart; the concealed storage space in the eaves; the foldaway divider should they wish to split the room in half; the stairs down to the first floor. Finally, they were back in the lift, pausing at the first floor briefly to take in the small reception area furnished with a corner sofa, oval coffee table and virtual parlour palm before continuing to ground level, out through the doors and into…

"What on earth…?"

Andy looked past Josh and Sean and nodded. "I'll hand over to my associate to take you through the next part."

Josh glimpsed a movement on the stairs and turned his head, expecting to see Dan and jumping to his feet in surprise.

"Shaunna? Lib?"

"Mr. Sandison-Morley." Fighting a grin, Shaunna shook his hand. "Doctor Tierney."

Sean responded to that all right, as in he was straight out of his chair for a hug, and Josh's hackles rose. Was this why Sean had been so quiet? Had he known Shaunna was coming? From the questions he was asking, he seemed equally surprised, although by now it was clear why Shaunna and Libby were here, and as long as Josh wasn't the only one being kept in the dark, all was well. Brilliant, in fact.

"So..." Shaunna wiped her palms on her thighs and took the laser pointer from Andy. "Before I start, you need to know this is only a proposal. It's entirely—"

"Yes," Josh interrupted.

"Rude," Libby said.

Josh grimaced. "Sorry. But it's amazing! I'm excited. Aren't you?" He nudged Sean with his elbow as Sean put his cup to his mouth, and it bashed his teeth. Josh grimaced again and folded his arms, but his legs were jiggling, so he sat on his hands. "I'll be good now. I promise."

"May we continue?" Shaunna asked. Lips pressed together like an over-eager schoolchild, Josh nodded. "All right then. So, the backyard is functional as it is. The flags are even and fairly clean. But as the lift will be the main entrance to the Daisy Foundation headquarters and there's no access from the front of the building, we're proposing some simple, low-maintenance landscaping. First of all, here's the ground plan." Shaunna nodded at Libby, who had taken over from Dan at the computer and brought up a drawing with shaded circular areas covering around two-thirds of the containing rectangle, representing the backyard, with a grey curvy stripe running diagonally from bottom right to top left.

"This is a path from the gate to the lift." Shaunna pointed at the diagonal stripe. "Here, we'd like to put some miniature fruit trees in planters." She indicated the three small circles bottom left. "And here would be the patio—" the two largest circles "—with a couple of picnic tables. This would be a small water feature—" the blue circle next to the patio "—just water bubbling over pebbles. Not a naked nymph spouting water out of her mouth."

Josh clenched his teeth and nodded tightly, quite sure Shaunna was trying to make him giggle. It would be the perfect revenge for his interruption, which he did feel bad about. He'd known he would love whatever idea she and Libby came up with. However, this was more than sprucing up what was a serviceable but fairly dull bit of land. This was an intervention, and it was working a treat. In less than two minutes, all his worries about ghosts, pranksters and Sean's distractedness had taken a back seat, and he was impatient for the construction work to get underway.

"Are you ready for the 3D version?" Libby asked.

"Oh, yes, please!" Josh said.

Libby narrowed her eyes at him. "I wasn't asking you."

Shaunna snorted. "Yes, please, Libby."

The plan disappeared from the screen, and the next thing, he was strolling along a stone-paved path, a blue-grey slate bed on either side, small leafy trees in large pots providing a screen against prying neighbours, to his right the patio, a pleasant bubbling sound coming from a blue stone urn filled with smooth, dark pebbles, apple, pear and plum trees on his left, and finally the sheltered entrance to the lift and his building.

The 3D image faded into a white screen overlaid with the Daisy Foundation's logo—a heart-shaped hug within a daisy-chain circle.

"What do you think?" Shaunna asked.

"I love it. The garden and the rebuild. It's perfect. Beyond anything I imagined. You people are just..." Quite certain he'd make a fool of himself if he went on, Josh nodded and smiled and said no more. The project had veered in an unexpected and wonderful direction, no longer entirely within his control.

He still had power of veto and was confident his say would be final should he choose to exercise it, but he could see no reason to do so. From the familiar placement of virtual furniture in his consultation room to the garden's circle motif, all of it was possible because his surgery had never been his alone. His friends had been there all the time.

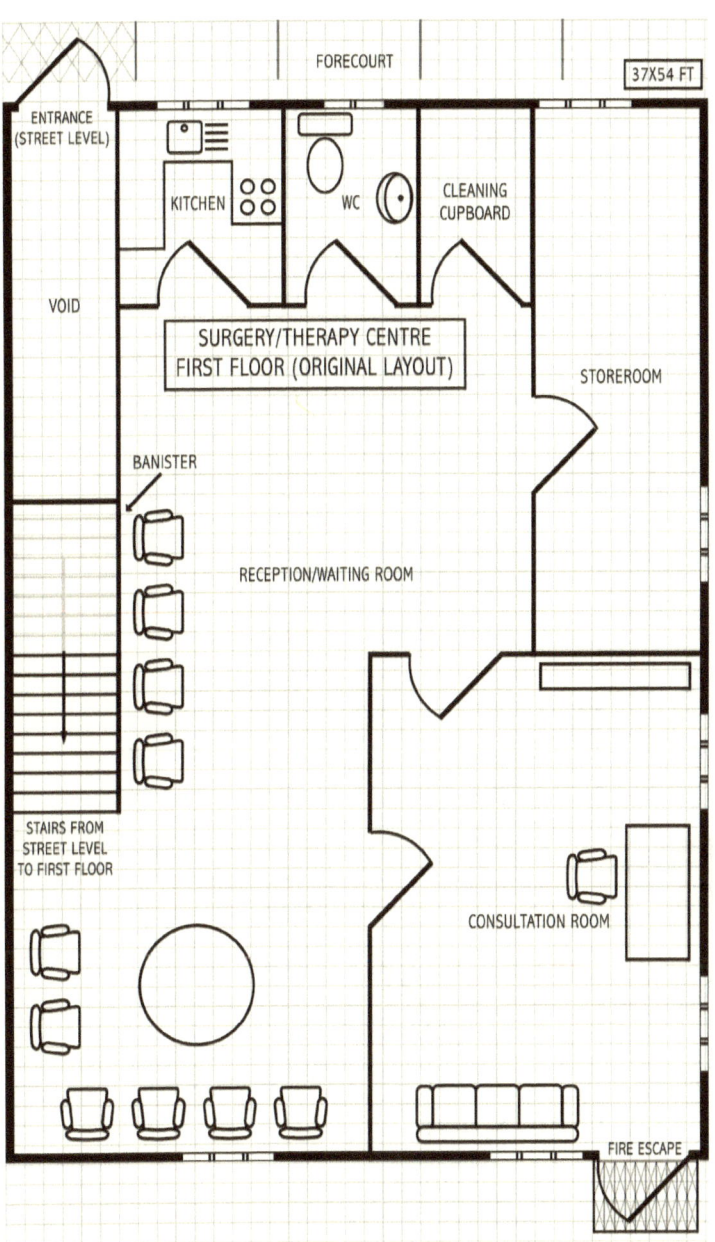

FORECOURT

37X54 FT

ENTRANCE
(STREET LEVEL)

KITCHEN

WC

CLEANING
CUPBOARD

VOID

SURGERY/THERAPY CENTRE
FIRST FLOOR (ORIGINAL LAYOUT)

STOREROOM

BANISTER

RECEPTION/WAITING ROOM

STAIRS FROM
STREET LEVEL
TO FIRST FLOOR

CONSULTATION ROOM

FIRE ESCAPE

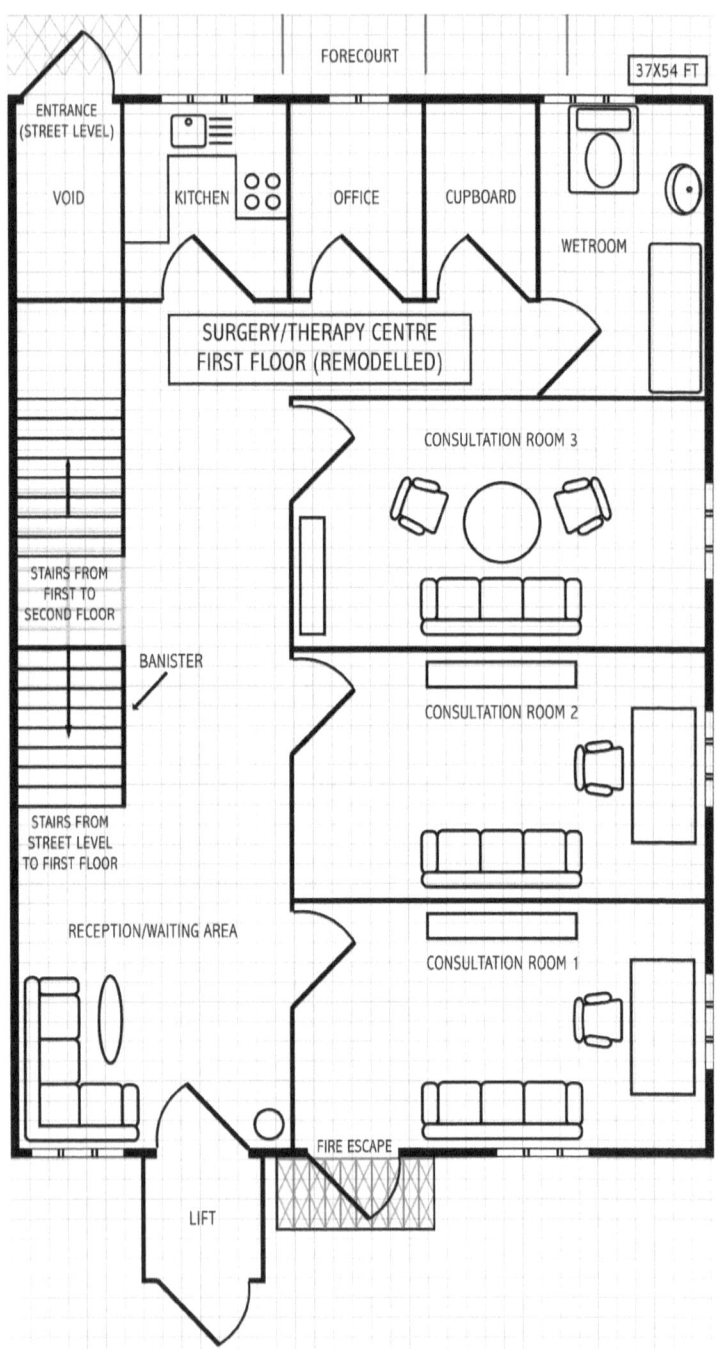

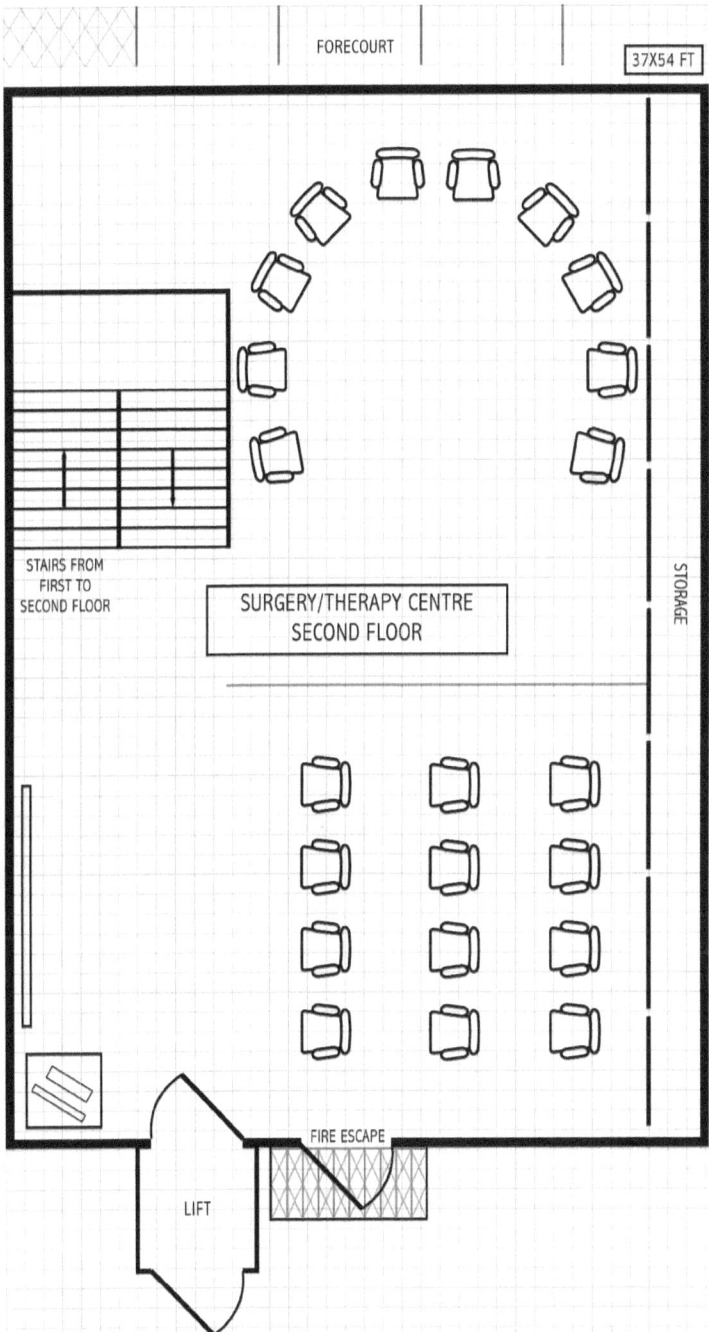

FORECOURT

37X54 FT

STAIRS FROM
FIRST TO
SECOND FLOOR

STORAGE

SURGERY/THERAPY CENTRE
SECOND FLOOR

FIRE ESCAPE

LIFT

LIFT

SURGERY/THERAPY CENTRE
GARDEN

27: By Degrees

"THAT'S…" GENIE TOOK off the headphones, not sure how to politely describe what, to her admittedly unmusical ear, was a noise akin to hammered first-year undergrads tripping over dustbins on their way back to campus. Beyond a means to avoid answering a question, she wasn't sure why Jess had forced her to endure listening to it at all. "Who's it by? Anyone I know?"

Jess made a show of pressing stop on her Discman and took back the headphones, her scowl all the darker for the heavy black eyeliner she'd recently taken to wearing.

"Oh dear God. You've become a groupie, haven't you? Throwing your underwear on the stage, tits on display…"

"Ha!" Jess yanked a drawer open and chucked in the headphones and player. "What do you take me for?" She slammed the drawer shut and stayed where she was, back turned to Genie, staring at seemingly nothing.

"So…" Genie began again, aware she wasn't being especially gracious, but it was almost Friday evening. "*Would* you be OK with—"

"I suppose," Jess interrupted airily.

"Thank you. And it is only for tonight. I don't envisage he'll even stay for breakfast." *Unlike Andy.* Genie didn't need to say it. Since he'd bought that car, Jess's…whatever he was had come down to see her once a month, every month, arriving Friday afternoon, presumably once Jess had given him the all-clear, and hanging around until Sunday lunchtime, filling their house with the stink of sex and sandalwood that lingered despite Jess opening all the windows. Then she'd go back to bed, leaving Genie to come home to a lonely ice box.

In all that time, the closest Genie and Andy had come to crossing paths had been at Sean and Josh's place. What pissed Genie off most was that Jess had known she was staying there yet expected her to keep out of the way, like she expected Genie to vacate their house without complaint one weekend in four while acting as if it were a massive inconvenience when Genie asked her to return the favour.

"I'm sorry if I upset you," Genie said.

"About?"

"The band."

"Which one?"

Genie sighed. "The one you just made me listen to."

Jess waved nonchalantly. "There's no accounting for taste."

Genie muttered lowly, "You can say that again," and instantly wished she hadn't. It was horrible when they weren't getting along.

A further moment of tense silence passed.

"Who's your date?" Jess asked.

Don't tell her, Genie's conscience implored petulantly. *She started this.* "Marcus," Genie answered, overriding it, and braced for the inevitable response.

Jess whirled around, a Maypole swirl of blonde tresses. "Marcus *the lecturer*?"

"He's a postgrad student."

"He's still one of our lecturers."

"So?"

"So you're an undergraduate."

"And the daughter of an earl," Genie pointed out. "One could argue that, in itself, negates any power imbalance."

"One could," Jess agreed. At last, she came over to the sofa and sat side on, her bent knee pressing against Genie's hip. "Want me to do your hair for you?" Shuffling closer, she gently tugged on the elastic band holding Genie's hair in a loose, short ponytail at her nape. She'd never grown it before, preferring the ease of styling a bob, but between study and partying, she hadn't had a chance to get it cut. She wasn't sure she wanted to anymore, a sentiment reinforced by the delectable shiver that tickled down her spine when the elastic band slid off and Jess scooped up Genie's hair, delivering a fingertip massage to her scalp and a breathy kiss under her ear.

"Or..." Jess murmured, rising to her knees and easing into the space behind Genie, moulding her front to Genie's back, "we could have a night in." Her palms crested Genie's shoulders and skimmed her collarbones before slipping under her top.

Involuntarily, Genie's back arched, pushing her breasts into Jess's cupped hands, a moan escaping unbidden as her nipples were clamped between fingers and thumbs. It was manipulation— sexual and emotional—and the sensible course would be to escape now, while she had half her wits about her. Sadly, in Jess's hands, she was the proverbial putty and sagged into a pliable lump of libido, for the moment unconcerned that her dress for her date, which she'd draped over the arm of the sofa to save it from creasing, had fallen to the floor.

"Marcus is picking me up at eight," she said, the 't' of the eight merging into a sharp inhale brought on by Jess's fingers sliding inside her jeans and knickers. "You could at least shut the curtains."

Jess giggled wickedly and continued, establishing a slow, rhythmic rubbing that could hold Genie on the edge indefinitely. "Marcus will thank me," she said. "You'll go for hours after this." With those words, she upped her game, nimbly vaulting Genie and whipping off her lower garments before slithering down between her thighs, both hands at work, deeply probing, swiftly caressing, deftly bringing her to climax. The storm front rolled in, black clouds looming as the moment of all-encompassing nothing lifted her clear of the mêlée before crashing down around her. Elation turned to regret and confusion when Jess sprang lithely to her feet and fled the room.

"Wait!" Genie called, her thoughts not so bleary that she missed there was more going on here than a one-sided quickie to enhance her staying power later. Neither of them was that selfless a lover. Denied the chance to bathe in the afterglow, she struggled into her jeans on the move and followed Jess up to her room, brought to a standstill by the view that greeted her of Jess sitting atop the suitcase on her bed. "Going somewhere?"

Jess finished zipping the case—too large for a weekend—and jumped down. "To a hotel. I'm sure I mentioned it."

"No, Jessica, you didn't." A prickle of anger flittered through Genie, up into her scalp and down her arms. She clenched her fists, released. "Why suggest a quiet night in if you had plans?"

"I was teasing." Jess affected a girlish smile and tiny shrug. "That's all."

That's all? The flittering anger became a pulsing flow. Still, Genie suppressed it. "Are you staying there alone?"

Jess laughed, light and false. "Of course not! That's why I thought I'd told you. Andy won a competition, and—"

"What kind of competition?"

"Who cares? If he wants to spend his winnings on me, I'm not going to stop him."

"We have exams next week."

"And?"

"You can't go away on holiday now, Jess. They'll fail you."

"We're not going *away*. We're staying at that place just out of town. Walton Hall?"

"Wharton Hall," Genie corrected wearily, certain now that Jess hadn't said a word about her 'holiday'. In its previous incarnation, the grand hotel, with its ballrooms and conservatories housing a spa and a pool, had been the stately home of Genie's ancestors—a fact she'd shared with Jess in the earliest days of their so-called friendship, along with the suggestion she'd treat them both to a weekend there sometime. Andy having beaten her to it doubled her loathing of her competitor for Jess's affections.

While Genie's thoughts played out, Jess had stripped and put on her bathrobe. She advanced with a careless half-smile, fully expecting Genie to move aside, let her go and make herself all clean and pretty *for Andy*. Was it irrational to feel that way? Probably.

"Is it intentional? This playing us off against each other?" It was certainly irrational to pick a fight over it.

The half-smile vanished. "What *are* you talking about?"

"All the times I've suggested we go on holiday together—"

"It's a few days away from the house."

"And last summer? What was your excuse then?"

"You know I have a standing arrangement with my friends back home."

"Including Andy."

"He's one of them, yes." Jess propped her hand defensively on her hip. "I don't understand what the problem is."

"Really? You can't see anything wrong in what you did before?"

"You mean getting you off?"

"Staking your claim."

"I... *What*?" Jess's irises, usually a tranquil pale grey, gleamed like stark steel rings around her enlarged pupils. The effect was unnerving.

"And then walked off before I could stake mine."

"What the hell is this 'staking a claim'? I did it because I wanted to."

"Without reciprocation."

"Is there a rule that says it has to be reciprocal?"

"Tell me you aren't saving yourself for Andy tonight."

"For God's sake... Why are you being so ridiculous over him taking me to a posh hotel for the week?"

"Because every time I offer to do that, you reject me, and don't blame it on your friends back home. You go away with them for two weeks in the summer. We could go during any of the other fifty weeks of the year, but it's always *I've got to spend Christmas with my mum and dad* or *it's too close to the exams* or *I haven't got any spending money*. Well, Jessica, it's too damn close to the exams now, but here you are, doing it with Andy, who I'm not even allowed to meet. What do you think I'll do? Brag about how hard I can make you come?"

"Seriously?" With an angry shrug, Jess spun away from Genie, hoisted the suitcase off the bed and lay in its place, bathrobe yanked open, legs wide apart. "If it's so important to you, go ahead. Stake your claim."

For several seconds, Genie stared at the neat triangle of dark-blonde hair that bobbed up and down with Jess's fast, angry breathing. There was nothing sexy about this scenario, nothing she wanted less than to touch the creature turned ugly by envy. It had to stop. They had to stop.

A further minute or longer passed in silence before Jess once more wrapped her bathrobe around her. "So we're clear," she said, standing and tugging the belt tight, "I've never stopped you from meeting Andy."

"That's bullshit if ever I heard it. The first weekend he stayed, what did you do? You kicked me out of the house, said you'd make it worth my while."

"I didn't kick you out. You stormed out and hid in Sean's pit for days. Mind you, it's no wonder you got lost in there. He's a tramp."

"Leave Sean out of this. He's been a good friend to me. To us both."

"A good fuck, you mean."

Genie laughed. She wanted to punch Jess so hard. "Yeah. That too," she spat. "How does he measure up to darling Andy?"

"Oh my god. You know what—"

Genie put up her hands, cutting Jess off, and backed out, forcing herself to walk, not flee in tears, to her room.

She was within touching distance of sanctuary when Jess caught up and grabbed her by the shoulder. "I'm sorry."

"Forget it."

"I didn't know you felt that way, but there's no need for you to be jealous. Andy's just a big kid in a grown-up's body. He's no threat to you...to us. I want you to meet him. It's just..." Jess chewed her lip.

"Just what?" Genie prompted. "A lie so you can go off on your jollies without feeling bad?"

"I totally get why you'd think that, and yes, it would make me feel better if we made up before I left, but that's not important right now. What you and I have is good, isn't it?"

"It was."

"It still can be. We never have to worry what comes next, like one of us getting pregnant or suddenly declaring our undying love and dropping to one knee. It's uncomplicated and fun, or I thought it was. Now—"

"Except I *do* love you, Jess."

"And I love you. Surely you know that." When Genie didn't comment, Jess added a doubtful, "Don't you?"

Genie nodded mutely. She didn't know anything anymore, other than how much she wanted to murder Andy.

***

As Genie had predicted, Marcus didn't hang around long enough to shower never mind eat breakfast, and she couldn't blame him for that. In her effort to get into the spirit of the evening, she'd drunk too much and eaten barely a thing and was thoroughly plastered before midnight. The painful sex that followed went on for almost two hours and only ended after she faked an orgasm. Then she'd gone to the bathroom, stuck her fingers down her throat until she vomited, thereafter spending the night wallowing on the sofa. By eight a.m., she had the house to herself and a long, empty day ahead of her.

It was all too much and yet nowhere near enough. Alone with her thoughts, she parried regret but couldn't beat it into submission. Why did Jess being with Andy get to her so much?

She didn't care about any of the other people Jess slept with, and really, she should have been more bothered about Jess and Sean when the three of them were sharing each with the other. Somehow, though, it worked. There was no jealousy, no possessiveness, no insecurity or need to compete. In another world where such relationships were not scandalised, Genie imagined she could have been content with their arrangement for the rest of her life. But it was not another world; it was this one, in which Jess vehemently resisted the possibility of a real long-term relationship, other than, of course, whatever this thing was with Andy.

What it all boiled down to, Genie surmised, was the way Jess kept them all in little boxes as if they were toys that must be tidied away before she took out something new to play with. Friends, lovers, parents—if it was within Jess's power to stop them coming together, she did so, yet there was no expectation of exclusivity, and that made Genie the biggest fool ever for moping in her dark little box, waiting for her turn to come around again. Jess had dictated the limited terms of their engagement, and Genie had accepted them, convinced that any kind of affection was better than none.

No more.

She couldn't switch off her feelings or switch between people the way Jess did, but she had other friends—friends she'd neglected when she'd become fixated on this one-sided relationship, and she was sick of keeping her misery company. She had the house to herself, and it was Saturday evening. Why shouldn't she invite those friends over for drinks?

It took three phone calls to set her plan in motion. An open invitation: "Any time after eight—bring your own booze." That left two hours to party-proof the house, which consisted of sticking a no-entry sign on Jess's bedroom door and throwing blankets over the sofas. She had an entire week to deal with the aftermath—if she chose to. On the one hand, she hoped her party guests would have more respect for a private house than they'd ever shown for the law students' halls of residence; on the other, this felt like her last hurrah, and she could be packed and moved out before the end of the weekend. For now, she was going with the flow. Party. Drinks. Fun.

Everyone turned up fashionably late, of course. First to arrive were Gabby and her boyfriend, whose mumbled name Genie missed the first and second time. No embarrassing third try, she smiled and accepted the half-gallon of scrumpy from the small, quiet boy in black who shadowed Gabby into the living room.

"I'll stick this in the freezer," she said, heading for the kitchen, and very nearly dropped the bottle when the volume of the stereo shot up.

That was but a prelude, as half the rugby team arrived next, post-victory thus quite drunk. Simon slobbered a kiss across Genie's cheek on his way past and up the stairs, calling back, "Bathroom's up here, yah?" as he pulled a small plastic bag from his pocket.

"Yes," Genie confirmed, second thoughts setting in hard. The other players had glanced into the living room and, having spotted Gabby and her boyfriend, congregated in the kitchen, where they popped the lids from their beer bottles, leaving them wherever they landed. James, the team captain and Simon's long-suffering so-called bestie, noticed Genie watching and quickly picked up the lids, offering her a 'See? One of us has manners!' smile as he deposited them on the counter, such difference as it would make by the end of the night.

A few more people arrived over the coming hour, including Sean and Josh, who apologised in advance for looming dissertation deadlines, stayed for one drink to be sociable and left, taking Gabby and her equally timid boyfriend with them. Had Genie not known the type of students all four were, she'd have hated them for leaving her with a crowd of people she realised too late were not friends but disrespectful fun seekers who, within a few short hours, trashed the house then crashed wherever they felt like it. Apart from James. But Genie didn't realise that until it was too late either.

Beyond his sweaty, bobbing head, the glow of streetlights sneaking in along the top of her curtains formed a scalloped stripe of yellow across her bedroom ceiling. With each grunt of his, she winced, her vulva swollen and sensitive from the dry, uninspiring sex of twenty-four hours ago. It was more an irritation than a violation because aside from the pain, she was numb and bored and could've cheered when he rolled off and zonked out next to her. With care not to wake him, she slid from beneath his leaden arm and made a dash first to the bathroom to clean up a bit, then to Jess's room, where she flopped face down on the bed and sobbed drunkenly into Jess's pillows.

James hadn't forced himself on her. He was good-looking, muscular, smelled of expensive aftershave, and she was fairly sure he'd have accepted it if she'd said no—both then and in the early hours, when they shagged again in Jess's bed. Genie had come that time, almost out of spite, and relished the sting of mingling bodily fluids. She wasn't surprised to discover the following morning as she stripped the bed that her blood was on the sheets.

How different it would've been if Sean had followed her upstairs instead of James. Three years at university equated to a lot of sex with many different people, and Sean was far and away the most considerate—the only one to whom she could've said, "I'm really sore," and known he would go gently, do whatever she felt comfortable doing. The only one who didn't insist on penetration.

The hangover lasted all of Sunday, but Genie refused to give in to it. The shower helped, while also forcing her to acknowledge she'd used herself as an emotional punch bag; her breasts and stomach bore a litany of tiny purple love bites, and the soap stung like acid between her legs. Pat-dry, she pulled on a band T-shirt she'd borrowed from Sean and her softest leggings and curled up on the sofa with her revision notes on constitutional and administrative law, only moving to make tea or restart the washing machine. Symbolic as it might have been to spill her blood on Jess's sheets, Genie put them through a 90°C cycle three times before she was satisfied they were clean, then hung them over the banister on her way to bed at eight p.m.

She slept a solid ten hours and was sure she could have slept longer were it not for the thump of feet on the stairs, the call of her name and, "Are these my sheets?" That was all the warning she received before Jess's head poked around the door.

"You're still in bed."

"Yeah, and you're not meant to be here."

Jess sighed. "May I come in?" Genie didn't reply, but Jess came in anyway and perched beside her.

"Hotel not up to your exacting standards?" Genie joked with the tiniest touch of venom, eliciting a pained smile from her housemate, lover. Heartbreaker.

"The hotel's lovely, but I couldn't stop thinking about you—what you said. I'm sorry. I didn't mean for you to feel rejected."

"No, you expect me to take it on the chin."

"That's not what I meant!" Jess hissed the words, angry but keeping her voice down. Genie held her breath, listening for clues. A sniff.

"Is he here?"

Jess nodded. "I want you to meet him."

"Why?"

"Because you're important to me. You both are."

"Does he know about us?"

"God, no!"

Genie gave Jess a sharp nudge with her knee. It was the best she could do, pinned under the covers as she was. Jess laughed at her effort—silently—then whispered, "I'll tell him if you want me to, but he'll think his luck's in."

"Maybe it will be," Genie said, nudging Jess again so she'd get up. "I need to pee."

"I'd reserve judgement if I were you." Jess headed for the door. "Remember that *bloody awful* music I *made* you listen to on Friday? That's Andy's band."

***

Grunge, it was called, apparently, and after a week of hearing about the etymology of the term, the genre and its attendant fashion, complete with musical interludes, Genie was feeling every bit the out-of-touch aristocrat she strived not to be. She supposed Andy was all right. She could even see, beneath the greasy mess of shoulder-length hair, hole-ridden woollen jumper with sleeves down to his fingertips and tattered jeans that hung off his arse, what Jess saw in him.

He'd have been a sight more handsome if he shaved that square jaw and dimpled chin, but aside from the testosterone overload, Jess was right. Andy was a child in a grown-up's body. He sprawled, took over the TV, left the toilet seat up and the towels on the bathroom floor. He sulked when Jess and Genie had to leave to sit their exams and zoomed around like a puppy reuniting with its owner when they returned. Without a doubt, he'd have begged for a threesome if he'd known about the two of them. Lord knew, he ogled them both enough without, although that was as far as he went.

For all of that, the longer Genie spent in Andy's company, the less of a threat he seemed, which was perhaps what Jess had banked on. Genie could've tied herself in further knots wondering for whose benefit Jess had done it, but she settled for knowing their house-share would be secure and amicable for the remainder of their studies.

"Bet you'll be glad to see the back of me!" Andy grinned, startling Genie in the bathroom doorway on Sunday morning.

"Not at all!" she lied through gritted teeth and pulled the belt a little bit tighter around her bathrobe. He was fully dressed, his holdall slung over his shoulder. "You're not heading off this early, are you?"

"Yeah. Got footy at ten."

"Right. Well…" Genie attempted to sidestep at the same time as Andy went for a hug but for some reason backed off at the last second. The sudden movement dislodged his bag, and it swung at Genie and whacked her in the boob.

"Shit. Sorry. I'll er…go."

"OK." Genie grimaced out a smile. "Safe trip."

"You too," Andy said nonsensically. He couldn't have cleared the stairs faster if they'd transformed into a slide.

The front door slammed behind him as Jess came out of her bedroom, took one look at Genie, and the pair of them burst into laughter.

"He got me in the boob!" Genie said, rubbing at the tender spot that was sure to blossom into a tremendous bruise before the day was out.

Jess frowned in sympathy. "He's an idiot. Want me to kiss it better?"

28: Law and Disorder

Sandison-Morley Residence
Present Day
Saturday, 27ᵗʰ – Monday, 29ᵗʰ April

*S*IMON HENDERSON. As if Josh needed the man's CV to start checking his credentials. It had arrived the morning after their phone conversation, and Josh had filed it unopened in his 'pending' folder, his curiosity only piqued now because researching Simon Henderson was the lesser of two evils. The Ouija board's rightful owner could wait.

Both Simon's covering email and attached CV were succinct. No gaps in employment, he had joined Lincoln's Inn and completed his bar training immediately after graduating, stayed with the firm at which he'd undertaken his pupillage for ten years before taking in-house positions with property companies alongside his pro-bono work for youth charities. He'd helpfully provided a link to an online reference-holding service, and to say his references were glowing was like describing Venus as a bit on the warm side. Whoever that suave, arrogant buffoon at university had been, the man he'd become was, on paper, exactly what the Daisy Foundation needed, but it wasn't enough. Aside from Josh's instinctive dislike of the aristocracy, everything about Viscount Henderson had infuriated him from that first day at university when he'd captured Jess's attention and her common sense.

Josh closed the references service website and typed Simon's name into the search bar. He was the son of an earl, so naturally, the entire family was listed on Wikipedia. Josh was also aware that prior to his friendship with Jess and her convincing him to come out, Simon had been betrothed to Imogen Rowan—Phee's mother—and the two had grown up alongside Gabby Bowes and her cousin, Xander Etherington-Bowes. That all four had chosen the same common-or-garden university over Oxbridge suggested a closeness beyond shared social position: every one of them had, in a way, rejected class tradition, and that rebellious streak had come from somewhere—genetics or upbringing.

He was right on both counts. Gabby's father was Simon's maternal uncle, and Simon's father was, according to a third-party article, Xander's paternal uncle: Xander's parents had divorced when his mother's involvement with Simon's uncle came to light. However, it had never been proven Xander was the result of that affair, and Lord Etherington—named as father on Xander's birth certificate—had accepted him as heir apparent. After the divorce, Lord Etherington married Genevieve Bowes—Gabby's aunt— hence Gabby's contention that Xander was her step-cousin, but if Simon's uncle *was* Xander's father, then Gabby, Xander and Simon were, biologically, first cousins.

"The peerage has no genetic imagination," Josh murmured, though he was alone in his study, having abandoned George in the living room. Libby was babysitting the twins for Shaunna and Andy and would stay over, giving Josh his first evening to himself in two weeks, not counting the one he'd spent stuck in a loft. His stomach lurched at the reminder, and he quickly refocused on his research.

The three families were so closely interwoven, they were, essentially, one and the same, and whichever links he clicked, he could, with relative ease, navigate back to his starting point. All in all, Simon's and Xander's absence of offspring was a good thing, even if it did mean that after Simon, the next in line was his nephew, and there was no direct descendant in Xander's line. Also fortuitous was that Gabby's husband, whilst a peer, was not English, which hopefully meant he'd introduced some much-needed genetic variation into a very small pool.

Likewise, Sean having fathered Imogen's daughter had brought in new blood and quashed the likelihood of the Hendersons pushing Imogen's parents to pursue their daughter and Simon's marriage but had left Sean and Jess equally culpable for any repercussions Simon had faced for coming out to his parents. The betrothal wasn't the only close connection between Imogen's family and Simon's: after Simon's parents divorced, Isla Rowan, Imogen's older sister by some ten years, had married Lord Henderson. Had Simon and Imogen gone along with their arranged marriage, Imogen would be both his wife and his aunt.

It was an hour later before Josh realised he'd been sucked back into the world of genealogy. Stranger still, George hadn't come up to complain about being left to watch TV alone; he'd either found a film he liked or fallen asleep.

"OK. Five more minutes," Josh told himself and set a timer before he moved on to what he was supposed to be researching: Simon Henderson's professional life. As part of the peerage, he didn't have ordinary online profiles or atrocious self-taken photographs and had no presence whatsoever on the main social networks, but he was on several sites relating to his legal career. Most of those concerned his previous cases, but the one of greatest relevance was his former position as trustee to an organisation called Aspire Youth Trust.

"Let's see where this goes." Josh clicked the link and waited. The connection was slow, and he was half expecting it to time out or go to a 'page not found', but it did eventually start to load. First the logo, then a text description—

"LGBT—wow!" The page filled with rainbow colours, latest news, events, a helpline number and, at last, the navigation. Josh went straight to the 'about' page: 'Aspire is committed to supporting young LGBT+ people to successfully pursue their ambitions…' Josh read on, and on, until he'd read every word on every page. The charity worked with youngsters who came from less than supportive backgrounds—precisely Simon's situation when they were undergraduates.

And yet, he was *Viscount* Henderson, first in line for the earldom he'd been so sure he'd lose if he came out. Did that mean he was still in the closet? If he had been a trustee to Aspire, surely not.

Unfortunately, that information would have to wait; Josh's five minutes were up, and whilst only he was there to police whether he stuck to his limit, he'd be cheating himself if he didn't. Before he knew it, it would be three a.m. and pointless going to bed. One night without sleep would lead to another, and another, and on it would go until his brain slammed on the brakes. For his own good, he shut down his computer and returned to the living room, where George was lying on the couch but surprisingly still awake. He sat up and followed Josh's progress across the room.

"What've you been doing?"

"Investigating Simon Henderson."

George frowned. "Why do I know that name? Is he a lawyer or something?"

"Yes. An alumnus of Jess and Gabby. I didn't know you'd talked to her about the trouble we were having finding one."

"Did I? I don't remember."

Josh squashed into the corner of the sofa and squinted at the TV. "What are you watching?"

"A really bad movie. The guy exchanged places with his son's goldfish when he was about to flush it down the loo. The goldfish is definitely having more fun than the guy is."

"Hasn't that story been told a dozen times already?"

"Yep." George picked up the remote and switched the TV to standby. "So, what happens next?"

"Simon sent me his CV and suggested we meet."

"That's good."

"Is it?"

"Well, you did say you were having trouble finding a lawyer."

What Josh had read online was all positive, but he knew very little about Simon on a personal level. They'd studied at the same university for four years, yet they'd spoken only once in all that time.

"What are you thinking about?"

"Simon when we were at uni. I don't remember seeing him around after the first semester. I assumed he'd dropped out." By which he meant he hadn't given Simon a second thought once Jess had moved on from their short-lived, farcical relationship. "He asked Jess to marry him."

"Another man whose heart she broke, eh?"

"Not exactly. He's gay, and he needed a wife or he'd have lost his title, or so he said. Last I knew, Jess persuaded him to tell his parents the truth, and now he's a viscount. She never mentioned him after that. I wasn't aware they'd remained friends until Gabby asked if she could tell him Jess had died." Josh sifted through his memories of Simon from university, their phone conversation and his online search, looking for answers. Why had he offered his services? There had to be more to it, something else between him and Jess that Josh didn't know about. "I've no idea what to make of him."

George smirked. "Guess you'll be taking him up on that meeting, huh?"

***

"I'm home!" Libby called. As she came through the front door, the cat flap in the back door beeped and Jinja pushed through, meowing loudly.

"Tattle-tale," Josh muttered into his coffee.

Across the kitchen table, George laughed and buttered another slice of toast. "Morning, Lib. Do you want some breakfast?"

"No, thanks. I had blueberry pancakes at Shaunna's. Have you fed Jinja yet?"

"He wasn't here," Josh protested defensively.

"I was only asking!" Libby collected the cat's bowl and food. "How were the twins?"

"Asleep. I ended up watching one of those body-swap films about a goldfish."

"I watched that too," George said at the same time as Josh said, "George watched that too."

"Rubbish, wasn't it?" Libby said. George nodded in agreement. Josh sighed in mock dismay. For the first few months of Libby living with them, he'd worried that she was mimicking their traits and preferences as a means of gaining approval, to the extent he'd looked forward to their first parent-child disagreement. It went without saying that he was no longer worried.

"Shaunna's gonna call you later, by the way."

"OK."

"She got an email from that charity commission woman."

"That doesn't sound good. I'll give her a call now."

"She was getting in the bath as I left."

"Bugger." Josh had acted decisively and Shaunna had already picked up. "Hey. You're in the bath. I'll call back."

"No need. Did Libby tell you I've had an email from our advisor?"

"She did. Problem?"

"Kind of. She was following up on our interviews and wasn't very happy that we failed to appoint. She suggested we readvertise or she can put us in touch with someone."

"Suggested or told us that's what's going to happen?"

"Yeah, that's what I thought too. We need to meet, all four trustees, and look at our options."

"I agree," Josh said, turning his chair so he couldn't see George's expression, which was telling him loud and clear what he needed to do. "Actually, I might have a solution. It's a long shot, but can you leave it with me for a day?"

"With pleasure! Enjoy your Sunday."

"You too." Josh made sure the call had ended and turned back to a very smug George. "I guess I will be taking him up on that meeting after all."

***

Monday morning, after a surprisingly restful night's sleep, Josh made the call—audio and video. He could interpret intent better that way, but he was also curious to see how the years had treated Viscount Henderson.

Josh pushed his glasses up his nose then took them off, straightened his shirt and adjusted his posture, chin up, shoulders back, all while waiting for the call to connect. Perhaps Simon was doing the same at the other end, or perhaps he was as arrogant now as he had been back then. It was poor form to keep a prospective employer waiting. Very poor form indeed.

As is the way of these things, the moment Josh's attention wandered from the call window back to his inbox, Simon answered, filling the screen with an obscene close-up of his beaming, glistening, barely-aged-a-day visage.

"Thanks for getting back to me." He was a little breathless and dabbed at his face with a dark garment of some kind. "I wasn't sure you would. Certainly not outside office hours."

A quick glance at the top of the screen confirmed it wasn't yet eight o'clock. "Sorry about that. We're early risers here."

"Good for you."

The absence of sarcasm from that statement was unexpected and further revised the profile Josh had constructed in his head. He was prepared to accept he had misjudged Simon. With the intention of building rapport, and to give the man time to catch his breath, Josh said, "It looks like a lovely, sunny morning there. Are you still based in the UK?"

"Yah. I'm not far from you, in fact. Just on the Welsh side of Chester, which makes this a remarkably lovely morning!" Simon grinned, and almost against his will, Josh returned it.

"You do seem to get more than your fair share of rain over there. It's handy you're nearby—is there a day that's convenient for you to come and meet for a chat? I'll have to check when the other trustees are available, of course."

"I understand. One moment." Simon's camera paused. "Checking my diary. I know I'm in court tomorrow...Wednesday's a bust...Thursday...no. Damn." He reappeared. "I'm afraid I'm solid till Friday. How does today look for you guys?"

"I'll see who else is available this afternoon." Sean would be, as they had an appointment with a flooring swatch this evening, and they could handle Simon between the two of them. "Shall we say one o'clock?"

"Great. One o'clock it is. I have the address for your offices— I assume that's where I need to go?"

"Campion Trust head office, yes," Josh said to make sure Simon had the right place. "See you then."

"Looking forward to it."

***

He was prompt, Josh would give him that. Few people arrived earlier than Josh for appointments, for which Simon was to be commended, although it also meant he either hadn't received or had ignored Josh's message putting back the meeting to two o'clock. He could only hope he'd had more success in requesting Sean's presence at Campion's ASAP, as Alice was taking her lunchbreak, leaving Josh with Simon, whom he dumped in the boardroom before fleeing to make coffee. That was his plan, but having searched every unlocked cupboard and the fridge, and remembering Alice's aversion to the smell, he concluded Campion's was a coffee-free environment and made a pot of tea instead. He carried it through to the boardroom and went back for the cups, saucers and milk, which was when he found the coffee, swathed in cellophane and shoved to the back of the salad drawer.

"Oh, well. Too late now." He shut the fridge door and returned to the boardroom, where his guest was still standing. "Have a seat, Simon."

Josh set the cups on the table, half attending to arranging them on their saucers while watching Simon pinch up his trousers at the thighs to avoid putting knees in them when he sat. It was a long time since Josh had seen someone—his dad, possibly—do that. Simon noticed him watching. "I don't come here often," Josh said as if that explained his surveillance, not that he needed to. Still, he felt compelled to make it relevant. "Hence we're having tea, not coffee."

"Either is fine."

They went through the usual motions of establishing how each took their tea, with some stilted small talk about their preferences—Simon hated Earl Gray but enjoyed a lightly smoked Lapsang Souchong when he could get it—before they hit an impasse of sorts. Josh was regretting his decision to sit on the same side of the table; in the interim silence, he was too close and too aware of Simon's immense, powerful presence, which derived as much from his profession as it did his physical size. He was well-built, well-dressed and well and truly in command of the moment, and Josh didn't like it one bit.

"We'll make a start as—"

"May I speak candidly?" Simon asked simultaneously. "Sorry. Go on."

"I was going to say we'll make a start as soon as the other trustee arrives. Do you remember Sean Tierney?"

"The Irishman? He and Jess—"

"Yes," Josh interrupted. "He shouldn't be too long now."

Simon nodded. He was complying with Josh's shutdown, his previous request left hanging.

"What was it you wanted to say?"

"I had a feeling you'd reject my offer outright, so thank you for hearing me out."

"I haven't yet, although it would be foolish not to."

"Let's hope you still feel that way after this interview. Before we start proper, I should explain why I'm offering my services."

"Perhaps you should wait and share with all of us?"

"If you wish, but I'd prefer the other trustees base their considerations on my professional standing alone. This is personal, about what Jess did for me. She may well have told you. Suffice to say, she guaranteed my gratitude for all eternity. I neither need nor expect remuneration, should you decide I am a good fit for the foundation. It would be my honour to serve you."

Simon's grand and very generous assurances did not appease Josh, although his suspicion had been surpassed by his curiosity. He could recall no instances of Jess's benevolence toward Simon during their time at university, or none of a significance that warranted *eternal gratitude*. Surely he couldn't mean her convincing him to tell his parents he was gay?

"What Jess did for you—" Josh had intended to inflect it as a question, but Simon interjected before he got that far.

"Much as you did for Gabby Bowes."

Josh's vision blurred, the mental onslaught catching him unawares. What he'd done for Gabby—goading her to go against her parents and change her degree route—he'd regretted ever since, not because it had gone awry. Gabby would not be where she was today if she had ignored his advice, but he could not have predicted it would end well. The right course of action for him might not be for someone else. That principle underpinned his professional conduct—to guide, not advise—for how could he or anyone know which path others should choose?

There was no dodging the fact that at seventeen, Josh's words had been unmeasured, unrefined and irresponsible. His beliefs had not changed; the underlying urge to tell people what he thought persisted, but he understood his power now, and he exercised it with great caution. He could not dictate the path a person should take, merely highlight the alternatives should they wish to pursue them.

Nonetheless, had he foreseen what lay ahead of Jess, he'd have tried his hardest to talk her out of becoming a lawyer, because it was easier to imagine she had been tarnished by a profession that valued self-service and greed than to accept she had possessed those attributes in the first place. That was the path Jess had freely chosen. Loathsome, duplicitous, sweet, sweet, Jess who, it seemed, had saved two wretches.

Josh broke free of the tendrils and cleared both vision and throat. "Sorry. I was…" Dumbed, he lowered his eyes to check he was not imagining Simon's hand covering his own.

"I'm sorry for your loss, Josh."

He drew back in his chair, anticipating Simon would move his hand away, but he did not, and instead it hovered an inch above Josh's knee.

"I know you were very close," Simon added.

"Do you know what she was? What she did?"

"Yes, though I didn't know for certain until her associates were on trial. I was in one of the other courts, and the gossip was rife. I hadn't made the connection—Jess and I lost touch some years ago. After her co-conspirators were convicted, I read the transcript." He smiled, and there was sadness, but admiration too, then shook his head. "She was clever. Always so damn clever. Had she lived, the way she'd covered her tracks, she'd have walked free."

"She left me her confession," Josh said, aware he'd done so out of bloody-mindedness.

"Which you immediately handed over to the police?" Simon asked with a sarcastic but playful, lop-sided smirk.

"What use would that have been? The police had all the evidence they needed from their undercover operation, and Jess had already dispersed her share of the money. The lead investigator said they couldn't trace it back to the fraud ring. It was to all intents and purposes her life's savings."

"And you—Jess's friends—made the necessary arrangements to ensure her soul was redeemed."

Josh bristled at the religious overtone. "It has nothing to do with redemption. We abided by her wishes. If you've come here to make a point about the foundation's funding coming from ill-gotten gains—"

"Not at all! As I said, I'm hoping you'll permit me to pay my dues."

"So after all that, you didn't forfeit your inheritance."

Simon laughed. "Quite the contrary, but it was a hard slog to win my parents round, and Jess stood by me, talked some sense into them. They still think it's a pity—she would've been the perfect wife, according to them—but they accept who I am, and these days they're on good terms with my partner. That's all thanks to Jess. She said you knew from the start."

"That you're gay? Yes, I did."

"How's that? Gaydar?"

"I beg your pardon?"

"Gabby mentioned you have a husband."

"Oh! Right, yes. I do. That's not how I knew." Josh wasn't sure if that were true. It was a new consideration. "I was a psychologist before I was a psychologist."

"Much like Jess was with law."

Josh pushed away a smile derived from happy days far in the past when he'd believed he knew Jess. Yes, she'd always been a lawyer at heart. As to the rest of it...

"I must tell you about the dream I had," Simon said, and this time Josh had to suppress a groan rather than a smile. After twenty-plus years of study and work as a psychologist, he couldn't have put a number on how many times people had told him their dreams, but he assumed an attentive pose and waited to be regaled.

"It was almost a premonition. Jess and I were having a picnic by the river, and she knelt in front of me. I thought she was going to kiss me, but instead she dropped something over my head. I looked down and saw it was a daisy chain. The very next evening was Gabby's exhibition. She asked if any of my junior associates might be interested in working with the Daisy Foundation. I'd never heard of it. When she told me it was set up with Jess's money and named after her little sister, I wanted to pinch myself to make sure I was actually awake. Bizarre thing, the brain, isn't it?"

"Yes, it is," Josh said and could have cried with relief when he heard the outside door open, followed by Eleanor and Sean's polite chatter. He hadn't known Eleanor would be sitting in but couldn't say he was sorry. His surface calm was barely holding. A dream was just a dream, a meaningful manifestation of the unconscious at best. Or so he kept telling himself as he introduced Eleanor and Simon and then watched Sean and Simon reunite like former soldiers of some great war. His 'haunting' and Simon's dream had occurred on the same day; a disturbing coincidence, but that was all it was. What more could it be?

29: Tethered

I'M GOING TO have an abortion."

Genie kept her eyes on the road ahead but nodded to confirm she'd heard. At least, she thought that was what she'd heard. With the windows open and the volume on the stereo cranked up to compensate, she couldn't be sure.

She'd kept her promise and not initiated conversation about it, not even when the aromatherapist had asked them to read the disclaimer about pre-existing conditions, one of those being pregnancy. It went against her instinct, but Genie had to trust Phee to know what was best for her body.

"You're not going to say anything?"

"One moment." Genie signalled to pull into the inside lane, slowing down and therefore reducing the road noise. "That's better."

"It'll take us ages to get home at this speed."

"I know, but I couldn't hear properly. What did you say?"

"You're just trying to get me to repeat myself."

"I'm really not."

"Whatever, Mother."

"Come on, darling. We've had a lovely week away."

"I'll shut up then, shall I?"

"Don't be silly." Genie kept her tone light. Both of them flouncing would get them nowhere.

"I said…I'm going to have an abortion."

"OK."

"Is it?"

"Is it what? OK?" A lorry overtook them, filling the car with hot hydraulic air. Genie wafted at it uselessly. "Yes. I'm here for you."

"What if I change my mind?"

"I'll still be here for you." Another lorry chugged past, belching exhaust fumes their way. Genie coughed and closed the window. "If you're not one hundred percent sure, you should wait. There's time yet."

"I know. Up to twenty-four weeks, but it's safer if it's earlier." The residual damp smell from the cleaned back seat became prominent again. Phee turned on the air conditioning. "Have you ever had one?"

"Yes."

"How old were you?"

"Younger than you are."

"How much younger?"

Having already thought about the subject coming up and how she would answer, Genie had decided on honesty. Even so, in the face of her feelings about Phee's pregnancy, it was difficult to admit. "I was fifteen."

"Mum!"

"What?"

"That's…really young."

"I was once, you know."

"You're not that old now."

"Thank you, darling…I think."

Phee was quiet for a while but every so often drew a breath then released it without a word.

"Services in a mile," Genie said. "Should we stop?"

"Do you need to?"

"No. I thought you might."

"I'm fine."

"OK."

The silence resumed. Phee skipped several songs in a row, then switched off the stereo. "Was it bad?"

"Not really. Mine was surgical, but I believe the medical option is more common these days."

"Yeah. It says that online."

"You're lucky to have all that information. I had to put up with a leaflet from the family planning clinic. Terribly grim stuff."

"Was it illegal back then?"

"No, it's been legal since the sixties, but it was still heavily frowned upon." The nurses had been quite callous in their treatment of the abortion patients, who were admitted to the antenatal ward, along with women going through spontaneous miscarriages or other pregnancy complications. For Genie, despite being certain she wanted to terminate, that had been the most traumatic part of the process, which was probably the point: to teach wayward girls a lesson in the sanctity of life.

"Please will you come with me?" Phee asked, sounding so very small.

"Of course I will!"

"Thank you."

"I'd also understand if you'd rather Sarah was there."

"She doesn't know, and I'm not going to tell her."

That was…curious. Genie was under the impression Phee and Sarah confided about everything.

"Since her mum, she's gone all pro-life."

"Ah." That explained it. "You sound like your mind's made up."

"Yeah, I think so. Unless…" Phee paused.

"Unless?" Genie prompted.

"Are you ready to be a grandma?"

"I've never given it any thought."

"Then stop driving like one."

"Cheeky toad."

Phee reclined the passenger seat and put her feet up, tapping her toes on the dashboard. "Home, Jeeves."

"And don't spare the horses!" Genie finished and indicated to overtake the slow coach in front.

***

Something was off. Genie sensed it the moment she and Phee entered the house, although Margaret had whisked their bags away to their rooms and returned to her preparations in the kitchen before Genie worked out what was different. No paintings, no photos, no ornaments on the bureau by the front door; it was as if someone had taken it upon themselves to pack up their belongings while they were gone. The realisation gave way to a memory of the day she and Jess had moved out of their student house—the day she'd pleaded with Jess to give them a chance. Tears threatened, but nothing short of a good cry in privacy could release the strain of the past fortnight, so Genie sniffed them back and concentrated on resolving the immediate puzzle.

"Margaret?"

"Going for a shower, Mum," Phee said and scooted up the stairs as Margaret appeared in the kitchen doorway, wiping her hands on a tea towel.

"Yes, my lady?"

"Where *is* everything?"

"Ah. You should prepare yourself." Casting aside the towel, Margaret approached the closed door to the drawing room and knocked.

"Come in!" Jonathan called.

Margaret opened the door and gestured for Genie to enter. She did so, tentatively, expecting some untold horror.

"Oh! Well…that's not…so dreadful. I mean, it is, but—" Now she saw what had happened to the paintings and ornaments, and that wasn't all. Their linens, perfumes, cosmetics, jewellery— everything other than the furniture—had been brought from the rest of the house into the drawing room. As if that wasn't bizarre enough, Xander picked up a porcelain doll and, holding it in both hands at arm's length, stepped over the pile and bowed stiffly, thrusting it towards the piano stool.

"No," he said.

A scratching somewhere to the left of where Genie stood speechless snagged her attention away from Xander, who exchanged the doll for a threadbare hobby horse, both childhood toys that had been stowed in the back of her closet. The scratching was that of a pen against the clipboard Jonathan was holding.

"No," Xander repeated and dumped the hobby horse back in the heap. Genie finally found her tongue.

"What on earth is going on?"

"His Lordship is—" Jonathan began but Xander talked over him.

"There has to be a reason this boy won't leave."

Genie nodded as if that made complete sense though it made none, not even after she'd replayed Xander's statement several times. She had, however, latched on to one aspect. "He's still here?"

"Hm. Who?"

"The ghost boy! Who else? You said *this* boy…"

"Yes, he's still here." Like a mechanical butler lacking knee and elbow joints, Xander advanced towards the piano stool once again, bowed and thrust forward a bone China floral teapot that had belonged to Genie's grandmother. "No," he said.

Jonathan marked an X on his clipboard. "That's everything, my lord."

Xander set the teapot on the sofa and looked around the cluttered room. "How unfortunate."

"Excuse me?" Incensed, Genie took a step closer, but Jonathan put out his arm. She batted it away. "How *unfortunate*? You've destroyed my home and you're telling me it's still haunted? What the hell have you been doing for the past week?"

"If I may—"

"No, you may not, Jonathan. I called you three hours ago, yet it didn't occur to you to warn me?"

"I'm sorry, Your Ladyship." He ducked his head, seemingly contrite.

"It's my fault," Xander said.

"Yes, it is." Genie was so angry she could barely think.

"I should like to take you out for that lunch now."

"Would you indeed?"

"A splendid idea," Jonathan concurred. "While you're gone, I'll return your possessions to their proper places."

"I'll help you," Margaret said behind Genie. She must have been there all the time.

"I was looking forward to a shower and a nap in my own bed," Genie complained, but it was three against one, and whichever way she turned, she was confronted by disarray. "All right. I'll come willingly, but you will tell me everything you know, Xander. Do we have an accord?"

"Yes."

"Good. I need to freshen up. Be right back." Genie marched from the room and up the stairs, conscious of the unfamiliar, naked wall in her peripheral vision. Who'd have thought she'd miss those ghastly portraits? She made it to her room and slumped on the side of the bed with her head in her hands. How was she going to freshen up when her toiletries were in Xander's hoard? The onslaught of tears nudged closer, staved off by a light rap on the door. Genie glanced up and smiled gratefully at her assistant, who had pre-empted Genie's requirements and flitted about the room with a quiet efficiency, putting everything back where it belonged.

"Margaret, thank you." Genie reached out and grasped the woman's hand. "I don't know what I'll do without you."

Margaret gently withdrew her hand and took a step back. "I haven't yet accepted the position."

"Are you...having second thoughts?"

"No."

"Oh." Genie sagged again.

"I'm sorry, my lady, I'm not making myself clear. I didn't want to leave in the first place, but I felt I had no choice." Margaret was wringing her hands.

"I asked Vic if I'd upset you in some way."

"He told me, but it's not you. It's always been a pleasure working here. You are so generous."

"And you are worth every penny, Margaret."

"How kind of you to say."

"Truly, you are a treasure. I don't want to lose you, so please, whatever it is, I'm sure we can resolve it. Tell me."

"It's Mr. Harper."

"Paul?" Somehow, that didn't come as a shock, although his messiness hardly seemed enough to make Margaret leave. "I appreciate he takes advantage of your good nature—"

"That is not the issue." The hand-wringing stopped; Margaret took a measured breath. "You and he may have an arrangement that it's acceptable to engage in intimacy with other people, and it is none of my business, but I have to tell you, as a Christian—"

"Let me stop you there, Margaret. Paul and I have no such arrangement, I can assure you."

Genie left a gap for Margaret to elaborate, but the poor woman was distraught, and there was only one reason she'd have jumped to the conclusion she had. It would be an unnecessary cruelty to have her confirm aloud that Paul had brought another woman into the house.

"I'm sorry, my lady."

"No. *I* am sorry you were put in this position. I wish you'd been able to tell me sooner instead of feeling you had to find other work."

"As I say, it is none of my business."

"You spend a good deal of your life under this roof. You have a right to feel respected and safe here. To that end, I will call Paul this evening and tell him to find alternative accommodation."

"Please don't do that on my account."

"Our relationship has run its course. This has merely brought it to a more timely end. So will you stay, Margaret?"

"Yes, my lady. I would be delighted to."

"Wonderful! Well, I'd best get a move on or Xander will think I'm not coming."

"Is there anything else I can do for you?"

"No, thank you, Margaret. For everything."

With a small nod, Margaret left and returned downstairs.

So very weary, Genie hoisted herself from the bed and leaned on her dressing table, staring into the mirror. It was a particularly unflattering pose that accentuated her crow's feet and fledgling jowls, but she was loath to apply make-up after a week without. Instead, she moisturised and spritzed with the first bottle she picked up—a light, floral scent that had a frivolous quality to it.

"I love that perfume."

Genie shifted her gaze to Phee's reflection. "That's why there's hardly any left."

Phee came into the room, perching on the end of Genie's bed. "So you and Paul are splitting up?"

"More making it official. We've been growing apart for a year or two."

"I'd noticed."

"Had you?"

"It's like he's a mate who comes over for a beer and stays the night."

"Yes, that's a good description. I think we both realised some time ago but couldn't be bothered to break it off."

"I told Sean that, then realised how tactless..." Phee trailed off and started picking at her nails. If she hadn't done that, Genie may not have thought anything of it, but it was all falling into place.

She turned to face Phee. "*When* did you tell him that?"

"We had dinner with him last Monday, Mother."

Clever girl. Like Genie, Phee was an expert bluffer, blurring the lines of truth, building a narrative until the other person filled the blanks and would swear they'd heard it straight from the horse's mouth. It was a cunning and necessary strategy because when it came to telling an outright lie, they instantly gave themselves away.

"Where did you go the first week of spring break?"

"I stayed at Sarah's. You *know* that."

"To clarify, you left here on Monday morning and went to Sarah's, came home Wednesday, stayed one night and went back to Sarah's."

"If you say so."

Still dodging the lie.

"Did you go to see Sean?"

"How would I get there?"

"Train? Coach? A lift?"

"And stay where?"

"Travel Inn perhaps? You seem to know an awful lot about them all of a sudden."

"You're being paranoid."

"Please answer the question, Phoenix. Did you go and see Sean the week before last?"

Phee jumped to her feet, yelling on the move, "Yes, I went to see Sean! Happy now?" The door swung violently shut behind her.

Genie clenched her fists and growled, beast-like, ready to kill the next person she saw.

Except the next person she saw was already dead.

30: Into His Own Hands

Campion Trust Boardroom
Present Day
Monday, 29th April

IT WASN'T FAIR on the man. Simon was riveting—amusing, charming, knowledgeable—but Sean's sleep was all over the place and he could think of nothing useful to say, while Josh was at his obnoxious best, asking all the right questions in completely the wrong way. That left Eleanor at the helm of a very rocky ship missing its red-haired captain, and Sean hated not pulling his weight. With that in mind, he poured the dregs from the pot into his cup, knocked back the bitter, strong tea, gave his face a vigorous rub and sat up straight, question ready for the next lull in Eleanor and Simon's dialogue.

"All right, so, here's a scenario for you. Let's say you're midway through a big case, tied up in hearings and what-have-you, and we have an emergency that needs your input. What can we expect from you?"

Simon sat back and folded his arms, holding Sean's gaze as he considered his response. He took his time, too, letting a good minute pass before he unfolded his arms and extended them in an expansive shrug. "It's a reasonable concern, Sean, and thanks for raising it, as I'm sure it's one your fellow trustees share. I can't guarantee I'll always be available at a moment's notice. That being said, my team is quite capable of handling a case in my absence."

"Abandon them a lot, do you?" Josh asked.

Simon pursed his lips, his amusement showing in the crinkles around his eyes. "I'm Queen's Counsel. The star of the show.

However, I can assure you…again…that is not how I conduct my pro-bono work."

"This isn't pro bono."

"The honorarium is pocket money even for the likes of you three generously salaried professionals, but you know my motivation for volunteering my services and why it guarantees you my fullest commitment to the Daisy Foundation."

Josh drew breath, and Sean jumped in fast. "Thanks, Simon. I don't think we have any more questions, do we?" He looked to Eleanor, who shook her head, and chanced a swift glance at Josh, whose nostrils flared with the effort of tamping down whatever snipe was brewing in that brain of his, but he shook his head too. "Grand," Sean said.

"Nothing further from me," Simon confirmed without Sean asking and rose to his feet. "Thanks for taking the time to meet with me today."

Sean got up to show Simon out. "Thanks for coming. It's good to see you again. We should catch up properly sometime."

"Yes, we should," Simon agreed, smiling warmly as he shook Eleanor's hand. That smile became an impish grin when he reached Josh. There'd be fireworks for sure if they brought Simon in, but even Josh would know that when it came to his versus Simon's contributions to the foundation, it was no contest. The only question remaining was how much fuss he'd make before he conceded.

***

"We could do with Shaunna's input," Eleanor said. She extracted half a ream of A4 paper from her folder and fanned it across the boardroom table.

"What's all that?" Josh asked.

"Hold that thought." Sean shifted to one side and pulled his phone from his back pocket.

Josh went to pick up one of Eleanor's papers, and she smacked his hand away.

"*My* notes," she said.

"On Simon Henderson?"

"For all the applicants. Where are yours?"

Smirking, Josh unlocked his tablet and waggled the screen in front of her face.

Sean chuckled to himself and proceeded to poke at his phone screen.

"See? Even Tierney's with the times."

"What's that now?"

"Digital notes on the applicants."

"Not likely." Sean tapped the paper notepad in front of him. "Mine are in there. I was laughing at the text Shaunna sent earlier. It says, *Just give the posh twit the job.*"

"How does she know he's a posh twit? She's never met him."

"I wonder!" Eleanor muttered and went on before Josh claimed it hadn't come from him. "So that's one vote for Simon Henderson. Who else is left?" She ran her pencil down a neatly numbered page. Josh leaned over to read it, and she flipped it against her chest so he couldn't see. "Use your own list!"

"I want to know who's on yours."

"You first."

"Dorothy Lomax."

"Applicant number six." Eleanor shuffled her papers and pulled out Dorothy's form. "I was reading her application last night. Her name's familiar."

"Is it?"

"Yeah. Not sure where from or why." Eleanor's eyes followed whatever route her thoughts were taking for a few seconds before she shook her head. "I don't remember. I'll stop trying and it'll probably come to me."

"Adele recognised the name too."

"But you didn't?"

"No. I'd never heard of her. When we're done with these—" he flicked one of Eleanor's little piles "—I'll have a look through Jess's stuff. Maybe they knew each other."

"Good idea," Eleanor said, distracted. Her attention had shifted to Sean, who couldn't have been more engrossed in his phone if he'd been fifteen with a new girlfriend. "How did she interview?"

"Very well. Her husband died the week before, but clearly their relationship ceased to be a marriage some time ago. She'd hired a twenty-four-hour care team."

"What was up with him?"

"Heart disease, diabetes, dementia, rheumatoid arthritis, pancreatitis, cancer of the prostate, ingrown toenails… The list grew throughout her interview. It was a *very long* hour."

Eleanor laughed at Josh's doleful tone. "So he was a drinker."

"Oh, yes, I forgot that one. A-bottle-a-day man, apparently."

"OK. Well, out of the ones I interviewed…" Eleanor picked up her list again and tilted it so she could read it but Josh couldn't. "Rafe Parker was fresh out of law school, which is no use to us. We need someone with a bit of experience behind them. Donna McGill worked for Strang and Partners—"

"Next!" Josh said.

"Yep." Eleanor made a dramatic show of crossing that name off her list, as if there were ever a likelihood of them appointing someone who'd worked for Jess's corrupt cronies. "Who interviewed Basil Lawson?"

"Shaunna and me," Sean said, still thumbing away at his phone. "Too expensive and not a nice fella."

"That leaves— Oh! I've remembered how I know Dorothy Lomax!"

"Do tell!" Josh lifted out of his seat, craning his neck. Eleanor bopped him with the papers in her hand and then put them face down on the table.

"She was on the Prince's Youth Trust panel when Charlie applied for her start-up loan for a women-only sports club."

"She didn't get it, presumably?"

"No, and I'll tell you why. Dorothy rejected the application on the grounds it endorsed positive discrimination."

Josh nodded. "That sounds like the woman we interviewed. Should we readvertise?"

"What's wrong with Simon?" Sean asked. Josh gave him a look, which he didn't see because he was *still* bowed over his phone.

"What *are* you doing, Tierney?"

"Hmm?" At last, eye contact. "Sorry. It's…never mind." He locked his phone and put it back in his pocket. "Why not Simon?"

"Because…he…"

"Is a posh twit?" Eleanor finished for him.

"Yes. No. Which is to say, he is a posh twit, although less of a twit than he used to be. I just…don't like him."

Sean laughed, but there was no joy to it. Indeed, anger was the predominant emotion rolling across the table. "Anything else to add to that?"

"Nothing. I know it's ridiculous—"

"D'you think so?" Scratch anger. Sean was sweating pure fury. "You sat on his CV for a fortnight—"

"I hadn't had a chance to look at it."

"That's a load of shite. What do you think, Eleanor? The same as your man?"

"Sean!" Josh admonished.

"Don't tell me you haven't noticed whatever you want goes around here."

"That's nonsense!"

"Let's see, shall we? Eleanor, do you think we should readvertise?"

Josh couldn't believe what he was hearing. He'd never seen Sean act spitefully before, which made it even riskier to ask, but he had to. "Is there something going on?"

"Don't push this back on me! You're suggesting we dismiss the only decent candidate we have, and by decent, I mean damn perfect for the job, because you *don't like him*?"

"Actually," Eleanor said, and it did sound like she would have spoken in Josh's defence, but Sean wasn't done.

"You were the same with Gabby and Xander at uni. And Genie. All that ballax about them being stuck up, but it wasn't them. It was you, mate."

"All right, wind ye neck in, Tierney," Josh joked, but any illusion he had that his dreadful attempt at Northern Irish slang would neutralise Sean's ire was vaporised by a hateful and, it had to be said, terrifying glare.

"Am I laughing?" Sean asked. His voice was dangerously quiet.

Josh shook his head. He didn't dare utter the word 'sorry' lest it be the spark to light the powder keg sitting less than six feet away. He might not have packed the gunpowder, but he'd nailed down the lid and attached the fuse.

"OK." Eleanor edged forward and pushed her papers back into a single pile. "I think we need to adjourn this discussion, at the very least to hear what Shaunna thinks."

"A wise move," Sean agreed. "I'll walk you out, Eleanor."

She opened her mouth to respond, but Sean was up and already waiting at the door. She grimaced at Josh and mouthed, *Speak to you later.*

He nodded and watched them leave, too stunned to do anything else and with no real idea of what had prompted Sean's outburst. Granted, Josh was being unreasonable about Simon. He'd admitted as much and would have backed down if Sean had let him get that far. Equally unreasonable was Sean's suggestion that Eleanor would agree with whatever Josh wanted to do, which simply wasn't true. If it were, they wouldn't fall out as frequently as they did because Eleanor had *no* trouble saying so when she believed Josh was wrong, and Sean had refereed their fights often enough to know that.

Sean's reaction—overreaction—made little sense when the massive stuff—being blackmailed into doing research to appease their professor, having his work plagiarised, finding out Jess was a fraud—just got him a *bit riled*. No doubt at times, there was a seething sea behind that cool, calm exterior, but even with his brother's antics, which pushed him close to his limit,

Sean had never snapped, so whatever this was, it was about something far bigger than Josh's petty resistance to appointing Simon Henderson.

Still pondering, Josh gathered the cups onto the tray and carried it back to the kitchen. Alice had told him to leave the washing up to her, but it felt like taking advantage, so he set the hot tap running and returned the milk to the fridge, sneering at the coffee lurking in plain sight. Still, tea made a nice change, and if nothing else, Sean's hissy fit had stopped Josh dwelling on Simon's dream, except now, of course, he was thinking about it again.

Dreaming about dead people wasn't unusual; in his experience, it was commonplace for those dealing with bereavement to recall dreaming about their lost loved ones. While there were plenty of solid psychological explanations for why it happened, Josh generally left his grieving clients to appreciate the small solace they found in imagining the dream was a visit from the recently deceased. But Jess *wasn't* recently deceased, and the fact Simon had mentioned his dream at all implied it wasn't a usual occurrence for him to dream about her. Something had triggered it. Not a visit from beyond the grave or some kind of precognition—maybe Simon had seen the Daisy Foundation ad but not registered that he had, or—

"Shit!" Josh dashed back to the sink and turned off the hot tap, and in the nick of time. The steaming meniscus was level with the surround. Tugging his sleeve up his arm, he plunged in and pulled the plug, fidgeting as he waited for the water level to drop enough that he could turn on the cold tap instead and bathe his scalds before the pain in his wrist had him attempting to sever his arm at the elbow with a teaspoon. It was a slow drain, and when the water level reached the halfway point, he chanced turning the tap to emit a trickle and braced. Typically, his phone, in his trouser pocket, chose that moment to judder against the steel lip of the sink. Josh pulled it out, switched hands and answered. Not Sean. George.

"Hey."

"Hey, yourself. You OK?"

"Sort of. Why?"

"Sean's just arrived home and you haven't."

"Ah. We had a bit of a set-to."

"Yeah. I figured. He stomped up the path like the Billy Goats Gruff's troll."

"I don't suppose you know what's up with him?"

"How would I?"

"You talk to Sophie."

"I haven't spoken to Sophie since the party. I don't like to hassle her when she's in London."

"Maybe that's why he's short-tempered. I'll pop in and see him when I get home."

"I'd give him a chance to cool down first."

Josh grunted. That was the same advice George had given him with Libby. He was seeing a pattern he didn't like. "It was about appointing Simon," Josh admitted. "I don't want to."

"Why not?"

"Because..." Ghosts. "It's hard to explain." Ghosts and practical jokes and... "It's like reliving university, George, and I...I just..."

"You can't," George finished for him.

"No."

"Really, you can't. Because I can't either."

Josh sighed, surprised by the shudder in his breath. It was a relief, in a way, that this phone call hadn't gone as he'd expected, but for once, Josh wasn't being stubborn for the sake of it. As Sean had noted, Simon couldn't have been a more perfect fit for the Daisy Foundation, and Josh wanted desperately to defer to his fellow trustees, all three of whom were ready to appoint. It was only now, talking it through with George, that he understood the real reason for his resistance, and it was nothing so petty as disliking the man, particularly as present-day Simon Henderson came across as an affable, decent human being. It was the potential destabilising effect he'd have on Josh's health.

"Are you still with me, ma moitié?"

"Yeah." George sounded a little spacey, but he'd answered straight away.

"Good. I need to…" Josh considered his words carefully, aware of how close they were to trigger territory for George. "I'm going to the surgery on my way home."

"I'll meet you there."

"No. I want to do it on my own." However afraid he was of the unexplained, or practical jokes masquerading as the unexplained, his greater fear was causing George further damage. It was time to reinstate some sense of rationality and move forward with both the plans for the surgery and objectively fulfilling his obligations to the Daisy Foundation. "I won't stay long," he promised. "OK?"

"OK," George agreed, though it was with reluctance. "I love you."

"I love you too. See you soon."

***

"This…is…" Josh gave the handle another aggressive rattle, to no effect, followed by a hard kick that hurt him more than the sturdy external and, crucially, still-locked door to his surgery. "Ridiculous!"

So much for facing his fears. Josh took out his phone and scrolled back through the long, autocorrect-error-riddled messages from Andy, first briefing him on his inspection of the timbers, then his noon meeting with the architect and, lastly, confirmation that he'd been in with the construction crew manager that morning. That last message had arrived in the aftermath of Simon's interview, and Josh had only skimmed it, completely missing the part about the key breaking off and the lock having to be drilled out and replaced. They must have passed in transit, as Andy said he'd drop the new keys off at Campion Trust offices.

Josh returned to his car and quickly typed a reply, explaining he'd left Campion's and would pick up the keys later, glad to have one mystery explained. Seat belt on, he shifted into reverse and glanced up at the building.

A dark shadow shifted across the kitchenette window and then was gone, leaving only the reflection of a few sheepish cumulus clouds drifting in the otherwise clear afternoon sky.

31: Bleeding Out

Heading to Rowan Mews
Present Day
Monday, 29th April

SEAN TURNED INTO the road and slowed to a crawl so he didn't miss the house a second time. He was devastated, still reeling at what he'd done—or hadn't done. He'd been so mad, he was halfway to Genie's before he'd given his son a thought, and even then it was prompted by a call from Unitots, where he'd left Dylan with a promise he'd be back before three. That call had extinguished Sean's anger in an instant, and he'd gone into a full-blown panic trying to figure out if there was a quicker way to drive back when it had been going on for four o'clock by then.

Thank Christ for Sophie's mum, who'd happily agreed to pick up Dylan from the nursery and offered to keep him overnight. Sean said yes, please, then nearly rear-ended the van in front of him. After that, he'd pulled over to gather his tattered wits. Almost two years of this parenting malarkey, he should have had it nailed. He'd *thought* he had, but apparently he was incapable of looking after himself let alone a child. What the hell he'd achieve by racing off to Genie, well, he'd know soon enough, as there was her house again, her car in the drive.

Sean drove a few yards past the gates and parked so he had a clear view between the laurel bushes, although there was nothing to see other than the low sun glinting off the enormous piano conspicuously displayed in the bay window and the intermittent flash of light on the alarm box above. It was almost like a dare— *do you have the ingenuity to steal this grand piano? If you can get it out, it's yours!* Of course, anyone with the space for a grand piano would also have the money to buy one, and it wasn't the sort of thing you could flog down the pub. Sean grinned, amusing himself with the thought. That or he was losing his marbles. Seeing Genie always made him a bit giddy, even knowing what he was walking into. He got out of the car and blipped the locks on his way up the drive to the imposing front door.

Sean smiled genially, his "Hello" lost to the prolonged ring of the doorbell. The woman who'd answered was as smartly dressed and austere as a Tory MP—Genie's housekeeper, he recalled. It would've been handy if he could've remembered her name, as she didn't appear to recognise him at all and kept an iron hold on the half-closed door as if she expected him to attempt to barge past.

"Can I help you, sir?" she asked once the bell had stopped ringing.

"I hope so. Is the lady of the house available?" Sean felt like a teenager on a first date trying to bypass his potential girlfriend's parents.

"She is not." The woman stared at Sean, then past him, then back at him, an unspoken suggestion that he should about turn and go back whence he'd come, although she hadn't shut the door in his face yet, so he pushed his luck.

"Any idea when she might be home?"

"I can't divulge that information, sir. However, if you give me your name and a contact number, I'll pass those on to her."

"Right, yeah, fair enough. The name's Sean Tierney, and my number is..." Sean dug out his mobile phone and was midway to getting the number up on screen when from inside the house came his rescuer's voice.

"It's all right, Margaret, you can let him in."

Same as Mrs. Thatcher. I remember now.

Margaret's nostrils twitched in suppressed defiance as she complied with her young mistress's order and opened the door a few inches further. Phee's smileless face appeared in the gap.

"Hello, Sean. Thank you, Margaret. I'll take it from here."

Margaret wasn't pleased about it, but she let Sean in and quick-marched away, casting a stern eye over him as she shut herself in the kitchen. To be fair, being bossed around by a seventeen-year-old would've irked Sean too.

"Are you all right?" he asked Phee.

She nodded. "Yeah, I'm OK. I'm so sorry. It just slipped out."

"Never mind that now. Where's your mum?"

"She went to the pub with Xander—for lunch. They've been gone for ages." Phee beckoned for him to follow her into the room where he'd slept the last time he'd visited, the night Phee had been rushed to hospital with suspected meningitis. The room itself hadn't changed much—the piano was still there, as he'd seen from outside—but he did a double take at all the stuff piled around the perimeter. Paintings, ornaments, even clothes and shoes, as if someone was preparing for a bric-a-brac sale.

"What's happened here?" he asked.

"Xander."

That wasn't much of an explanation, but Sean became sidetracked by the picture that had once hung on the wall of the café where he'd worked in his student days. "I can't believe she's still got that."

"What?" Phee asked.

"That miserable painting of the cliff. I remember her buying it." He carried on with the story of how he'd convinced Cassandra who owned the café to get rid of all her drab paintings and twee ornaments and instead display art students' work with price tags so customers could buy it. Cass kept a small commission, thus could afford to keep Sean on all year round, the art student got the rest. Everyone was a winner, and Sean was still impressed that he'd come up with the idea, although he probably wouldn't have done anything about it without Genie's encouragement. He'd have told Phee that, but he was talking to himself. She'd drifted across the room to the bay window and was looking out, as desolate as the house atop the cliff in that painting.

"Right, young Phee, you'd better get on and tell me exactly what happened that sent your mother off on a bender with Xander."

"Where's Dylan?"

"With his grandparents."

"Your mum and dad?"

"Sophie's. My mum lives in Derry—too far away for babysitting, unfortunately, but she's coming in June for Dylan's baptism."

"What about your dad?"

"He died."

"Oh. Sorry."

"No need. We weren't close. So—"

"Derry...that's in Northern Ireland, isn't it?"

"It is. Listen, I understand you don't want to talk about it—"

"It's not that."

"No? Because to me, it seems you're dodging the subject, and I'd like to prepare before your mum gets back, give meself a fighting chance."

Phee managed a small laugh at that. "I need to tell you something first."

She turned around but still wouldn't look at him. When, at last, her eyes met his, he knew what she was going to say. Normally, he'd have made sure he was open, non-judgemental, but he was so far off his game, he couldn't raise his guard in time.

"I'm going to have an abortion." As she said it, she shrank back in shame, and if that hadn't kickstarted Sean's nurture drive, her tears surely did. He went straight over, wrapping her in a big hug, and like all those who'd come before her, she managed to grab a few chest hairs along with his shirt as she clung on and sobbed. "I'm sorry, Sean."

"You've nothing to be sorry for." Whether for dropping him in the stink or her decision, it was true either way.

"But you don't want me to."

"Why would you think that?"

"Because you're a Catholic."

"Well, I'm more your lapsed Catholic, which sounds like I just forget to go to church of a Sunday when in truth I only go to weddings and funerals or if my mum nags me. Now she's the real deal—never misses mass or confession—but even she understands that sometimes pregnancy isn't a blessing. And so what if we agree with your decision or not? What matters is that you do what's best for you."

"How do I know it *is* best for me?"

"What—because you're young?" Sean asked. Phee nodded against him. "I met your mum when she wasn't much older than you, and sure, you and she are different people, but you inherited so many of her strengths. You know your own mind. You're astute, determined..." There was movement outside the bay window. "And formidable—did they get a cab?"

Phee lifted her head from Sean's chest, but not before wiping her nose on him. He sighed and found a tissue for her, and they watched together Xander and Genie's meandering progress to the front door.

"So, you've got about ten seconds to tell me everything before you mother has me guts for garters."

"I don't think you need to worry. She's a soppy drunk, but you probably know that."

"I do."

"And she only knows I went to see you, not anything we talked about."

"OK. It might not be so bad then." Still, Sean straightened his shirt and smoothed his hair in preparation for Genie's entrance, and it was a grand one. She skipped into the room, dragging Xander along by his hand and releasing him suddenly when she saw Sean and Phee.

"Well, well!" Swaying, she closed one eye and leaned closer. "Not seeing double. You *are* here."

"You've had a skinful, have ye?"

"Absolutely! It was glorious, wasn't it, Xander?"

"Excuse me." He almost ran out the door; the slam of a second door was followed by muffled retching.

"I should get Jonathan," Genie said, miss-stepping as she turned. Sean lunged and caught her before she went down.

"*I'll* go and get Jonathan," Phee said.

"Thank you, darling!" Genie gushed.

"Drink some water!" Phee instructed on her way out.

"Water? Pfft!" Genie batted at Sean to release her. "I can stand perfectly well, thank you."

"Is that so?"

"Yes!" She pushed away from him, and he tried not to smirk as she slopped like custard back into his arms. "Harrumph."

"Maybe you should sit down."

"I've been sitting all day! Xander's been terrific company. And do you know…" She poked Sean in the midriff. "I have a housekeeper!"

"Yeah, I know. She wasn't for letting me in."

"Not Margaret, silly. She's my assistant. Well, that's the same thing, but we don't call them servants anymore."

"All right." This very drunk Genie was preferable to the raging banshee he'd expected, but she was heavier than she looked and couldn't stand unaided. "Let's take this to the sofa." He didn't give her a choice, steering her across the room.

"Oh, yes. The sofa. Mmm." She tried to kiss him, but he dodged and ended up with alcoholic slobber down his cheek. "I have many fond memories of you and I and a sofa."

"Likewise," Sean said, upping his efforts. A couple of feet from the piece of furniture in question, he spun and gently launched Genie so that she plopped down onto the middle cushion, then quickly sat beside her so she stayed upright. "I'm sorry for not being honest with you, Genie."

She smacked his arm. "I'm telling you about my housekeeper!"

Sean raised his hands in surrender.

"Her name's…" Frowning, Genie turned and hollered, "Xander? What's her name again?" Xander didn't answer, but Genie seemed already to have moved on. "She worked for my grandmother."

"She must be quite an age then."

"Grandmama would have been ninety now. She died. Did you know that?"

"I did," Sean confirmed. She'd died while he was completing his PhD, and supporting Genie through her loss was part of the reason he'd decided to pursue bereavement counselling as a specialism. So in a way, he had her dead grandmother to thank for his career.

"She's dead," Genie said.

Sean nodded sympathetically. He was pretty sure it was the drink talking.

"Not Grandmama! Her housekeeper!"

"Ah! So is she your err...poltergeist?"

A loud, wearisome sigh tore Sean's attention from his drunk companion to the only slightly more sober-looking man clinging to the doorpost.

"Are you all right there, Xander?"

"No. I'm tired of explaining that poltergeists are fictitious."

"My mistake. I thought that was what you called ghosts that move stuff around."

"I don't. Hollywood does."

"There's a whole folklore that goes with it, isn't there?"

Xander's eyebrows peeked above his glasses. "Yes. And one can see how that folklore appeals, especially in a case like this." He pointed towards the piano. "That boy, however, is no poltergeist."

Sean would've dearly loved to turn and look where Xander was pointing, if only to prove there was nothing to see, but fear had him in its firm grasp, and he couldn't even move his eyes. Had he and Phee been standing next to a ghost all that time?

Xander ambled across the room, and Sean heard him say, "I haven't given up."

"I would hope not!" Genie said. Grappling against Sean, she pushed up from the sofa and weaved her way after Xander.

It seemed to break the spell on Sean, who didn't dare move from his seat but could now twist so he could see what was going on. Xander was upright, more or less, his elbows propped on the curved back of the piano, while Genie, remarkably, managed to land on the stool without falling off.

"Am I sitting on him?" she asked. Xander shook his head.

"He's over there, with Beatrice."

"That's it! That's her name." Genie waved in Sean's general direction. He nodded slowly, neutrally, the way he would if he was in the middle of a conflict situation in a healthcare setting rather than a drawing room with two posh people he'd swear were barking mad, but how could he be sure it was them and not him?

"You'll stay for dinner, won't you?" Genie asked. "Both of you."

"I cannot," Xander said. That was it. No reason given. Sean wished he could so brazenly disregard an order disguised as an invitation because a bollocking now would have been a whole lot easier to take than whatever emerged once Genie sobered up. She was, as Francesca would've said, vibrating with anxiety, but he'd driven all this way to say he was sorry. Irrespective of whether she accepted his apology, he needed to stick around and lend his support, however she chose to use it.

"I'm staying," he said.

"Oh, good! I'll let Margaret know." It took a couple of tries for Genie to get her bum off the piano stool, and on the second, the stool scooted away from her. Xander—closer and having thought the same as Sean—dashed around the piano and caught Genie before she fell back into thin air.

"Tell you what," Sean said, "I'll let Margaret know on my way out—I need to get my stuff from the car. Are you all right here for a minute, Xander?"

"Yes." He was in the process of walking Genie back to the sofa.

Sean waited until she was safely seated. "Won't be long."

The kitchen door was open, but he knocked on it before entering. Margaret was sitting at the centre island, a laptop in front of her. She took off her glasses. "Doctor Tierney."

"Hello, Margaret. Genie wanted to let you know she has invited me to stay for dinner."

"I see. Do you have any specific dietary requirements?"

"Well, I'm supposed to be watching my cholesterol, but I'm not a faddy eater, so whatever you're making will do me."

"And will Miss Rowan be joining you?"

"I couldn't say. She went to find Jonathan, whoever he is."

"His Lordship's assistant. I believe he's in their room. I shall go and find out if they plan to stay also."

"Xander—His Lordship says not. I need to get something from my car. Will you let me back in if I leave?"

Despite her aloofness, Margaret apparently had a cheeky side and said with a smirk, "I might."

***

"I brought someone with me," Sean said. He and Genie were sitting on the sofa, post-dinner coffees cooling on the low table. Xander and Jonathan hadn't stayed; Margaret had gone home; Phee had gone to a friend's. The old house ticked peacefully, marking the passage from sunset to late evening; they had the place to themselves—other than the ghosts and Sean's hitchhiker.

"That old fleabag's still alive?"

Sean glanced sideways at Genie, making sure she didn't really think he had Sphinx stowed in the car. "Jesus, if you heard him when he has to see the vet, you'd know how unlikely it is either of us would survive a three-hour drive together. Although I'll have you know, he was treated for fleas, ticks, worms, the whole *kitten caboodle* last week."

Genie groaned at his joke. "He must be getting on a bit now, surely?"

"Fourteen, he is. Plenty of life in the old boy yet." That was Sean's hope, anyway. Both Siamese and Persian breeds were long-living, and Sphinx was fifty-fifty.

"Well?" Genie prompted.

Sean reached forward and picked up their coffees, handing Genie's to her. "Well what?" he asked, sipping innocently.

"If it's not your cat…"

Sean hummed appreciatively, taking his time to swallow. "Good coffee," he said. Genie poked him in the side. Laughing, he set his cup back on its saucer—both gold-rimmed—and struggled up out of the sofa, cursing and delighting in how comfortable everything was in Genie's abode as he left the room.

"Don't take all night!" she shouted.

"I won't," he promised. He was only going as far as the wee bathroom across the hall, where he'd stashed his 'conference bag'—a soft case he kept on standby that contained a toothbrush, toothpaste, deodorant, rechargeable shaver, a change of underwear, phone cable, notepad and pen. He wasn't being presumptuous in bringing it with him; he'd been in no state to reason how this trip might pan out beyond making reparations to Genie and needing a bag of some sort. Retrieving what he'd come for, he left the bag where it was and returned to the drawing room, shaking his head and smiling to himself.

"What's amused you?" Genie asked, watching his progress with interest and leaning to the side in an attempt to see what was behind his back.

"I was just thinking how daft I am."

"Tell me something I don't know."

"I could tell you a lot you don't know, but I don't like to show off."

"You'll take that knowledge to the grave if you don't stop terrorising me."

Sean grinned. Genie was so much fun to torment. "So…a little context if I may?"

"Keep it short."

"I'll do me best. So as you know, when Phee came to see me, she had to stay in a hotel, and I felt awful about it, especially as I think she read more into it than it being due to having only the two bedrooms for Dylan and me. I had the attic converted a while back, but it was so full of junk I couldn't swing Sphinx in there. After I saw Phee off on the train home, I decided to clear the space, not for her specifically, although I'd welcome her anytime. Same goes for you."

"I'll keep it in mind," Genie said drolly and signalled with her hand for him to wind up his story.

"Cutting to the chase because there was a bit more I wanted to share, but—"

"Sean!"

"All right! Look who I found lurking behind the boxes." Sean brought his arms in front of him, cradling the small, white teddy bear with its heart declaring *Love You Always*. Genie gasped and covered her mouth with her hand, her eyes showing fear and anguish—not the reaction Sean had envisaged. She shook her head quite violently, the tears that had fallen zigzagging down her cheeks. Sean quickly set the bear on the table and sat, pulling Genie to him.

"I'm sorry," he murmured into her hair. "I'm so, so sorry. I don't know what I was thinking."

"It's OK," Genie assured him, but it wasn't. Not at all. He'd been there at the time and since wasted years reflecting, wishing he could've pre-empted it, told Jess to choose her words with more care because she *had* loved Genie; he was sure of that. Throwing the bear back in her face, insisting Genie had known all along they were 'just' friends with benefits and she should never have allowed herself to fall in love as if it could be switched on an off at will—it was all part of an act that was brutal and loaded with lies yet was the kindest, most honest thing Jess had ever done. She'd had her own agenda, even back then, not necessarily for a life of crime, but it was a life with no room for significant others.

However much her rejection had stung, Sean now understood that Jess had tried to protect Genie and him.

"I want to hate her," Genie said, still inconsolable. Sean rubbed her back, breathed deeply through his better-late-than-never empathy and blinked the tears from his eyes so he could scowl at that bear.

"No," Genie amended, "I don't want to hate her." She sat up and tugged a handful of tissues from somewhere, scrubbing angrily at her cheeks. "I want to not give a damn, get rid of this pain like a punch to the sternum whenever my denial wears off. She used me, Sean. She used me over and over again, her literal puppet on a string—housemate, fuck buddy, classy whore with bargaining power. I meant nothing beyond what I could do for her, yet I can't shake the vision of her wasting away, dying alone."

Sean the psychologist nodded and hummed, encouraging his patient to go on. Sean the friend and lover wanted to take a chainsaw to that bear, hack right through its lying heart.

As if she'd read his mind, Genie picked up the bear and sat it on her knee, tracing the embroidered words with her finger. "I've had nightmares where she's a wizened, bald hag, shrunken and grey amid a mass of snowy sheets, and I can't reach her. I try to climb onto her bed, but it's too high, too wide, and getting wider all the time." Genie laughed bitterly, hopelessly. "I certainly don't need a psychologist to interpret that for me. All those years I resisted, made her beg for my help when in truth I'd have done anything she asked, and when I offered it willingly, she rejected me. The harder I tried, the further away she pushed me. Sometimes I relish it—that vision of her dying alone—and I think, *serves you right, you bitch*. But I never really wanted that for her. She didn't die alone, did she?"

"She didn't," Sean confirmed. "We were all there the night she passed."

"Who's all?"

"Her mum and dad, boyfriend, friends—there's this whole big group of them. It's a bit mad. Unbelievable. Never in all my years at the hospice have I seen anything like it, more's the pity. Support like that does wonders for a patient's prognosis—if the patient lets it. But, you know, our girl kept us all at arm's length."

Genie leaned against Sean and slid her hand into his lap for comfort, no ulterior motive. "At least it wasn't just me."

Sean adjusted position so that her fingers nestled between his. "She didn't fight it, Genie. She delayed diagnosis, refused treatment, fought me tooth and nail over going into the hospice…"

"I know."

"Did she tell you why?"

"No. She never told me anything except that she didn't love me." Genie closed her eyes, breathed awhile, cleared her throat. "Her boyfriend…"

"Andy."

"Husband then."

"Ah, see now. You said she never told you anything," Sean teased lightly. Genie pinched his inner thigh, and he hissed at the sting. "He's all right, is Andy."

Genie pinched harder. "And I'd almost forgiven you."

"Ouch!" Sean grabbed her hand and moved it out of his lap. "Always shooting the messenger, aren't ye?"

"Well, there's a perfect solution to that, isn't there?" Letting the bear fall to the floor, she rose to her knees and straddled Sean's thighs.

"What's that?" he asked, praying that his arousal, which had simmered all through dinner, would hold out.

"Stop playing errand boy to everyone else, and for once, do what *you* want." She leaned in, her lips trailing up his neck to his ear. "What do you want, Sean?"

"You," he answered without hesitation, then sighed in unabashed joy as she whipped off her top and placed his hands on her bare breasts. He wasn't sure he could deliver, but he'd be damned forever if he didn't try.

32: Exorcises in Love

Rowan Mews
Present Day
Tuesday, 30ᵗʰ April

S OMETHING AWFUL HAD happened last night, something so
awful Sean had left without saying goodbye. Not their love-
making, although it hadn't been earth-moving either. At their
age, Genie didn't expect the acrobatics they'd enjoyed in their
youth—the kind of energetic sex she could still get from Paul if
she so desired, and she did not. She'd made up her mind about
that; Margaret's revelation yesterday merely confirmed it as
the right decision.

No, making love with Sean had been like returning to
one's own bed after a trip away, which, of course, was the case.
It seemed so much longer than a day since she'd arrived home
to the mess that still filled the drawing room, despite Jonathan
and Margaret promising to put everything back. None of it was
their fault. She'd have rather liked to blame Xander, seeing as
she wouldn't have been open to the possibility of ghosts at all
without him egging her on, and then she wouldn't have seen her,
that bloody housekeeper, standing at the stove, bold as brass.

Genie had been too busy shrieking like a loony to remember
the order of what followed, but she and Xander had somehow
made it to the local hostelry, where he'd plied her with alcohol
until her heart stopped trying to escape through her mouth. So,
for that part, Xander was to blame. Had she been sober, she'd have
told Sean exactly what she thought of his deception and thrown

him out on his ear instead of asking him to stay for dinner and then taking him to her bed.

It had all felt so natural and right, and they were well into some very delicious foreplay before Genie even considered they might be cheating on Dylan's mother. She'd halted the proceedings right then and there, but Sean had assured her there was nothing to worry about and then pulled her on top of him, watching her the way he always had as she rode out her first orgasm. By the second, she'd forgotten all about Dylan's mother, other than thanking her and whomever else had helped Sean develop his stamina over the past two decades, or perhaps it was just another benefit of life after forty.

What had remained the same was the affection he lavished upon her after he'd joined her for her third and final orgasm of the night, telling her how much he loved and admired her, how much he missed her and that he wouldn't be letting her slip so far away again. Now here she was, alone in this big, old house, wondering if she'd done something to upset him or if he had wooed her simply to dodge a telling-off and fled at the first opportunity. If it were any other man, it wouldn't have surprised her, but Sean wasn't like that. Correction: he hadn't been the last time they'd spent the night together.

There was little point dissecting it now. Little time, also, as Margaret was due any moment, Xander and Jonathan were coming at nine-thirty, and Genie was still in her dressing gown. She'd call Sean later, if only to check he'd arrived home safely. Returning upstairs, she set the shower running and stood in the doorway, surveying the scene of last night's revelry, which was when it registered—the 'something awful'. Two glasses, a pool of dregs in each, and an empty wine bottle.

"Oh God. Oh…*shit!*"

Three years off the booze, Sean had said, hadn't he? Three years. Why hadn't he refused when she'd offered him the glass? She wouldn't have been offended. Surely, he would have known that! Perhaps he had known, but the temptation had proved too great. Or neither of those things were true, and he'd accepted the glass but then poured it away while Genie was otherwise occupied. That was the best-case scenario; she tried not to dwell on the lack of anywhere to discard a glassful of red wine because Sean hadn't left the room, not even to use the loo, and the possibility she was responsible for him falling off the wagon was so awful she felt sick thinking about it.

She called; he didn't answer, but she couldn't very well leave a voicemail relating to such a sensitive matter. Instead, she sent a general well-wishing text message—*Have a safe journey. Speak later. G x*—and left it at that.

By the time she was showered and dressed, the aroma of coffee had filled the house, along with the sound of Margaret singing to herself. That would usually have put a smile on Genie's face; she hadn't heard Margaret sing in ages and took it as a sign that their troubles were behind them. Another positive: the usual text from Phee had arrived, wishing her a good morning and saying she'd be home around lunchtime, love you and kisses. And perhaps this would be the day Xander finally cleansed the house or whatever it was he did. Sending spirits into the light seemed too religious or too Hollywood—too un-Xander-like.

On her way back downstairs, Genie studied the naked wall, the slightly darker rectangles left by her ancestors' portraits.

"Good morning, Margaret."

"Good morning, my lady." Margaret beamed a smile at Genie as she poured coffee into a mug. "How are you today?"

"Quite well, thank you." It was less of a lie than it would have been twenty minutes previously. "How are you?"

"I'm marvellous, my lady, thank you for asking."

"Oh, good!" Genie sat at the island, her back to the stove. As usual, her newspaper lay folded and waiting. Margaret placed the mug of coffee next to it. "Thank you. I…ah…I don't suppose you've ever noticed anything strange occurring in here, have you?"

"Do you mean in the same ilk as what happened in Miss Rowan's room?"

"Yes."

Margaret pondered a moment, but she was already shaking her head. "Nothing comes to mind, although…" She pursed her lips.

"What is it?" Genie asked.

"I can't say, I'm afraid. It would be unprofessional, as it relates to my former employer."

"I understand." As desperately as she wanted to know more, she wouldn't push the woman, who was so flustered by having almost broken her own rules that a flash of red had spread up her chest and neck. A change of subject was in order. "I was wondering…would Vic be able to come and paint the stairwell?"

"I'd imagine so. Should I ask him?"

"If you wouldn't mind."

"Not at all."

"Wonderful! There's no rush. Whenever suits him." Genie opened the paper and pretended to read, aware of Margaret loitering nearby when normally she'd have left to make a start on the day's duties. After a couple of minutes with no change, Genie looked up and smiled, hopeful Margaret had decided to share after all. No such luck.

"Did you manage to speak to Mr. Harper yesterday evening?"

"I didn't, unfortunately. Which is to say I called but had to leave a voicemail."

"Oh dear me." Margaret's eyebrows arched in distress.

"I will speak with him, Margaret, you have my word."

"I trust you will, my lady. I was thinking how awful it must be to receive a voicemail like that."

"Well, I was a little more cryptic," Genie said, realising the significance of choosing to wait to speak to Sean when she'd had no compunction leaving what amounted to a Dear John voicemail for Paul. "He knows it's coming," she justified.

"He's due back from his trip on Thursday, so perhaps you could take a couple of days' leave? Paid, of course."

"That's very kind, thank you, my lady." She took off her apron and was halfway to the door when she said, "Oh! I almost forgot!" and came back. "There were two telephone calls yesterday afternoon. I believe it was the same man who called twice. He didn't want to leave a message but said he would call back today."

"No name?"

"No, and the number was withheld."

"OK. Thanks, Margaret."

This time, she made it out of the door; a moment later, the vacuum cleaner whirred into action.

Genie drank her coffee and flicked through the newspaper, wondering who had called. On balance, it was likely one of her former clients. Most had moved on to pastures new, but those she'd seen less regularly, who were either unaware she was no longer in the escort business or pushed their luck by playing ignorant, called now and then. She always took the time to catch up and make appropriate recommendations, ending their association on a pleasant note before she blocked their number. She'd had mercifully few troublesome encounters in her twenty-year career, but that part of her life was firmly behind her.

"Gosh, Genie you *are* distracted this morning," she chastised herself, having reached the crossword on the back page without reading or even seeing anything else in the paper. *1 ACROSS: Cabinet ensures in part sobriety. (10)* That was surely her cue to try Sean again.

The line rang out, intermittently becoming louder than the vacuum with each sweep Margaret made along the hallway. Sean's voicemail kicked in. Genie ended the call and hit redial, absently turning back through the newspaper. If Sean didn't answer this time, she'd wait for him to call. Although, maybe that wasn't such a good idea with his track record; under the circumstances, whose turn it was hardly mattered.

Still no response, not even from voicemail, Genie threw down her phone, and it spun across the marble counter, knocking over her mug, splattering the last inch or so of coffee across the newspaper's double spread. Genie leapt from her stool and grabbed the paper towel, tearing off a couple of sheets to blot the spillage, noticing as she dabbed a byline towards the bottom of the last column.

New evidence emerges in Met Police hunt for fraud victims' missing millions.

The roll of paper towel toppled and fell off the island, unfurling in a slow diagonal line across the tiled floor before it was halted by the toes of a pair of low-heeled black shoes. Next came the doorbell's loud *ding-dong* followed immediately by the ringing of the landline phone in the hallway. The vacuum powered down, and Margaret shouted, "One moment, please!" To whom, Genie didn't wait to find out. She snatched Margaret's keys from her bag and fled to the wine cellar.

***

Genie set her glass on the cabinet and crouched next to the piano, waving her arm underneath it and concentrating on 'being open'.

"Are you sure he's gone?" she asked again.

"Yes, I am certain," Xander confirmed.

"That's...disappointing."

"You still have Beatrice."

"Ah, yes. Dearest Beatrice." If she sounded blasé, it was because what she'd lost in propriety earlier, when she'd taken Margaret's keys without permission, she'd since found in Dutch courage, though it had taken something a little stronger than wine. "She's a permanent fixture, is she?"

"For as long as you live here, yes—perhaps beyond. It's not unknown for ghosts to tag along when their loved ones relocate."

"So I could be stuck with her forever," Genie mused. It was a surprisingly comforting thought, like having a housekeeper in reserve, although it was as well Xander's gift was rare. One sniff of a planchette and Beatrice would be spilling all their secrets, whereas Margaret was the soul of discretion and, as she had more than proved in recent times, indispensable.

As if the thought had summoned her, Margaret appeared in the doorway. "Victor's left with the recycling now, my lady."

"My goodness, that was jolly efficient of him. Do pass on my thanks, won't you? And thank *you*, Margaret."

The woman nodded meekly and left.

Genie returned to the sofa, picking up her glass and the Scotch on her way. "Anyone else for a top-up?" She raised the bottle; Xander and Jonathan both declined. "Of course," she said, generously refilling her glass and ignoring Jonathan's inquisitive frown, "the question remains of why the boy was here in the first place. You said it wasn't he who was playing the piano, Xander."

"Correct. He covered his ears, like this." Xander clasped his hands to the sides of his head. "He was crying. He wanted it to stop."

"Who *was* playing?"

"I still cannot tell you, but there were two of them, playing one hand each. A male and a female. What did your grandmother look like?"

"She was...well." Genie indicated the portrait, restored to its place above the mantel. "That's her, or an excellent likeness."

"Then it was not your grandmother, unless she tinted her hair."

"She did, but only to maintain her natural colour. Dark like mine."

"No. This woman was blonde and young. She may even have been adolescent."

"The boy's mother?"

"I don't think so."

"And the male?"

"Ah, now, he could have been related to the boy. But it might also have been the boy at a different age."

"I don't understand how that's possible," Genie said.

"Nor do I," Xander admitted.

"Are they gone too?"

"Yes—" He looked to the left of the fireplace. "Did they?"

"What's Beatrice saying now?"

"That they left with the boy. She knows more about it, but…"

"But?"

Xander stood and fastened his blazer. "We must be on our way. Jonathan? Genie, thank you for your hospitality." He was already at the door.

"Wait! Xander!" Genie raced after him. "You can't leave now!"

"Your…poltergeist is gone—"

"I haven't even had a chance to thank you."

"I didn't do anything. Now, we really must go."

Genie blocked his exit. "Not until you tell me why you're suddenly in such a hurry to leave." She looked to Jonathan, but he shrugged, as puzzled as Genie was. Xander tried to edge past her. She moved with him. He stepped back. "Talk to me, please, Xander."

"I was wrong," he said. "I don't like being wrong."

"About what?"

"The boy being tethered here. Jonathan—bring the car to the tradesman's entrance."

"Yes, my lord." Xander's obedient little footman quick-marched off down the hall.

"The *tradesman's entrance*?" Genie borderline shrieked and started to laugh. The day had been a farce from the start, and she was well on her way to writing it off as a prolonged flashback. That or Xander had slipped something into her wine yesterday— an idea so ludicrous she was almost wetting herself. "So not only are you in a *tremendous* hurry to leave, you're being sneaky about it!" she shouted, once again chasing after Xander, who had followed Jonathan to the side door—the 'tradesman's entrance'— and stood, blinking, watching Jonathan reverse the car up the side of the house. As Genie reached Xander, the doorbell sounded, its echo joined by the sound of Margaret's sensible heels trotting along the hall.

The voices were muffled, but Genie heard enough of the exchange to put it all together. Xander was right: he needed to leave. With that thought, she shoved him off the step and almost into the car's path. "I'm sorry," she hissed. "Go!"

"Call your father!" he urged as she shut the door in his face and locked it. Then, with a quick smooth of her hair and pat of her cheeks, she went to face the metaphorical music she'd spent almost two years listening for.

"Good morning, Officers. How can I help you?"

"Lady Imogen Rowan?" The question came from the younger and taller of the two, a detective dressed in a black suit, white shirt and blue paisley tie, while the shorter, older man was in uniform.

"Yes, that's me," Genie confirmed.

"I'm Detective Inspector Thompson, Ma'am, from West Mercia Police, and this is Police Constable Hanlon. We're here on behalf of our colleagues in the Metropolitan Police. They believe you are in possession of evidence of significant value to an ongoing investigation. I trust we have your cooperation to search your premises?"

Genie knew the drill, and it had nothing to do with having a degree in law—a career she'd ditched for motherhood and one that didn't require prostitution of her soul. If she didn't cooperate, they'd assume she had something to hide and get a search warrant from the magistrates.

"What is the nature of this evidence?"

"Documents pertaining to criminal activity."

"I see. Margaret, please accompany the officers to the vault and anywhere else they wish to search."

"Yes, my lady. This way, please."

The detective inspector followed Margaret down the hall, while the uniformed constable started pulling out drawers from the bureau.

"Would you like a drink, Officer?" Genie asked.

"No, thank you, Ma'am."

"All right, well, I hope you won't mind if I finish mine. Excuse me." Genie went into the drawing room and sat on the sofa, the trauma of having her house turned over numbed by her inebriation.

Finished with the bureau, the constable went upstairs with Genie's permission, into her room, Phee's room, the guest rooms—she hadn't considered before how distinct the sound of each door was—and up to the attic before returning downstairs and searching the drawing room. He was much more efficient than the detective inspector, or perhaps less thorough, as he checked inside the piano and stool and glanced up the chimney but left the rest of the furniture and Genie undisturbed. Empty-handed, he moved to the doorway and stood at ease, his gaze fixed on a point across the room, keeping Genie in his peripheral vision. She rose and went to the drinks cabinet for a refill. At this rate, she'd need to restock on whisky as well as wine.

"Can you tell me more about this investigation, Officer?"

"I can't, I'm afraid, Ma'am." He offered an insincere half smile. Genie sighed and returned to the sofa, nursing her glass and wondering if Xander had managed to escape without being spotted. A politician of his standing could be ruined if they were caught up in a criminal investigation. The same would be true of her father, if she were to take Xander's advice and call him, which she had no intention of doing. Still, it was nice of Xander to consider her welfare.

It was perhaps a quarter of an hour later before Margaret and the detective inspector emerged from the vault, the latter carrying Genie's crate of legal documents, which he offloaded onto the constable.

"Did you find what you were looking for?" Genie asked.

"To be frank with you, Ma'am, I'm not sure what we're looking for. Are there any other documents on the premises?"

"No. I keep everything in the vault."

The constable nodded, confirming Genie's statement.

"In that case, here's a receipt detailing what we've taken." The detective inspector handed over a printed list, which Margaret had already signed.

With her heart once more attempting to flee and hoping she was successfully concealing her anxiety, Genie looked over the items listed.

"Don't worry, Ma'am, I'll lock these away myself," the detective inspector said.

Not successful then. Genie folded the list and passed it to Margaret for safe-keeping. "What happens now?"

"We'll scan the documents and return them to you as soon as our colleagues have reviewed them."

"How long will that take?"

"I can't say, I'm sorry." The detective inspector moved along the hall, his colleague moving with him as if the two were leashed together. Margaret stepped past them and opened the front door. The constable, already panting with the effort of carrying the heavy crate, went ahead. The detective inspector shook Genie's hand. "I will let my colleagues know that you cooperated fully, Ma'am."

"Thank you." Genie kept up her smile until Margaret closed the door and the police car, parked in the driveway, was out of sight. Genie slumped against the wall.

"What a morning! I think we both thoroughly deserve a stiff drink! What say you?"

Margaret didn't argue with that.

33: The French Have a Phrase for It

On Campus
Present Day
Monday, 13ᵗʰ May

"A FAMILY EMERGENCY."

The Dean of Psychology and Counselling peered over her glasses, briefly making eye contact, although her attention ostensibly remained on the papers in her hands rather than on Josh, who was beginning to feel like a naughty pupil called before the headteacher when that honour belonged to his errant business partner. Of course, the business with said partner was contingent on him showing his face again. As to when he might do so, that was very much the question of the moment.

"How long does Doctor Tierney envisage this emergency will continue?"

"I couldn't say, Dean. What I *can* say—" and had already said "—is that I will continue to cover Doctor Tierney's duties until his return."

The dean grunted, pulled open a desk drawer, shoved the papers inside, shut the drawer, opened it again and withdrew a small cyan-and-white-striped paper bag. "Mint imperial?" She popped one into her mouth and pushed the bag across the desk.

"Thank you." Josh took one out of politeness and was soon glad he had. The smooth, mildly minty sweet nestled pleasantly on his tongue, evoking cherished childhood memories from before he'd known the dangers of tooth decay and enamel erosion. It appalled him that he hadn't visited a dentist until he was six years old—

one of many cultural differences that came with being brought up by an older French woman who considered no meal complete without dessert and contended that dentists, like doctors, were for emergencies only.

"You surprise me, Josh." The dean crunched her mint and washed it down with a generous slurp from her coffee mug. "You left us less than a month ago, having resisted my every effort to coax you into staying. Now here you are, a willing volunteer."

"Well, I do expect you to pay me," Josh joked thickly around the sweet. The dean chuckled.

"How is your therapy service progressing?"

Josh crunched. "Very well." A sharp fragment stuck in his throat, probably caught on the lie. True, the renovations were underway, and the utilities were connected—they'd never been disconnected—but he needed Sean's input on fixtures and fittings, directory listings, when they'd start advertising, web presence, booking systems…the list was endless. But none of that would matter if he choked to death on a mint imperial.

The dean opened her drawer again and handed over a bottle of water. Josh took a grateful gulp, dislodging the shard.

"What's your completion date?"

"The official opening is the first of October."

"So if Doctor Tierney were still on leave at the start of the next semester—"

"He won't be." He couldn't be.

"Hypothetically, if he is, can you continue covering for him? If not, I'll have to appoint someone fixed term."

"Really, he won't be, but *hypothetically*, I'd be able to oversee the counselling diploma, not the rest."

"All right. I'll get something in place for Sean's other duties, but can you tell him to call me, please? He should've done that instead of making his own arrangements."

"I'll let him know," Josh said, shifting his eyes to the bag of mint imperials as he stood.

"Take some with you."

Shameless, he grabbed a few and left, heading back to Sean's office to collect his laptop and wondering if Sean would receive a formal reprimand for going AWOL and also if he'd care, seeing as he hadn't actually asked Josh to cover for him. He'd left both the university and the hospice in the lurch, the latter especially troubling when Sean loved his work there and Josh wasn't qualified to step in. As it was, Josh was supervising doctoral candidates when he didn't have a doctorate, but he'd expected Sean to be gone for a few days at most. In their almost twenty-three years of friendship, he'd never known him to storm off, just like he'd never seen him throw a paddy the way he had over appointing Simon. Storming off and paddy-throwing were very much Josh's domain, and he wished now he'd had it out with Sean right away instead of going to the surgery, intent of facing his demons alone.

That was two weeks ago, and he hadn't been back to the surgery since. Nor had he tackled Sean, as within minutes of Josh arriving home, Sean had marched out of his house, slung an overnight bag in the boot of his fancy, bigger-than-a-runaround car, paused briefly to cast a thunderous glance at Josh's office window, then driven away. Other than texting Libby to ask if she'd feed Sphinx, that was the last they'd seen or heard from him. Josh had no idea where he'd gone or for how long, and if Shaunna or Sophie knew, they weren't sharing.

The three mint imperials he'd snagged from the dean were gone before he reached his car, and they'd given him a taste for more. He left the campus and drove straight to the nearest sweet shop, bought two bags and took a detour to the rest home to see his grandma. She picked up the bag he placed on her tray and dropped it again, unimpressed, although little impressed her these days. Josh expected he'd have seen and heard everything by the time he was ninety too.

"Did you say you'd visit today?" she asked in French.

"No," Josh answered, also in French, and went on to tell her about his meeting with the dean, which had prompted him to buy sweets and come to see her. Josh didn't speak the language well, but the stroke that put her in a rest home had also taken away her comprehension of English, so he soldiered on. Before he realised it, he was telling her about his 'haunted' surgery and Sean's disappearing act. As he talked, his grandmother sucked noisily on mint imperials, occasionally grunting in acknowledgement. He wasn't even sure she was listening, but the stream of words kept coming. It was cathartic yet strange when theirs had always been a relationship of silence, communicating through gestures and actions.

"L'appel du vide," she said when at last the stream ran dry.

"Who? Sean or me?"

Her reply was a predictable, enigmatic shrug. That was how she'd raised him—to discover the answers for himself. The rattle of the advancing lunch trolley, however, made one decision for him.

"I'm going now." He kissed her cheeks; she pinched his. "Be nice to the nurses." She pursed her lips, her eyes twinkling playfully. He had it on good authority that she gave the rest home staff no trouble, or not since they'd moved her to a room with a patio so she could occasionally go out for a cigarette.

He pondered all the way home over what she'd said. L'appel du vide, the call of the void, could be anything from the urge to jump the red light at a junction to a full existential crisis, and the therapy centre—he was thinking something related to Shaunna's circle motif, name-wise—was a leap into the unknown for him *and* Sean, but they'd taken it months ago. Fearlessly, even. So why the delayed reaction? Was that why Sean had buggered off? Could it explain Josh's ghosts? Or had his grandma meant Sean was having some kind of personal crisis that was bigger than their business venture? Was the business tied to it? Had it triggered it somehow?

There were no answers, only more questions.

He parked the car outside the house and went straight up to his office, thinking back to the day of Simon's interview and whether there had been any clues to Sean's state of mind. He'd been communicating with Shaunna via text messages and seemed no different than usual, a little tired maybe, but in good spirits up until the moment he'd snapped. He could've shut Josh down with some of that cunning Tierney persuasion. Instead, he'd set it up as 'us and them'—him and Shaunna versus Josh and Eleanor—when that wasn't the case. Eleanor had liked Simon and would have sided with Sean if he hadn't attacked her.

Was that what this was all about? A flounce to get Josh to back down? It was extreme, and since when did Josh give in to tantrums?

A light thud on the desk stopped him replaying Sean's departure on repeat, the waft of coffee steam alerting him to the full mug beside him and his husband already halfway down the stairs.

"George, hold on."

George stopped and peered over the banister, eyebrows raised.

"I…" Josh had no idea what he wanted to say. He was used to a certain amount of disorientation when he was cycling and his perception of reality was skewed, but his moods were stable, he thought. Sean would have been able to tell him, except…

Except it was always Josh relying on Sean to tell him he was stable or make him so. In theory, they sponsored each other through difficult times, but Josh wasn't sure that had ever been the reality, not when it came to a real crisis, when Sean felt *l'appel du vide*.

"Have I been conning myself all this time, George?"

"About what?"

"Sean."

"I'm not sure what you mean."

"I've always assumed he's more resilient than I am, but I think he's just better at hiding it from people."

George backtracked and sat on the top step. "He taught you that emotion suppression technique, didn't he? So I guess he'd be pretty good at hiding his feelings, but didn't he have a bit of a blip the day Dylan was born?"

"Yes! George, that's it! Because that blip, as you called it, wasn't about becoming a father per se. It was the new responsibility, and Jess was dying—you know she and Sean were involved at uni, don't you?"

"Yeah, you told me."

"He admitted he took the hospital job here so he'd be near Jess and me, yet he never tried to contact us. I only found out because I had a psych appointment and saw his photo on the unit staff board. Jess didn't know until we dragged her to quiz night a couple of months before she died, and by then it was too late. I don't know why he didn't tell us sooner. Well, I can understand him not telling me. We hadn't spoken since he left for Bristol to do his PhD, and it was an...acrimonious farewell."

"That's one way of putting it," George muttered, and Josh chuckled. Poor George and Sophie had caught the brunt of his and Sean's spiteful bickering back when they thought they could work together and ignore their past. They'd fought less since they'd had it out, but two people as bloody-minded as they were would inevitably butt heads from time to time.

"We wanted to be students forever. We used to talk about it, usually when we'd pulled an all-nighter and were caffeinated to the hilt. We'd graduate and do our Master's, take years to complete our PhDs, apply for research fellowships—anything that would keep us in academia. It was a nice dream, but Sean couldn't afford to be an eternal student, which is why he changed to the clinical track. Then I became ill, and Sean buggered off to Bristol, not because I was ill, although it felt like it at the time. There were other things going on that he refused to talk about, and I think in the end it got too much for him, so he hatched an escape plan."

"You're worried he's done the same thing again."

"I am. If you'd seen him at that meeting, George... I admit I'm at fault and he had every right to be pissed off, but his reaction was disproportionate. Maybe seeing Simon again so soon after Phee turned up reignited his feelings for Jess." It was speculation and conjecture without hearing from the man himself. "How do I get through to him?"

"You're asking me? You're the—"

"Psychologist. I know. But you're a better friend than I could ever hope to be. What would you do?"

George rubbed his chin as he thought about it, the light rasp of work-roughened fingers against stubble familiar and reassuring. "I'd get on his case."

"He's ignoring my calls."

"Then leave voicemails, send texts, call his mum, Sophie, his brother, Shaunna—anyone you can think of who might be in touch with him."

"If someone harassed me like that, I'd rip their head off."

"Yep. But Sean isn't you. Don't forget, Joshua, he…" George zoned out.

"He saved my life against my will. Twice," Josh finished. He sat next to George on the stair and put his arms around him in case he toppled, but the episode was brief, an absence rather than a seizure. "You're getting better."

George nodded.

"The art therapy's working."

"Desensitisation."

"In art therapy?"

"No. You. Tub-thumping."

"Tub… Ohh! I see!" Reckless disregard for his own survival was finally paying dividends. Josh leaned his head against George's. "Are you all right?"

"Yeah. Are you?"

"I am. I'm going to start my Tierney harassment campaign, but a bit of stealth is called for. I'll send a group text message to him, Ellie and Shaunna, seconding his proposal to appoint Simon as legal trustee."

"For real?"

"Yes. I can handle it, George. If you can."

"Even if Sean rips your head off?"

"Even that. I'm invincible. You just said so. I get knocked down—"

"Yeah, I'm an idiot. Go send that text."

***

When the landline rang later that evening, Josh felt a surge of panic. All his friends called his mobile phone, Sean included, usually, but in the absence of any response to his messages, Josh was primed for bad news.

"Hello?"

"Hello, is that Joshua Sandison-Morley?" The caller spoke upper RP, almost certainly Oxbridge-educated, with a round, deep register, the whole effect putting Josh in mind of a sumptuous purple velvet.

"Whatever you're selling, I'm not interested." He moved the receiver away from his ear, about to end the call.

"I'm not a salesman. My name is Jonathan Reardon."

Josh gave him the benefit of the doubt. "How may I help you?"

"My apologies for not introducing myself first. You are Mr. Sandison-Morley, I presume?"

"Josh, yes."

"Ah. Good evening, Josh. I'm calling on behalf of Lord Etherington-Bowes."

Xander? Was it paranoia that Josh's first thought was his web search on Simon Henderson had been traced by the Secret Service? Perhaps not, considering Xander sat in the House of Lords. Surely, if a government agency had been monitoring Josh's internet activity, wouldn't they have also hacked his email and seen he and Simon were corresponding about the Daisy Foundation? It seemed far-fetched, but Josh could think of no other reason for the call when Xander had ditched their university at the end of Freshers' Week and fled to Cambridge, where presumably he'd met Jonathan Reardon, whoever he was.

There were more commonplace connections between them, such as Gabby being both Xander's cousin and George's art therapist, but that didn't explain a call on Xander's behalf any better than Secret Service snooping did. So why?

Jonathan Reardon's next statement answered that.

"A mutual acquaintance informed His Lordship that you may wish to utilise his gift."

"*Which* mutual acquaintance?" He didn't need to ask which gift.

"I'm not at liberty to—"

"Imogen Rowan." That was Xander, and with his utterance, the pieces fell into place then ignited in a whoosh of flaming fury. *Bloody Tierney.* It had to be.

"Imogen and I are alumni, but I hardly knew her," Josh said. "Could you put Xander on, please?"

"I'm afraid not. He doesn't use the telephone."

"I see." *Sensible man.* "In that case, could you tell him— actually, forgive me, but I don't know who you are in relation to Xander. His husband?"

"Good gracious!" Jonathan laughed. "No, I'm his personal aide. Perhaps—"

Xander's voice, as loud as Jonathan's, interrupted, "Ask him when he's available for us to call in on him."

"He can hear you, my lord."

"I can," Josh confirmed levelly. He was livid but containing it so far. Clearly, Sean had blabbed about the haunting. He might even have contacted Xander directly and asked him to be discreet. Either way, Josh had no intention of agreeing to have Xander 'call in on him'. "I'm sorry, you've been misinformed."

"What about Sunday?" Xander said.

"Am I not making myself clear? I do not need to *utilise your gift*. Goodbye!" Josh hung up and ripped the phone's cord out of the wall socket.

All the grovelling he'd done, admitting he'd been pigheaded in not wanting to appoint Simon, telling Sean not to worry about work and take as long as he needed, only for this betrayal. Sean knew how Josh felt about Xander, or *had* felt for that one week of university. Sean had even brought it up after Simon's interview, accusing Josh of snobbishness like his lowly status meant anything to Lord Xander Etherington-Bowes. If he was that much of a snob, he wouldn't have married George or befriended Sean, and he certainly wouldn't have inconvenienced himself to cover for Sean with the dean.

No, however tough life was for Doctor Tierney right now, this was unacceptable. Josh marched upstairs for his mobile phone and fired off a text message telling him exactly that. He didn't expect a reply. Sean had read but not responded to the group message about Simon and hadn't picked up when Josh called earlier. Still, he stood with his phone in his hand for a full five minutes and would have continued to do so indefinitely had the front door not opened to admit a cheerfully whistling George, back from his art therapy session.

Josh left his phone and went to warm George's dinner, greeting him with a light, "Hey, you," and a kiss as he raced past.

"Hey, yourself." George hung up his jacket and followed Josh into the kitchen. "Mmm. Is that moussaka?" He squinted at the plate spinning in the microwave.

"Yes. It's only a ready meal, I'm afraid."

"I don't care. I'm starving." George took a half-full milk bottle from the fridge and swigged from it. "So, my painting's destroyed."

The microwave pinged; Josh removed the moussaka and slid it out of the container onto a plate, depositing it and a fork on the table. "Two minutes' standing," he warned and then shook his head in dismay when George dived straight in without waiting and *hoo-hoo-hooed*, chimp-like. "That's a radical approach."

"Huh?" George swallowed and followed up with a glug of milk.

"I've always thought it was a peaceful, gentle process. Granted, it's not my area of expertise—"

"Joshua, what are you talking about?" Undaunted, George scooped up another great, steaming forkful of moussaka.

"Not the same thing you are, it seems. *You* didn't destroy your painting?"

"No. Why would I?" And another.

"As part of the treatment."

"Right." George didn't comment further, intent on wolfing down his dinner before it fell below the temperature of molten lava. Fearing for his husband's oesophagus, Josh staved off asking further questions for as long as he could. He didn't quite make it to the empty plate but not far off.

"If you didn't destroy your painting, who did?"

"Vandals. It's all been cleaned up now, obviously, but they smeared paint everywhere and threw white spirit on the walls." George scooped up the last morsel of moussaka, chewing and swallowing on the way to the sink. He rinsed his plate and put it in the dishwasher, then picked up the milk bottle and sipped casually as if he were recapping something they had discussed before when, in fact, Josh was completely lost.

"What vandals?" he asked.

"The ones who broke into Gabby's studio."

"I beg your pardon?"

"She didn't tell you?"

"I haven't spoken to her since our party."

"I thought…wasn't that what you were talking about?"

"When?"

"At the party?"

"No. We were talking about Simon Henderson. Could you start at the beginning? *When* was Gabby's studio broken into?"

"The day of the party. Well, the night before. She arrived for work Friday morning and the place was trashed."

"Bloody hell. Did they take anything?"

"There's nothing to take—unless there's an underground market for art supplies."

"They could've been solvent abusers."

"The good stuff was still locked in the storeroom, and white spirit and turps substitute don't get you high."

It was no mystery how George knew that. Drug abuse was a major problem on the estate where he and his mum had lived, not surprisingly. The residents were poor and their life chances were grim. By contrast, Gabby's studio was in a well-to-do rural town where, one could safely generalise, there were fewer addicts and a lower crime rate, which begged the question of why someone would break into an art therapist's studio.

"Had she forgotten to lock up?"

"Nope. Both the front and back doors were still locked."

"Someone with a key?"

"Only Gabby and Howard have keys."

"An open window?"

"That's what the police reckon. None of the windows were open when Gabby got there, but whoever broke in could've closed the window and then left through the door."

That seemed unlikely. "What else did the police say?"

"Not much. They recorded the incident, gave her a load of crime prevention gubbins and said they'd chat to some local teens who've been causing bother, but there's no security cameras and too many people's fingerprints on everything. She reported it to her insurance, but it was less than the excess—about fifty quid's worth of damage."

"Discounting personal injury to Gabby and her clients," Josh argued.

"I guess, but it's not like we're creating masterpieces, is it?" George downed the rest of the milk and rinsed the bottle. "So how was your evening?"

"Unexpected."

"OK?"

"I'll tell you tomorrow or I'll be dwelling on it all night."

"Fair enough," George said. "I'm going to bed. You coming?"

"I'll be up in a second. I'll just put this out and check the doors." Josh picked up the bottle and went out to the recycling bin, his mind not on the task. Now he understood Dustin's remark about Gabby almost not making it to the party, and he could also appreciate why Gabby hadn't wanted to talk about the break-in. Even after all these years, recalling the moment he'd known for sure someone had been in his room at uni evoked an acute sense of violation.

Still, he couldn't shift his growing unease. First the surgery, then Simon's dream and Gabby's break-in all in the same week? Objectively, he kept telling himself he was seeing links that didn't exist, but why would yobs with no respect for others' property go to the trouble of closing the window and locking the doors behind them? And how did they lock the doors without a key?

Josh was still clinging, by fingertips only admittedly, to the hope of finding a perfectly normal explanation that involved neither sabotage nor ghosts, and maybe Sean was trying to help, although a warning would've been nice. At least with Xander, he would have a definitive answer and wouldn't be ridiculed for entertaining the possibility of a supernatural cause, which, he supposed, couldn't be ascertained remotely.

He startled at the faint clicking noise from above and looked up. George poked his head out the window.

"Have you fallen in?"

With a sheepish smile, Josh released the bin lid and went back inside, reconnecting the landline and dialling out the last number that called.

"Sunday, you said."

"Ah, Josh. Hello. Yes."

"It's a long way for him to come just to see me."

"It would be. However, His Lordship is visiting his cousins this weekend."

"Josh is an atheist too," Xander said in the background.

Josh sighed heavily. It was a prime example of why he found Xander so infuriating. "Any time after ten," he said.

"May I take down your address, please?"

"Certainly, it's—" Josh stopped and listened in growing horror as Xander reeled off their address, postcode and all. "Yes, that's it."

"I'll call Sunday morning to confirm the exact time, but it will be about eleven o'clock."

"It *will be* eleven o'clock," Xander stated.

"I look forward to it," Josh lied and ended the call before Xander gave him an aneurysm.

34: Getting Up Again

A Park in Southwest London
Present Day
Tuesday, 14ᵗʰ May

Daddy!" Dylan waved from the top of the slide and then threw himself on his bottom, kicking his feet, and down he came, giggling as he flew off the end into the wood chips surrounding the cabin-style climbing apparatus. "Again!" he said and raced off, up the stairs, through one tiny house and across the rope bridge to the next before appearing once more at the top of the slide. And down he came. And up he went.

"How does he keep going?" Sean muttered. As his mother would've said, he was exhausted from watching, but it was worth it to see Dylan enjoying himself, and they both slept better when he'd burnt off some of that boundless energy.

It was a shame there were no other kids around for him to play with. For an inner-city park in a fairly poor area, it was well-tended but quiet most days: after two weeks staying in a budget hotel that kicked them out of the room between ten and four, Sean had bench slats imprinted on his backside and was glad today's play session was almost over.

On Dylan's next crash landing, he went over to intercept. "Come on, fella. Time to go and meet Mummy from work."

"No!" Dylan scooted out of reach, making Sean work for it. He gave chase and caught Dylan by the back of his coat, which he didn't like at all and tried to break free.

"That's enough now. Let's go." Sean picked him up, ignoring the screaming and sharp kicks to sensitive places while they fought each other over pushchair straps. Dylan was at that age when tantrums could erupt out of nothing, although it was hardly nothing when his entire routine had been disrupted. Sean didn't think either of them would've survived without Sophie's calm, reassuring presence, which was why he'd gone from Genie's to Sophie's parents to fetch Dylan, then headed straight down to London.

The twenty-minute walk to the university hospital was mostly one long, residential road made up of terraced houses slightly larger than Sean's and around eight times the market value. Not that he'd ever consider moving—his mother would've worried herself to death if she'd known they were here at all—but he was amazed the hospitals had any staff when just feeding the two of them for a fortnight had wiped out his last NHS pay packet. He reminded himself he still had his lecturing money coming in and some savings and kept his cold feet moving at a steady pace, even putting on a bit of a sprint when he rounded the corner and saw Sophie coming towards them.

"Hello, you two!" She crouched in front of Dylan. "What're you covered in?"

"Wood chips," Sean said.

"Have you been sawing down trees?"

Dylan shook his head vigorously and pointed back the way they'd come. "Park!"

"Ohhh!" Sophie straightened up and smiled at Sean. "Everything OK?"

"Grand," he confirmed, swinging the pushchair around, heading for the local juice bar that had become their daily haunt. "Josh called again."

"Another voicemail?"

"Aye." That brought the running total to seven voicemails and twenty-four text messages, not counting the abundance of missed calls and the calls to Sophie and to Sean's mum, the latter of which had resulted in Sean lying to her for the first time in his adult life and seriously pushed the limits of their friendship.

"What did he have to say this time?"

"That he's still angry, but he understands what I was trying to do."

"Sounds almost like an apology."

"Almost." It was a step in the right direction compared to the previous day's messages, which went, in the space of a few hours, from *I'm here for you* to ranting in fury because Sean had told Xander about the surgery being haunted, which he hadn't. He and Xander had been too busy keeping Genie from falling flat on her face to have a conversation of any kind, but Sean supposed he must've mentioned it to Genie or else how would Xander have known? Then there was Josh's group message proposing they appoint Simon as the foundation's legal advisor, listing the reasons why as if the other three trustees were the ones who'd been against it.

"Have you heard anything more from Genie or Phee?" Sophie asked.

"Not a word." The day he'd left Genie in bed, he'd replied to her message confirming he'd made it home in one piece—true if he stuck to the physical—and she'd sent back an essay that threatened to send him completely off the rails. Paul was history, which was good news, and Phee was booked in for her termination the following week—the day after her eighteenth birthday. So really, Genie need never know that Phee was pregnant because of Paul, but the compulsion to tell her was driving Sean mad.

Genie had signed off her lengthy message with *I'm sorry if I made you do things you didn't want to*, and he wished he could've assured her, told her he'd been a willing participant, but that wasn't a discussion he could handle right now.

A shrill whistle snapped him out of his woeful thoughts; Sophie was standing outside the juice bar several yards back along the pavement. He turned the pushchair around and went to join her, keeping his head down. She was watching him so intently he felt stripped naked. He knew what was coming. He'd been waiting for it since he'd told her what had happened. As he reached her, he looked up and gave her a wan smile, turning it into a wide grin as they went inside together.

"Bout ye?" he called cheerily to Freya, one of the owners and a Belfast ex-pat, they'd established two weeks ago.

"Ah, if it isn't himself!" Unlike his, her grin was the genuine article, but she wasn't addressing Sean. "Hello, big man! What've you been up to? You look like a macaroon, so you do!"

She thumbed at the tray of desiccated-coconut-covered cakes in the display cabinet. Sophie and Sean laughed. Dylan wriggled in his seat, smiling coyly. He was the same every visit: once they were settled at a table, there'd be no shutting him up.

"What'll it be? The usual?"

"Yes, please," Sophie confirmed and dug out her purse while Sean went to find a table.

"Whisht!" Freya shooed Sophie away. "Pay when you're leaving."

"OK, thank you." Sophie put her purse back in her bag and grabbed a high chair on her way over to join Sean and Dylan. "Speaking of leaving…" she said. "Not that I'm trying to get rid of you or anything."

"Says you!" Sean protested. "You'll be pleased to know we're going home tomorrow."

"Thank goodness for that!"

The whole conversation was conducted in jest with a gentle undercurrent of truth. Sophie hadn't complained, not even once, but Sean and Dylan were getting in the way of her research.

Serious now, she asked, "Are you sure you're up to it?"

"I'm not resolving anything hiding out here, am I?"

"No, that's true, and I know you know this, but you need to be in the right mental space or you'll relapse."

Sean nodded but kept his head bowed in shame. Half a bottle of wine—a glass and three-quarters—was all he'd had, and not his usual tipple, but he'd come so close to raiding Genie's liquor cabinet, desperate to put on the old comfort chain mail, that he'd known the only way he wouldn't was to leave. That was how it had always felt, the booze; invincible armour. He'd maybe get jolted by the force of a particularly nasty blow, but none of the sharp points could penetrate. He'd worn it for so long, he'd stopped noticing how heavy it was, but by God he'd felt it the day after the wine, less for the hangover than the voice in his head telling him he was a useless piece of shite, which was a stupid way to think. Addiction was a mental illness—an easy concept to grasp intellectually. Not so easy was remembering that wanting to start every day with a drink was because he was sick rather than morally corrupt and irresponsible.

"Was it a one-off?" Sophie asked.

"The wine?"

"You and Genie."

"Ah." This was the conversation he'd been waiting for. "Hard to say."

"Do you want it to be more?"

"I don't know. Maybe." Sean grimaced. "It feels odd, you know? Talking with you about this."

Sophie shrugged. "Well, don't interpret this as anything other than a statement of fact, but you've never taken Viagra for us."

"Because I don't feel under pressure to perform."

"Whatever the reason, whatever happens with you and Genie, it doesn't have to change what we have."

"How can you be so sure? Actually, never mind." She could be sure because her being with Grant hadn't changed their relationship. "At the very least, I owe her an explanation, but one thing at a time, all right?"

"Yep." Sophie smiled and took his hand. "I love you, very much."

"Likewise."

"And if things develop with Genie and we leave us behind, I'll still be here for you."

"Thanks. That goes both ways. Plus we'll always have this wee man." They both smiled at Dylan, who was bashing the table with his palms but stopped and eyed his parents suspiciously, which made them laugh.

"Don't forget I'm home Friday," Sophie said. "If you and Josh need a referee—unless you want me to come back with you tomorrow?"

"God, no. I've caused you enough trouble already. And anyway, I'll be seeing Shaunna on Thursday."

"She'll soon have you both whipped into shape."

"That she will." Sean chuckled. It was something to look forward to, their weekly date at Milky's. He'd missed it— Shaunna's company more than the yoghurt not-smoothies.

"Two frappés and a strawberry milkshake!" Freya shouted from the counter.

"I'll go," Sean said. That was the other thing he'd missed. Table service, and the metal bistro chairs here weren't a patch on Milky's cushioned bench seating. To Sean, it seemed everything in London was designed to keep people moving swiftly along. Maybe when he was younger, he'd have enjoyed the hustle and bustle, but he much preferred the laidback, sedentary busyness of his lifestyle, which would remain the same whether he worked for the NHS or himself.

"Yeah," he said, returning with their drinks. "I'm ready to go home."

***

Milky's Milk Bar
Thursday, 16th May

"KIND OF A successful trip then." Shaunna sucked the straw in her drink, scowling around it when it failed to deliver. She changed tactics, blowing instead, which cleared the cherry blockage and splattered pink yoghurt up into her face. Sean tactfully averted his eyes as she grabbed some napkins. "Don't you laugh at me!" she scolded, shaking them at him and then dabbing at her cheeks.

"Laughing *with*," he said with a wink. Her antics had taken the heat off him for a moment, not that she'd given him the third degree, or not about his failed abstinence. She'd listened without comment, hugged him and then told him she expected the full lowdown on him and Genie before the day was out. While Sean wasn't eager to go over it again, perhaps her perspective would help him get it straight in his head. For now, though, she left him to savour the quiet comfort of a few hours away from Dylan and, most importantly, in her fine company.

In the mid-afternoon lull, the background music became more than its beat; the young guy behind the counter hummed along as he disinfected surfaces and restacked cups. Milky's must've taken on more staff, as he was another unfamiliar face. He paused his in-tempo wiping to look around, subtly eyeballing his few customers: aside from Sean and Shaunna, there were three others, each sitting at their own high table along the window, an illusion to passers-by that the place was packed. It would become true soon enough when the senior school kicked out. After the students came the commuters, a flash mob routine with rucksacks, phones and fold-up bikes, in, coffee, out, then the parents of Scouts deposited at the church hall, the daily concerto of town life that Sean had missed so much.

"Come on then, spill. Tell me why you look like your cat died while you were away."

And there was the prelude to a rousing overture.

"He didn't, did he?"

Sean chuckled. "No."

"Phew!" Shaunna's relief didn't mean he was off the hook.

He sat forward, rubbed his chin, the roughness of the grey bristles and the creak of his old bones at odds with his imagined self. "It was like travelling back in time, undoing history."

"She makes you feel young again."

"She does. She's not changed. Women don't."

"We do. You're seeing her how she was, not how she is. I did the same with Andy."

"But you don't anymore?"

"Most of the time, which is as well. I couldn't stand him when we were younger. He'll tell you himself he was an idiot, and it took a long time for me to see past that."

"What convinced you?"

"The last big group holiday we had in Wales, when he found out Jess had gone behind his back. He handled it so well. I mean, the rage was pouring off him, we could all feel it, but somehow he kept a lid on it so he didn't ruin the holiday for everyone else. That was when the attraction kicked in."

"And you spent the night together," Sean recalled.

"Yeah, but it was a one-off, and we were hammered. Neither of us remembers a thing. You didn't drink that much with Genie, did you?"

"No, thank Christ, and I remember every second of it."

"Was it good?"

"Amazing."

"So the problem is…what? That you still see her as a sexy undergrad who drinks and parties too hard?"

"That's just it. I don't see her like that at all. I do think she's sexy, obviously, more so now than when she was younger. When we left uni, she was deeply unhappy and doing too many drugs. All that stopped when she got pregnant."

"It sounds likes she's changed to me," Shaunna said.

Sean nodded miserably.

"Then why the long face? Because you had a drink? I know that's a massive thing, but you seem to be taking it in your stride. Do you feel like you cheated on Sophie?"

"I did at first, but we're OK."

"So…Genie doesn't want to take it further and you do? Or you don't and she does?"

"We both do."

"Hmm." Shaunna studied the air, frowned, pursed her lips, fixed her hair, homed in on him again. "Tell me who you are."

"What?"

"Introduce yourself as if we've never met."

"Er...I'm Sean, and..." He cleared his throat. "God, this is hard."

"It's not."

"All right." He scrubbed his face, switched on the smile. "Hello there. I'm Sean Tierney. I'm a psychologist, currently in between jobs. I have two kids, one who lives full time with her mum, and I have joint custody of my son. I have a house, a cat who's still alive..."

"And a full-scale identity crisis," Shaunna finished for him. While he'd been floundering, she'd taken his hands in hers, and she shook them until he looked up and met her gaze. "These big changes—you've got a bit lost, haven't you?" He nodded. "It's understandable. The first thing you said—I'm a psychologist. Your work is who you are, and without it, you don't feel like you're anybody."

"Pathetic, isn't it?"

"No. We all have something that drives us. For me, it was being a mum, and then Krissi grew up, and I was a bit lost too."

"Now you're a mum again."

"True, although it's not the same with the twins. I have the Daisy Foundation and my counselling course. I found myself in other ways, and you will too because you can't go back, Sean. That's why you had a drink, maybe even why you slept with Genie. You're not that person anymore."

"So I have to leave it all behind?"

"That's up to you. Genie could be part of your future if you want her to be. You make it work with Josh, don't you?"

"If by make it work you mean tiptoe around his ego..."

"Yeah, you kind of did do that with appointing Simon, but look what happened when you asserted your opinion."

"The world imploded."

Shaunna laughed. "Dramatic much? I get that you and Josh have a really traumatic past and it's easier to pretend it didn't happen, but if you ignore it, you can't move forward. The two of you went into this business without setting ground rules or divvying up responsibility, and Josh doesn't always want to lead, but he will if no-one else does. So it's on you to take the wheel sometimes, even if it does mean the world implodes."

"I'm not sure I'm up to it. Romance or business. That's the problem."

"Whose problem? Yours or theirs?"

"Theirs if I screw up."

"Yours too, if you keep pretending everything's *grand* when it's not. What is it you say? Honesty's a good thing?"

Sean grunted. "I don't know what I'm talking about half the time."

"Yeah, you do, and you need to follow your own advice. Be honest with Josh and Genie. Tell them you're struggling. They won't think any less of you. If you can't do that, then at least be honest with yourself. Drop the act. Get some help."

"From you?"

"From someone qualified who isn't personally invested in your recovery."

A stranger, in other words, and there was nothing stranger than the folks in their profession.

"You're a wise one, Shaunna Hennessy."

"And you're a flatterer."

"I mean it."

"So do I. Also…"

"Hmm?"

"My smoothie's melted."

"Another?"

"I wouldn't say no."

"I bet you would."

"Then you'd lose. Again."

35: Entropy

Libby peeked around the living room curtain. "A car's stopped outside. Is it them?"

George joined her at the window; Josh huffed and went to open the front door. It was eleven o'clock on the dot. Of course it was them. He reached for the handle, his fingers less than an inch from it, as he was struck by a ridiculous thought. Well, all his thoughts were, frankly, ridiculous right now, or else why would he have called upon the services of Lord Xander Etherington-Bowes?

"Are you gonna open that?"

Josh glanced behind him, where George was leaning against the living room doorframe, casual and relaxed.

"Or are you worried it works the same way as vampires?"

George was being facetious, trying to ease the tension that had almost resulted in two arguments this morning, and theirs was usually such a peaceful home, but that was *exactly* what Josh had been thinking.

A two-headed, hopefully human silhouette formed on the other side of the obscure glass, and while Josh considered whisking the door open to capture the element of surprise, George made his move, opening it for him.

"Hi. Xander and Jonathan, I'm guessing? I'm George—Josh's husband. Come on in." He stepped aside, simultaneously bumping Josh out of the way so the two men could enter. In the time it took George to shut the door and direct them to the living room, Libby scooted behind their backs and shot up the stairs. Josh watched her go before trailing after their guests, who had obediently accepted George's invitation to sit and were doing so side by side on the sofa.

"And you must be Josh," Jonathan said, half rising again with arm extended.

"Yes." He leaned over the coffee table and shook the man's hand.

"Hello, Josh," Xander said with his unique, grimace-like smile.

"Hello, Xander." Josh maintained his focus on the thick, round lenses covering Xander's tiny eyes while taking in other details peripherally. In his wool jacket and slacks, Xander was less of a scruff than he'd been at university yet still carried the air of an unkempt student, largely due to the old school scarf loosely knotted beneath his chin and the worn, curly flapped, tan leather satchel clutched to his side. "It's been—"

"Twenty-two years and seven months."

"Yes, that long."

"Wow," George uttered in surprise. Whether it was at the passage of time or that Xander knew precisely how much of it had passed was unclear, but he shook it off to ask, "Can I get anyone a drink?"

"Yes, please," Jonathan answered. Xander didn't. He was staring into the hall.

"A girl resides here. I saw her."

"Yes," Josh confirmed. "Our daughter, Libby."

"Is she still alive?"

"Erm…yes." Bewildered, Josh looked to George, who shrugged and addressed Jonathan again, and who could blame him? He was the only other sensible person present.

"What would you like? Tea, coffee, juice, water…?"

"Tea would be lovely, thank you, George." He glanced at his boss, who paid him no heed. "Perhaps I could lend a hand?"

"Sure," George agreed.

The two of them left Josh at Xander's mercy or vice versa, judging by Xander's discomfort, although it didn't dampen his forthrightness.

"Should we get down to business?"

"Yes, let's." Josh quickly sat in the armchair.

Xander shuffled the satchel into his lap and flipped open the buckles with ease to extract a notepad and pencil. "I like to take notes," he said.

"That seems wise."

"Not as an aide memoir, you understand."

Josh really wished he didn't understand quite so well.

"Tell me what's been happening, please."

"Before I do that, what is it that you actually do, Xander?"

"I investigate unexplained phenomena and, if they're caused by paranormal activity, I establish why the activity is occurring and find a resolution."

"You lay ghosts to rest."

"One could call it that."

"I don't know that my unexplained phenomena *are* paranormal."

"That is why I am here, is it not?"

"Yes," Josh conceded. "Should I give you some background context first?"

"If it's pertinent."

"I think it is."

"Please, continue."

"OK. I recently bought the property in which I previously leased the first storey for my counselling work. I'd been there for fifteen years but retired from private practice to focus on academia. Then a few months ago—" Josh amended, knowing Xander would want him to be specific. "Six months ago, I decided to buy the building with a view to reopening my private practice as part of an expanded service." Josh noticed Xander inhale and paused to permit him to speak.

"How much time elapsed between your retirement and your decision to come out of said retirement?"

"Eighteen months."

"Did you regret your original decision?"

"In some respects, yes, but it was the right one at the time."

"You don't have a doctorate."

"No. Is that relevant?"

"No." Xander turned the page and wrote a couple more lines. "Go on," he said.

"Erm. Well…actually, can we backtrack a moment? Why did you mention my lack of doctorate?"

Xander peered over his thick glasses—to correct myopia, apparently, because his eyes weren't so small after all. "I expected you would become a clinical psychologist like Doctor Tierney."

"What gave you that impression?"

"You did."

"Oh." Josh thought about the handful of awkward interactions he and Xander had endured in that one week they'd spent studying at the same institution and mostly consisting of Xander showing off how clever he was while Josh failed to demonstrate they were nothing alike. There was only one that would have led to Xander's conclusion. "Is it because I asked if you're autistic?"

"Yes."

Josh nodded, gearing up to doing what he should have done but was incapable of at the time. "I'm sorry for prying. It was none of my business."

"I didn't mind you asking."

"I appreciate that, but it doesn't make it right."

"It goes against your codes of conduct," Xander said.

"Outside of a clinical environment, yes. Even inside one, I wouldn't ask unless it was necessary to therapeutic goals. And I confess, I was showing off a bit, testing my understanding of diagnostic criteria."

"You said you were just curious."

"I *was* curious, but not *just* curious. The thing is, Xander, and please forgive me for saying so, you're not easy to get along with. I was looking for distinctions because I saw all the ways you and I were similar—"

"You aren't autistic. You told me so."

"No. Or, should I say, I don't have a formal diagnosis." At Josh's request, Sean had informally assessed him while they were postgrads, using the old criteria, and confirmed what Josh had already known: he had a number of so-called 'autistic traits' but was not 'significantly impaired' on all three axes. If he were assessed again with the new criteria, there was a good chance he'd get a positive result, but he didn't need a test to tell him his brain was atypical.

"I didn't like myself very much back then, Xander. I hated being different—cleverer, younger, asocial, asexual. I wanted to want the same things as everyone else. And then there was you, the cleverest person I've ever met, and on the one hand, it was a relief to no longer carry that pennant. On the other, I was undermined by your intelligence. But I also realised I didn't want to be like you either. Not because you're autistic and see ghosts—"

"You still don't believe they're real."

Josh shrugged, unperturbed by Xander's interruption. As it had been when they were undergraduates, something about Xander compelled Josh to share far more than he would with even his closest friends, and it would serve neither of them well to admit aloud that for the longest time Xander had represented everything Josh loathed about himself. "Let's just say I'm more open to the possibility than I was twenty-two years and seven months ago."

Xander removed his glasses, blinking rhythmically as he polished the lenses on his scarf. "Tell me about your business premises." He put his glasses back on and picked up his pencil.

"It's a two-storey property, formerly residential, built on public land in the mid-1850s. That's as far as my research has taken me.

I'm waiting for access to the electoral registers to find out who the previous residents were."

Xander continued writing for a minute or so, then said, "You are much more open-minded than I remember."

"Thank you. However, I'm not trying to identify my alleged ghost. A former resident left some of their belongings in the loft, and I'm hoping to locate their next of kin so I can return them."

"Valuables or personal items?"

"Neither. Erm…" Josh chewed his cheek. "Victorian spiritualist equipment."

"How interesting." Xander made a note of that. "Did you attempt to use it to resolve the problem yourself?"

"How absurd!" Josh said indignantly, realising too late that Xander was tormenting him.

"Sorry. I meant it as a joke."

"I know." Josh pulled himself together. "It was kind of funny too." Movement in the hall caught his eye: Libby scooted past on her way to the kitchen, the cat in pursuit.

"Are you sure she's corporeal?" Xander asked doubtfully.

Josh laughed. "Absolutely positive." Although the question had piqued that pervasive curiosity of his. "Are ghosts solid like people?"

"They *are* people."

"Like living people."

"If they're self-perpetuating, they're quite solid."

"Self-perpetuating? What does that mean?"

"Some have what is commonly termed unfinished business. Matters they must attend to before they accept their lot. Those are self-perpetuating and retain an element of consciousness. The rest are best thought of as an after-image of how they appeared to their family, friends, colleagues et cetera. They vary in how solid they appear and are usually repetitive in their actions."

"I see," Josh said. "That fits with my experience of treating bereavement and relationship breakdown. People are more likely to report seeing ghosts in the early stages, when they're subjected to emotions intense enough to distort their perceptions. Hence they interpret the sudden draught from an open window as a cold spot or shifts in light as spectral shadows, and understandably so. Who wouldn't want to invest in evidence their loved ones haven't simply popped out of existence?"

"A flawed hypothesis," Xander said, once again jotting notes in his pad.

"You don't know that."

"I do." He wrote a couple more lines and set down his pencil in the groove of the open spine to give Josh his undivided attention. "The first part is right. People *are* more likely to see ghosts when they are subject to intense emotions, but it's because those emotions are…" He wiggled his fingers in front of his face, trying to pin down the right word. "Energy."

"Psychic energy?"

"Yes," Xander confirmed curtly; he hadn't missed the sarcasm. "Ghosts are always here, but they can't manifest in any tangible form without fuel."

"So they don't pass into the light then? They just run out of fuel."

"That depends on their beliefs." Xander's tone was decidedly smug. He'd caught on to Josh's game and was playing his trump card. "As atheists, it is unlikely you or I will be, ah, passing into the light."

"We'll simply pop out of existence," Josh mused.

"Fade rather than pop," Xander corrected. "Along with our integrity of self."

"Entropy," Libby said. Both Josh and Xander turned their heads sharply toward the door. "The person's energy disperses and becomes more and more disorganised until it's no longer them."

"Yes!" Xander clapped his hands, his face a picture of untempered delight as he turned to Josh to state, "One presumes you are biologically the girl's father."

"One presumes wrong," Libby said. She advanced into the room and perched on the arm of Josh's chair. "Also, my name's Libby."

"My apologies, Libby." Xander's gaze flitted between them, comparing, contrasting, until eventually he said, "Regardless, your similarities are striking."

Josh looked up at Libby, beaming proudly. Libby grinned back at him.

"Have you figured out who our ghost is yet?" she asked.

"No, not yet," Josh said.

"We have been catching up," Xander added.

"You—" Libby stared at Josh, then Xander, then shook her head. "I…I dunno," she said, suitably bamboozled because truthfully, his and Xander's conversation couldn't have been more different from the factual, stilted briefing Josh had predicted. It was, as Xander suggested, a catching-up, although it had also been one-sided so far, and Josh was prepared to address that, but first he wanted to confirm his suspicions regarding the whereabouts of his husband and Xander's personal assistant.

"Where's George got to, Lib?"

"He and Jonathan are in the garden playing with Blue."

"Who or what is Blue?" Xander asked.

"Our German shepherd dog."

"Oh. Yes. Jonathan is very fond of dogs. He often brings his to work. A Labrador by the name of Bertie. Very placid thing."

"Can dogs see ghosts, Xander?" Libby asked.

"I believe so. Why do you ask?"

"No reason. Just curious."

"Hm." Xander did that peering over his spectacles thing again, directly at Josh, who must surely have been a blurry blob without lens correction. The thought amused him, disproportionately so. To Xander, it would seem Josh was laughing at the astuteness of his observation, which was as insightful as it was sobering. Xander's quirkiness was the sum of his parts, and in the years since they'd last seen each other, both of them had matured, mellowed, achieved self-acceptance, a more turbulent journey for Josh than for Xander, perhaps. Josh also acknowledged that he liked Xander now. Better still, his theory on ghosts was grounded in good, solid science, and it was plausible, worthy of further discussion.

"Do you drink coffee, Xander?"

"Yes, I do."

"My machine makes Italian coffees. I'm going to make a cappuccino for myself. Would you like one?"

"I would, thank you."

"Me too, please," Libby said.

"I'll be right back." Josh rose from the chair, and Libby slid into it. As he left, he heard her ask Xander if she could tell him about 'their ghost', followed by Xander's assent. The rest of what was said was obscured by the grind of beans, the hiss of steam and a minor pang of jealousy at the sight through the kitchen window of George and Jonathan laughing together. It wasn't born of insecurity or mistrust; Josh was as sure of George's love for him as he was of his love for George, yet he envied the easy interaction, the way George got along with almost everyone.

It was silly, really. Josh didn't desire any more gregarious a social life than the one he had. When he spoke candidly, his friends knew how to take him and set him right if he was way out of line; he could communicate confidently with his clients, students and colleagues. The trouble was, interacting with strangers took so much filtering and required such a high level of concentration to keep track of what he'd said rather than what he'd thought, it was exhausting, thus he avoided it whenever possible. In that respect, he wouldn't have minded being a bit more like Xander, whose filters were as flimsy as his ghosts in the final throes of entropy, but perhaps that was a function of occupation rather than sociability. After all, it would do Josh's clients no good if he were to share his unfettered thoughts. Likewise, beating around the bush was all well and good for career politicians, but Xander's articulate speeches and research as a proactive parliamentary lord had contributed to real and significant social change.

With the coffees made, Josh set the three mugs on a tray, and as he did, he glimpsed George looking his way. George gave him a questioning thumbs up, and Josh nodded. They had made remarkably good progress, and all was well.

He returned to the living room, where Libby immediately relinquished his seat to join Xander on the sofa, the two of them acknowledging him long enough to accept their drinks before continuing their discussion. Critical debate was a more accurate description.

"If it's energy, why hasn't the Large Hadron Collider detected it?" Libby asked.

"It may very well do so in time," Xander said. "There is much the LHC has yet to detect."

"Also, why does it create cold spots? Shouldn't it create hot spots?"

"Quite right. Cold spots are folklore…"

And on they went while Josh played fifth *I'm a social scientist not a real scientist* wheel. He could no doubt have held his own, or convincingly bluffed at any rate, but for once he chose not to. Libby was an exceptional physicist, which came from her extracurricular studies, as she was determined to pursue a career as a psychologist, but no ordinary psychologist. No. She wanted to work for the European Space Agency, supporting astronauts' well-being on that inevitable long journey to Mars. She was explaining all this to Xander when Josh's phone buzzed: Andy calling. He reluctantly excused himself from their riveting discussion.

"Don't hate me for this, will you?"

Andy's opening gambit instantly put Josh's back up. When it was good news—and he likely had Josh's number on speed-dial for such occasions—Dan delivered it. Otherwise, he shirked and left it to his brother.

Rather than ask if Andy was aware he'd drawn the short straw again, Josh went with a quietly diplomatic, "What's the problem?"

"Turns out the original loft insulation was loose-fill asbestos, and there's still a fair bit lurking under the new stuff."

"That's the dangerous kind, isn't it?"

"It is, unfortunately, but the lads who were working up there had their gear on and damped it down straight away. We've got an HSE contractor coming out to assess tomorrow morning. In the meantime, we'll have to down tools. Sorry. You're not gonna be able to get in there this afternoon."

"Oh, well. It can't be helped," Josh said philosophically. "Apart from that, how's it all coming along?"

"Good, yeah." Andy's answer was typically vague.

"Do we have a lift yet?"

"Pretty much. No stairs, though—that's how we discovered the asbestos—and the spark still needs to do the wiring, but we'll be good to go once we've got the all-clear."

"No other structural problems? Doors not shutting properly, deathwatch beetles…"

"Nope. Everything's spot on now, and any dodgy timbers have been replaced. If you can give me a week, I should have a consultation room in some sort of usable shape for you."

"OK. That's great. So do you think you'll still complete on time?" *Please say no.*

"No problem, mate."

Damn it. "Excellent. Thanks for keeping me posted."

"No worries. Have a good one."

The call ended, and Josh spent a moment ensuring he would seem suitably disappointed when he broke the news. He was sorry Xander had made a fruitless excursion, but the longer he could put off going back into that building the better.

36: A Good Thing

"WAS EVERYTHING ALL right at the uni?" Sean followed Josh into the kitchen and looked around in puzzlement. He'd expected that the table would be loaded with printouts and notes, or Josh's laptop at the very least; instead, there was a salt-and-pepper cruet and a slender, glass vase containing a single, stamen-less, white lily.

"Yes. No problems at all. Zsa Zsa seems to be settling in well."

"That's good to hear."

"And we started off the diploma students with their logbooks, made sure they could access the VLE and whatnot. All twenty attended the induction session, which bodes well. A couple of placements still need to confirm…"

Josh's flat, factual report went on and on, became a drone like a distant plane. It was all information Sean needed to know but not right this second. The greater part of him wanted to interrupt Josh just to get his back up—the part that would throw away everything for another drink—but he'd kept it at bay this long. He could last a few minutes more.

"…nothing else to feed back," Josh finished. "On the university side of things, that is."

"Well, thanks for stepping in."

"It's not like I could do anything else with the renovations stalled." Not a flicker of frustration, disappointment.

"I was looking forward to having a gander at the progress," Sean said.

"Yes. Sorry about that." No remorse, anger. Nothing. It was probably a good thing. Sean had plenty for the both of them, and it was rearing up, ready to erupt into the emotion void.

"I've got to say, Josh, you don't sound sorry."

There it was, a tiny spark of alarm; Sean could've laughed at how predictable his old friend was. All these years insisting he hated being called Joshy. All these years of lying—to each other and themselves.

"Good grief. Anyone would think I planted the asbestos."

"I'm not saying you did, but you're not sorry it's in there, are ye?"

"No, quite honestly. I'm not. In fact, I'm having serious doubts about the whole project. I told you, Sean, I can't do this without you."

"Is that right? Because you've done a grand job of it so far!"

"Erm…excuse me? You're the one who's been gone for almost three weeks! Even before that, you weren't really contributing anything."

"Because you wouldn't let me."

"That's utter nonsense, and you know it. When Dan and Andy gave us the virtual tour, I asked you what you wanted to say, and you said you didn't want to say anything."

"On that occasion."

"And you cried off on looking through flooring swatches. Then there was our planning meeting when you claimed you'd come up with the exact same points as mine—"

"Hey now, slow down there, fella. I *claimed* I came up with them?"

"All right." Josh backed off, though not much. "I wasn't suggesting you plagiarised."

"I damn well hope not! You seem to be forgetting I hadn't seen your notes until I was sitting there with your laptop in front of me."

"Then how do you explain it? Telepathy? Oh, I know! I'll get that pendulum back from Adele and see what it has to say! Or maybe we could ask Xander? You and he are mighty pally these days."

"There we have it."

"What? You think I'm jealous that you have other friends?"

"It's not always about you. But seeing as you mentioned it, you *are* jealous of Shaunna and me."

"No, I'm not."

"Yes, you are. You can't stand the idea of me confiding in her instead of you. It was the same with Jessie at uni."

"You're wrong, Sean."

"Am I? Prove it."

"Well, obviously I can't. She's dead!"

"Maybe we can ask Xander to have a chat with her?" Sean mocked with so much spite he could almost taste it. It must have hit Josh full force too, as he turned away and started faffing with his coffee machine, wiping it down, running it through a cleaning cycle, his stance rigid. Sean pulled a chair from under the table and sat, focusing on breathing and letting go of as much of his anger as he could. There were things he still needed to say—needed Josh to hear—but it would be futile before they'd both calmed down.

"Anyway," he said, once he thought he could say it without turning it into another accusation, "I fell off the wagon."

Josh's faffing continued a bit longer, coming to a gradual stop. "Bugger." He sighed and turned around. "What happened?"

"It crept up on me the week I finished at the hospital."

"The week Phee turned up."

"It was, but it wasn't just to do with what Phee's got going on or giving up the job I spent a decade getting the qualifications to do. It's…" Sean shrugged.

"Me?" Josh suggested.

"There ye go again, thinking it's all about you."

Josh inhaled sharply, but Sean held up his hands.

"Just listen, OK?"

Josh let the breath go. "OK."

"See, I made that mistake too, blaming you. I won't lie. I properly hit the bottle after…you know what, but I was depending on it to get by before that day I came back from the conference and found you. After, when you were in the hospital, the uni nagged me, trying to get me in to see the campus counsellor, but that's the thing with you and me. We think we can do it on our own, then something comes along and shows us we can't, and so we run away."

"*You* run away," Josh contended. "I don't."

"No. You withdraw like a wee hermit crab. And we can't keep doing it, not if we're really intending to make a go of this therapy centre. So…cards on the table, all right? I'm scared."

"Why?"

"Because you still don't talk to me or involve me in what's going on with you. Before you say it, I don't mean what the builders are up to or where the hell the lift's going, or even Shaunna and Libby's magical garden. I didn't even care that you got shitty over Simon. It all just looks like you flouncing and lording it if you never talk to me about why."

"You don't talk to me either."

"I'll remedy that right now if you can hold off on getting all high and mighty."

Josh spluttered indignantly, but Sean ignored him and went on.

"Phee's pregnant. She couldn't tell Genie because the father is Genie's boyfriend. That's why Phee came to me, then she dropped me in it, and I got a furious message off her mother while we were deliberating over Simon's interview, so maybe I did overreact to your nonsense, but I meant what I said about you being stuck up, even if I was just trying to get out of there so I could fix things with Genie."

"So that's where you were," Josh said. "At Genie's."

"No. I was in London with Soph, but I did go there first, and yes, I saw Xander briefly while I was there."

"And told him about my haunted surgery." Josh flinched. "*Our* haunted surgery."

Sean chuckled half-heartedly. "Don't worry about it. I'm pretty sure it's habit, not a Freudian slip, but we should clarify where we both stand."

"Agreed."

"And for the record, I didn't tell Xander. I don't remember telling Genie either, but I must've done. I'm sorry."

"I'm sorry too," Josh said. "Not that you somehow brought Xander my way. I might owe you thanks for that yet. While this clearly isn't all about me, I still wish I'd never put you through what I did, and I'd take it back if I could—for your sake, not mine, because I'm not sorry it was you. There was nobody else who could have done what you did for me."

"Arguable." Sean winked, trying to joke and instead releasing a tear. That was a real apology, raw and honest, and he wanted to revel in it, have a good wallow, but he'd save that for later. For now, he swiped the tear away and pushed on. "So what's this about owing me thanks?"

"Xander came to the house yesterday to discuss applying his talents to my...our haunting."

"Nooo! He never did!"

"He's coming back to take a look around as soon as we get the all-clear from Andy."

Most likely to avoid further scrutiny, Josh set to making coffee for them both while Sean watched on, quietly astounded but also feeling his hopes lift a little, knowing Josh was prepared to do whatever it took to get their business off the ground.

"I must admit," Josh said, "I'm a little insulted you think I'd judge you by Phee's behaviour. Or even that I'd judge Phee when it sounds like she's a victim."

"She says not. Either way, she's decided on an abortion, and Genie's sent the boyfriend packing, so he's out of the picture.

But that wasn't the bit I expected you to take issue with because when I say I went to Genie's, I meant that Genie and I..." Sean paused, thinking how best to say it. 'Spent the night together' was ambiguous, 'had sex' too coarse and dismissive, 'made love' too sentimental, and it was more monumental than any of those phrases conveyed.

A cup appeared in front of him, and he looked up, meeting Josh's gaze, inquisitive at first, then surprised, finally settling on mildly annoyed.

"Again, why would I judge you for that?"

"Well, the way you were about Jessie and me—"

"I was seventeen, Sean, for goodness' sake. I'm a grown-up now, with a lot more experience of relationships. My problem with you and Jess was what would have happened if it had ended badly. You assured me it wouldn't come to that, although...at the risk of making it all about me again, is that why you didn't tell her how you felt?"

There were times Sean hated how well Josh could read him because he'd known long before Sean that his feelings for Jess ran deeper than the friends-with-benefits limit she'd set on all her romantic relationships. Even if she'd allowed more, Sean had promised to put an end to it if that was what Josh wanted. In retrospect, that was probably at the root of the dynamic that was still causing them trouble. Josh's mental health was more stable now than it had ever been, yet Sean was so scared of tipping him over the edge that he course-corrected his own life rather than chance it. For all of that, his reason for not telling Jess he loved her was not Josh's delicate sensibilities. It was witnessing Genie self-destruct after she'd done the same.

"You and Genie feels like something more serious," Josh said, keeping up with Sean thought for thought. "Is it?"

"If I say yes, are you going to give me grief about Soph?"

"It's none of my business, but you're a grown-up too, so let's assume you know what you're doing."

"Christ, I wish I did, Joshy."

Josh brought over his drink and pulled out a chair, facing Sean and ready to listen.

Sean took a big gulp of coffee and got it straight in his head. "Soph and me are fine, by the way. The same as always. We're Dylan's parents first and foremost, and we love each other. That won't change, whatever happens, but I'm not sure anything can. Being with Genie again…there was always a spark between us, but there was also Jess, and…well, I'll spare you the blushes and just say we were young, frisky and loved each other freely. But it was also hedonistic and tied up with drinking. If I pursue anything with Genie, I risk relapsing, and I'll lose everything—Dylan, my career, the business, our friendship…"

"You're not going to lose our friendship or the business," Josh said confidently. "You functioned perfectly for years while tanked up, but you're not doing this alone, Sean. I'm here for you, as is everyone else."

"Everyone as in that whole big circle of friends of yours?"

"Are we really going down that road again? They're your friends too."

"You say that, but if it came to it, we all know whose side they'd take."

"Ha! These days, Shaunna is a paid-up member of Team Tierney. As for the rest—I could probably count on George, maybe Dan and Andy, Adele at a push—"

"We're getting away from the point here, Joshy."

"Yes, we are."

"All right, so." Sean still felt like he was going through the motions, but putting it into words would, even if not legally binding, solidify their commitment. "If we're doing this, we're doing it together, right?"

"Yes."

"We talk, we listen, we don't run away or hide."

"No."

"And none of this Team Tierney shite! *We* are a team, you and me."

"We are."

"Because if we're not in this together, we might as well call it quits now, and I don't want to do that."

"Neither do I."

"Good. Then we're in agreement so far."

"Yes."

"One last thing. We should appoint…not a business manager but…"

"An overseer?" Josh suggested.

"That's it. Someone to keep us in line, who'll step in if it all goes to the dogs."

"You mean if I hack off my hands or you drown in a vat of whiskey."

"I admire your flippancy."

"Cards on the table, you said. We both live with chronic, sometimes acute, mental illness. We need someone who can handle that. Do you have someone particular in mind?"

"I do, as a matter of fact."

"I see." Josh studied the air between them as if it held clues to the identity of this 'mystery' overseer. Finally, his gaze settled on Sean's. "I support your proposal," he said. "That is, if Shaunna wants the job."

37: Big Air

M ORNING, YOU TWO." Giving Genie's hip a hard nudge, Jess squashed in beside her and lifted the half-boiled kettle. Satisfied there was enough water in it for three, she set it down again and swirled smoothly on thick-socked feet. "Sleep well?" she asked with a wicked grin. "Or *at all*?"

A dark, hairy arm curled possessively around Genie, followed by the burn of rough stubble on her neck, hot breath and a kiss. The burn spread to her cheeks, and she cursed inwardly. Last night should *not* have happened, but once they'd polished off a bottle of vodka between them, it was inevitable. Her mistake: she'd assumed they'd have a threesome, and it was bloody good sex, honestly, but it was *Andy*, the man-child whose social repertoire had only become more dreadful since he'd graduated and replaced his *History of Grunge* lecture with *The Scuba Monologues*.

Accordingly, Genie now knew the difference between scuba and free diving and that there was a huge marine conservation project in Thailand, where Andy would be spending the summer. She should have been delighted, knowing he wouldn't come between her and Jess for two months, but by then, they, too, would have graduated, and Andy's trip merely pressed home how little time was left to convince Jess that what they had was worth keeping.

The kettle clicked off, and Genie peeled Andy's arm away from her chest, missing it immediately; the morning was bitterly cold. She reached for the cups at the same time as Jess, meeting her gaze long enough to read her amusement, before lowering her eyes—another mistake. The satin of Jess's pyjamas clung to her breasts and draped tantalisingly from her erect nipples, sending Genie into a trance that held even after Andy announced he was "Going for a crap" and left.

"Now you know why I keep him around."

"Hmm?"

Jess eased the cup from Genie's hand, breaking the spell. "I said—"

"I heard," Genie interrupted, although it took a second for her brain to catch up. "Why didn't you join us?"

"I thought you might like to have him to yourself. Besides…" Jess paused to spoon coffee granules into the cups, one—"last night"—two—"he told me"—three—"he likes you." She bashed the lid of the jar shut. "As in *really* likes you." She zipped off to the fridge for the milk, added it to the cups, then back to the fridge, then back to stir the cups. She rinsed the spoon and dried it, finally looking at Genie. "What?" she asked.

Genie shook her head, stunned. Jess really didn't care about anyone—not Andy or Sean and certainly not Genie. "You were trying to set us up."

"*Trying*? I could hear you fucking each other's brains out! I'd say I succeeded!"

"So now you've got us both off your conscience, you can move on."

"Move on?"

"Stop repeating me like you don't know what I'm talking about!"

"I really don't! Literally, the only thing I did was go to bed when I saw the two of you getting horny."

"Why? Andy comes here to see you."

"Because he fancies you, and clearly you fancy him, so why not? It's just a bit of fun. I don't see why that's a problem."

Because it's not just a bit of fun to me!

Genie swallowed, smiled her sweetest smile. "It isn't a problem," she said and picked up her tea, sipping calmly, falling apart.

"Good." Jess looked at the clock. "Shit. I need to shower." She was already on the move. "Simon's picking me up at half ten."

"Wait!" Genie chased her to the hallway. "Where are you going?"

"That charity event his parents are putting on. There'll be judges and barristers there." Jess paused at the top of the stairs and leaned over the banister. "Aren't you going too?"

Genie laughed in disbelief, although not at her lack of invitation to one of the Hendersons' business soirées. "This is the first I've heard about it."

"Oh! Well…" Jess bit her lip as if she was considering not going. It was all an act, but Jess endearing herself to Simon's parents had inadvertently done Genie a favour because while Jess was going to all those boring Henderson parties, Genie didn't have to.

"Enjoy!" she said, raising her cup of tea in a toast.

Jess grinned. "I'm going to network my stockings off."

"Quite." There would be plenty of old letches at that party who would get off on helping her with that. The toilet flushed, reminding Genie she had her own letch to worry about. "Does Andy know?"

"I did tell him, but he's probably forgotten." Jess moved off again, calling back from her room, "I'm sure you can keep him entertained for a day."

Genie sighed and muttered, "Fantastic."

Andy came out of the bathroom, but that was the last Genie heard, as she went into the lounge, shut the door and put on the television. There she stayed, her senses under assault from loud, brash, Saturday morning kids' TV, until the door opened and Jess poked her head in.

"See you tomorrow."

"You're not coming back tonight?"

"No. It'll be too late."

Genie turned her attention back to the TV. "See you tomorrow then."

Jess loitered a moment longer then left, pulling the door shut. Next the front door opened and closed, and Genie sagged back into the sofa. *Five, four, three, two…*

"Just you and me, huh?" Andy flopped down right next to her.

"Yes. Just you and me."

"What d'you wanna do? I mean, we can sit and watch telly all day. That's cool with me—"

"I have a better idea. Have you been to the ski centre?"

"Where's that?"

"About five miles from here."

"Never been skiing."

"No, you strike me as more of a snowboarding type."

Andy nodded enthusiastically. "I'm gonna do that after Thailand."

"You can snowboard at the ski centre. Are you up for it?"

"Totally!"

***

Genie stopped outside the house and braced for the gearbox crunch as she shifted into neutral and pulled on the handbrake. Andy's car was a heap of junk—his third since passing his test, the others written off, each time hiking his insurance premium until all he could afford was this…death trap running on vapours. She'd had to call her father to check she was covered to drive it—perish the thought that he allow her to take out her own policy—because Andy was a maniac with a pathological love of danger and was lucky he'd come away with only a dislocated shoulder. But, as he'd told the doctor in A&E, it was "worth it for some serious big air," and in any case, this wasn't his first rodeo, so "whack that sucker back in place and I'll be outta here."

His inhuman roar when the doctor did just that was not a sound Genie ever wanted to hear again.

Now Andy was off his face on painkillers, and she was stuck with him for the night. In fairness, he'd called his brother the second they'd left the hospital; after much swearing and calling him an idiot, his brother had agreed to pick him up but couldn't get there until the morning. No matter. Andy was a creature of simple habits.

"Pizza?" she suggested once she'd settled him on the sofa with the TV remote, a glass of juice and all of Jess's pillows. Jess wouldn't be needing them, after all.

He nodded and grimaced. "Hurts like a bastard."

"I can imagine. Won't be long."

Feeling a little stiff herself, she drove Andy's car to the pizzeria, returning via the petrol station where she endeavoured to shrink out of sight when the gearbox once again made her out to be incompetent behind the wheel. When she got back to the house, Andy was asleep and comfortable for the time being, so she sat on the floor and had a proper look at him while she ate her pizza. With those long lashes and smooth skin, only the stubble on his square jaw and the sheer size of him gave away that he was a grown man.

She'd skied beside him on the dry slope as he'd wobbled along on his board for a couple of descents, toppling many times, but it hadn't taken him long to find his groove and move on to the jump ramp. Then she'd watched with her heart in her mouth while he'd flung himself upwards, flying for a few seconds before he somehow, miraculously, landed the right way and punched the air, shouting "Woohoo!" On his second attempt, he grabbed the rear of his board and, managing to land that, tried a spin. He didn't land that one, or not on his board, and he'd paid the price. She'd have said it served him right, but there was no cockiness involved, just a desire to make the most of the experience. He was also a lot of fun to be with, so yes, she could see now why Jess kept him around, although for Genie, it was less about his sex appeal than the latent mothering instinct he stirred within her. She hoped he never lost that innocent sense of adventure.

Roused by the smell of the pizza, his nose twitched, rabbit-like, a few times before he performed a one-armed stretch and squinted at Genie.

"Alright? How long have I been out?"

"Not long. How are you feeling?"

"Sore. Nothing a beer and pizza won't cure."

"We'll discuss beer after you've eaten." Genie knelt up and placed his pizza box on his lap. "Can you cope from there?"

"Yep. Cheers." He flipped the box open and tried to extract a slice, flinching with the effort. Genie was itching to help but waited until he peered at her hopelessly before she went to his aid.

Now he was awake, she moved to the other end of the couch and sat cross-legged, her pizza box on the seat between them so she could keep an eye on him. Watching him eat was not a pretty sight, and by the time he was done, strings of mozzarella decorated his stubble and his chin glistened with grease. Genie took away his empty box, returning with a damp cloth, which he squished around in his hand before giving it back to her. She sighed and cleaned his face for him, becoming uncomfortably aware of the way he was looking at her.

"There," she said, giving his chin cleft a final dab before she moved out of his reach, not that she thought he'd push his luck, but she didn't want to encourage him. She did bring him a beer though, and they spent the evening watching TV—a rom com of all things—which had Andy rapt. The heartache was too close to Genie's reality for her to find it entertaining. The end credits rolled.

"Genie?"

"What do you need? Another beer?"

"I think I'm in love with you."

"You barely know me."

"I..." Pink circles appeared on Andy's cheeks, and he slapped his hand down on his head, scrunching his hair. "Well...shit."

"I'm sorry." She'd had a feeling something like that was coming—not quite the L-word, but still. She felt awful for him. "The thing is…you're a good-looking guy and very sweet, but I have feelings for someone else."

Andy sighed. "Story of my life."

"Is it?"

"Yeah. There's this girl I really like. Have done for ages. Years. I thought she liked me back…" He paused, the painful memories pulling at his angular features. "Thing is, me and my brother—people mistake us for twins because there's only a year between us and we're the same height, same build, eye colour, this…" He jabbed at the cleft in his chin. "We got into shitloads of trouble when we were at primary school—it was pretty hairy at times. Then I moved up to high school, but Dan was a year behind, and we'd been together as long as I could remember." Andy paused again and picked up his beer bottle, swigging on air. Genie took it from him.

"I'll get you another," she said and left to do so, wondering if he was aware he'd gone off on a tangent. He tended to jabber on, but she'd never heard him talk so openly about himself—probably a side effect of the painkillers, although they should've been wearing off by now. The hospital had sent him home with a couple of days' supply, which was in Genie's bag in the hall; she checked the packet on her way back to the lounge.

Do not *drink alcohol. Take with water.*

"Oops!"

Popping two pills from the bubble pack, she went back to the kitchen, exchanged the beer for a glass of water and returned to the lounge. "No more beer for you, I'm afraid. Doctor's orders."

He chuckled glibly and took the pills, handing back the glass. "Sorry for going off on one."

"I don't mind." Genie re-joined him on the sofa. "How's the shoulder feeling now?"

"Nothing I can't handle. I do need a piss, though."

Genie grimaced. Andy chuckled again, more cheerfully this time.

"I'll manage," he said and grunted his way to the edge of the sofa, onto his feet and all the way up to the bathroom while Genie waited for the call of *help!* It didn't come, and he arrived back downstairs in jogging pants rather than jeans, grinning proudly. Genie giggled and beckoned him over.

"You're all in a heap," she said, fixing his pants and becoming aroused by the proximity of his groin to her mouth. But when she looked up at his face, she saw only fatigue. She patted his belly. "There you go."

"Cheers." He didn't move.

"OK?"

"D'you mind if I go to bed?"

"Not at all. I'm a little tired and achy myself." Genie gathered Jess's pillows and followed Andy up the stairs, surprised when he bypassed Jess's room and stopped outside Genie's, waiting for her. When he realised, his good shoulder slumped.

"I'm happy sharing," she said, "but I thought you'd be more comfortable on your own."

"No worries." He shuffled back along the landing to Jess's room, looking so dejected, Genie couldn't stand it.

"Come on." She pulled Jess's door shut. "You can stay with me."

"Are you sure?"

"Positive."

"I just…I dunno." That good shoulder shrugged.

"Need company? Me too."

It took a bit of wriggling and rejigging pillows, but they got there eventually. Andy lay on his back, his dislocated shoulder to the wall, his other arm around Genie, who cuddled close. It was cosy and platonic and not what Jess would've had in mind when she set them up.

"I'm curious," Genie said. "You started with the girl you've liked forever and ended up talking about your brother."

"Ah, yeah." Andy laughed quietly. "I asked her out and she turned me down. Said it wouldn't be fair on me because it was Dan she fancied. All the girls at school did."

"That's harsh."

"Yeah, it was. I get it, though."

"Didn't you say you look alike?"

"We do, but he's cleverer than me and works his arse off, whereas I'm a lazy turd. Plus my mates were all dickheads. Took me a while to figure it out. Girls…women want someone with prospects, not a loser like me."

Genie reached up and stroked his cheek. "That's a terrible way to think about yourself."

"It's the truth."

"Jess seems to like you well enough."

"Yeah, well, you know Jess."

"I do," Genie agreed ruefully. Long-term prospects were irrelevant when she'd set her sights on a single life dedicated to her career. "She doesn't think you're a loser, Andy." Genie lifted on her elbow so she could look him in the eye, but he'd already fallen asleep. She kissed his cheek, whispered, "Neither do I," and snuggled down next to him.

***

Genie woke to the sound of the doorbell ringing three times in quick succession and rolled over to check the time.

"Andy?"

He grunted.

"Are you awake."

"Kinda."

"What time did your brother say he'd get here."

"He didn't. What time is it?"

"A quarter past nine." The doorbell rang again.

"Huh. Yeah, that's probably him."

Genie swung her legs off the bed and sat up. "I'll go and let him in."

"Cheers."

Pulling her bathrobe around her, she headed downstairs, shivering, and opened the front door. "Hello—oh, goodness! Dan, I presume?"

"Er, yeah." Dan's frown, while very much like Andy's, was darker, more serious.

"I'm Genie. Andy's not up yet. Come in."

"I'd better not. My mate's in the car."

Genie glanced past Dan, making eye contact with the guy in the passenger seat of the dark-blue BMW parked behind Andy's car. "He should come in too. It's freezing." Bare feet weren't helping.

Dan shrugged and beckoned to his friend, who stepped out of the car. He had an eighties-pop-star vibe—moody yet glamorous.

"I'm just going to put some clothes on," Genie said, already on her way upstairs; the cold had made her desperate for the loo. "The lounge is the door to your left. Make yourselves at home." She dashed into the bathroom for a pee and a quick brush of her teeth, then back to her room, where Andy was right where she'd left him.

"Hey, wake up!"

He groaned and shuffled across the mattress, eyes still shut, while Genie raced around the room, tugging on her clothes.

"Come on, Andy. Dan's waiting downstairs, and he's brought a friend with him."

"Kris?"

"No idea."

"Skinny, good-looking, blonde highlights. Looks like the dude out of A-ha."

"Yes! Now will you *please* get up?"

"Doing it." Finally, he struggled to the side of the bed and sat, teeth gritted. He'd woken Genie at four a.m., not intentionally: he'd been crying in pain. She'd given him another dose of pills, and he'd drifted back to sleep.

"You can have more pills now if you want," she said. He nodded, and she popped them out of the packet onto his palm, then realised there was no water left in the glass. "Won't be a moment."

"It's fine." He dry-swallowed them. "Can you give me a hand with my jeans? They're in Jess's room."

"Of course!" Grabbing Jess's pillows, Genie crossed the landing and nearly dropped the lot when Jess's door swung open. "What the hell…?"

"Morning!" Jess stretched and yawned.

"When did you get home?"

"Six-thirty, seven…not sure." She squinted at Genie. "I looked in on you. So cute!" Jess yawned again. Genie wafted away the champagne breath.

"Andy dislocated his shoulder. His brother's come to pick him up."

That jolted Jess out of her sleepy-drunk stupor. "Dan's here? Superb." She didn't mean that. "I'm going for a shower," she said, grabbing her robe from the door before scooting away to the bathroom.

That was the last Genie saw of her until Andy had departed, a passenger in his brother's car while the pop-star friend was saddled with driving the rust bucket.

"Andy said he'd call you later." Genie handed Jess a cup of tea. "How was the party?"

"Excellent. Pierce introduced me to a barrister friend of his." *Pierce.* AKA Lord Henderson. Simon's father. "He said I can do my pupillage with him if I want."

"Jolly good."

"Yeah, I don't think I'll take him up on it. I'd rather find somewhere myself."

"So much for networking."

"Oh, I still made plenty of contacts, but I want to do it on my terms, Genie. You understand."

"I do." Far too well.

"Anyway, enough about me. Did you have fun yesterday?"

"We did, as a matter of fact. Andy and I really hit it off."

"Oh! That's…nice." Jess smiled, far too brightly.

"Yes," Genie continued, loving and hating how jealous Jess was. "We're going to do it again sometime before he goes to Thailand."

"Just don't break his heart," Jess warned.

"I'll try not to."

"Or let him break yours." Jess reached out to stroke Genie's hair. She dodged sideways, laughing.

"Unlikely!" It was hard to break something that was already in smithereens. "Well, I have work to do. How about you?"

"I need to sleep off this hangover. Join me later?"

"Maybe."

Or maybe not.

38: Reconstruction

HALF IN THE space, half on the road, Josh stalled the car, startled by the avalanche of rubble that slid down the chute into the skip in front of him. The second load had him smacking his knees on the steering wheel, and he called the builders a choice name or two, but it behoved him to exercise some patience. Andy had been on site every day, overseeing the asbestos removal, and the builders had put in overtime to have the building accessible within a week.

From where Josh was sitting, it didn't look anywhere close to accessible, but what did he know? He'd stayed well clear, even taking a longer route to the university to avoid driving past, happy to accept the Jeffries brothers' assurance that work was well underway—irrefutable, given the nuclear fallout of evidence all around. They'd also promised one of the rooms would be useable by noon; there was only one way to find out if they'd been true to their word. Josh waited for the dust plume to slowly settle in the skip, and all over his car, before he got out and locked the door, muttering ventriloquist-style, "Well, this should be fun."

Dan was on his way downstairs as Josh approached the outside door, which was held open by half a breeze block. Josh stepped over it and drew breath to say hi, then quickly covered his nose and sneezed into his hand.

"Oh…*oh!* Yuck." He wiped the dark-pink residue on the rag Dan handed him.

"Sorry. Should've warned you it'd be dusty. One of the lads is just giving your room a quick vacuum. We've stuck the furniture in but left the plastic on."

"Thanks. How's it all going?"

"I'll show you." Dan led the way. "We're ahead of schedule, mostly thanks to Andy. They managed to contain the asbestos to the loft so got the all-clear by Wednesday. First floor—structural work is done." He gestured to the area at the top of the stairs, which bore very little resemblance to the image in Josh's memory but matched Andy's 3D computer model. The large landing that had been Josh's waiting room was now half the width, with plastic sheeting covering a wide gap in the middle of the wall on one side; along the other, two of the three rooms were doorless, giving Josh his first glimpse of their new consultation suite. Despite his disorientation, he thought he liked it, and if he didn't, well, tough luck. He couldn't very well ask Dan and Andy to put it all back the way it was.

Behind the closed door to Josh's consultation room—it was and always would be because bugger was he giving it up now he'd got it back—a vacuum cleaner powered down. He looked to Dan for guidance and received a nod of encouragement, but the door opened before he reached it. A young man in overalls and tan boots exited, dragging an industrial vacuum cleaner along by its power cord like a reluctant robot dog. Josh waited for man and machinery to pass by before entering. The vision stopped him in his tracks, and for a moment, all he could do was stare in astonishment. Then he shook his head and laughed. "Did you put the furniture in, perchance?"

"Yeah. Why? Is it in the wrong place? No worries—I'll move it for you."

"No, no. It's…perfect, as if you marked the positions on the floor beforehand."

Frowning, Dan peered into the room. "Ah. I see what you mean." He chuckled self-consciously. The desk, chairs and sofa were all brand new but, as the 3D render had suggested, in exactly the same formation they'd been in the old surgery. "Will it do you for today?" Dan asked.

"Absolutely!" Josh went over to the chair by the desk and sat in it, ignoring the crinkle of plastic as he sank back and the tension left his body. "Thank you." He noticed the waver in his voice after the event.

Dan smiled. "No problem. Nice to have you home."

"It's nice to be home." His new chair was incredibly comfortable, as Dan had said it would be, and he foresaw a future spent napping between appointments, pending this afternoon's spiritual cleansing or whatever it was. Xander hadn't volunteered any details, and Josh hadn't asked.

"Right, gonna get the guys off site and leave you to it. Give us a call when you're done."

"Will do."

"Oh, and the kitchen's in working order too. Or enough for you to get your fix, and there's fresh milk in the fridge."

Josh grinned. "You're a star."

With a nod that most would have interpreted as arrogant but which Josh recognised as pleasure for his client's happiness, Dan strode from the room, his feet echoing on the carpetless stairs. The door at the bottom clicked shut, the draught lifting the paper runner from the door to Josh's desk. He watched it ripple and waited for it to come to a standstill before he dashed along the corridor to the kitchenette, as eager to see what it looked like as he was to get to the coffee.

'In working order' was accurate if somewhat disappointing. To his right, the wall was bare plasterboard with no sign of the cupboards or hotplate that had been there prior to the renovation. To his left, the cupboards, fridge and counter were as they had always been, other than someone had swiped them with a damp cloth, leaving rosy swirls of plaster dust across the plain white melamine; it was an aesthetically pleasing effect but not one Josh planned to keep.

Not so pleasing were the grotty fingerprints all over the polished-steel kettle plugged into the only outlet in the room, and the sink, currently free-standing under the window, had taken on a matt appearance other than the tea-stained plug hole. Josh ran the cold tap, rinsing the kettle a couple of times before he filled it and switched it on, then inspected one of the four mugs upended on the drainer. A builder's mug. In other words, disgusting.

A quick search of the cupboards confirmed that there were four more mugs, never used, as well as instant coffee, teabags, a bag of sugar and half a packet of chocolate digestives, the open end twisted to keep them fresh. Josh retrieved two of the mugs and the coffee but left the biscuits, not prepared to risk his gut health more than was necessary on the poor hygiene of Dan and Andy's crew. In fairness, the place would've been in a far better state had he not sprung this on them, and unless Xander or Jonathan had a severe allergy to dust, it was clean enough for their purposes. The kettle was a fast boiler too, as it had switched off before he'd finished rinsing the mugs and located a clean teaspoon.

A cold breeze whisked across his face, and he stopped dead, the spoonful of coffee granules suspended above the mug, a few tumbling into it as Josh wondered why on earth he'd decided to wait here, in his 'haunted' building. Every creak it made, the flap of the blinds against the frame of the open window, the click of the kettle cooling, he could explain it all, yet his heart refused to slow down, and he was clutching an empty spoon. He couldn't stay there, not alone. Very carefully so that it made no sound at all, he put the spoon in the mug and walked as calmly as he could along the corridor and down the stairs, patting his pocket to confirm he had his keys.

Back in the confines of his car, Josh concentrated on slowing his breathing, and when it and his heartbeat reached a closer-to-normal rate, he started the engine and reversed out, pointing the car towards the coffee shop. He had an hour to fill and no intention of entering that building again without Xander.

***

"Jessica Lambert is dead." Those were the first words Xander said as he reached the top of the stairs.

Josh had walked ahead of him purely because he'd had to unlock the external door and would have felt foolish saying *you go first*, but he stopped outside his consultation room and turned back, noting Jonathan hadn't followed them in. "Yes, she is. Why do you ask?"

"It wasn't a question." Xander rotated on the spot, still only a foot from the staircase. "Gabby told me."

"Oh! I thought…never mind." Josh tilted his head and leaned in the direction Xander was turning—clockwise—as if that would grant him a better understanding of what Xander was doing, quickly straightening up as the man completed his next rotation and came to a halt facing Josh. Every so often, he met Josh's gaze; mostly, he was looking anywhere but.

"I'm sorry for your loss," he said.

"Thank you." As it had been with Simon, it seemed more than a nicety, although they'd spoken for almost an hour the previous Sunday, so why hadn't Xander given his condolences then? Unless he'd been waiting until they were alone lest he breach a confidence. Better that than, as Josh feared, because Xander had seen something in the surgery. If only Josh could scrape up the courage to ask, it would alleviate his worries. Or confirm them. Was that worse than hanging in limbo? He had no idea.

"This is my consultation room. Please, come in." It took Xander a few seconds to comply, and Josh wasn't looking his way, yet he knew the moment Xander set foot over the threshold. Perhaps there was something to ESP after all.

"She's not here."

423

Josh pulled his chair out from under his desk and stalled, hand clutching the back. "Erm…" *Take control, Joshua. This is your office.* "Let's sit and then talk."

"As you wish." Xander headed for the plastic-covered sofa and sat, one leg crossed over the other. With his hands clasped around his knee and fingers locked together, it was hardly a relaxed pose, and the unexpected rapport they'd found the previous weekend was absent. Whether it was because they'd both gone into professional mode or Xander was picking up on Josh's anxiety, they'd struggle to make progress if they were acting like a couple of stiffs.

"Before we begin, would you like a cup of tea or coffee?" Josh asked.

"Coffee, thank you."

"It's only instant, I'm afraid. How do you—"

"With a dash of milk. Twenty millilitres."

"Should I measure it with a spoon?"

"Is that a joke?"

"No, it's not."

"Then yes, if you wouldn't mind."

With a nod, Josh departed to the kitchenette, which was precisely how he'd left it. The kettle was still warm, and the breeze through the open window was still cold; he pulled the window shut and switched the kettle back on. The coffee granules he'd abandoned were now a brown puddle in the bottom of the mug, which he rinsed and started over. He should've asked Xander if it made a difference whether he added the milk first or last but went with milk before everything, measuring out four teaspoonfuls and then, out of intrigue, free-poured milk into the other mug and compared the two.

Great. Something else to add to the list of things Xander and I have in common, but it didn't gall him as it had in the past. In fact, it was comforting in ways Josh had not been emotionally mature enough to process at seventeen but understood now he was older and had a better sense of self. The kettle switched off, and he finished making their drinks based on his own preferences for strength and amount of stirring and carried them back to his consultation room, where Xander remained on the sofa but with his notebook and pencil at his side.

"I'll leave this on the floor," Josh said and crouched to do so. It went against his better judgement, but while he was down there, he took a peek at Xander's notebook. The lettering was neat and orderly, but it may as well have been the doctorly scrawl Josh had expected. Without his glasses, he couldn't read it. He retreated to his desk and waited for Xander to make the next move.

"My cousin suggested it would help if I told you about Lucy."

"Who?"

"Lucy Everett. She led me to her body."

"When?" Josh asked.

"Eleven years ago, at twenty-five minutes to four in the morning. The information is publicly available." Xander stared pointedly at Josh's tablet on his desk. "You can check that I'm telling the truth."

Josh didn't doubt it. Nevertheless, he picked up his tablet and activated the screen. "I *am* going to look it up—not because I don't believe you."

"I know. You should watch the interview with her mother," Xander advised.

It was the first item that came up in his search; Josh obediently clicked the link and turned up the volume.

Daytime TV, distinguishable by the sofas and the picture window behind the male and female presenters. A meek woman sat to their left—Lucy's mother—talking while they offered sympathetic frowns and nods and asked tactful questions. The woman's self-containment was impressive; the interview was dated two years after her daughter's body was found—no mention of who found it—and seven years after Lucy had gone missing, a far shorter time than the one case of child murder for which Josh had acted as counsellor, not to the grieving mother but to her partner, the murderer. Ten years in prison, remorse, regret...

and fantasies so pervasive that he'd begged the police to take him back into custody before he acted on them again. They wouldn't— couldn't without the man committing a criminal act—and in the end, he'd taken the matter into his own hands. Josh, along with the man's mother and brother were all who attended the funeral.

Lucy Everett's murderer was dead too, and the parallels were striking, other than her stepfather had died from natural causes a few days after her body was found and before the police had identified him as her killer. Such injustice, no-one to punish, but her mother wasn't seeking retribution. She pressed for a change in the law to enforce a legal duty on family members to report abuse, had the backing of a member of the House of Lords—

Josh paused playback. "Do you believe that's why Lucy made contact with you?"

Xander's smile was condescending. "She was four years old and a ghost."

"What does that mean? She was too young to articulate what had happened to her?"

"Perhaps. Ghosts like Lucy's don't answer questions. One cannot engage them in conversation. It is much as it appears there."

"A recording?"

"Yes."

"I see. So…" He wasn't sure how to word his questions.

"I will tell you what happened," Xander said.

"I'd appreciate it if you would. Thank you." Josh set his tablet aside and picked up his coffee.

"May I begin?"

"Please do."

"I like to walk home when I work late. My apartment is thirty minutes from Westminster, between the two locations a children's playground. That was where I saw Lucy, dressed in school uniform, though it was not that kind of playground. I looked into the history. The site was formerly a primary school, which Lucy had attended for only seven weeks. It was in the autumn half-term break that her stepfather killed her.

"I didn't see her again for more than a year. I generally don't work past midnight—"

"Why didn't you go back the next night?"

Xander pressed his palms together and moved them slightly apart, then together again. "I see ghosts all the time. Too many to count or keep track of."

"I'm sorry, that wasn't an accusation."

"I didn't take it as one."

"And I'll try not to interrupt again. It's being in this chair."

"You're creating a therapeutic dialogue."

"Yes. Force of habit."

"I like your direct approach. You don't pretend you believe me or to understand my extra-sensory perception."

"Is it extra-sensory, though?" Josh speculated and then, realising the potential for misinterpretation, clarified, "I do believe that you believe you're seeing ghosts."

"But science tells you otherwise."

"Science tells me nothing. There is no empirical evidence to support the concept of life after death. However—"

"The existence of ghosts is not necessarily evidence of life after death."

"Precisely. Our senses and perceptions are still largely beyond scientific understanding."

Xander gave a stilted nod. "If I may continue?"

"Yes, of course." Josh settled back in his chair, mentally pulling a zip across his lips.

"The second time I saw Lucy was almost a year later, and I did go back the next night, and every night thereafter until I found her body. At half past three every morning, she ran across that playground, straight through the play equipment, but disappeared before she reached the other side.

"I watched her for a week before I followed her. There was nothing notable about the spot where she vanished, nothing notable about the path she took. It was merely an echo of the weeks leading up to her murder. What do you make of that?"

The question came as a surprise, and at first, Josh thought it was rhetorical, but Xander was waiting for him to respond.

"Erm…well… You say she only attended the school for a few weeks?"

"Seven."

"Therefore it must have held some personal significance for her. Was she murdered there?"

"No, she was not. Why would echoes of the deceased reside where they died?"

"A residue of powerful emotions?"

"That is logical, but it's not how it works. Do you recall what we discussed last Sunday morning?"

"About self-perpetuating ghosts versus after-images, yes."

"Those after-images are sustained by other people's energy, not the ghost's."

"I think I see," Josh said. "Lucy was an after-image."

"Correct."

"Hmm. And the school no longer existed, so it wouldn't have come from former teachers or pupils. Other children perhaps? Or their parents—did Lucy play there before she died?"

"She did not."

"In that case, it has to be the one person who knew where her body was—her stepfather."

"Bravo!" Xander clapped his hands, not quite in applause, but Josh still basked in the praise.

"I think I'm getting the hang of this." He sat forward, a sponge open to absorbing Xander's knowledge. "What happened after you found her?"

"The police arrested me. As we have established, the murderer knew where she was, so naturally, they assumed I was the murderer. I was incarcerated for almost two weeks while they tested the DNA found on Lucy's body against her stepfather's blood relatives. That was also when the stepfather's mother came forward and admitted she'd suspected her son was abusing his stepdaughter."

"How awful."

"Yes, it was. Harrowing."

"Thank you for telling me."

"You're welcome, as they say."

Josh chuckled. "It is an odd phrase."

"May I share what I have learned about the presence here? Have I opened your mind sufficiently?"

"I think so, yes." Josh's hands turned clammy, his cup sliding out of his grasp. He set it on the desk and wiped his palms on his thighs. "Can you see them?"

"Yes."

"They're here now?"

"Yes. They've been here all the time."

That presence could have been throwing furniture and slamming doors, and Josh wouldn't have heard or felt anything, the rate his pulse had reached. An aneurysm was looking more likely by the minute. For a few seconds, he fought the impulse to look over his shoulder, then he was doing so and concentrating hard on seeing *something*, but, of course, he saw nothing except patchy plaster walls and dust. "Where are they?"

"He, I believe, is in constant motion, as if he's looking for something." Xander's eyes tracked movement across the room, towards the door. "He'll be back in a moment."

"What does he look like?"

"Slender build, light-coloured hair. Here he is again." It was like Xander was watching cars race from the door to the far end of the room and back. "I can't describe his features. He's too fast."

"How is he dressed?"

"Contemporary attire, based on the colours. Shirt and slacks perhaps. I would usually ask for a list of those who have spent any amount of time on the premises so I can research further."

"I'm sorry, I can't provide that without breaching client-practitioner confidentiality."

"I understand."

Nevertheless, Josh scanned his mental records of his former clients for a match, and there were a couple of possibilities, but as far as he was aware, both were still alive. He had their contact details at home; it would take only a short phone call to each to find out.

"Your father is dead, you told me," Xander said.

"Yes, when I was six, but he had dark hair and was quite a large man. He also never came here."

"Ghosts are attached to people, not places, although they can become tethered to objects of significance to their loved ones."

"Those spiritualist tools I mentioned—could they act as a tether?"

"Perhaps. Show me."

"They're at a friend's house. I could call her—"

"Then no, they're not tethering this ghost or he would have gone with them. The furniture is all new, yes?"

"Yes," Josh confirmed. "Other than the kitchen units, everything is new."

"In that case, he must be attached to you." As he uttered the last word, Xander startled. At the same moment, Josh was overcome by a gasp, shuddering and deep and vital as the first breath of a rescued drowning victim. It flooded his lungs with dusty air and sent him into a coughing fit.

"You felt it," Xander said, unmoving while Josh fought to catch his breath. "He passed through you, and you felt it."

Josh clutched at his throat, pressing his finger and thumb into the muscles to stop the spasms, although the way his hand was trembling there was a good chance he'd pass out before he succeeded. That might even be preferable if it took away the aching and nausea that had descended on him as suddenly as a bout of flu.

When the coughing abated a little, Josh attempted to pick up his coffee cup, still half-full, or it had been until he sprinkled most of it over the floor. Good job it was covered in plastic.

"Let me help you," Xander offered, already standing over him. He held the cup steady for Josh to drink and when he'd had enough took it away. Josh nodded his thanks.

"Would you mind if we leave this for today, Xander?"

"Not at all. I had hoped to depart soon, as I must attend a dinner in Southwark this evening. Never fear, Jonathan will continue our research while I'm indisposed, and he is an exceptional historian."

Never fear? Josh was too...too *something* to point out it was a bit late for that. He spent a few moments breathing and visualising, a practice he had learned from his primary school counsellor and which he'd taught to every client since, and it had the desired effect, as it was only when he heard the sound of running water that he realised he was sitting on his own.

He trailed Xander out of the room and waited at the top of the stairs, watching helplessly as the man he'd once considered a nemesis—a member of the landed gentry at that—gave the cups a cursory rinse and left them on the draining board.

"Thank you, Xander. You didn't have to do that."

"I disagree. You are clearly quite shaken." Xander wiped his hands dry on his blazer and went back into the consultation room, returning a moment later with his satchel and Josh's tablet, handing over the latter and then gesturing for Josh to go ahead down the stairs. "I'll let Jonathan know I'm ready," he said once they were outside. "Shall I call George for you too?"

Josh pulled the door shut and dead-locked it. "Why?"

"You should not drive in your state."

It was a reasonable observation, although George was such a nervous driver it was arguably safer for Josh to drive himself.

"Or perhaps you could leave your car here and we will take you home if George doesn't drive."

"He does. He just doesn't like to, but I'll manage. It's not very far."

"Are you sure? It really is no trouble."

"I'm…" *If we're not in this together, we might as well call it quits now.*

A car stopped at the kerb; Jonathan got out and walked around to open the back door.

"Actually, yes, please," Josh said. "I'll ask Sean to bring me back. He needs to see how work's progressing here anyway."

"Doctor Tierney?"

"Yes. We're business partners."

Xander moved towards the car but paused before getting in and looked back at Josh. "You are fortunate to have such a good friend."

"I am."

"All the more important then, that we get to the bottom of your haunting as quickly as we can."

39: Hair of the Dog

A ND THE LIFT will be in by the end of the week, Andy
...said, so we might not need to hold off until October for
the official opening..."

Sean stopped at the top of the stairs while Josh continued,
both walking and with the monologue that had begun in the car.
Understandably, he was nervous: he hadn't told Sean what had
happened over the weekend with Xander, but it had to be bad for
him to abandon his beloved 'runaround' for three days.

So this was it, their new therapy centre, and from where Sean
was standing, it was a bit of an anticlimax. Bare, white walls; plain
wooden doors; a line of low-energy spotlights along the corridor
ceiling. Behind one of those doors was Sean's consultation room,
but it wouldn't have felt any more like his if his name had been
emblazoned in neon. The space was blank, soulless, didn't feel
like it belonged to anyone, not even Josh. It could've been any
building anywhere.

Of course, it was all symptomatic. The little wine he'd
drunk wouldn't have done any further damage to his body, so it
wasn't like last time, when he'd had to get through the physical
dependence first, but Sean had still done the sensible thing and
kept away from stress and temptation for those first two critical
weeks, in his case a wealth of knowledge proving more dangerous
than a little. Three years clean, but the odds dropped further the
longer he stayed so, and that incessant voice in his head was all

for logical fallacies. Most people relapsed early on, and it was easier to say *oh, well, I'll start over after this wee drinky* than to keep going.

He was into the recovery period now, and thankfully the booze had lost most of its salience, but it had left a bog of apathy that he waded through every morning just to get out of bed. It would take time to rekindle his enthusiasm for the things he'd always enjoyed, never mind this new adventure that he'd been so sure would succeed only a few weeks ago. Right now, it was hard to believe he'd ever care about it or anything again.

"Sean? Where—oh!" Josh appeared at the end of the corridor. "I thought you were right behind me. Do you want to see this wet room?"

If it comes with a wet bar, he wanted to say but stuck with, "Sure," and kept on trudging through that bog, nodding and making the right noises as Josh prattled on about the new additions—the office and storeroom next to the kitchen—"same as always"—and the wet room around the corner—"much bigger than the old loo"—then back again to the corridor with the consultation rooms on one side, the stairs up to the loft on the other. There was also an almighty draught blowing from what Sean presumed was the empty shaft beyond the closed lift door up ahead. Josh continued towards it, while Sean stayed where he was, next to the new staircase.

"Are we not allowed up there?"

"Hm?" Josh turned back, his frown one of innocent puzzlement.

"The loft," Sean said, quite sure Josh had heard and understood.

"What about it?"

"Is it done?"

"I believe so."

"Don't you want to see?"

"Erm…" Josh chewed his cheek and peered past Sean, then smiled too cheerfully and reached for the nearest door. "I had in mind that this would be your room, but you can take your pick out of the two that aren't mine." He pushed the door open and went in. Sighing, Sean followed him and continued his performance of nodding and being interested, waiting for the stream of babble to run its course. The room was nice. It even had furniture. And more of those blank, white walls. Sean looked around them gloomily.

"Can I paint in here?" he asked.

"No."

"No?"

"What I mean to say is…yes, if you must."

"It's…clinical. Cold. Devoid of personality."

"Ah, but we have those fancy lights, don't we?" Josh said. "Or we will have."

"Fancy lights?"

"The ones Adele and Dan have in their kitchen. We talked about them when we met with Dan and Andy. Remember?"

"Right, yeah. Of course." That would be the meeting when he'd bitten his tongue instead of giving Josh an earful for leaving the Jeffries boys to consult with the architect. Fair enough if Josh wasn't interested in doing it, but Sean had wanted to and had made sure Josh knew that. There was no point being bitter about it now; it was a done deal, same as the white walls, white ceilings, white tiles in the wet room. No doubt the kitchen would be all white in the end too. All considered, Sean probably didn't need to see the loft either, but he had to stop rolling over like a puppy expecting punishment. Josh had run the show long enough.

"I'm going up to see the loft. Are you coming?"

"No, no." There was that too-breezy smile again. "Shall I make coffee?"

"Good idea. I'll join you in your room when we're done, all right?" He was confirming his intent, not asking permission, and didn't wait for an answer but caught a glimpse of Josh's stricken expression as he left.

As he'd expected, the loft was an expanse of bright white—dazzling, actually, with the large skylights—and still under construction. The void along the bottom of the external side wall had been boxed off with a timber frame and was awaiting boards or doors; on the rear external wall was a lift door matching the one on the first floor, next to it a control panel with its innards hanging out. It had the potential to be a fantastic space, but…

There it was again. *But.* Never mind getting rid of the ghost. The whole building needed an injection of spirit, soul, energy—*anything* other than this emotional whiteout, an illusion of wiping the slate clean and starting over that was typical Josh, and Sean was done with it. Done with it and then laughing because he was mad as hell and it was a huge relief to shake off the mental numbness.

Ready to go and have it out with his business partner, Sean turned to leave and near died of shock when a figure appeared from nowhere.

"Jesus!" the figure said. "You frightened the life out of me!"

"*I* frightened *you*?" Sean asked, incredulous. "Did you do that on purpose?"

"Do what?" The figure, whose attire of a 'Browns Electric' polo shirt and cargo pants placed them firmly in the realms of the living—although Sean considered giving them a poke to be sure—pointed to the corner of the loft. "I've got to rerun a cable because of you and your stupid guffawing." They brandished a pair of wire cutters, snipping them in front of Sean's face. "What was so bloody funny anyway?"

"Ah." Sean grinned, suddenly sheepish. "Sorry about that. I'll get out of your way." He scuttled back down the stairs, feeling much better for the interlude but no less determined. "Right, Joshy, get your arse in here," he said, heading straight for 'consultation room 1'—Josh's room—and taking up residence on the new sofa.

Several minutes on, he was still on his own.

"Are you growing the beans yourself?"

"No," Josh answered from close by. Sean turned and saw he was standing in the doorway, a mug in each hand, not moving.

"What's up?"

"Can we do this next door?"

Sean considered backing down for all of a second. "No. Whatever happened with Xander—"

"A ghost walked through me."

Sean processed that statement. Not 'Xander claimed' or 'Xander saw'. "In here?" he asked.

"Yes."

"Right. Well, that's…er…"

"Terrifying," Josh said. "It was absolutely terrifying."

"But you don't believe in ghosts."

"Oh…shut up, Tierney." The mugs started to tip in Josh's hands. Sean sprang up and went to rescue them.

"So what d'you want to do? Swap rooms?"

"No. This is *my* room! I want it back."

"Then take it back."

"I…" Josh swayed dangerously.

Sean looked around for the closest place to dump their coffees. "Shite." There was only the desk across the room. A light thud made him turn back to Josh, who had come to a rest against the doorpost. "Let's do this in my room, shall we?"

Josh smiled glibly and kind of rolled around the corner into the corridor, inching his shoulder along the wall to the next door, which Sean reached first and nudged open with his knee. He waited for Josh to enter then followed him in, finally offloading the mugs and blowing on his slightly scalded forefingers.

"Did I tell you what the hospital bought me as a leaving gift?" he asked, his intention being to distract Josh long enough for him to shake off his mortal fear so he could talk about it. "A clock for in here." Sean gestured to the couch; Josh complied and sat. "It's brilliant."

"Why would you need a clock? You can't tell the time."

Sean chuckled. Josh's delivery was flat, but his joke suggested he was coming round. "Wait till you see it." Now Josh was seated, Sean handed him his coffee, then brought over his own and sat on the other end of the couch.

"Where will you put it?" Josh asked.

"I don't know." Sean looked around the blank white walls but this time saw them adorned with his certificates, a noticeboard, a couple of arty posters... "Up there, maybe." He nodded at the wall opposite. "Unless it'll get in the way of those fancy lights. You'll have to tell me about them again sometime because, I'll be honest with you, I wasn't paying much attention that evening at Dan's place. I'm still having a problem with you leaving it to them to deal with the architect."

"I'm sorry, Sean. I didn't think. Well, no. I thought that as seeing as we'd come up with identical lists, it would save us both the hassle, as it was just a case of passing on the information along with the sketches of the layout, which I realised too late were solely my vision. I've been so worried you'd come here and hate it. That wasn't unfounded, was it?"

"I don't *hate* it, but it feels like a new build. D'you know what I mean?"

"No residual energy?" Josh asked, and he wasn't even being sarcastic.

"Your ghostly encounter says otherwise."

"Don't remind me."

"On the plus side, you know it's not what's-his-name pulling a prank."

"Tony Baines? I'm not ready to rule that out, but if it is him, once he sees we're not prepared to give in, *he* will, and Xander's investigating the ghost angle. One way or another, it *will* stop."

At last, there was a hint of the Josh that Sean knew, the determined, reasoned man who didn't kowtow to pranksters, ghosts or anyone.

"All right, so, that's all in hand, and the Jeffries boys are cracking on with the building work. What's next on our agenda?"

"Knock, knock!"

Sean didn't need to look and couldn't have stopped his grin if he'd tried. "Well, well, if it isn't our new boss!"

Shaunna cackled. "You have *no* idea!"

"Oh, we do," Josh said. "And your timing is perfect, as usual."

"Just one of my many talents," she bragged, then admitted, "Andy called to tell me my decking's arrived, and he said you were both here, so I thought I'd pop up and say hi." She gave the room a visual once-over then leaned back and did the same with the corridor. "It's looking great!"

"Haven't you seen it before?"

"No. Well, not since the old days."

"You make it sound like the 1800s," Josh said. "It was five years ago you last came here."

"Really? I didn't even think it was that long. But anyway, who's giving me the guided tour?"

"Sean?"

"How about both of us," Sean suggested.

"Excellent!" Shaunna grinned. "Come on, minions!" She swirled, the flames of her hair licking at the doorpost as she marched off down the corridor, out of sight.

"Get a move on, Tierney," Josh called on his way out.

"Jaysus, what have I signed up for here?" Sean muttered to himself and traipsed after them, to the plumbed end of the building and then back along the corridor to lift end and what Sean presumed would be a reception area. In its present form, it bore a troubling resemblance to the secure observation room in the hospital's psych unit, and he didn't have the creative juice left to imagine it with the low-profile corner sofa and table Josh was describing to Shaunna, or the parlour palm she insisted would complete it.

The pair of them were still swapping ideas as they headed back along the corridor. If Shaunna noticed Josh's distraction tactics as they passed his consultation room, she didn't react, but she did when they reached the loft stairs.

"Oy! Where are you going?"

"I'll make drinks for us all, shall I? Tea for you?" He'd already reached the kitchen door.

"But—"

Sean coughed once to get her attention and indicated upwards with his eyes. Shaunna frowned briefly but got the message.

"OK," she said. "I'll have coffee too—keep it simple." She winked at Sean—all the tea drinkers in their midst agreed that Josh made the worst tea ever—and led the way upstairs. The electrician almost bowed before her while she fluttered her eyelashes in flirtatious interest as they explained they were fitting the control panels for the lift, blinds for the skylights and loads of other stuff Sean didn't hear because his phone buzzed in his pocket, rattling his keys. He had a missed call from Genie, followed by a text message:

> Nothing to worry about. Just letting you know the procedure went well and Phee's in recovery. Will call again later. Hope all's good with you! G x

"Sean?"

"Hmm?"

Shaunna circled with her finger, telling him to turn around.

"Are you done here already?"

"Yep." She threw a big cheery smile in the electrician's direction and bundled Sean back down the stairs, catching hold of his arm before they reached the bottom to whisper, "Is everything all right?"

He nodded, his initial response of *I'll tell you later* supplanted by his agreement to communicate better with his business partner, who was, above all else, his oldest friend, without whom Sean could not have stayed in England, would never have completed his studies, pursued his career, met Genie and Sophie or had Phee and Dylan, felt the safety and comfort of unconditional friendship or the sorrow of its loss. All that from a single gift of kindness from one lonely undergraduate to another.

Predictably, that once lonely undergraduate was loitering outside Sean's consultation room, which was roughly opposite the stairs to the loft. He flashed them a swift smile and turned to go in. "The drinks are in here."

"Phee went for her termination today," Sean said.

Josh turned back. "Is she OK?"

"She's fine."

"Are you?" Shaunna asked.

Sean gave it some consideration. He *was* fine, maybe a bit more than that. "Aye," he confirmed. "So, this is my office..." He gestured across the corridor.

"It's not," Shaunna argued.

"If you'd rather have it—"

"It's too clean and tidy to be yours."

"Hey, I resemble that remark. Although...that's a good point." Sean looked behind him at the stairs and then in through the open door. "I might be better in the next one along."

"Or you can learn to tidy up after yourself," Shaunna chided lightly.

"If I may..." Josh interjected and waited for his colleagues' consent. "I think you should keep this office and fill it with as much clutter as you want. Your messiness is part of your charm."

"You know, Joshy," Sean slung his arm around Josh's shoulders, "for a caustic, stuck-up so-and-so, sometimes you say the nicest things."

"Shall I leave you to your bro moment?" Shaunna asked, which turned Josh rigid. Chuckling, Sean gave him a pat on the back and released him.

"I tell you what you can do, if your man here's all right with it. Give him some ideas for what to do with his consultation room."

"Ideas like...plants and pictures for the walls or...?"

"Yes," Josh said, meeting Sean's gaze to confirm he was on the same wavelength. He went and opened the door, then moved back to give Shaunna space.

She made it a few steps inside before she stopped. "This is exactly how it used to look."

"Yes, it is," Josh confirmed. "Smaller."

"Everything's in the same place."

"Except for the bookshelf that used to be against the back wall."

Shaunna walked over to the wall in question and ran her hand over the plaster. "It's…" She froze. "Brrr." She shuddered dramatically. "You know that feeling like someone…"

"Walked over your grave?" Josh finished and looked at Sean, resigned but perhaps also relieved. "So it *is* a ghost."

"Is that what you want to believe?"

"No, but we've eliminated every other explanation. Multiple independent witnesses—"

"Not so fast, Mr. Scientist." Shaunna re-joined them in the corridor. "You know my beliefs, Josh."

"Yes, but—"

"And you know I wouldn't usually fight you on this, but Libby told me what you and she saw, so I'm hardly an independent witness, and neither are you and Libby. You're being… reductionist!"

Josh's eyebrows rose; Sean smiled proudly and barely stopped short of saying *that's my girl!*

Shaunna ignored them both and went on. "What other explanations have you ruled out?"

"Dan tested the electrics—all fine. Andy checked for subsidence and deathwatch beetles—nothing to report."

"Ah, but did he check for infrasound?"

"Why would he… Ohhh!"

Shaunna nodded smugly.

"What are yous on about?" Sean asked.

"Infrasound. Ultra-low frequency—"

"I know what it is, but how's it relevant here?"

"There's been a few studies of the physiological and psychological effects on humans, none of them recent," Josh said. "Small samples, inconsistent and non-significant findings…"

"Which show?"

"Some very limited evidence to indicate sound below human hearing range might account for alleged psychic experience."

"Very limited but you're still considering it."

"It's that or a ghost, Sean. Which would you prefer?"

"Neither, if I have a choice."

"OK, well, it won't do any harm to ask Andy to look into it."

"Good idea. What about Xander? When's he coming back to you?"

"Erm…" Josh glared at Sean.

"Open and honest, remember?"

"Oh…fine." He told Shaunna, "Xander sees ghosts. He offered his help, and I agreed—but you already knew that, didn't you?"

She nodded. "I did, and I haven't told a soul."

"Thank you." Josh glared at Sean again, making it clear he wasn't forgiven for blabbing.

"While we're being honest," Sean said, "Genie had a poltergeist. That's why Xander was at her place."

"Did he get rid of it?" Josh asked.

"I didn't see any shenanigans while I was there."

Shaunna cleared her throat. Josh snorted.

Sean shoved his hands in his trouser pockets and stared at the floor. "Or not of the supernatural variety."

Someone patted him on the head, and he peeked at them through his eyebrows; both were close enough to be the culprit.

"Do we have a plan?" he asked.

"Yes," Josh said. "I'll give Xander a call in a moment."

"I can talk to Andy," Shaunna offered.

"Perfect. Any other business?"

Simultaneously, Sean and Shaunna looked through the door into Josh's seemingly empty consultation room and repeated, "Any other business?"

"Not funny," Josh grumbled and then ruined it by laughing and shaking his head. "Sean, anything further from you?"

"Nope," he confirmed with a grin. "But thanks for asking."

40: Dirty Money

A Hospital in Shropshire
Present Day
Tuesday, 28ᵗʰ May

G ENIE CLOSED THE magazine and put it back on the overbed
table, wondering when she had become so *old*. Granted,
it wasn't the kind of thing that would appeal to Phee either,
but the patient whose bed she'd taken over had ordered it, the
newspaper-trolley woman had said, adding with a kindly smile,
"It'll keep your mind off things for a while." Genie had accepted
the magazine and made a show of reading it, but nothing was
holding her interest today.

Phee napped fitfully, still recovering from the anaesthetic.
She'd been too far along for the 'lower risk' medical procedure
and her heart rate was a little high so she was being monitored
overnight, but the dangerous bit was over. The surgery had gone
well; Phee's pain was under control. That was all that mattered for
now. The rest they could deal with later, although what it might
entail was so distressing, Genie felt sick every time she thought
about it.

The bell rang along the ward, indicating the end of visiting
hour, but Genie didn't want to leave and spend another night
alone in an empty house. It had been quiet for almost a month,
not a trace of the ghostly housekeeper since the day the police
turned up and Xander had made his swift exit. Genie had
pondered at length whether it was his presence that had made it
possible for her to see Beatrice. Or perhaps she'd been so eager
to please him that she'd conjured Beatrice from her imagination.

Unexpectedly, she'd discovered she enjoyed Xander's company; alas, he was not one inclined to socialising for the sake of it, and she no longer had an excuse to call him.

"I hate to intrude, but…" A young nurse smiled at her from the doorway.

"Visiting's over. I know. Sorry." Genie picked up her bag and rose, leaning over the bed to kiss her daughter's forehead. "Sleep well, darling, see you tomorrow," she whispered and left, glad of her flat pumps as she hurried along the corridor of the main ward, at the end glancing back to Phee's private room. The uneasy fluttering started up again, and she quickly walked on, keeping her head down all the way to the car. Collapsing gratefully into the driver's seat, she took a moment to collect her thoughts and remind herself that she'd done it for Phee, to shield her from the guilt others would have imposed on her, as they had done to Genie.

How could she have known Phee would be admitted to a general surgical rather than antenatal ward? Would it have made any difference if she *had* known? Genie's experience had been driven by the need to keep her termination from her parents, who most likely wouldn't have made her see the pregnancy through, but they would have seized back the little independence she'd found at school. That was why she'd gone it alone on the NHS, quite the culture shock and not one her daughter need be subjected to when they could afford private healthcare. But at whose expense?

It was this question that had played on her mind since Xander had told her the ghost boy was gone, along with his adolescent companions. Or were they his tormentors? No doubt those two were responsible for the other, more destructive incidents—the flying lamp, the erupting sheet music and the smashed bottle—typical teenagers, even in the afterlife. As to who they were, Xander might have failed to identify them or what had brought them into Genie's home, but she'd had her suspicions the moment she'd seen the title on that score, and everything that had happened since seemed to confirm she was right.

You know what you must do.

Manifestation of her conscience or uttered by a benevolent spirit, it mattered not; those words had led her to do what she ought already to have done, saved her and others from facing recrimination, but her hands were far from clean.

Back home again, she poured a glass of wine and put on some music, normally enough to soothe and distract. She'd let the algorithm select on her behalf, yet every random choice took her deeper down the dark path of loss and loneliness. For the first time in eighteen years, the mantelpiece was bare; Phee's birthday cards were still in their envelopes, all celebration postponed until the procedure was out of the way. Even then, she didn't want a big fuss. *No surprise party, Mother.*

If things had been different, Genie might have ignored that and planned one anyway. It was too long since this house had seen a celebration of any kind, and her grandmother would have approved. Or perhaps not. Her eternally captured gaze seemed particularly disparaging this evening. Largely to avoid it, Genie picked up her phone and opened her address book, staring at her most-recent contacts until the names remained when she closed her eyes. Sean, Phee, Xander, Paul. Sean had promised they were fine, he was just tied up with the business, but he hadn't answered her calls. Phee needed to rest and recover. Xander—it would be ludicrous to attempt a conversation via Jonathan, if Xander would even entertain that much—and Paul…

She had so much to say to Paul.

She opened a text message, typed *We need to talk*, then stared at it on her screen, vacillating between hitting send and deleting it in favour of calling him tomorrow without prior warning. The screen dimmed before she reached a decision: her attention had wandered again, this time to the piano, her father's lieutenant standing in silent judgement. She should get rid of it too.

"I can't tell whether you're here, Beatrice, and I'd probably die of fright if you showed yourself, so I'd rather you didn't..." Genie swallowed hard but lost the fight, and the tears fell. "I'm in such turmoil. I know I should only be concerned for my daughter right now, but that boy..." Why that boy had been anchored here was, to her shame, all she could think about.

"I was a fool. Still am. But the heart knows only what it wants, not what's best for it, and I loved Jess with all of mine." Genie took a glug of her wine and held the glass up to the light, admiring the clarity of both vessel and liquid, despising their symbolism. "I regret destroying those documents, Beatrice. I'm afraid all I did was banish that poor child to suffer elsewhere rather than bring him peace, and I *should be* held accountable. This house, the wine cellar, the money—I'm not entitled to any of it."

A sob of anguish caught her unawares, and more followed. She sobbed at the prospect of giving herself up to the police, of years behind bars away from her daughter, the scandal that would topple her father, all because of her love for a woman who was too cold and selfish to love her back and had died before she could face justice herself. No-one else should suffer for their weakness. Phee was an innocent, born into a situation she had accepted mostly with grace. It wasn't Genie's father's fault he was rich and powerful; he'd been born into it too. What he did with it, though, that *was* a choice, and he chose to enjoy it to its fullest, sitting on his committees, attending dinners and galas, unlike Xander, who'd dedicated his life to helping tortured souls, the living and the dead. Genie also had a choice, but that she knew how to exercise it.

She was so lost in her thoughts she only saw the incoming call as it ended; nor did she have an opportunity to call back, as they beat her to it. Grabbing a tissue, she gave her nose a quick blow and answered. "Now this *is* a surprise!"

"I hope you were sitting down."

"I was. It's so good to hear your voice, Sean."

"Likewise. How are things?"

"OK. Phee was sleeping when I left—they kicked me out of the hospital."

"Appalling."

"I know!" Genie laughed, dispelling a little of her sadness. "Damned NHS."

"Ah, she's in the commoners' hospital, is she?"

"Yes, although she has a private room. People judge, and she shouldn't feel guilty for her decision. It's her body, her life."

"I'm with you on that. And how are you doing?"

"None too well, to tell you the truth. It's too quiet here. Too much opportunity for ruminating."

"Do you want to talk about it?"

"Yes, but it can wait for another time. How are you?"

"I'm all right. Getting through the days."

"I'm so sorry, Sean. I didn't even think."

"Why would you? It's not your job or anyone else's to keep me sober, and so we're clear, you didn't make me do anything. I wanted to be with you."

"Wanted…"

"Past, present and future. I love the bones of you and always will, but if you're intending to reciprocate the sentiment, hold off, as I've something I need to tell you."

"Did you steal from the dying?"

Sean chuckled. "No."

"Then it's unlikely anything you tell me will change how I feel about you when that didn't stop me loving her."

"You make a good case, Genie."

"So I do."

"So you do. Now, I know you hate me rambling…"

"Since when has that stopped you?"

"I just thought maybe if you understand where I'm coming from…"

"*Sean.*"

"Right. Sorry. So, as we've established, Phee came to see me, and when she told me what had gone on, I was torn between my

449

professional duty of care for her and my loyalty to you, but I also wanted her to tell you herself. So I held off saying anything, and then you said she was ending the pregnancy and…"

Sean sighed heavily, and Genie wanted to save him the misery of continuing, but she knew how he operated. *One can take the boy out of Catholicism…*

"Paul got her pregnant, Genie."

"I know."

"She told you?"

"No. She left her phone switched on when she went to surgery, and I wasn't snooping. I'd never do that to her. But the screen unlocked when I was turning it off, and it was open on her messages. I saw the last one she sent him—a week ago. I'm so angry and sad for her, not just that she told him what she was doing and he didn't bother to reply let alone ask if there was anything he could do. She's always had so many friends, yet that message was the third one from the top. She's eighteen years old, and her inbox is more barren than mine. It's all wrong. She's isolated herself these past months, and I can't bear the thought of what that means."

"Are you suggesting he groomed her?"

"It's crossed my mind, yes. But it's also my fault, for cutting her off from her family. Outside of school, she only has her best friend and me. Well, she has you too, but only because she sought you out, and I'm so thankful she did. The idea of her going through this alone…"

"I'll always be here for her—for the both of you—in whatever capacity you need me. And what's this about it being your fault? You're an incredible mum. You've done a fantastic job of raising your daughter—without other people's interference."

"Hmm. I'm not sure I agree. Maybe it's time my parents and I resolved our differences. Phee's eighteen now, after all."

"She told me you still weren't talking. Has she ever met them?"

"No. Nor her aunt Isla, although that's no bad thing. She's so mercenary she makes Jess seem saintly."

"That bad, is she?"

"Put it this way. She didn't marry Simon's father just for his dashing good looks. Nor he for hers, but that's by the by. I'll worry about that once I've dealt with Paul. Do *you* think he's a…" Simply having the word in her head made her murderous.

"I don't know, but Phee says it was consensual."

"Am I an awful mother for hoping that's not true?"

"You don't mean that."

"No, but I miss how it used to be. She was such an oversharer when she was young, it was embarrassing at times, and I've felt her pulling away from me as she's found her place in the world. It's the old adage of setting someone free, isn't it? I have to let her go to keep her. But I never expected her to betray me like this."

"Would it help to know she's devastated by it?"

"A little." Hurt as she was, Genie didn't want Phee to suffer more than she already had.

"Listen, lovely, I need to go as Dylan's not settling, but I'll call again in a couple of days if that's all right with you?"

"Anytime, Sean. And thank you."

"No need. You know where I am."

I do. Good night."

"Good night, sleep tight."

Genie moved her phone away from her ear, catching sight of the call-ended notification before it disappeared, landing her back in her address book.

She scrolled down to J, where there was only one entry. She pressed the name and brought up the contact information: such a silly photo, it had to be fifteen years old; huge sunglasses, skimpy bikini, a cheeky smile on lush lips pursed around a straw poking out of a fruit-filled fishbowl glass. It had been taken on one of those holidays Jess had raved about, fun in the sun or the snow or whatever, just a whole big group of friends, nobody special. He'd have been there, perhaps right beside her, but it no longer hurt the way it used to.

With a fleeting thought, dismissed as always, that she should take the final step and delete Jess from her address book, Genie returned to the main view and scrolled back to the top, tapping the name before she could talk herself out of it.

"Hello, is that Andy?"

"Genie? Alright, mate! Blimey, it's been a while! How's things?"

"Fine, thanks. And with you?"

"Yep, all good here."

Pleasantries over, Genie searched for a natural lead-in to why she'd called. It took her too long, and Andy jumped in first.

"Is this a social call or…?"

"After a fashion. I, ah…" Genie picked at her cuticles. She was starting to think this was a terrible idea—more so when she heard a woman's voice ask him who was calling.

"One sec," he said into the phone, then to whomever was with him, "Genie—a mate of Jess's from uni."

"Oh, *really*?" The woman sounded overly surprised but added nothing further.

"Sorry about that," Andy said. "You were saying?"

"I haven't caused trouble for you, have I?"

"Nah."

"Oh, good. Is that your girlfriend?"

"Yep. We've been together a couple of years."

"After Jess."

"Kinda before too. Long story. You seeing anyone?"

"Not at the moment. Listen, I don't want to keep you, but there's been…a development, shall we say?"

"Let me guess. The police?"

"Yes! How did you know?"

"Got a mate on the local force, but they've been sniffing around here too."

"That's worrying."

"It's pretty stressful, yeah, but you're in the clear."

"Are you sure about that, Andy?"

"Anything that could be traced back to you was destroyed—wasn't it?"

"Yes, of course." He didn't need to know when.

"Then you've nothing to worry about."

"Thank you for the reassurance." She sighed as if that had lifted all the weight from her conscience and asked casually, "The victims' families received what they were owed, didn't they?"

"Yeah. Well, some of them didn't have any family or their next of kin couldn't be located. Police put you on a guilt trip, eh?"

Genie laughed glumly. "I manage that perfectly well on my own."

"I get you. That's why I offloaded everything the first chance I got."

Andy's girlfriend said something, and he came back with, "I mean handed the responsibility to someone who knows what they're doing." His tone was playful, but there was no question of who the boss was in their relationship, and it made Genie laugh for real.

"You sound happy," she said.

"I am."

"You wouldn't dare tell me if you weren't."

"True that."

"I don't want to harp on, and I hope you'll trust I have a good reason for doing so and not ask me to elaborate…"

"Go for it."

"Was there a young boy among the victims?"

"No idea."

"Damn."

"The solicitor's got a list, though. I can ask her to check or send you a copy?"

"Would you? That would be wonderful!"

"No worries. I'll get on it first thing in the morning."

"Thanks so much, Andy."

Genie paused, gearing up to the final thing she needed to say, which would bring the conversation to a close, and she didn't want that. Her younger self would never have believed it. However, the babble of a small person close to the receiver confirmed it was time to wind things up.

"I must let you go, but before I do, I want to apologise for using you."

"When was that?

"Can your girlfriend hear me?"

Andy cleared his throat, his voice dropping to a deep murmur. "Is this gonna get juicy?" Either his girlfriend was very understanding or she'd left him to his phone call.

"Not a chance."

"Thought my luck was finally in."

"One woman not enough for you?"

"If you were seriously making the offer—"

"You'd run a mile."

"You're not wrong. I've already got the girl of my dreams."

"That's what you said about that girl you liked at school."

"Because she is that girl I liked in school."

"Oh my goodness! Who knew fairy tales came true?"

"I'm guessing Jess told you I was a lost cause?"

"No. You did. I take it you don't remember very much about the day we spent at the dry slope?"

"Good day, that."

"Other than the part where you dislocated your shoulder."

"Ha, yeah. Did I talk your ear off?"

"A little, but it was nice getting to know the real you. I only wish I hadn't entered into the occasion under a false pretext."

"What d'you mean?"

"I hoped it would make Jess jealous."

"Aw, mate. That's shi...atsu."

Genie snorted a laugh at his censoring.

"Sorry. This one's a little parrot."

"My daughter was the same."

"Phoenix, yeah?"

"That's right."

"We've got twin girls. Rosie and Sorsha."

"Lovely names!"

"Cheers."

"Now I have to ask—did Jess tell you?"

"About Phoenix? Yep. And about you and her."

"Oh." It hadn't been a secret, but after they'd graduated it was never mentioned again. Were it not for Sean having been there, Genie could almost have convinced herself she'd fantasised the entire relationship. "I hadn't known that."

"It was near the end, like she needed to get it off her chest, make peace with it."

"The fraud or dumping me?"

"Both, I reckon. It's why she wanted to make sure you'd be all right. Money-wise, I mean. She never really got that there's more to life than that." There was a lot of sorrow in Andy's insight but no bitterness.

"I'm sorry she hurt you too, Andy, and I'm glad you made it with the girl of your dreams."

"Yeah…" He chuckled coyly, then followed up with a loud, nasal, "Ow! That's my nose!" His daughter giggled. It was so lovely listening to the two of them, Genie could, selfishly, have stayed on the phone all night, but she'd kept him long enough.

"I'll say goodbye now, Andy."

"All right, mate."

"You're a very sweet person. Don't ever change."

"No fear of that! It's been good speaking to you, Genie."

"Same. Take care."

"You too. Bye."

***

After a little too much wine and two impromptu but exceedingly pleasant telephone conversations, Genie had fallen asleep on the sofa and eventually made it to her bed at half past midnight. Thus, she was miffed when she was awake less than three hours later. As she came to, she was aware of the difference in the way the mattress felt, the warmth of someone behind her. *Paul*. Throwing off the duvet, she shot out of the bed and turned, the words *How the fuck dare you!* at the ready.

Phee startled, then froze and cried out in pain.

"What are you doing here?"

"I'm sorry, Mum. I didn't want to wake you."

"Why aren't you at the hospital?"

"I couldn't sleep, so I turned on my phone. I knew you'd seen my message to Paul. I had to come home and explain. I'm sorry. I'm so stupid." Phee's words dissolved into a heartrending mess of sobbing and wailing that instantly set Genie off too. As carefully as she could, she slid back into the bed and pulled the duvet over them both. Aching to comfort her daughter but afraid of causing her further pain, she held still while Phee inched closer, cocooning against Genie's chest. Even with her nose mostly blocked, Genie picked up the tang of blood and disinfectant.

"Did you sneak out, darling?"

Phee nodded. "I don't..." she began, but Genie shushed her and stroked her head. The information from those leaflets flashed warnings through her mind of infection, haemorrhage, reaction to anaesthetic, and all that on top of an elevated heart rate. She should insist Phee go back to the hospital, but she was so distressed, it seemed a far smaller risk to keep her home.

"I thought you and him were over..." Phee fought to get the words out between shallow, gasped breaths. "You weren't talking to each other or spending any time together...but then I saw Sean and Sophie, and I realised people can still be OK even if they're not full-on all the time."

"You were right, though, darling."

"No, I wasn't. I wrecked your relationship because of a stupid crush."

"No." Genie hugged Phee as tightly as she dared. "It's not your fault."

"But it is. I thought I really liked him, and I didn't want him to leave, but then I sent him that message, and I thought...

maybe he'd beg me not to go through with it or at least come and be with me, but he just ignored it. I've messed everything up. I'm so sorry, Mum."

"Oh, my sweet girl." Genie couldn't hold back any longer and gave in to the tears, crying harder than she'd cried in years—since Jess left her—as they cuddled together.

It was some time later before Phee relaxed from the tense ball into which she had protectively curled and her breathing evened with sleep. Genie withdrew her arm from beneath her daughter's neck to alleviate pins and needles but stayed where she was, watching the gentle pink of the new day spill beneath the curtains and cast a wide, warm sunbeam across the floor. The hour was still early; how early, she couldn't be sure. Her clock and phone were on the bedside table behind her. Soon, she would get up, make coffee, do what needed to be done. First things first: she'd call the ward, let them know Phee was safe and seek their advice on caring for her at home. Then she'd make sure her daughter was comfortable and knew how very much she was loved. After that...

Phee wasn't a child anymore, but there was no doubt in Genie's mind. Paul had taken advantage of Phee, used her fear of losing him to get what he wanted, and for that, he was going to pay dearly.

41: Loose Ends

Campion Trust Boardroom
Present Day
Wednesday, 29ᵗʰ May

BEFORE THE BOARDROOM door had fully swung open, Sean sighed and dug in his pocket.

"There y'are." He slapped a five-pound note down on the table. "Feckin' unbelievable."

Still catching his breath, Josh pulled out a chair between Shaunna and Eleanor and sat. "Sorry I'm late."

"You're not the only one," Shaunna grumbled, adding her fiver to Sean's. With a smug grin, Eleanor scooped up the money and shoved it in her pocket.

"What's happening?" Josh asked.

No answer forthcoming, he gave each of his fellow trustees in turn a narrow-eyed look. Across the table, Simon chortled. Josh's gaze homed in on him, but he was checking through the paperwork he'd come in to sign and either hadn't noticed or wasn't as intimidated as the rest of them, which was good news for the Daisy Foundation.

"Sean?" Josh pronounced with a slow, rising tone.

"Yeah?" Sean mimicked that tone exactly.

"Why did you give Ellie money?"

"That's right, pick on me. *She* did too." Sean elbowed Shaunna. She elbowed him back.

"Because he knows you'll crack."

"Yeah, Sean," Eleanor said, nodding.

"Seriously, it's like playtime at St. Mark's Primary," Josh muttered. "I can't imagine what you must think, Simon."

Simon looked up and grinned. "It's fabulous. Much more fun than I anticipated after our last meeting."

"Aye, well…" Sean felt his hackles rise, followed by a sharp, heel-shaped pain in his foot. He grunted but didn't let on otherwise. Shaunna gave him a sickly, sideways grin. "So, Joshy," Sean said, "you got held up, did ye?"

"Yes, I did. You won't believe—hang on a second. Were you betting on me being late?"

"Christ, no. I thought you'd be here half an hour before the rest of us."

"Well, I would've been."

"You don't need to tell me that."

"Or me," Shaunna said.

Eleanor shrugged noncommittally and then burst out laughing. Sean and Shaunna both leaned forward and glared at her.

"That was bloody excellent!" Simon said. "Not a single tell."

Shaunna whirled in her seat, whipping Sean with her hair and pushing Josh back so she had a clear line of sight to Eleanor. "You *knew*?"

"'Fraid so."

Now Josh was glaring at Eleanor too. "You didn't tell them I was going to be late?"

"That's cheating! Give me my money back." Shaunna held out her hand, palm up. Eleanor smacked it lightly, still grinning.

"You should've stated your terms more clearly than 'A fiver says he'll be on time.' If only we had a lawyer. Oh, wait!"

"On the matter of terms…" Simon said, flicking the catch on his snazzy attaché case and extracting a silver pen. "I'm satisfied that these documents are accurate facsimiles of the electronic versions you sent and which I reviewed previously." He uncapped the pen and flicked through the documents, signing each with a flourish and nary a scratch from the nib. He recapped the pen and slid the documents across the table to Sean, who pushed them along to Shaunna—not an act of chivalry or shirking. That the Daisy Foundation had come this far was down to her hard work and commitment to see through her promise to Jess.

The acceptance agreement needed the signatures of only two existing trustees, but all four signed—Shaunna, then Josh, then Eleanor and finally Sean.

"I'll go make a copy of this for you," he said, by which he meant he'd ask Alice to. He had more sense than to touch her photocopier, and Alice being Alice, she met him at the door as if she'd anticipated his request; more likely, she'd been eavesdropping. Either way, he was back in his seat in less than two minutes. He handed both copies to Shaunna, who passed one across the table to Simon and filed the other, along with the rest of the documents, in her bulging folder.

For once, Josh refrained from remarking on her insistence on printing everything. Not everyone was ready to go fully digital, and Sean was with Shaunna on that one. Admittedly, his reasons were more to do with never quite knowing what he was doing and having a knack for attracting gremlins, whereas Shaunna was a social media wiz and had typed all the foundation's documentation herself but made no bones about her opinion that people who put their trust in technology were asking for trouble. There'd been some very heated debates in their meetings since Josh had become a trustee, and the lack of one today was not down to him putting on a show for their newest colleague but because he was itching to share whatever was in the signed-for envelope he'd been clutching when he arrived. Sean figured it was about time someone put him out of his misery.

"So why were you late?"

"Funny you should ask." Josh waved the envelope. "I was on my way to the Post Office when Dan called to say the lift's up and running."

"How was it?"

"The lift? I don't know. As I said, I was on my way to the Post Office. I finally—"

"Aren't you even a wee bit interested?"

"Shut up, Sean."

"Yeah, shut up, Sean," Shaunna parroted.

Josh's nostrils flared. "I'll go and look at the lift tomorrow, OK?" Warning Sean and Shaunna off with a glare, he started again. "I finally tracked down the sole living relative of the owner of the stuff in the loft. You'll never believe who it is."

"Who?"

"Take a guess."

"No idea," Shaunna said.

Eleanor shrugged. "Someone famous?"

"No."

"Someone we know?" Sean asked.

"*Know of* in your case. And Ellie's, actually."

You could just tell us."

"Where's the fun in that?"

"It better be good after all this," Eleanor muttered.

Josh grinned and handed her the envelope. She gave him a dubious look as she fished out a single, folded sheet of watermarked vellum. That dubious look became incredulous when she read what was on it. She shook her head and handed it to Shaunna, whose eyebrows rose higher the further she read.

"Bloody cheek of her!" she said and thrust it at Sean. Fortunately, he'd pre-empted her ire and whipped his hand out of the way, avoiding a nasty papercut. The edges were sharper than his chef's knife, which he kept in a box in a cupboard, well out of Dylan's reach. It was a good, heavy paper, though. Substantial.

Aware the others were waiting for him so they could gossip about it, Sean stopped admiring the paper and got on with reading the letter, which at first glance appeared to be handwritten in blue ink but was in actuality printed in purple cursive font.

Dear Mr. Sandison-Morley,

I must confess: your correspondence falsely elevated my hopes. I expected that it would relate to other, professional matters between us that remain unresolved.

As regards what it does relate to, you are correct: Ethel Davison was my mother's cousin and a spinster. If my memory serves correctly, I met her only once, at my sister's wedding; I invited Ethel to my wedding three years later in 1983 but received no response because, as you note, she died in 1982.

Given my sister is also deceased, it would seem that I am Ethel's last living relative, and whilst I have no material or sentimental need for an inheritance, I would accept a modest sum as recompense. Alternatively, I can collect Ethel's property from you at your earliest convenience.

Sincerely,
Dorothy Lomax

"Am I right in thinking this is the woman you two interviewed?" Sean asked Shaunna and Josh, both of whom nodded to confirm it was. "Skint, was she?"

"Pfft!" Shaunna verily spat. "*And* we told her weeks ago she hadn't got the job. I sent out the letters myself!"

"Anyone I know?" Simon asked.

The way the other three did the same sudden head turn as Sean was a good indication they, like he, had momentarily forgotten Simon was there. Still, this was his official induction; it was no bad thing that he was getting to see them as they really were.

"Dorothy Lomax," Shaunna said. "She's a retired solicitor."

"With a purple fetish," Josh added.

Simon's eyes moved with his thoughts for a moment before he shook his head. "I don't recall crossing anyone of that name or—" he smirked at Josh "—matching that description. A purple fetish?"

"Clothes, shoes, nail varnish, ink…"

"Not a fancy clinical name for autoerotic asphyxiation then?"

"I think that's just autoerotic asphyxia, isn't it, Sean?"

"You're probably right," Sean said casually, as if he hadn't read everything *DSM-5* had to say about sex disorders during the past two years. That one was listed under 'Paraphilic Disorders', way down past 'Sexual Dysfunctions', a category he could've quoted with a level of accuracy that would have impressed even Josh *Photographic Memory is a Curse* Sandison-Morley. To wit: 'Erectile dysfunction is also strongly associated with feelings of guilt, self-blame, sense of failure, anger, and concern about disappointing one's partner'. It would've been grand if the APA could tell him something he didn't know, but he did feel as if he was finally making some progress. He'd taken that first, tentative step and called Genie rather than waiting for her to call him, and he was going to talk to Sophie about her relationship with Grant. Sean was genuinely OK with it, or he wanted to be, but he'd conceptualised it as rejection, Sophie going to Grant for what she couldn't get from him. Not only was that tremendously unfair on Sophie, it was also way off the mark. The bottom line was had they not had Dylan, their relationship may well have ended three years ago, before Sean's performance issues started in earnest, and he would still be drinking.

He'd also taken on board what Shaunna had said about talking to a professional, and his gut was telling him it needed to be a grief counsellor. However well he performed that role himself, and he thought he did a fairly decent job of it, he found ways to avoid processing his own grief. Losing Jess had psychologically kicked his feet from under him, perhaps because it called time on his dream of a life with her and Genie, or perhaps because it confirmed that it could only ever have been a dream. It made no odds. The process was the thing, and he knew enough to not expect a definitive answer by the end.

The mention of Genie in coincidence with him thinking about her pulled Sean out of his brief self-reflection, although he'd not been completely away in his head. He'd seen Shaunna move to the other side of the table, for instance, but her conversation with Simon had been background hum, likewise for Josh and Eleanor's. He spent a few seconds listening in on each and established who had mentioned Genie and why at the same time as Shaunna noticed him looking her way and beckoned for him to come over. He did so, with Josh's eyes burning holes in his back.

"Shall I make more tea?" Eleanor suggested.

"Actually, why don't we—" Josh began, but she cut him off.

"Come on, you can give me a hand."

Huffing, he followed her out of the boardroom.

"I was just telling Simon…" Shaunna touched Sean's arm to get his attention. "Genie phoned Andy last night."

"Did she?" She hadn't mentioned it to Sean. He was tempted to ask what time she'd called to reassure himself she hadn't kept it from him, but swiftly dismissed the idea. Why would she?

"She was asking about Jess's victims, whether one of them was a little boy."

"That's strange." Or it would have been if he hadn't known about Genie's poltergeist. "And was one of them a little boy?"

"We don't know. Andy called the solicitor this morning, but some of the records are sealed, which might be because those victims were minors or vulnerable adults." Shaunna looked to Simon for backup, and he nodded.

"I might be able to get access to them, but not without just cause."

"Any idea why she wants to know, Sean?" Shaunna asked.

"I think so. I can't tell you what it is, mind you, but I'll vouch for her if that helps with unsealing the records."

"I'll see what I can do," Simon said.

"See? I knew we made the right choice!" Shaunna winked but then followed up with a sincere, "Thank you," and squeezed Simon's hand. He dazzled her with his most charming smile, and Sean gave himself a mental clip around the ear for being an eejit. What did he think he was doing, getting jealous of a gay man indulging in a bit of light flirting with Shaunna? She was his friend, a close one, sure, and she'd snogged his face off not that long ago, but that didn't give him a claim over her any more than spending the night with Genie gave him the right to expect she'd tell him everything she got up to. As for Sophie, he didn't dare contemplate how many unrealistic expectations he'd placed on her lately.

Before he could get himself in even more of a tizzy over it, Eleanor and Josh returned, both empty-handed. Keeping his head down, Josh went back to his seat, while Eleanor held the door.

"Really, you didn't have to, but thanks," she said as Alice trotted in with an *oh, but I do have to* expression and a tea tray, which she deposited on the table before scurrying from the room. Barely had Eleanor closed the door when Josh bustled her aside and left again without a word. Sean raised an eyebrow, and Eleanor mouthed *phone call*, following up with a shrug. Sean moved over to the window and lifted the blind slats with his finger; he could just make out Josh getting into his car and putting his phone to his ear.

The tea brewed, Eleanor poured, and conversation around the boardroom table turned to foundation matters, consisting mostly of Shaunna's plans for the loft space in the therapy centre, which was now on schedule to officially open on 1st August—two months sooner than expected. The garden was almost done too—Simon gushed like the host of some TV makeover show at the photos she showed him, which once again rattled Sean. He needed to get that counselling on the go ASAP, although he was more worried about Josh, who, half an hour on, was still sitting in his car even though his phone call had ended five minutes after he'd gone out there.

"Will you excuse me a moment?" he asked, such as he was contributing to their discussion, and left the room, acknowledging Alice with a nod on his way outside.

Josh noticed Sean immediately and hid behind his hair. Then, with a sigh heavy enough for Sean to see it, got out of his car, blipping his alarm on his way back towards the building. He didn't look at all well, almost panda-like with those dark shadows beneath his eyes, but Sean still had to ask so Josh wouldn't feel compelled to share.

"Are you all right?"

"Xander thinks he's solved my ghost problem. He wants to come and see me tomorrow. In my consultation room."

"Ah." That said it all. "Do you want me to—"

"Yes, please."

Sean resisted saying, *Are you sure you don't want to think about that now?* and drew breath to ask the more practical question of what time he was needed but put it on hold as Simon was leaving, and the man had tact, Sean had to admit. Sean's car was parked next to Josh's, and Simon's was next to that, yet he went around the front of all three to avoid coming too close. He patted his attaché case, making eye contact with Sean to signal he had Genie's request in hand, then climbed into his flash electric convertible and silently drove away.

"Two o'clock," Josh said.

"On my mother's life, I'll be there by quarter to."

"Make it one-thirty."

"Now you're pushing it, Joshy, but all right."

***

"Hello, Genie?"

"Good heavens! Twice in as many days?"

Sean chuckled, despite the gravity of the news he'd called to deliver. Sophie had come back from London a day early and had taken Dylan for the night, and Sean had been looking forward to a quiet evening in front of the telly. Tea eaten, dishes done, he'd plonked down on the sofa, remote in hand, then his phone rang, and that was the end of that.

"I'm running messages again, I'm sorry to say."

"On whose behalf this time?"

"Andy's, or his girlfriend's actually."

"Now I'm intrigued!"

"You might be mad when I explain how it came about. She's a bit of a fixer, you see. After Jess passed, she set up a foundation offering support to families who've lost babies to SIDS—"

"Ah! That's what Andy meant by handing over responsibility."

The way she casually dropped in that they'd had a conversation was further evidence Sean had been acting the eejit earlier.

"I'd say so, and she's doing a smashing job. So, anyway, we just appointed—"

"We?"

"I'm a trustee of the foundation too. There are five of us in all, since we officially appointed Simon Henderson as our legal expert today."

"Is this a wind-up?"

"I know it sounds like one, but it isn't. He heard through a friend of a friend that we were looking for someone to take on the role and offered his services."

"You could've asked me."

"We could've, but…" She had a first-class honours degree and knew her stuff, but she wasn't a qualified solicitor. Whether that would've been a stumbling block for the Daisy Foundation, Sean couldn't say because the thought hadn't even entered his head.

"You didn't think I could do it," Genie accused.

"What? God, that's not it at all. It didn't occur to me, Genie, honestly. If it had, I'd have told you about it, but I'd also have tried to talk you out of it. Old wounds, you know?"

"You were close to her too, Sean, but whatever. It's done now." She was smarting. "So, Andy's girlfriend, the foundation, Simon…"

"Right." Back on track. "Shaunna—Andy's girlfriend, that is—mentioned to him that you were asking after one of Jess's victims, but the records were sealed."

"Sean! Do you have *any* idea of the trouble this could cause?"

"It's fine, Genie, I promise. Simon's treating it as foundation business, so it's privileged and there's no way of tracing his query back to you."

"I'd like to say I believe you, but the Simon I know wouldn't hesitate to throw me under a bus if it was to his advantage."

"Then he must've changed since you last saw him because he's giving his time and expertise for free."

"For the kudos, more like."

"Or for credit with the big man upstairs," Sean added curtly. Time had kindly fuzzed out the bits where Genie had dug in her heels when they were younger, but it was all coming back to him now. "D'you want to hear what he discovered or not?"

She didn't answer for a minute or so, but Sean could still hear her huffing down the line, so he waited in silence for her to relent. "Go ahead," she said.

Stubborn and rude, but Sean wouldn't be telling her so.

"He confirmed that one of the victims *was* a young boy, aged three. He died of leukaemia following a botched transplant with bone marrow from his twin brother."

"Oh, how awful!" That was more like the Genie he loved.

"It gets worse. The twin brother was killed in a car accident in March this year. He was driving—doing eighty in a forty zone. No other casualties other than him and his girlfriend."

"How old were they?"

"Eighteen."

"So it *was* them. My poltergeist—or geists."

"The details certainly fit."

"Their poor parents, losing two children like that."

"Aye, well, God forgive me for even thinking it, but maybe they're better off without him."

"Surely you can't mean that, Sean."

"No, but he only turned eighteen in February and blew through his trust fund in a month, most of it on the car. That was the compensation for his brother—the parents hadn't kept a penny of it for themselves."

"Teenagers can be terribly self-absorbed, can't they?"

"That they can. How's Phee doing today, by the way?"

Genie laughed at his segue. "In pain and feeling sorry for herself. She's wrapped up warm in bed with all her gadgets and her TV. She discharged herself. Can you believe it?"

"Sure I can. I know her mother."

"Hmm. She told me the truth, finally, at three o'clock this morning, and I think we both now have the measure of Paul. I spoke to him earlier."

"Did you rip off his balls?"

"Figuratively, yes. I told him if I ever catch wind of him chasing schoolgirls again, I'll have the Home Office on him faster than he could say Section Ten of the Sexual Offences Act 2003."

"Good on ye, Genie. So I can tell Shaunna her services aren't required—she offered to do it on your behalf."

"Good God, she knows about that too?"

"I tell her everything. She's a great friend—if you ever come for a visit, I'll introduce you. You'll love her to bits."

"Yes, well, I can't say I'm not grateful to her for finding the information when nobody else could."

"Has it put your mind at rest?"

"A little. I'm relieved the boy's family received the money they were due, although it doesn't explain what the three of them were doing here."

"Maybe it was to help you through a tough spot."

"Maybe. I suppose I must accept that I'll never know." She sighed. "Thank you, Sean."

"No thanks needed. I'm only the messenger."

469

"And I shot you again."

"I'm sure I deserved it."

"No doubt. But please do pass on my thanks to Shaunna—or I might wait and deliver them myself."

"You're going to come and see me?"

"If you'll have me."

"Always."

"Mmm. I'll hold you to that."

Sean's body stirred promisingly, but he ignored it. "As I've said before, you and Phee are both welcome anytime. I'd love to see more of her—if it's all right with the both of you."

"She's an adult now, so it's up to her, but yes, I'd love that too."

42: Size Medium

A DELE WATCHED XANDER's back all the way down the stairs, and then, in time with the slow-close of the door at the bottom, swivelled to face Josh and perked one of her perfectly honed and tinted brows.

"A friend of yours?"

Alarmed he'd almost said yes, Josh prevaricated for a few seconds and went with, "Alumnus."

"Is that a secret society for psychologists?"

Her question—an educated guess and not that far off, he supposed—released a good deal of his tension. "Adele, you really do make the world a brighter place."

"I do?"

"You do." He moved off towards the kitchenette. "Cup of tea?"

"Yes, please, but…"

When she didn't finish the sentence, he looked back and startled. Her heels were unexpectedly quiet against the new light-oak floors and he hadn't heard her following, yet there she was, less than a foot behind him. "But what?" he asked.

"Can I make my own?" She grimaced. He laughed.

"Of course!"

"No offence."

"None taken. I make terrible tea."

"I wouldn't say that…"

"No, but George's mum would, and has, so by all means, make your tea, I'll make my coffee, and we'll adjourn to the foundation's office slash group therapy suite."

"The penthouse!" Adele said. "How super!" Pinky raised, she plucked a teabag from the jar and dropped it into the chunky, not in the least bit pretentious mug Josh slid her way.

After that, they worked silently side by side in the small kitchen, which was still dusty, although less so each visit. Also different from last time was the one-cup filter he'd purchased— a steel, funnel-shaped contraption that, once he'd wrestled it from its packaging, sat on top of the mug and meant he didn't have to endure the builders' cheap instant coffee. He'd have offered Xander a cup earlier, but after that bombshell, he was more than happy to palm him off on Sean for the rest of the afternoon.

Sean had come through in every way today, arriving dot on one-thirty as promised, listening without interruption while Josh rambled nervously for a full thirty minutes about how unfair it was that Xander received no credit for what he did even if Josh could appreciate why it was necessary for Jonathan to carefully manage Xander's image for the media. Nor had Sean interrupted when Josh's line of reasoning devolved into questioning whether, given the lack of evidence, Xander had the talent he claimed. He'd known as he was saying it that he was finding ways to dismiss in advance whatever Xander had to tell him in case he didn't like it, and he very much didn't like it.

Then Xander and Jonathan had arrived, and Sean had taken Jonathan aside, treating him to the Twisty Tierney technique, friendly banter that shifted imperceptibly, persuasively, until the recipient would've given Sean all their passwords and PINs if he'd asked for them. Accordingly, while Josh stood petrified in his office, unable to move yet distressingly aware of Xander pacing around him and repeatedly muttering, "I've never seen this before," Sean not only established that there was, in fact, an abundance of evidence in the database Jonathan had compiled detailing Xander's every case and its outcome, but he also secured Xander's agreement to give Josh access to it.

His coffee finished dripping around the same time Adele fished out her teabag and then pirouetted, looking for somewhere to dispose of it, but there was no bin nor even a plastic bag, and Josh had the same problem with his spent grounds. Adele improvised by spreading the filter's packaging flat and plopped the soggy teabag onto it. Josh followed suit, tipping the funnel upside down. The wet grounds broke apart and tumbled across the counter.

"Ooh!" Adele lifted the mugs while he tidied his mess. "Now I know what to get for your office-warming gift!"

"Do people buy those?"

"Who knows? I'm doing it anyway because a kitchen composter is a must-have. They're amazing."

"I have a gift of sorts for you too."

"Oh?"

"The Ouija board, tarot cards and whatnot? They're yours now."

She gasped and stared at him, her eyes sparkly wet. "Are you sure?"

"Absolutely!"

She hugged him, sniffling in his ear and filling his nose with her perfume. Not purple. If he'd had to put a colour to it, then it was a warm yellow, like a hazy, summer meadow. "Thank you so much!" She released him, took a step back—there was no space for more than that—and ran her finger under her eyes. He nodded to confirm her mascara was still where it should be.

"Now please don't take this as ingratitude," he said, "but will a composter fit in here? It's a bit smaller than yours."

"A tiny bit." She grinned, rightfully proud of her beautiful kitchen, in which the kitchenette would fit eight times over and there'd still be room for appliances. "The composter isn't too big. You can leave it on the counter or hide it in a cupboard like I do. You chuck all your food waste in it, add some stuff that looks like sawdust, then empty it into a garden compost bin or ask the council to collect it."

Josh pondered on that as he led the way, checking she was following, into the uncharted territory of the lift up to the loft. Adele pulled the door shut behind her, he pushed the button, and slowly and smoothly, they began their ascent.

"That's a really good idea, Adele."

"I have more if you'd like to hear them?"

"I'd love to!" he said. "Thank you again for doing this."

She shrugged. "It's what friends are for. Plus, I get joint first ride in the lift. Well..." Her nose twitched in dismay. "After Dan."

"Contractors don't count."

She seemed to like that.

Josh had anticipated a panic attack, going up to the loft for the first time since he'd got stuck in the hatch, but as he'd hoped, Adele's presence kept him calm. It helped that being closed in, the height didn't trigger his acrophobia, even if he did still expect the lift to open onto a dark, cobwebby expanse filled with unidentifiable shapes and shifting shadows.

Through the door's small window, the upper storey came into view: no lumpy silhouettes or shadows; the moth-eaten furniture that had created them was long gone, leaving a light, clean space, empty except for a pair of garden chairs with a note attached to them. Adele opened the door and stepped out.

"Wow, this is roomier than I thought it would be." She traversed the perimeter, nodding and humming to herself as she examined the bare, white walls, following them upwards and then tracing the path of the metal beams across the ceiling, shielding her eyes when she reached the vast skylights. "Bright too."

"We wanted it to be suitable for art and other creative therapies."

She circled back to Josh, frowning as she reached past his left ear. "What does this do?" A switch clicked, activating the blinds, and the space darkened until he couldn't see her even though she was inches in front of him.

"Good for sensory workshops," she said.

"Yes. Those blinds are very—" *Effective*, he'd intended to say, but a noise across the room cut him off.

Now came the panic attack. The silence filled with his rapid breaths, the thrum of his pulse so loud in his ears Adele must surely have heard it too. His vision started to adapt, then tunnelled, and he shut his eyes, refusing to believe this was happening again.

Another click, and the darkness ebbed; Josh felt the shift through his eyelids, but he didn't dare look. There were no strange noises now; only Adele's soft footfalls retreating from him.

"What was it?" he asked in a warbly old-man voice, all a-dither.

"One of the chairs." The scuff of plastic against wood echoed in the space, and Josh chanced opening one eye. Adele gave the chair a light shake. "Wobbly legs," she explained. It certainly wasn't alone in that regard. She picked up the note. "Conference chairs coming tomorrow. D." She drew breath to say something else but abandoned it when she looked back at Josh. "You've turned ever such a funny colour. Do you want to go back down?"

He shook his head. "I'm OK." It was a blatant lie, although his fear was being swiftly overwritten by frustration.

"You'd best sit down," Adele advised, and he nodded in agreement, but his feet stayed stubbornly stuck to the spot. Without passing comment on his predicament, Adele set her mug of tea on the floor, came and plucked his coffee from his hand, deposited it next to her tea and then returned for him, hooking her arm through his and leading him across the room as if he were indeed a doddery old codger. She kept hold until he was securely seated on the chair that hadn't toppled then bravely perched on the other one herself.

"I'm sorry," she said.

"What for?"

"I never got how scared you are of heights until you were stuck up here. I should've known when you told me about that nightmare."

She meant his recurring dream about the water slide—not a nightmare as such, more an infuriatingly indecipherable message from his unconscious. He'd resolved it eventually, thanks in part to Adele's maverick interpretation, but it was best not to encourage her.

"Thank you for apologising, but it doesn't bother me when I can't see how high up I am."

"Then why have you got the collywobbles?"

"Because...I don't know."

"Is it the Ouija board?"

He didn't want to think about how she'd homed in on that item as the one most likely to give him *the collywobbles*.

"It's not here anymore," he said.

"But it *was*, and then the chair fell over, and..." Adele's hand shot up to her mouth, showing off her full manicure—a lemon-lilac gradient, fanning from her thumb to her little finger. "There's something here, isn't there?"

"No." Josh tried to say it wearily, dismissively, but Adele had more than proved she was no fool.

"You don't believe in the Spirit World." She stared at him, then through him, processing...processing. "The chair wasn't the first thing, was it?" She wasn't asking him, so he didn't bother answering. "You saw something, and then you found all the spiritualist stuff, and you couldn't explain it away, so... Ohhhh! Is he a what-d'you-call-it...one of those psychologists in *Ghostbusters*?"

"A parapsychologist?"

"Yeah."

"Who?"

"Your aluminus."

"*Alumnus*," Josh corrected.

"Nothing to do with the Illuminati?"

"No."

She shook her head. "Why am I so stupid?"

"You're not. You're dyslexic."

"Same difference."

"No, it's not." She hadn't had the help she'd needed at school, and while she was getting it now with her business diploma, she still had to work twice as hard as other students to keep up. Learning came so easy to Josh, he couldn't imagine what that was like, but for Adele, his patience was endless—as long as they stuck to safe subjects. "An alumnus is someone who attended the same school or college as you."

"So we're alumnus too?"

"We are. Well, alumni—that's the plural."

"Alumnus, alumni…" she repeated with a smile. "You and…?"

"Xander."

"You and Xander are alumni."

"That's right, although he's not a parapsychologist or psychologist of any kind. He's a historian."

"Oh! That makes sense. He's trying to find out who lived here in the past. Figure out who passed—"

"No," Josh interrupted before Adele got carried away. Her smile dwindled, and because he hated seeing her so disappointed, even though it was absolutely not a safe subject, he added, "But he was here doing some research. Xander is…sensitive."

"He's a medium?"

Josh laughed. The term was a very poor fit for Xander, not that he could think of a better one. "Kind of, although not a Gary the Russian type of medium. Xander believes he can see and hear gh…spirits."

"No way! Like, actually sees and hears them?"

"So he says."

"Can he talk to them?"

"You'd have to ask him that."

"Did he see yours?" That was disturbingly on the nose.

"Who says I have one?" Josh bluffed.

Adele hummed. "He's a proper medium, then."

"Are you finally admitting Gary was a charlatan, Adele?"

She ignored him and picked up her tea, sipping and thinking. That was one of the things Josh liked most about her—her lines of reasoning were straightforward. Thus he had a good idea what she was going to say next.

"We could hold a gathering here."

"I'm not having a séance in my new surgery."

She pooh-poohed him in no uncertain terms. "Don't get me wrong. I love, love, *love* all that Victoriana, but it's not *real* spiritualism."

"What's the difference?"

"Why d'you always have to be like that?" She'd taken offence to his question, but he wasn't criticising. For all the reading he'd done, his knowledge of psychic research was significantly lacking because truly empirical studies were also lacking.

"I really do want to understand, Adele."

"How can you understand when your mind is so closed? Even Dan is open to the idea of life after death."

And if it was good enough for Dan…

"Please, Adele?"

She pushed at her hair as if to brush it out of her face, yet not a single strand moved. "No interrupting," she warned.

"Promise."

"And no smart-alec smirking."

Josh nodded in solemn agreement.

She narrowed her eyes and watched him for a moment. He didn't even blink. She seemed satisfied.

"Real spiritualism is personal. Like, you can be receptive to Spirit and receive communication inwardly, but there's nothing to see because they speak to you directly."

"Have you ever—" Josh began. Adele silenced him with a glare.

"All those things you found up here are about putting on a show." She tutted. "Trying to get the spirits to move tables and planchettes and blow out candles, like they're performing monkeys. Why would they? The spirits have lifetimes of experience and know things we don't. They understand the nature of the universe and how to restore balance. Make sense?"

"I think so," Josh said. Was her perfectly symmetrical living room what Adele meant by *balance*? He was curious but knew better than to voice his facetious thoughts. "But you've used a Ouija board, you said."

"Yeah. Shaunna and me and a few other friends used to mess around with it when we were younger and didn't know better. Sometimes we use them in gatherings if there's no medium and we're struggling to understand a message coming through. But communing with Spirit comes from within."

"Do you *commune* with spirits?"

"Spirit," Adele corrected. "I try. It's hard with the kids and Dan. I have to do it while I'm in the bath or on the loo, and even then they don't give me a minute."

"The spirits?"

"The kids. I just get into the right state of mind and then Robbie's nappy needs changing or Shu wants to show me a picture and Daddy's working. He thinks I use it as an excuse to get some peace and quiet because it doesn't look like I'm doing anything. This is why scientists don't think it's real. Like, I tell you I communicate with the spirits and you want proof, but I can't give you any. Only my word."

"It's not falsifiable," Josh said. Adele shrugged, and he explained, "Scientific research works by testing if something is false."

"I don't get it."

"All researchers are biased in favour of their own theories, and if they set out to prove their theory is true, they only collect evidence that supports it. Then another researcher comes along and calls attention to all the things they overlooked, and that's their reputation up in flames. However, if they set out to prove their theory is false and they can't, they can conclude there's a good chance it's true. The rest of the process is about establishing the likelihood of it being true."

"Seems very complicated," Adele said.

"It can be."

"I suppose if it makes your job easier, it's worth it."

"True." Josh wasn't sure it always did. "Most of the psychology I do isn't like that, but when I'm figuring out a treatment programme, I know which approaches have worked in the past because they've been tried and tested."

"How do *you* know, though? You've only got those other researchers' word for it. Doesn't it come down to your experience in the end?"

"Well, yes…" She was pushing him into a corner, and it wasn't one he was prepared to defend. Not to Adele. Not today. "Listen, I know this will seem like I'm changing the subject—"

"Because you are?"

"I really would like to hear your ideas."

"Fine. OK then." She sighed with fake reluctance, but that was as far as she got before she was cut off by a whirring as the skylight blinds rolled into action.

"Please tell me you're holding the remote control," Josh said.

"What remote control?"

Josh looked down at Adele's hands and even leaned back to check she wasn't doing it with her feet, convinced she was playing a trick on him, but it was already too dark to see. The blinds clicked into their fully closed position and immediately began rolling back. Even in the initial dim light, Adele's expression told him it was no joke. For a few seconds after the blinds came to a stop—fully open—she didn't so much as blink, then she took in a very deep breath, held it and moved her hand down over her solar plexus in a classic chi-centring motion.

"Can't you feel him?"

"Who—" The pronoun registered and snipped off Josh's dismissal.

"He's looking for something."

Hearing that statement a second time, Josh's autonomic nervous system hit critical level, and his pulse slowed so drastically he concluded it had stopped in spectacularly prophetic fashion. Knowing it was homeostasis at work, not a sudden doubling of gravity, didn't make it any easier to move, but his coffee was slipping out of his hand and his eyes wanted to close, so he let them.

"You don't believe me," Adele accused, and he smiled knowingly at the shake in her voice, the slight shrillness to her tone. He was ahead of her, way down at the bottom of adrenaline hill, while she was cresting the brow. "It's not funny, Josh!"

"Not laughing." If only they'd been on the floor below, he could have reclined his chair and had a nap. Better still, stretched out on the sofa.

"Josh?"

"Hmm?"

"Are you…stoned?"

Now he was laughing. He'd never tried cannabis, but if it felt like this… The garden chair gave a dangerous creak, and he blinked back to semi-alertness. "Sorry. Just…" A yawn hijacked his jaw. "…been a weird day. That ghost—"

"Feels like he's gone."

Josh coerced his heavy hand into pointing downwards. "He'll be in my consultation room."

Adele sprang to her feet and looked frantically from side to side, more like she was checking for spiders than spirits.

"What happened to your Zen?" Josh asked.

She stopped and tilted her head, frowning at him. "I think you stole it. Can we go downstairs?"

"To hunt ghosts? Why not? In for a penny…" Josh leaned forward a couple of times, building momentum to get to his feet. On his third try, Adele hauled him off the chair and caught his cup mid-air. Coffee slopped onto the floor.

"I'll clean it up later," she said, towing him across the room, back into the lift. Immune to her urgent jabbing at the button, it moved off at a snail's pace.

"It's not going anywhere," Josh said. "The ghost, I mean, not the lift. Obviously, the lift is going down—"

"How are you so calm?" Adele interrupted.

"Honestly? I'm sick of all the obstacles to getting this business up and running."

"It's the law of attraction."

"The law of attraction is a myth. There's no scientific evidence it exists."

"Like there's no scientific evidence *ghosts* exist?"

"That's not *quite* what I said. There's no evidence of an afterlife or that mediums and spiritualists are communicating with the dead."

The lift stopped, and Adele opened the door, but neither of them moved to leave. Ahead of them stretched the empty corridor where dust motes swirled, caught in the ambient spring light spilling from the three consultation rooms. Closer to the lift, in the small reception area with its corner seating still in plastic wrap, someone—Shaunna at a guess—had placed a palm plant in a black, glazed pot. From his new perspective—literal and figurative—Josh felt like he was viewing the space for the first time. It was a beautiful renovation, perfect, pristine...and cold as the grave.

"What happens at a gathering?" he asked. Adele slurped in an excited breath, and he held up a finger. "I'm not necessarily suggesting we have one."

"But you're thinking about it."

"Yes, I am because, according to Xander..." He paused, weighing up the consequences of telling her and realising she'd never let that dangling thread go. "He thinks it's my ghost. Which is to say, it's me."

"But..."

"I'm not dead?" Josh nodded. "That confused Xander too. His theory is it's related to my near-death experience."

"You had an NDE?"

"Yes." They were talking at cross purposes: she meant 'seeing the light and hearing the call of lost loved ones', while he meant 'clinically dead and resuscitated by medics'. As regards the latter, the tally was closer to five—one would probably have sufficed for Xander's theory, which was plausible. Logical even. Josh wasn't putting any stock in it just yet, but the evidence was mounting. True, it was anecdotal: as Shaunna had said, she was not an independent witness; Adele's starting point was always supernatural explanations; Libby's agreeableness predisposed her to being suggestible. Likewise, while Xander's perception of ghosts was real to him, his greater-than-coincidence success rate in solving mysterious deaths and putting an end to so-called hauntings could be explained by his and Jonathan's extensive, evidence-based research.

Even Josh was fallible. He'd made the connections between his experience, Simon's dream, Gabby's break-in and Genie's poltergeist on the basis that they'd all happened around the same time and they were all alumni, specifically Jess's, as was Sean, which was why Josh had assumed Sean's current struggles were because of his unprocessed grief as opposed to the kind of major life changes that would have anyone cracking up.

One thing was clear, however, and undeniable when it was staring him in the face. From his insistence on white walls and keeping the same consultation room to his delight at Dan's positioning of the furniture and Sean's disconnection from the building and the business, Josh could see now that he hadn't built a new therapy centre. He'd modernised his old surgery and was labouring under the misguided notion that he could pick up where he'd left off, reconvene his former existence as Josh Sandison, the therapist too afraid to love, too proud to apologise, too selfish to take responsibility for someone else's well-being and too arrogant to admit to his mistakes.

Libby and Xander were right. He was, metaphorically or otherwise, haunting himself, but that was no longer his life nor even the one he wanted.

"Adele…I'd like you to arrange a gathering."

She squealed and hugged him but then must've decided he was tormenting her, as she released him and stepped out of the lift, glancing back, eyes narrowed suspiciously.

"Really," he said, following her, although he'd have made more progress wading through treacle, as she was heading straight for his consultation room. "The sooner the better," he added.

It was time to lay his ghost to rest.

Epilogue: Ellipsis

Therapy Centre
Present Day
Mid-June

WIND TURBINES," ANDY said. "No noise survey required."
He went over to the window and looked out. "You can
just about see them."

Josh joined him. "Oh, yes." In the distance, their blades
sweeping the horizon, were four wind turbines. "They weren't
there two years ago." The day he'd handed the keys back, he'd
stood right where he was standing now, taking in the view for
what he'd thought would be the last time. "Surely they're too far
away for us to hear them."

"Yeah, they are." To demonstrate, Andy opened the window,
and for a minute or so the two of them listened to the muted
hum of traffic and snippets of conversation from the street
out front, the many songs of birds, a jet flying high above,
the gentle trickle of water over pebbles in Shaunna's garden
below...not a whisper of whirring wind turbines. Andy shut
the window.

"Of course," Josh said like he knew what he was talking
about, "we won't hear it if it's infrasound."

"You would if it was loud enough, and they can be noisy
bastards close up. I got chatting to some anti-wind-turbiners
once. Nice enough bunch but bloody crackers. They reckoned
infrasound from turbines causes all sorts—dizziness, high
blood pressure, jellified organs, you name it. It's all bollocks.
Infrasound's only dangerous to health if you can hear it."

That was too reminiscent of 'if a tree falls in a forest...' for Josh's liking.

"Does that mean the soundwaves don't reach this far or they do but we can't hear them?"

"Depends how much background noise there is. We're what, two miles from those? The level here will be about twenty-five, thirty decibels. Unless you've got bionic ears or it's the middle of the night and there's zero wind, you're not gonna hear that."

"Could we still be affected by the noise even if we can't consciously hear it?" Josh pressed.

Andy shrugged. "That's more your department than mine." Pulling his phone from his pocket, he moved towards the door. "All I can tell you is the noise from modern wind turbines at this distance won't even come close to blowing your clients' eardrums. Sorry, gotta take this. See you this afternoon, yeah?"

The last Josh heard was Andy saying "'Lo?" on his way down the stairs. The door release buzzed, then the outside door clicked shut, leaving Josh alone in his consultation room for the first time since the day he'd come to meet Xander and agreed to Adele arranging a gathering, when even being there with someone else had paralysed him with dread. That was no longer the case, despite Andy effectively eliminating his last shot at finding a non-paranormal explanation, and a good thing it was too. If the turbines had been to blame, it would have meant either going to battle with the council to have them relocated further from the town or finding new premises. Josh would rather take his chances facing off his ghost.

The door release buzzed again. From his room, he still had a direct line of sight to the top of the stairs, but he recognised the swift, light rhythm of the footsteps long before their maker popped into view.

"Hey, Lib."

"Hey. The sign's done. Come see!"

"I will in a minute. Can you give me a hand?"

"Yep." She came into the room. "What're we doing?"

"Reorganising the furniture."

"OK." she agreed, although her frown asked *why?* "Where—"

Josh held up his hand to stop her and addressed the small, white cube on the windowsill. "Set consultation room one to…" He gestured to Libby. Her frown became an enormous smile.

"Green," she said. "For new beginnings and growth."

A pale glow spread, dust-free polished floor up, loft-hatchless ceiling down, slowly filling the white walls with a rich, forest green. Josh heard Libby's breath catch in excitement. She'd been right again: the place *had* needed brightening up, perhaps with something subtler for day-to-day operations, but for this moment, the colour was perfect, and Josh was overwhelmed with happiness, so much so it turned him tearful. Libby snuggled against his side, her arms looped around him, his around her.

"New beginnings and growth," he whispered.

***

"This is it." Sean brought the car to a halt, nose to the front façade of a building. He stopped the engine and unfastened his seat belt. "First impressions?"

"You've changed profession?" Genie suggested wryly. She hadn't had a chance to form any kind of impression, given the view through the windscreen consisted of two doors, one being held open by a girl around Phee's age, the other etched with a dentist's name and credentials.

"Are we getting out?" Phee asked from the back seat and, without waiting for an answer, did so. She approached the other girl, who smiled at her. Phee said something, half-turning to glance back at the car.

"She's Josh's daughter," Sean explained. "Libby."

Genie nodded in acknowledgement, aware she was remiss in not showing an interest, but she had nothing to anchor it to. She'd barely known Josh when they were undergraduates, which she'd always blamed on Jess. However, with Phee back at school for her A' Level exams these past few weeks, Genie had indulged in some very painful retrospection and come to terms with the possibility that what she'd thought of as 'being in love' was addiction or obsession. It had stopped her from keeping old friendships alive and pursuing new ones, out of jealousy when it came to the likes of Josh or Andy, and because every minute spent with someone else was a minute without Jess.

She wished she could say she'd had that epiphany all by herself, but it had come from Phee admitting she'd ditched her friends and 'even sold out my own mother' for Paul. Perhaps that was all love was in the end—an obsession to the exclusion of all others.

"So, *are* we getting out?" Sean asked.

"Soon."

The two girls had gone inside the building, revealing the etching on the other door, although it was too cryptic for Genie's anxious brain to make sense of.

"Three dots?"

"An ellipsis," Sean said as if that were explanation enough.

"What does it mean?"

"All kinds of things. An unfinished conversation, a pause, a missing detail—"

"Someone is typing a reply."

"Dead on. A subliminal *to be continued* if you will. Open dialogue. An always-listening ear." Sean turned in his seat and studied her awhile. This wasn't an ideal first meet-up post-coitus, and they needed to thrash out what they were now, but it would have to wait until they were finished here.

"Are you watching my ellipsis?" she asked.

"Sorry?"

She glanced sideways at him. "Waiting for me to say something."

"Ah. Sort of. I was wondering if you're all right."

"Hmm…" She breathed deeply, and again, and decided not to fudge it. "No. I'm not sure I want to take part in this séance or whatever it is."

"To be honest, I have reservations too, but I'm told it's more a group meditation kind of thing."

"Super." If she were with anyone else, Genie would have suggested heading for the nearest pub. She couldn't even claim she thought it was all bunkum, but she could think of better ways to pass a balmy Saturday afternoon than calling forth the spirit of Jessica Lambert.

"OK, look," Sean said, "how about I give you the tour and we see what's what. Then, if it's too much, we can make our excuses and leave."

That seemed bearable.

The door with the etched ellipsis opened again, and Shaunna peered out; they hadn't been introduced, but Genie recognised her immediately from Sean's reaction.

"We're being summoned," he said and couldn't have left the car faster had the engine been on fire. Laughing, Genie followed suit at a more sensible pace.

"Good afternoon, each!" Shaunna greeted them with a smile. "Genie, it's lovely to meet you at last!" She hugged her and kissed her cheek, a slightly more intimate gesture than the continental version Genie had expected but not unwelcome. Shaunna smelled of almonds and toasted coconut—good enough to eat—and the scent lingered as she moved on to Sean, her eyebrows arching in surprise when he returned the hug stiffly, patted her back and withdrew.

"Lovely to meet you too," Genie said, sharing a knowing eye-roll with Shaunna, although she did feel for Sean, whose two worlds were colliding in spectacular fashion. Between them, they knew everything about him, past and present.

"I was going to show Genie around," he said as they moved inside, entering a narrow hallway that led to a staircase, much brighter and more modern than the exterior suggested.

The murmur of multiple conversations drifted down to meet them as they ascended. "What's the plan?"

"Adele's setting up in the loft, so that's off limits. She wants to keep it low-key and not have an official *everyone must be sitting down ready to start* time. It's driving Josh nuts."

"I bet."

"But nominally, we're starting at half two."

"Right, so we've fifteen minutes," Sean informed Genie. She refrained from pointing out that she was quite capable of telling the time and instead took in her surroundings. Coming in to view above the banister on her left was a white-walled corridor punctuated by pale-wood doors in between which hung framed art, charcoal and pastel depictions of people and animals—dogs, horses, cattle—in the same fluid, almost sketch-like style. They were clearly all the work of the same artist and perfect for the space, which was light and cool, the ambience paradoxically clinical yet welcoming, in part due to the coffee aroma that didn't quite mask the smell of paint and something else; frankincense, Genie thought, as it reminded her of being in church.

At the top of the stairs was a small sitting area with a low table and sofa, where she found Phee and Josh's daughter. Astonishingly, they were talking to each other, not a mobile phone in sight, but paused their hushed conversation when a man approached and set two glass mugs of hot chocolate on the table.

"Thank you very much," Phee said, sending a thrill of pride through Genie, and she choked up a little. Every emotion seemed more intense than usual today.

Josh's daughter grinned up at the man. "No biscuits?"

"Watch it, you." He wagged his finger playfully at her and turned Genie's way. "Hi. I'm George." He held out his hand, and she shook it. "Bit much, isn't it?" She nodded, in her head cursing Sean for abandoning her. She peered along the corridor, but he and Shaunna were nowhere to be seen. "Can I get you a drink?" George asked.

"Yes, please, if it's not too much trouble."

"What would you like? Hot chocolate, coffee of some kind, green tea, normal tea, orange juice, water…"

"Normal tea with a splash of milk?"

"Coming right up."

As George headed back along the corridor, Shaunna materialised as if she'd stepped through the wall.

"Adele's ready for us," she called, loud enough to be heard over the various mumblings coming from behind those doors. She spotted Genie standing alone. "Where did Sean go?"

"I have no idea."

Shaunna shook her head. "So much for showing you around."

"It's fine, really. Just tell me where I need to be."

"We can go up together," Shaunna suggested.

"Perfect." Genie looked to see where George had gone so she could tell him not to bother with the tea, but a glimpse of a man through the doorway opposite the top of the stairs stopped her dead.

"Good lord!"

At her exclamation, Simon stopped crooning at whoever else was in the room and, with a grin, said, "That's me," and came out to greet her.

"Hardly *good*," Genie muttered against his shoulder, caught up in another unexpected hug.

Simon laughed. "Hardly a lord either these days." He stepped back and took her in. "You look fantastic, Genie!"

"As do you," she said truthfully. Of course, it was easy to stay fit and youthful when one enjoyed all the trappings of wealth and status, but it was more—dare she think it—his aura. He was positively radiating happiness, and it was having the strangest effect on her, as in she was aware of other people moving around yet she couldn't tear herself away, struck down by an unprecedented yearning for a catch-up. "How are you?"

"I'm very well, thanks. And you?"

"I'm doing great. I'm surprised to see you here."

"Really? I'm not surprised to see you. You're here for Jess, yah?"

"Well, yes, but…"

"She didn't tell me she was sick, Genie. I only found out last year that she was dead."

"Oh, Simon. I'm so sorry. For what it's worth, she kept it to herself for as long as she could. She asked me not to attend her funeral."

Simon shook his head sadly. "She was…an enigma."

Genie could think of at least a dozen less polite names for her, but she chose not to tarnish Simon's memory of the person who had turned his life around.

"So you know about the Daisy Foundation, I take it?" he asked.

"Yes. Sean told me about it. You're their legal team."

"A team of one." Simon's expression turned thoughtful for a second or two before he qualified, "Of course, it's a very small organisation."

"Of course," Genie said, still getting a bit of a kick from his discomfort in admitting he was involved in what must have been a mere trifle for someone of his stature. "And how are the family?" she asked while she had him on the backfoot.

"My partner and I are very happy."

That wasn't what she was asking, and he knew it.

"We've been together eight years and have a whole gaggle of feral cats. Piotr's a property developer—we met through work—and he found this delightfully rundown farm for us to live in. The cats came with it. Spiteful little monsters, but he loves them."

"Piotr sounds wonderful."

"He is. You must come for dinner sometime and meet him."

"I'd love to!"

Simon took out his phone and passed it to her with the number displayed. She added it to her phone's address book and zipped off a quick '*hi, this is Genie*' text message. Simon put his phone back in his pocket.

"Thanks. I'll talk to Piotr later and give you a call if that's all right?"

"Perfect."

"How about you, Genie? Anyone special in your life?"

"Ah…yes, I think so!" She couldn't help smiling as she answered his generously ambiguous question. Perhaps Sean had been right about him. Still, she couldn't let the opportunity pass by. "Do you see much of your parents these days?"

"Not if I can help it. Forgive me for saying so, but my father and your sister are a menace."

"How so?"

"They're trying to convince your father to sell them Wharton Hall."

"Why bother? She'll inherit it when he dies."

"Who knows?"

"*Ahem!*"

They both turned to see Shaunna standing where she'd been earlier.

"Sorry to interrupt, but we're ready to start—unless you want to give it a miss?"

Genie looked at Simon, and he at her, a moment of silent indecision passing between them. Jess had been important to them both, and she'd denied them the chance to say goodbye. It would be foolish to come all this way only to leave without doing so. Wordlessly, they went to Shaunna, who gestured to a gap in the wall that, now she was level with it, Genie saw led to stairs upwards.

"May I have a quick word, Shaunna?"

Shaunna's sympathetic smile became a puzzled frown. "Sure. Simon, why don't you go on up? We'll join you in a second."

***

"No Xander?" Genie asked out of the side of her mouth, taking the seat next to Sean.

"He declined the invitation. Where've you been?"

"Since you abandoned me? Talking to Simon."

"Sorry. I had to show Andy where I wanted my clock to go."

"Andy's here?" Genie squinted through the gloom at the others present, raising her hand a couple of inches in greeting when she found him, that same hand going straight to her nose to stifle a sneeze. "The incense is a bit much."

Sean nodded, glad his sense of smell was defunct because she wasn't the first person to comment, but for health and safety reasons, there was no burning incense. All around the room, Adele had placed small lights that flickered gold like candle flames and intermittently emitted puffs of vapour, presumably the source of the smell people were complaining about. With the blinds closed, it cast a hazy glow over the loft, which was sleep-inducingly cosy.

"I'd like for us to begin now," Adele said, her tone much slower, quieter and deeper than her usual speaking voice. "Is everyone OK with that?" She made eye contact with each person in turn, seeking their agreement. Sean followed the progression around the circle, a professional instinct drilled into him through years of case conferences, and it dawned on him all those present were Jess's alumni, not Josh's. Adele had specifically invited Genie and Simon, which got him wondering if Josh had misled her about the identity of his ghost.

After Adele had secured Sean's consent, Genie nudged him and whispered, "Where's Phee?"

"In the garden with Libby." He grimaced apologetically, even though Adele was in the zone and paid them no heed. "She's fine," he added hastily so Genie wouldn't worry. The girls had come up in the lift, but Libby had taken one look at the room and gone straight back down. Given her background, her reaction hadn't surprised him. She'd been forced by her biological parents to attend prayer meetings that would've looked a lot like this, and while George had stayed downstairs and would keep an eye on Libby, Sean had no qualms in granting Phee's request to stay with her. He was impressed by her compassion, even if he did suspect her motivation was more personal.

That left Adele, Shaunna, Andy, Simon, Josh, Genie and Sean, an intimate circle that would have fitted in one of the consultation rooms, but this was their group therapy suite, not to mention that holding the gathering up here meant Josh could avoid ever entering the space again.

"Thank you," Adele said in that same slow, quiet voice. "We come together today in love and openness to the wisdom of Spirit. Know that each of you has a guide who stands beside you and will keep you safe on this journey, just as they do every day. As you open your heart and mind, remember you are loved and safe. Listen and you will hear and be heard.

"We begin by breathing deeply, bringing sustenance into our bodies, concentrating on the feeling of our core, centring our thoughts." Eyes closed, Adele swept her arms towards her as she inhaled, leading them all to do the same, and then away from her as she exhaled, repeating the action twice more. "Continue taking in slow, deep breaths," she instructed.

"Full disclosure—I am not a medium, but I open myself to the Spirit World and offer what I have learnt to you. Some people find it easier to think about lost loved ones, bring memories to the surface. You can do that now."

Adele's voice faded into the silence, and Sean closed his eyes, expecting he'd need to make a conscious effort to do what she was asking, instead being presented with a vision as vivid as a dream, of the quiz night in the pub when he'd seen Jess for the first time since uni. In a wheelchair, she was thin and gaunt, in the advanced stages of her illness, yet then and now, his memory overlaid the image with the old Jess, curvy, glossy-haired, eyes bright, full of life and ambition.

It was that same vivacious woman he saw the day he'd taken her to the hospice to look around, with whom he'd stayed hour upon hour, chattering away about all kinds of nonsense while she drifted in and out of drug-induced sleep, and to whom he'd said goodbye the day she passed. His faith, such as it was, and his training had instilled in him the importance of remembering lost loved ones in their best light, and he had eternalised Jess's beauty in his mind, then twisted it into repulsion and rejection— a self-inflicted cruelty that reflected his feelings of inadequacy as a lover and friend, not the reality of their friendship, because somewhere in their past, he had forgotten the kind, vulnerable human being beneath that beautiful, ruthless exterior. Jess had fought the pain of loss every day, yet through those dark months when Josh was sick and Sean had almost thrown it all away, she had stuck by them both, travelling back to spend every free evening and weekend with them even though her workload, as a newly qualified solicitor, had been immense.

Would she have mocked his impotence? Maybe, but it would've been innocent fun aimed at taking the pressure off, not belittling him. Then she'd have pranced away, flashing that cheeky smile over her shoulder. *Come find me when you're ready—you know where I'll be.*

***

"Sean?"

"Hmm...yeah?" He yawned. "Shite." The room came back into focus. It was some solace that the others looked in much the same state as he was himself. "Did I nod off?"

Genie shrugged. "You might have done. I'm going to check on Phee. Are you OK here?"

"Sure. See you in a bit."

Genie's hand brushed his back as she passed behind him and went downstairs.

"I'm opening the blinds," Shaunna warned.

Sean felt the twinge of his pupils adjusting as light trickled in and shut his eyes. A moment later, when he opened them experimentally, Shaunna was sitting where Genie had been. He smiled; she didn't.

"What's up?" he asked.

She held out her hand, in it a folded piece of paper. He took it, unfolded it.

"Jesus, that's a lot of zeroes."

"What do I do, Sean?"

"Banks still accept cheques, don't they?"

"Well, yeah, but it's a huge donation. If it was from a stranger…"

"Why? Who… Ah." Now he understood. Shaunna's dilemma wasn't with the size of the cheque or whether the bank would accept it but the name across the bottom: *Imogen E Rowan*. He shrugged and handed it back. "We need to treat it the same as any other donation."

"A donation?" Josh's head appeared between them as he leaned in so he could read the cheque. "Wow!"

"From Genie," Shaunna said, her tone conveying an expectation that Josh would take her side.

"She is aristocracy. I'm sure she can afford it."

"I can," Genie said, reaching around Josh to unhook her bag from the chair. "I'm also going back to law."

"Really?" Sean said. "That's…grand."

Genie smiled. "It *is* grand, as was this gathering. Just what the doctor ordered." She held Sean's gaze for several seconds, long enough for him to process the significance of her donation and her decision. She'd made her peace with Jess. "So, about that tour…"

"I'll take you," Shaunna offered. She ushered Genie towards the stairs before Sean had a chance to argue.

Josh slumped onto the chair Shaunna vacated. "I'm glad that's over."

"Me too," Sean said. "Are you all right?"

"Yes, I think so. Are you?"

"I'm knackered but fine otherwise. It feels better in here, doesn't it?"

"The right residual energy?" Josh suggested dryly, back to his old cynical self.

"I'd be careful if I were you." Sean tilted his head towards Adele, who was chatting with Simon but kept looking over. "She'll be after making it a regular event."

"Not a chance." Josh took out his phone and frowned at the lit screen. "Here we go again." He hit answer. "Hello?" he said sharply. "Erm...wh...?" His frown deepened, shifting from annoyance to confusion, disappearing as his eyebrows rose and his eyes widened to comical proportions, although there was nothing funny about his reaction. "Yes, OK. Thanks, Lib." Trance-slow, Josh lowered his arm and stared at his phone. "That was Libby."

"I got that."

"Calling from our new landline."

"It's connected? That's great news!"

"Yes...great news."

"Is there a problem?" Sean asked.

"No. No problem." Josh smiled manically. "Just...you know how the phone company gave us one of the new batch of numbers rather than one that's been allocated before?"

"I didn't know that, no."

"Well, they did, or perhaps I should say they were supposed to, seeing as I've been receiving calls from that number for the past two months." He chewed his cheek. "Since the day Phee turned up at the university and Libby and I came here."

"Right." That gave Sean's pulse a jolt, although hopefully only back up to its usual rate. Coffee might not be a bad idea. "Look on the bright side."

"Which is?"

"At least we know who was calling you now, don't we, *Schrödinger's therapist*?" Sean grinned and gave Josh's forearm a light poke. "As I suspected before we opened the box. Definitely alive."

Josh's answering poke was not so gentle and got Sean right in the sternum. "That's more than you'll be if you call me that again."

"You'd best get after Adele, then. We'll be needing that Ouija board for staff meetings."

***

"Cappuccino." Josh set the mug on the new side table next to the sofa and resumed his seat on the desk chair.

"Thank you." Xander picked up his drink, sipped and put it down again. "That is a most agreeable blend."

"I thought you'd approve." It was Josh's favourite, which he wasn't ready to admit aloud, but having seen how in-depth Xander's data recording and analysis were, he'd come to terms with that and the many other traits they had in common. This visit was a follow-up at Josh's request, and he was eager to put his mind at rest before they went full steam ahead with the official opening of *Ellipsis Psychotherapy Centre*, but Xander seemed in no rush to conclude proceedings.

"Did your *séance* go well?"

"It wasn't a séance. It was a spiritualist gathering."

"*Si ad hominum communem opinionem attendamus, videbimus eos suae mentis aeternitatis esse quidem conscios, sed ipsos eandem cum duratione confundere eamque imaginationi seu memoriae tribuere, quam post mortem remanere credunt.*"

Josh blinked, dumbfounded, for a good minute after Xander was done. "You're fluent in Latin?"

"I've studied Spinoza," Xander stated as if all scholars learnt multiple languages purely to read classical texts.

"I've studied Freud, but I'm not fluent in German."

"Then you haven't studied Freud."

That aneurysm was threatening again. "Xander...please just give me the translation."

With a pitying grimace-smile, he said, "Most people, while conscious of the eternity of Spirit, confuse it with duration and ascribe it to the imagination or the memory, which they believe persist after death."

"You can't criticise Adele for believing in an afterlife when *you* believe the same, albeit in a metaphysical rather than spiritual sense."

"A séance has the express purpose of communing with the imagination and memory after death."

"It wasn't a séance—"

"And you are not dead."

The urge to snipe *ten out of ten for observation* was instantly snuffed by comprehension. "I see what you mean. So my ghost is still here, then."

"Your ghost…" Xander picked up his mug and sipped slowly, savouring before he swallowed. "This really is an excellent blend."

"Damn it, Xander, am I still haunting myself or not?"

"No, Josh. You are not."

Hearing the confirmation, Josh sighed in relief, but it was so much more than that, as if he were releasing stale air that had festered in his lungs for years, all the way back to discovering that first note left in his uni room by a so-called ghost. It was, astonishingly, easier to open himself to the possibility of persistent consciousness than accept the callous cruelty of those in his discipline who bent the rules to their own ends.

"Thank you, Xander."

"What for? I didn't do anything."

Perhaps he was right and everything that had happened was Jess's intervention from beyond the grave: bringing Simon to them when they'd tried and failed to appoint a legal expert for the Daisy Foundation; steering Genie and Sean back together at a time when both their lives were in tremendous flux; forcing Josh to face the past then shut the door on it. Josh accepted now that Jess had, in her way, loved them all unconditionally and would have done whatever was in her power to help them, but without Xander's insight, his mediumship, he would once again have dismissed recent events as mere coincidences, the products of compromised minds.

"You stopped me destroying my most important friendship and saved our business. That's far from nothing."

"Oh." Xander blinked, took off his glasses, polished them on his scarf and returned them to his face. "In that case… you're welcome."

"As they say," Josh added, for Xander's benefit and his own, and relaxed back in his chair, coffee in hand.

Welcome home.

• • •

Acknowledgements/Credits

As ever, I owe epic thanks to Nige, Andrea and Jor, my constant cheerleaders, my A-team, without whom my stories would be an absolute shambles.

Thanks also to Jen Burkinshaw for taking time out from launching her debut novel *Igloo* (which is awesome, by the way) to beta-read and offer brilliant feedback, and to Paul McDermott for proofreading my last-minute faffing.

Lastly, thank you to my readers, whoever you may be. Every so often, I receive an email or a comment on social media from one of you, and it truly makes my day.

References (because who doesn't include academic sources in a fictional novel?)

American Psychiatric Association (2022). *Diagnostic and Statistical Manual of Mental Disorders: DSM-5-TR. 5th Edition, Text Revision.* Washington, DC: American Psychiatric Association Publishing.

McGill College (A Student in Arts) (1879) 'Alouette' in *A Pocket Song Book for the Use of Students and Graduates of McGill College.* Montreal: McGill College.

Spinoza, B. (1677). *Ethica: Ordine Geometrico Demonstrata et in Quinque Partes Distincta, in Quibus Agitur.* Public domain, via Wikimedia Commons. Available at: https://upload.wikimedia.org/wikipedia/commons/6/6a/Benedictus_de_Spinoza_-_Ethica_Ordine_Geometrico_Demonstrata%2C_1677.pdf (Accessed 10 October 2022).

Spinoza, B. and Elwes, R. H. M. (trans.) (2017). *The Ethics (Ethica Ordine Geometrico Demonstrata),* Project Gutenberg EBook of The Ethics, by Benedict de Spinoza. Available at: https://www.gutenberg.org/files/3800/3800-h/3800-h.htm (Accessed 10 October 2022).

About the Author

Debbie McGowan is an author and publisher based in a semi-rural corner of Lancashire, England. She writes character-driven, realist fiction, celebrating life, love and relationships. A working-class girl, she 'ran away' to London at seventeen, was homeless, unemployed and then homeless again, interspersed with animal rights activism (all legal, honest ;)) and volunteer work as a mental health advocate. At twenty-five, she went back to college to study social science—tough with two toddlers, but they had a 'stay at home' dad, so it worked itself out. These days, the toddlers are young women (much to their chagrin) and Debbie teaches undergraduate students, writes novels and runs an independent publishing company, occasionally grabbing an hour's sleep where she can.

Social Media Links

Website: debbiemcgowan.co.uk and hidingbehindthecouch.com
Newsletter Signup: eepurl.com/b8emHL
Blog: deb248211.blogspot.com
Facebook: facebook.com/DebbieMcGowanAuthor and facebook.com/beatentrackpublishing
Twitter: @writerdebmcg
YouTube: youtube.com/deb248211
Instagram: instagram/writerdebmcg
Tumblr: writerdebmcg.tumblr.com
LinkedIn: uk.linkedin.com/in/writerdebmcg
Goodreads: goodreads.com/DebbieMcGowan

By the Author

I'm not a single-genre author, for which I make no apology. Nor do I write stories of a specific length; I believe a story should be as long as it needs to be.

Thus, to assist you in navigating my catalogue, I've also included the closest-fitting genres and types of publication.

Hiding Behind The Couch Series
(Contemporary/Literary Fiction)

The ongoing story of 'The Circle'…
Nine friends from high school;
Nine friends for life.

The Story So Far…
(in chronological order)

Beginnings (Novella)
Ruminations (Novel)
Class-A (Short Story – also in *Take a Chance* anthology)
Hiding Behind The Couch (Season One)
No Time Like The Present (Season Two)
The Harder They Fall (Season Three)
Crying in the Rain (Novel)
First Christmas (Novella)
In The Stars Part I: Capricorn–Gemini (Season Four)
Breaking Waves (Novella)
In The Stars Part II: Cancer–Sagittarius (Season Five)
A Midnight Clear (Novella – also in *Boughs of Evergreen* anthology)
Red Hot Christmas (Novella)
Two By Two (Season Six)

Hiding Out (Novella – CHO Crossover)
Breakfast at Cordelia's Aquarium (Short Story)
Chain of Secrets (Novella – also in *Love Unlocked* anthology)
Those Jeffries Boys (Novel)
The WAG and The Scoundrel (Gray Fisher #1)
Reunions (Season Seven)
Reverberations (Novel)
To Be Sure (Novella – also in *Never Too Late* anthology)
Tabula Rasa (Gray Fisher #2)
What A Scorcher! (Flash Fiction)
Goth of Christmas Past (Front of House #1)
The Lost Mitten (see 'Children's Stories')
The Advent of Reason (Novella)
Highlights ~ co-written with A.M. Leibowitz (Short Story – Notes from Boston meets Hiding Behind The Couch)
Not My Christmas (Novella)
Distractions (Gray Fisher #3)
Perfect Tenor (Novella)

Checking Him Out Series
(M/M and LGBTQ Romance)

Checking Him Out (Book One)
Checking Him Out For the Holidays (Novella)
Hiding Out (Novella – Noah and Matty – HBTC Crossover)
Taking Him On (Book Two – Noah and Matty)
Checking In (Book Three)
The Making of Us (Book Four – Jesse and Leigh)

Seeds of Tyrone Series
(M/M Romance)

~ co-written with Raine O'Tierney

Leaving Flowers (Book One)
Where the Grass is Greener (Book Two)
Christmas Craic and Mistletoe (Book Three)

Stand-Alone Stories

Champagne (LGBTQ Historical Novel)
'Time to Go' (Contemporary Short in *Story Salon Big Book of Stories*)
And The Walls Came Tumbling Down (Sci-fi Novel)
No Dice (Sci-fi Novel)
Double Six (Sci-fi Novel)
Sugar and Sawdust (M/M Romance Short Story)
Cherry Pop Valentine (M/M Romance Short Story)
Coming Up ~ co-written with Al Stewart (LGBTQ Short Story)
Of the Bauble (LGBTQ Fantasy Romance Novella)
So Long, Little Black Diamonds (True Short Story)
The Pastor's Last Drop (Ongoing Historical Novel – Wattpad)
When Skies Have Fallen (LGBTQ Historical Romance Novel)
A Snowy Ball (When Skies Have Fallen Novelette)
The Great Village Bun Fight (LGBTQ Comedy Novella – also in
Seasons of Love anthology)
'Oh No She Didn't!' (LGBTQ Short Story in *Upstaged!: an anthology of
women who love women in the performing arts*)
The Great Pretendo (Flash Fiction)
'Nina, Pretty Ballerina' (Short Story in *Play On…*: a collection of short
stories, poetry and prose, inspired by the songs of ABBA)
Meredith's Dagger (Contemporary/Historical Feminist/LGBTQ
Novel)

Audiobooks

And The Walls Came Tumbling Down – Narrated by Hannibal Mills
Checking Him Out – Narrated by Tim Larkfield
Of The Bauble – Narrated by Jack Hardman
The Great Village Bun Fight – Narrated by Jack Hardman
When Skies Have Fallen – Narrated by Tim Holbourne

Children's Stories (written as J.S. Morley)

The Lost Mitten ~ illustrated by Sofia Oxelstrand
Chompy the Velociraptor ~ illustrated by Kate Andrew
Zoom the Pterodactyl

Beaten Track Publishing

For more titles from Beaten Track Publishing,
please visit our website:

https://www.beatentrackpublishing.com

Thanks for reading!